Cover designed by MiblArt

Chapter artwork designed by Kevin Lemon

KATE VALENT

TROUBLE IS BREWING

Calamity in a Coffee Pot
By Charlotte Steepe

Chapter 13

Master Stonewall liked to throw a ball every year, but this year's was one of truly unprecedented scale and grandeur. There was not a soul in all of London who would wish to miss it, Cathy least of all. Her recent engagement to the fabulously wealthy coffee merchant, Marshall Brue, meant a most coveted spot on the guest list. As a mere tailor's daughter, she never would have dared dream of receiving an invitation on her own. It was a fact of which she was all too well aware, clad in her new lavender dress which had been bought with her fiancé Marshall's money.

She ogled the splendor of the beautiful manor, awash in ladies wearing colorful dresses dripping with lace and ribbons. Silver jewelry bedighted with all manner of precious gems glistened on their slender porcelain necks everywhere she looked. She reached for her own necklace, and could not suppress a feeling of shame that the simple pendant wrapped around her neck looked so homely in comparison.

Enough magic flowed through Stonewall's manor to give it a pretentious air that so perfectly encapsulated its owner's essence. The enchanted floor gave one the illusion of walking on water, and illusory fish with gold and silvery scales darted this way and that, retreating from her steps as she timidly walked across the ballroom.

Much to Cathy's chagrin, the guest list also included her fiancé's wretched cousin, Barnaby Brue. The detestable man caught her in his villainous gaze from the other side of the dance floor, and like a spider upon its web he strode out to meet her. His mustache curled just so as always, highlighting his rugged jawline. His suit showed off his impeccable taste in fashion and his long legs that moved with the grace more befitting a swan than a man.

Ladies both young and old fanned themselves at his passing. How naïve and foolish they were to swoon over him, dazzled by his carefully curated outward appearance. Little did they know that it was naught but a well-polished facade, hiding a sense of self absorption so endlessly deep as to smother any candle that might light his way out.

Cathy alone saw him for the fiend he was. She tilted her head from him and fanned herself to show him her disdain. As ever, her clear contempt for the loathsome man did little to dissuade him. Indeed, it was as if he fed on her reactions, like some manner of accursed creature seeking only to bring about tears and agony. Nothing it seemed, could satiate the void where his heart should beat.

Beside her, Marshall discussed business with the illustrious Master Stonewall himself. Compared to Marshall's modest suit, the stitching of the boisterous magician's garments glowed with magic. Both men turned and smiled when Barnaby greeted them, unable to see him for the scoundrel he was.

His wicked smile was like that of a wolf as he turned his attention to Cathy. "May I have this dance, Miss Grant?"

She did her best to keep a polite smile on her face, no matter how much her lips quivered and strained. The sinister Barnaby had timed his opening strike perfectly. With her fiancé and the host of the ball watching, it would be the height of scandal to turn down his offer.

"Why yes, of course, Master Brue." Blithely, she accepted his arm, and as she followed him to the center of the ballroom floor, she silently cursed that the floor was merely magic. Oh that she might see him thrown to the water with all the other bottom-feeding creatures of the deep. Perhaps he'd be more tolerable were he to dwell amongst his own kind.

A quartet of stringed instruments was suspended in air by unseen magical forces, and even without musicians to play them, the instruments sprung to life, beginning the next song. With that, the dance had begun, with all the ladies and gentlemen in attendance moving gracefully to the tune. Yet none moved with a more devious grace than Barnaby.

Cathy, by contrast, struggled to keep pace with her diabolical dance partner's footwork. She felt as though all eyes were watching her stumble, and she felt truly hopeless. She wondered how she could possibly persevere against a foe who so effortlessly masks his villainy. That Cathy did not belong amongst these socialites was obvious to her. Even the shoulders of her dress felt tight, squeezing her as her growing anxiety tightened her chest.

"Foolish little girl. You ought not to have so profaned this ball with your presence."

The wicked timbre of his voice brought her back from the edge of despair and stoked the flames of fury within her. Her shaky nerves had become as iron.

Yet even as righteous anger welled within her, still Cathy fluttered her eyelashes at him, determined to play the innocent. She would meet his gambit, and let him think he had the upper hand until it was too late. "Why whatever do you mean? Marshall himself asked me to accompany him, and it would have been rather uncouth to refuse such a request from my fiancé. Wouldn't you agree?"

The predatory grin on Barnaby's face faded, his jaw now hard set as he ground his teeth maliciously.

Cathy continued to feign ignorance, retorting to Barnaby's malice with a bright smile. "I'm ever so glad to be in attendance this evening. Just look at how beautiful this manor is! With the enchantments upon the dance floor, I must confess that I find myself believing we could be dancing on a real lake."

He squinted at the floor. "I've not brought you here to discuss the flooring. You are to tell me precisely why you are still engaged to my cousin. I had thought we'd come to an understanding that you were to leave at once."

"Then I must beg your pardon, but it seems we have not come to an understanding at all," Cathy said defiantly, "for I will not be leaving my fiancé."

His eyes narrowed, like a lion preparing to pounce upon its prey. "You will not marry my cousin."

"Why not? It's because you think my birth standing is too low, isn't it?"

"Exactly. You are a mere tailor's daughter, and I will not sit idly by while you defile my and my family's name and legacy. Neither I nor my cousin will have anything to do with gutter rubbish like you." The warm, welcoming smile he wore upon his face like a brigand's mask belied the cruelty of his words. Anyone casting an errant gaze their way would not have seen the two as being locked in a duel, grasping at one another's throats.

Cathy composed herself, refusing to give her adversary a reaction. "How peculiar indeed that you speak so harshly of my family, and yet you so frequently patronize our tailor shop. If my father's work is so far beneath you, what exactly does that make you who clads himself in it?"

Like a venomous snake, Barnaby sneered before catching himself, reverting back to his insufferable smile. "At least your father knows his place. He's not the one parading himself around pretending to be something he clearly isn't."

"I do no such thing." She stepped on his right foot. Hard. "My apologies. You know how clumsy we peasants can be."

"My point exactly. I'm glad we agree." His shoe scrapped her foot. She narrowly dodged the full brunt of it. "Only a fool would expect a strumpet like you to fit in with polite society. Therefore, I will once more politely ask that you do us both a favor and break off the engagement before I'm forced to resort to more... impolite measures."

"Impolite? What exactly do you mean by that?" Once more, she dodged another stomp intended for her foot, and with righteous anger, she stomped on his instead.

Barnaby bit his tongue, suppressing his pained groan. "Suffice it to say that it would be better for you to not test my patience. Now be a good girl before your poor father has to worry about losing his store."

She gasped, her mouth agape in shock. Once more she attempted to stomp on his foot, but this time it was he who avoided the strike. "You brute. You wouldn't."

He responded with a scheming smirk that would put the Devil himself to shame. "It seems you don't know what I'm capable of."

"I know precisely what you're capable of, you monster." The song ended. She took a step away from him. "And I know that it was you who stole from the orphanage before burning it down."

His eyes went wide at the accusation, appearing for the first time that evening to be the prey and not the hunter. "You can't possibly prove that!"

She clucked her tongue at him. "Perhaps not, but I'll not back down from you until I can."

He scowled, grumbling like a wounded, feral dog. "You're in over your head, little girl, and if you won't listen to reason, then you've given me no choice." He stepped toward her, hooking an arm around her waist to keep her from slipping away. He leaned toward her. "I'll see your reputation and your family's business laid to ruin."

She recoiled from his dry lips, unable to imagine a worse fate than letting them touch hers...

*Editor's note: Charlotte, I agree that Bertram (Barnaby) is insufferable, but perhaps you could dial him down a touch to make him more believable for readers? He feels a little too villainous — Mary

<h1 style="text-align:center">Chapter 1</h1>

An autumn chill clung to the crisp, clean air of the countryside. Colorful leaves made the narrow lane outside the carriage window idyllic. Laoise felt as though she'd stepped right into one of the landscape paintings hanging throughout the Steepe's London residence. Compared to the dirty, smelly air of London, the countryside was paradise.

Laoise could get used to living somewhere this pretty, even if it would only be for a few months. After the hard work of helping with Charlotte's wedding to Martin Steepe, a few months of relaxation in the countryside would help her recover.

There'd be no tea parties to prepare for every week, or large family dinners, and there'd be no little dachshund running around underfoot. Despite being such a small dog, Oolong was an ever-present tripping hazard, particularly when Laoise was carrying fragile teaware. She understood why Charlotte thought such a sweet creature was some sort of malevolent demon. After Charlotte's embarrassing incident with the Hammond dachshunds a few years back, Laoise didn't blame her.

She was also grateful to have a break from the cranky butler, who she was embarrassed to think she once harbored a crush on. Sure, his face would have been handsome if he ever smiled, but it was difficult to stay enamored while being lectured about shining the silverware.

Yes, time away would do her some good. She would relax, recuperate, and best of all, she'd be paid handsomely to do it. There'd be no more worrying over how to afford all the medicine and doctor visits for her little brother Sean. Not with her salary more than doubled during her stay in the countryside to tend to the exiled Bertram Steepe, Martin's cousin.

Her nose wrinkled in disgust. Bertram. He was the catch in this little plan to relax. In her opinion, he deserved far worse than exile after his attempt to frame Charlotte and Martin for robbery at The Great Exhibition. All because he didn't approve of his cousin Martin marrying Charlotte, a baker's daughter and Laoise's best friend.

As if Martin could do better than sweet, naïve Charlotte. Those two fit together like an adorable, awkward pair of puzzle pieces that no one else quite understood. Last time she'd seen Charlotte, she'd been hunched over her new writing desk scribbling faster than Laoise could read. A sign Charlotte's latest story was going well.

The carriage pulled up to a large estate over twice the size of the Steepes' London house. Laoise stepped out, gaze locked on the house. "Are you sure this is the right place?" she asked the driver, but the man was already off his seat and pulling her bag out, eager to get rid of her.

The manor looked far too nice for a man to spend in exile. Then again, when you had the wealth of the Steepe Family from their successful shipping business and now from their popular new tea shops, she supposed even exile was done in style.

"Aye," the driver confirmed as he set her suitcase at her feet. He reached into his coat pocket and pulled out a small onyx stone. It was adorned with elaborate inlaid brass filigree, and an ancient looking rune carved into one side. "You'll be needin' this."

Laoise took the stone. It was heavy despite its small size. "What's this?"

"A summon stone. Just give 'er a tap and I'll know to come get ye." He tapped his finger on the rune. It thrummed with energy and glowed a faint light blue. Reaching into his other pocket, he produced an identical stone whose glowing rune matched the first. It let out an eerie hum like the sound a wine glass makes when running a finger around its edge.

"Pretty fancy magic," Laoise said. "Did you make it yourself?"

The driver chuckled. "That Steepe boy gave it to me a while back. Decent fellow." He gestured toward the manor. "Not that one. The other one."

Laoise snorted. Obviously Bertram hadn't made it. If he had, it would have exploded in their faces.

"Suppose I'll be seein' ye in a few weeks." He shook a brown leaf off his lumpy flat cap before plopping it back onto his head. "Might be snow on the ground by then."

"I'm staying for three months." Until early January, giving her a late Christmas celebration with her family. She hated to miss any holidays when she didn't know how many more she'd have with her brother, but being a few weeks late was worth being able to afford his medicine. She suspected the doctor didn't need to specially make the medicine like he claimed, but with no other doctor willing to take on another poor client, they had no other choice but to comply.

The carriage driver snorted. "We'll see." He jerked his thumb toward the maid stomping down the walkway toward the carriage, a battered valise in hand. Leaves crunched under her feet. Shannon. She'd come a month ago.

"Take me to the train station," Shannon demanded as she tossed her bag into the carriage.

"Where are you going?" Shannon had always been her favorite maid. They shared a room together at the Steepe residence in London, and they both came from Irish families. She related to Shannon more than any of the other staff members. Even when being teased for liking the butler.

"Mr. Steepe is all yours. I'm leaving. Good riddance to him and good riddance to this house." Shannon climbed into the carriage.

"You're leaving now? You've got two more months left out here." Losing her would make the household short a maid. She would be the one left to pick up all the extra work.

"I refuse to stay another day." Shannon spit at the house. "You should do yourself a favor and come with me. Leave the rat bastard to rot out here on his own."

The driver turned to Laoise, eyeing up her bag. "Ye stayin' or goin', Miss?"

"Staying."

"Ye'll regret it."

"Probably, but I have to stay. I need the money." She wouldn't let Bertram Steepe scare her away.

Shannon shook her head. "Then good luck. You'll need it. I left the instructions on the kitchen table. That's all I can do for you. Driver, get me out of here. I never want to see this damned house again." Shannon slammed the door shut.

The driver tipped his hat one last time to Laoise. "You can send for me when you need a ride to the station or village."

"Will do."

"Until then, goodbye, Miss." The carriage rolled toward the road. Shannon stuck her head out the carriage window to make an impolite gesture at the house. She'd never been one to hide her opinions.

Standing alone with only one bag in front of the large house made Laoise feel small. The windows were dark. Only a few on the main floor sported open curtains. It made the house look empty and quiet compared to the liveliness of the London residence. Part of her reveled in the silence. The rest of her feared it. She was too used to the crashes of Oolong bumping into people and objects. And little mechanical hummingbirds zipping past and over her head. Plus all the servants hurrying here and there. Silence felt...wrong.

She knocked once to the servants' entrance, and then twice a minute later when no one answered. She tried the knob, and finding the back door unlocked, let herself in.

Not surprising. The butler who'd spent the last two decades at the manor had retired a few months ago. If there was no new butler yet and no Shannon, she supposed answering the door would fall onto her shoulders now if the housekeeper demanded it. She'd never much liked that job. Guests were too often impatient, pushy, and worst of all, rude. Serving them was bad enough without welcoming them in with a smile too.

Fortunately, Laoise thought, a man in exile doesn't get too many guests. Perhaps Montgomery Steepe, Bertram's uncle and head of the family, would come visit to yell at his nephew and remind him of his shortcomings. Even though she rarely saw the man, that would be a guest she'd relish in welcoming to the manor.

Inside, silence greeted her. Dim light filtered in through the closed curtains. She slid her bag to her left hand and stepped deeper into the house. Large paintings depicted the fleet of ships that got the family their start in business. The wooden floors sported a sparkling shine that came from magic instead of maids. Light floral wallpaper decorated the walls. The decor was similar to the family home in London right down to the large house plants.

There was no doubt she was in the right house. Except the London home was only ever this quiet when the family was gone to the countryside. Then again, Bertram was the only Steepe in residence. The spoiled brat got exiled to a mansion to be waited on hand and foot while his uncle covered up his misdeeds. She bet he hadn't learned anything. He was no doubt reclining somewhere with a book in hand while he waited for a maid to serve him. Not a strong enough punishment in her opinion.

A thump echoed down the hallway, followed by a curse. She left her bag at the door and followed the noises. If she got any say in it, she'd open more curtains. The light in the hallways was too dim.

Another curse, this one gruff and laced with frustration. Definitely Bertram. She'd recognize his voice anywhere with how often he visited his cousin. He seemed to take sadistic pleasure in ordering her about whenever he showed his face.

Ticking filled the air as she approached one of the few rooms full of sunshine. The purple curtains clashed with the awful green wallpaper, or at least with what little of the wallpaper she could see. Clocks of all sizes and ornamentation hung all over the room, occupying nearly every inch of the walls. There had to be at least a hundred of them all ticking in eerie unison, with a stately grandfather clock as the centerpiece of the room. Besides the empty fireplace, only a few chairs decorated the middle of the room.

"Where is it?" Bertram growled out. He prowled along the far wall, his back to her as he inspected a cuckoo clock. Instead of his usual fashionable suits, he wore a silk dressing gown. The belt hung loose, trailing down one side as he moved on to the next clock. His hair stuck up at odd angles.

She'd never seen him disheveled before. Then again, she'd never seen him in anything but fashionable suits tailored to show off his lean figure. She paused, struggling to accept the sight in front of her.

"Can I be of service, sir?" Laoise put on her cheeriest smile. She hadn't even had time to unpack and her work had already begun. She'd have to have words with the rest of the staff later.

His head whipped around at the sound of her voice. She sucked in a breath. Bloodshot eyes met hers. His unshaven chin matched his dressing gown and rumpled clothes. He looked more like a vagrant who'd snuck in rather than the charming man who made the young ladies of London blush. It was only his jawline, still perfect as ever, that gave away his identity.

"Do you hear it?" he asked, voice rough from lack of sleep. His left eye twitched.

"The clocks?"

"The clock. One clock." His unfocused gaze raked over the wall of clocks to his right. "The one that's different."

No two clocks in the room were the same. The room must have been designed by a madman. There was no reason anyone needed this many clocks. Bertram looked tortured as he held an ear up to one clock, teeth gnashing when he wasn't pleased with it.

"Wha—" The clocks cut her off, chiming the hour in one great cacophony of noise. She clapped her hands over her ears. Nothing could be done to drown out the cuckoos, chimes, and dings. Bertram stood frozen. His gaze darted from clock to clock.

The tolling of the hour ended, plunging the room back into silence and leaving her ears ringing. Then a cuckoo clock to Bertram's left began to chime, the little wooden bird chirping its mocking tune.

With no hesitation, he ripped the clock from the wall and threw it onto the wooden floor. He stomped on the clock again and again, each stomp changing the pitch of the cuckoo's song. It sounded as though he were throttling a bird in front of her.

Finally, a small slate tablet spilled out of the wooden housing of the clock, the runes still glowing with magic. Bertram descended on the tablet, dashing it against the floor until it broke in two. The chirping stopped abruptly, leaving only the sounds of the ticking clocks and Bertram's panting. Then he straightened up, huffing as he regained his composure.

"Finally. Peace." He took a step forward. The clock stuck to his foot. He bounced backward on one leg until his back hit the wall. He steadied himself against the wall. Then two shakes of his leg and the clock came free. He straightened his dressing gown, as if that would somehow improve his appearance.

Laoise took a step back when his attention landed on her.

"I'll take dinner in my room today."

She shuffled out of the way, keeping her distance as he left the room.

Well then. She'd be serving a man who'd lost his mind.

Chapter 2

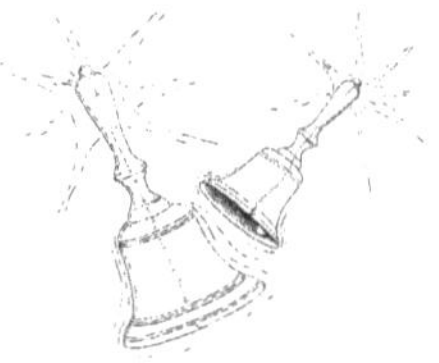

A quick exploration revealed a large parlor, a second smaller sitting room, and two other smaller rooms too dark to make out. The hallway ended at a glass door leading into the greenhouse. Laoise peered through the door, finding thick unkempt greenery stretching from one end of the room to the other, sprinkled with colorful flowers. It was like a jungle inside, and knowing the Steepes and their eccentricities, it wasn't hard to imagine hidden surprises waiting in the vegetation. Unexpected magic or fearsome creatures. Oolong could be quite fearsome when he attacked his favorite ball.

Gertrude Steepe, Martin's mother, often spoke of the greenhouse. Building it had been her husband's wedding gift to her. She would gush to her guests about her prized collection of exotic orchids, listing off names that Laoise could swear she was making up on the spot. Looking over at the colorful blooms now, Mrs. Steepe's boasts didn't seem like an exaggeration, though she couldn't for the life of her name a single flower she saw.

Unlike the rich ladies she served, Laoise had no time to waste on flower arranging or gardening. The best she could do was to shoot poor Charlotte sympathetic looks whenever her mother-in-law prattled on about the meaning of each individual orchid. That, and stand behind her mocking her mannerisms to make Charlotte laugh.

She turned and retraced her steps. At the stairs, she turned to try the other side of the house. Her bag remained in front of the door where she'd left it. There were no signs of anyone having rifled through it. Not that there were any valuables worth stealing. The bag itself was worth more than the clothes inside. She headed for the servants' quarters to find her room.

"Hello?" She wandered up and down the hallway. The butler's door hung open, but the room was empty save for a scattering of empty whiskey bottles on the desk. The housekeeper's room sported a drawn portrait of Mr. Steepe. It was a fairly accurate likeness, save perhaps for the devil horns and crossed eyes. The fork stuck through the face pinning the drawing to the wall was also an interesting creative liberty. A pity the housekeeper hadn't done the same to the real Mr. Steepe.

There really was no one else except her. Not today anyway. There was supposed to be permanent staff at the ready year round. Had Bertram truly been so frustrating as to make everyone quit? Or perhaps they had been given the day off from their duties. It was a dull hope, but it was far better than the alternative.

The missing cook worried her the most. It'd been years since she helped her mother in the kitchen. While her mother had always been an excellent cook, those skills never came naturally to Laoise. Practice did little more than make her food palatable.

She decided to explore the rooms and pick one. With no one else about, she could claim any bedroom she wanted in the servants' quarters. She had just stopped at a room with a surprisingly large window to the outside when a ringing bell stopped her short. She eyed up the wall of bells that would tell her which room the request was coming from, but by the looks of the wall, someone had torn them all down in a fit. The tinkling grew louder and faster. Impatient even. She double checked the bells. None were attached.

Then a floating bell appeared from around the corner, a little silver one, heading right for her head. She sighed and set her bag down, still unable to unpack.

She reached out her hand to grab the bell and stop its irritating jingling, but like a shy cat, it remained just beyond her grasp, beckoning her to follow. She followed the bell upstairs. It never stopped ringing, although it quieted down a notch. She grit her teeth as it led her down a hallway to a room at the back of the house. The bell finally went silent as it passed over the room's threshold.

Mr. Steepe stood inside in front of a mirror as he fixed his cuffs. The robe was gone and his suit was back. Although his shirt had been misbuttoned, making it crooked toward the bottom. In London, she imagined his valet never would have stood for such a thing. He had also shaved and combed his hair. He no longer looked like a deranged lunatic but rather like his usual handsome, smug, insufferable self.

"Shannon!" he said as soon as he spotted her in the mirror. "My porridge has gone cold. How many times do I have to tell you I want hot porridge. Bring me a new bowl."

"Yes, sir."

He finally turned from his reflection and frowned. "You're not Shannon."

"No, sir, I'm Laoise. Just arrived." The bed was a mess with sheets and pillows on the floor. Open books littered the desk alongside an umbrella. A large magnifying glass rested against it.

"About time I get another maid. Warm up my porridge, Lisa."

She gave him a curtsy, mouth twitching against the way he botched her name. "Right away, sir." She'd always preferred serving Martin. He didn't get her name right either, but he couldn't get anyone's name right. At least he was more polite, almost always requesting either tea or something to put in it. An easy enough task unless Oolong was prowling the halls.

The breakfast tray sat on the corner of the desk despite the late morning hour. She grabbed it and headed back downstairs. When she reached the bottom of the staircase, she hesitated. Which way was the kitchen? She'd expected someone to give her a tour. This place was enormous enough that she could lose Oolong in it.

The dirty porridge pot sat on the stove. She plopped the porridge back into the pot and heated it up, an easy task with the kitchen's magically powered stove, one of the few amenities afforded to the servants. Having demonstrated the extent of her culinary prowess, she plopped the porridge back into the serving bowl and started back on the long journey back to Bertram. With a slight chill in the air, she half expected the porridge to be cold again by the time she reached his room.

Truly this house was far too big for only one man. In the dim light, it felt as though the portraits on the wall were watching her. To be fair, if they were enchanted they likely were. But in the cold dim light, it was far more unnerving. She preferred her portraits silent and frozen.

The carpets running down the center of the hallways silenced her footsteps. Passing all the dark rooms made her wish she hadn't heard Charlotte's friend Mary whispering about haunted houses and seances. She'd never been one to dwell on ghost stories, and yet walking through an empty house made her worry the stories were true. Then again, a ghost would make a better house guest than Mr. Steepe.

"Finally," he said as she entered his room. He'd moved to his balcony despite the chill. An old newspaper sat on the little table. The headline declared The Great Exhibition a smashing success. The scowl on his face put her on alert. In the past, that look was usually followed by some impassioned speech and wild gesturing that often knocked over his tea.

The sunshine beat down on the table. Knowing him, he'd complain about it any second. She reached for the closed umbrella over the table. "Let me get that for you, sir."

"Get what?" He looked up from his newspaper. "No," he objected as he reached for her arm. The umbrella opened with a swish and water poured out of it. She gaped as the umbrella rained down on the newspaper and porridge. A dark little cloud hovered underneath the umbrella, flashing with what looked like lighting. It even had the sound of distant, muffled thunder. The blurry edges of the cloud unculated, but it continued pouring down with no signs of stopping or dispersing.

Mr. Steepe shot up and closed the umbrella, water dripping down his arms. His eyes closed. He grit his teeth as he lowered himself back down. "No touching the umbrella. Ever."

The umbrellas had to be his work. Though seemingly gifted in wealth, status, and looks, he'd never had any talent for the gentlemen's pursuit of magic. She'd seen his umbrella back in London do something similar before Martin fixed it. Evidently, whatever Martin had done continued to elude his cousin.

"Sorry, sir. Can I get you anything else?" she asked, adding a false sweetness to her voice to hide how much she enjoyed seeing him soaked. His miserable expression brought a genuine smile to her face. She also didn't mind the way his white shirt clung to his chest and broad shoulders.

"Has the newspaper come yet?" He scowled as he tossed the ruined one onto the porridge tray. A layer of water floated above the porridge.

"I don't know. I'll have to check."

"Well, go check." He waved her off, annoyance written all over his face. "And have the cook start dinner. Beef Wellington."

She hesitated a moment, unsure of how to say that she couldn't find the cook. She wasn't even sure if there was one. "Right away, sir," she said, thinking better of it.

She went off in search of the newspaper. By the time she found it, the little ringing bell was back. It bumped into her shoulder and then her head. The ringing didn't cease until the newspaper was in Bertram's hands. She let out a frustrated sigh. With floating bells, there'd truly be no escaping his demands.

In the empty kitchen, she flipped through the lone cookbook sitting near the stove. "I'm a maid, not a cook. I should get paid triple for this," she grumbled as she searched for a beef Wellington recipe. Finding it, she read through the instructions. "This is going to take all day!" she dropped the book with a huff.

Silence greeted her. It was eerie talking to herself. She held out some small semblance of hope that the cook would appear from the doorway laughing at her predicament but still joining in to help. With each passing moment, the silence and loneliness crept further and further in. The kitchen in London was always the busiest room in the house. A kitchen wasn't meant to be this quiet.

Maybe there was some sort of similar, easier dish she could prepare. She flipped through the cookbook, but each recipe was somehow more complicated than the previous one. She returned to the beef Wellington and sighed. Finding no way out, there was nothing left to do but grit her teeth and start work on the complex dish. Besides, even in exile Bertram still had some clout. Getting soaked with his umbrella and served the wrong meal for dinner on her very first day might result in complaints to his uncle and cousin, which might result in a cut to her pay. Better to try and appease her employer for now, no matter how ridiculous his demands might be.

She groaned after reading through the recipe a second time. A roast beef was easy enough, but wrapping the beef in mushrooms and pastry? Charlotte could probably cook up a dish like this in her sleep, but Laoise was still struggling to figure out what the hell "duxelles" were. Even so, the thought of making Mr. Steepe eat her cooking brought a smile to her face. For the first time in her life, she was glad she didn't have her mother's talents. If he was set on being a demanding prick, she'd play his game and make him suffer right back.

She got to work, humming as a rush of energy invigorated her. The recipe played out as she'd expected. While the food baked, she searched through the pantry and read Shannon's instructions. She spent a few minutes attempting to fix the wall of broken bells before giving up.

Laoise reached into the oven and pulled out her creation. She could almost hear her mother groaning in agony at the sight of the thing. Not fit to serve to a dog, she'd probably say. The top of the crust was burnt to a crisp, and the bottom was a soggy mess. It looked like an old log floating in scum. Surely Bertram deserved nothing less.

By the time she cut away the burnt and soggy bits, there wasn't much crust left. She cut the beef into slices and put it on a tray. She added a glass of water and headed back to Mr. Steepe's room.

This time he was so absorbed in checking several feathers with his large magnifying glass that he didn't notice her at first. Not until she put the tray down beside him. "Dinner, sir."

He dropped the feather. "What's this?"

"Beef Wellington, sir. As requested."

"This is decidedly not what I requested. There's no Wellington here." He poked at it with his fork. "Not much beef either. Send this mess back to the cook."

"There is no cook, sir."

"No cook?" He dropped his fork onto the plate with a clang. "So she actually did leave after all..."

"Seems so, sir."

"Just as well I suppose. Her last batch of biscuits were harder than rocks." He picked his fork back up, cutting off a bite-sized piece of the beef and tasting it. "So this is your doing then?"

"It is indeed," said Laoise with a curtsy. "It's my first time cooking it. I made it just for you, sir."

"It shows. This is dreadful." Clearly there'd be no sympathy for her predicament. Bertram's spoke curtly, not looking up from his plate as he cut off another piece and inspected it. "The pastry is inexplicably both under and overcooked, and the duxelles mushroom stuffing is slimy and musty."

Even though she had intended for him to hate the meal, his words cut her more deeply than she'd expected. Back in London she got backhanded remarks when Mr. Steepe was displeased, but at least he tried to maintain a polite facade. Apparently there was no need to maintain appearances in exile. At least now she knew how to pronounce the word duxelles. Like "duke cell," and not like "duck sells" as she had been reading it to herself. Her mind wandered, imagining a duke cell. A fancy prison for wealthy noble brats. The complaints of one such brat snapped her back to the real world.

"...and as for the meat itself." His nose wrinkled as he chewed, clearly not enjoying the experience, yet evidently his hunger was winning the battle against his sense of taste. "Well, it's difficult to ruin a good cut of beef, but you forgot to even season the thing. Fetch me the salt. Now."

"Of course, sir."

"And bring me another portion. I have no intention of starving myself for your failure."

Laoise raised an eyebrow. "Even though you don't like it, sir?"

"I'll make do. I'd have you prepare something else, but you've done enough damage in the kitchen already." He choked down another pink cut of the beef, pushing the pastry and stuffing to the side. "You're to stick to simple fare from now on."

Laoise bit her tongue and held in the smart remarks threatening to burst out of her. Instead, she'd offer an olive branch to smooth things over. "Perhaps you would like some tea as well?"

"No, I would not," his voice was full of disgust, far more cold and bitter than when he spoke of his meal, "Not now. Not ever. You will never ask me that question again." He lifted his fork, using it to shoo her toward the door. "Now fetch the salt."

She waited to roll her eyes until she had her back to him. Life in the countryside was supposed to be relaxing and rejuvenating. Instead, she was ready to grab a fork and make Bertram's face match the drawing in the servants' quarters. She'd heard plenty of women swoon over the man and his perfect jaw. A moment with him would surely make them come to their senses.

She wasn't the swooning type. Or the type to give up easily. It would take more than an impolite employer to drive her off, and if he insisted on making her life miserable, she'd be more than happy to return his generosity in kind.

Chapter 3

Morning came too soon like it always did. At least she got a quiet, warm room. Having a full room to herself felt like a luxury. She'd always shared a room with another maid. And before that she'd shared her room with her siblings.

With a few minutes to spare before getting to work, she took advantage of the free time. She set up a picture of her family on her nightstand. Her Da had paid for the photograph around Christmas as a present to her Ma. The picture included everyone, with her smashed in the middle between all three of her brothers.

Everyone looked somber in the photo, but only because they had to stay perfectly still for so long. The ghostly wisps around her brothers' hands were all that remained of the constant fidgeting and muffled laughter as they punched one another in the arm. She could recall how her father stood motionless and spoke through clenched teeth as he threatened to toss all of them into the river if they didn't behave.

Only her mother delivering her own punch to his arm had kept him from making good on that threat. Laoise couldn't help but smile looking at the picture as the memories of that day came pouring back, even if it looked like they were all gathered for a funeral.

Next came the folded drawing, which her youngest brother Sean had made. It showed the two of them together a few months ago with all the artistic talent one could expect from an eight-year-old. Their heads were far too big, but they were all smiles. Almost literally.

She also kept a short note from her middle brother Rian wishing her luck. He would be embarrassed if he knew she still had it after all these years. He'd given it to her during her first few months living away from home during her first job working for the wealthy Mrs. Hammond. She'd been struggling more than she let on with the change, but seeing her brother's sloppy handwriting always made her efforts feel appreciated. She'd carried the note with her wherever she stayed ever since.

Her attention lingered on Sean's drawing. Every time they thought he was past the illness for good, it would return and render him bedridden. She knew better than to hope he could keep beating back his sickness forever. But she'd help him beat it for as long as possible. Unfortunately, the new medicine their doctor had suggested was expensive. Without her extra money from looking after Mr. Steepe the family wouldn't be able to afford it. They were counting on her help.

She straightened the photo, and the rush of warmth that always came with looking at her prized possessions hit her right in the chest, working its way to her face. Laoise would do anything for her brother, including spending three months meeting Mr. Steepe's pompous and rude demands.

She shoved her spare set of clothes into the wardrobe. The little room looked sparse with her meager belongings and no roommate. At least Shannon had left behind a schedule on the desk. The simple schedule included meal times and food deliveries. It wasn't much, but it was a start. Back in London, the housekeeper would mete out their duties and change them as needed. Here, Laoise had to be everyone and do everything. An impossible task, which meant she'd have to decide what was most important.

She got to work on a fresh batch of porridge, humming the tune of *The Rising of the Moon* while she worked. She always hummed Irish folk songs when she worked, an old habit she had picked up from her mother. It certainly helped chase away the silence which permeated the house like a crypt. While the porridge cooked she took better stock of the pantry.

The shelves were sparse. She wished she'd made better use of that beef. A stew or something that would have given them more meals. Despite there being plenty of tea, there was no coffee. She checked twice to be sure. Water it was then. After his reaction the day before, she suspected he wouldn't appreciate her slipping him a pot of tea.

She took the tray up on a cart, taking the walk slow to keep from getting lost in the servants' passageways. As she opened the door to the dusty, dim hallways designed to keep the servants out of sight, she suddenly felt quite silly. With no one but Mr. Steepe around, why shouldn't she start waltzing around the house as she pleased? Staying out of sight of one person was easy enough, particularly one who didn't seem interested in maintaining even the illusion of the nicety typical of a normal household. She pushed the cart confidently out into the gorgeous main hall, illuminated by the bright, soft rays of the morning sun.

She made her way to his bedroom door and knocked quietly. "Breakfast, Mr. Steepe." No answer came. She thought back to the schedule left for her in her room and the small note that said he preferred his breakfast delivered to his room. As a maid, she shouldn't go into his room while he was still in there. But there was no butler or valet to wake him. If she didn't wake him, she'd have to listen to him complain about cold porridge again.

She squared her shoulders and knocked once more before opening the door and pushing the breakfast cart inside. "Good morning, sir. Breakfast is ready," she called in the most chipper voice she could muster. The closed curtains dimmed the light streaming into the room. More books had joined the ones on the desk. Bookmarks jutted out between the pages. Some bookmarks were nothing more than scraps of paper with notes scrawled across them. The body of a pocket watch sat in the midst of the mess, its internal gears and springs strewn around it.

Muffled, unintelligent words floated to her from the bed. She spun around. Mr. Steepe lay in bed on his stomach. Shirtless. Blankets tangled around his lower half. The wet patch of drool on his pillow kept her mind from straying onto an impolite path. A plain gold bracelet adorned his left wrist. She wondered if it was a gift from a sweetheart. After all, he was older than Martin. He should have been married off first.

"Are you all right, sir?" Both Mr. Steepes at the house in London were early risers. Half the time, Martin Steepe would already be up and out of the house by now. That man hated to waste the morning. She'd assumed his cousin would be the same. Apparently not.

"Get out of my room," he said, voice muffled against the pillow crammed against his head. She kept her attention on his face to avoid looking at the way his back muscles clenched as he moved.

Annoyance trickled through her as she left, not bothering to shut the door. She should know better than to expect any gratitude for cooking for him. Men like him were used to ordering the servants about. They saw nothing to be grateful for.

With him lazing about, she did more exploring to better get her bearings. She ran the duster over paintings and portraits she passed. The housekeeper wasn't here to lecture her for not cleaning if she had time to wander, but old habits died hard. Looking like you weren't busy enough always came with a new list of work to be done. Plus, if Mr. Steepe caught her wandering, she'd pretend to be working. Servants hard at work might as well be invisible. Sometimes she thought the rich would make them invisible with glamour if they figured out how.

The silence felt stifling and heavy in a way she didn't expect. Then again, she got little of it in the city. This wasn't the peaceful silence she'd dreamed about. But more of an empty, lonely silence of a house that was meant to be full of family. And dachshunds.

To distract her away from the quiet, she hummed to herself, running through her favorite folk tunes as she made her way through the house, *The Rocky Road to Dublin* this time.

Without knowing which room was which, she took to calling them each by the color of their wallpaper or furniture that stuck out to her. There was the obvious parlor, followed by, the blue room, the daisy room, the clock room with enough clocks to drive anyone mad with existential dread, and finally the room with the ugliest armchair she'd ever been sorry to lay eyes on.

A faded green and yellow floral pattern covered the cushioning on the seat and back of the chair. A patch of mismatched fabric marred the front of the seat cushion. The light wood didn't pair well with any of the fabric. Worst of all, ticking from the clock room next door infiltrated the room. A conversation would drown it out, but the annoying ticks and tocks of time would be there in the moments of silence.

When she reached the stairs the duster tried to pull away from her. She yelped at the sudden movement and let go. Free, the duster got to work dusting the banister.

"Magic. Of course." She relaxed. In the city the Steepes didn't use cleaning spells during the day because the magic didn't care who or what got in the way. Oolong was bad enough to have underfoot without having brooms and buckets getting in the way too. That's to say nothing of the chaos that could arise if even a single rune was smudged. Back at Mrs. Hammond's a new footman once inscribed the wrong runes on a mop handle and nearly flooded the entire kitchen. But the duster didn't seem to be causing much havoc. Not yet anyway.

At the top of the stairs the duster fell over and she caught it before it toppled down the staircase. In the upstairs hallway she passed by a broom sweeping the floor. She gave it a wide berth. The duster yanked her toward the dusty paintings lining the stairwell. She dusted them as she went.

Downstairs magic was more on display than upstairs as if it was meant to impress guests. The hallway wallpaper moved, the trees and flowers on it swaying as if blowing in a wind. The effect made her go cross-eyed as she tried to watch all the details. Funny how the upper classes would waste magic on their wallpaper, but continue to hire a small army of servants to look after them. Servants were a status symbol as much as magic.

As she made her way through the first floor toward the back, the ticking of clocks grew louder and louder.

The clocks never quieted. Bertram didn't understand how Martin slept through them. Or how the butler could stand to keep winding them all up. It had to take that man an hour each day just to tend to the clocks.

"Bertie, can you fetch me another clock? A cuckoo one this time."

"You already have two. Isn't that enough?"

"Hardly!" Martin looked to the two clocks hanging on the wall across from his bed. He looked smaller than his eight years with the pile of blankets his mother had covered him in, declaring he would sweat the fever out. Judging by his red cheeks and the sheen on his forehead, his fever wasn't over yet. Yet feverish or not, his spirits certainly hadn't dampened. He smiled brightly, swaying from side to side in time with the pendulums of the clocks. "Tick. Tock. Tick. Tock."

Bertram put his hand on his cousin's shoulder to stop him from swaying. "And you don't get sick of that sound?"

"Never! I like thinking about all the things inside spinning and whirring..." He pet a dachshund who slept beside him, tongue lolling out. Delicately, he lifted up the dog's floppy ears in each hand, lifting them to match the rhythm of the clocks. "And Oolong likes them too! Tick. Tock."

The dog stirred a moment before yawning and shutting his eyes once more. He was very mild-mannered for a puppy. A suitable match for a bedridden young boy. Surprising seeing as how the dog came from a Hammond litter.

Suddenly Martin dropped the dog's ears and looked up eagerly. "Ooh! You know what would be perfect? That big clock with the hummingbird in it! Will you bring it up here?"

"That giant thing?" The clock was too massive, easily twice as tall as Bertram. Even the footmen would have a hard time lifting it. "How am I supposed to do that?"

"You can levitate it up the stairs, can't you? Pleeeease?" Martin clasped his hands and smiled. It was hard to say no to that face. Even so, Bertram had only recently learned the runes to levitate small objects. He wasn't confident in his ability to lift the massive clock, even less so in his ability to fix it if he dropped it. He reached for the washcloth and wiped the sweat off Martin's forehead, dipping it into the pan of cold water and then laying it back over his forehead. "I have something better than that old clock."

"Like what?" Martin patted the bedsheets in excitement. Oolong lifted his head at the commotion before rolling to his side.

"Something I made just for you." Martin's birthday was still a few months away, but Bertram wanted to give him something early. Just in case... No. He wouldn't contemplate that. Martin would see his birthday. He had to. He reached into his pocket and pulled out the gift. It was a small metallic bird, barely big enough to fill the palm of Bertram's hand. "A hummingbird of your very own."

Martin's eyes widened. "A real live hummingbird?"

Bertram chuckled. He'd thought the brass screws for eyes and the wind up key sticking out of its back would have been a giveaway. "Mother says we can't buy a real one, so I made one for you. I built and enchanted it myself." He'd taken some inspiration from all those damned clocks for this project and a spell he'd found in one of his school books. He offered the brass-plated bird to Martin. "And now you have the only hummingbird in all of England. Want to wind it up?"

Martin gasped and nodded rapidly. He reached out with both hands, straining a bit as he turned the stiff key in the machine's back. The bird started to emit a rapid clicking sound and a faint bluish glow appeared from between the seams of the brass plating. With jerky, mechanical motions, the bird's head started to turn left and right. Then its wings started to flutter.

Bertram held out his hand, and the bird sprung to life, hovering in mid air. It did one loop around the bed before stuttering and crashing into the headboard of the bed. Oolong started awake, giving the machine a quick sniff before rolling back over.

Bertram's cheeks burned with embarrassment. That wasn't the surprise he'd meant for his ailing cousin. "I'm sorry. I'll fix it." He reached for the bird, but Martin scooped it up first. His mouth opened in awe. Bertram recognized that look. It was the same look he had the first time he saw fireworks. Or the first time he saw his mother apply glamour to her face. Or whenever Oolong did something cute.

"Wow! It flew! It really flew just like a bird!" The wings twitched like a dying insect in his hands. "And you did it all by yourself?"

"Y-yes," said Bertram, scratching the back of his neck sheepishly. Coming from anyone else such praise would sound sarcastic, but Martin was incapable of anything but absolute sincerity. For a moment, he forgot that the machine had broken down in a matter of seconds. "I'm glad you like it."

"Like it? I love it!" Martin pulled the tiny bird to his chest. It gave one last twitch as a gear sprang out from under its wing. "You're the best, Bertie!"

Bertram smiled at his cousin until a spring suddenly shot out of the bird's neck, hitting him on the cheek. "Will you at least let me fix the thing?

"No. Not 'til you show me exactly how it works." Martin's eyelids drooped. The day's excitement had clearly been too much for him. He and Oolong yawned in unison. "I want to learn to make wonderful things like this."

"Tomorrow." He patted Martin's legs. The boy needed his rest. "For now, let's put this thing away before it explodes."

"It explodes?"

"Hmm..." Bertram pondered as he placed the remains of the bird in a small wooden box. "Probably not."

"Wow," muttered Martin as he laid back his head and closed his eyes. "An exploding humming bird."

Bertram crept out of the room, nearly closing the door behind him before hearing the hummingbird fall completely apart, its components clanging against the inside of the box. He sighed. It would take him forever to put them back together. But this time he'd do it with Martin. They'd have plenty of time to make it even better. The endless ticking of the clocks in the room reminded him of that.

The duster dragged Laoise into the hideous room. All the ticking from the clocks made her wish she had earmuffs. Even the crackling of the fireplace had been drowned out by the endless march of gears and pendulums. "Not the clock room," she groaned.

"It's called the green room, not the clock room." Mr. Steepe shifted in an arm chair to her right, startling her. She hadn't noticed him there. He gestured to the nearest wall at an area where the clock from yesterday had been. "After the wallpaper."

"I see. How can you be sure the walls are green when you can barely see them? And why are there so many clocks?"

He wrinkled his nose. "You ask a lot of questions for a maid."

"My apologies, sir. Just tryin' to get to know the house better. I've never been here before."

The apology appeared to appease him. He leaned back. "The clocks all belonged to my grandfather. He liked clocks. Unfortunately for him, once you start collecting something, you get saddled with always collecting it. Since no one knew what else to get him every Christmas, he got plenty of clocks. From family, business partners, and anyone else trying to please him. Needless to say, he was never a man to be late. He also took 'Better three hours too soon than a minute too late' literally."

"Is that a saying?." She let go of the duster, letting it float up to get the tops of clocks too tall for her to reach.

"It's from *The Merry Wives of Windsor*."

"I don't know that one."

He scoffed. "No, I don't suppose you would know your Shakespeare, would you?"

She bit her tongue. Better to be diplomatic for now. She could always slap that smug face of his later. "With all this ticking to deal with, I'm not surprised he'd leave three hours early for an appointment to escape."

"They aren't so bad. This is the best room in the house to think in."

"Really? I can't hear myself think at all over all this racket."

"Exactly." He propped his feet up on the ottoman and closed his eyes.

Once, he'd been sitting in a similar manner while visiting Martin. A new maid, a girl who couldn't have been more than sixteen, had nearly set her skirts on fire when she got distracted staring at him. She hadn't seen the logs roll when she added one to the fire. Nor had she noticed the sparks that popped right at her skirts, leaving scorch marks. After the incident, the other maids teased the girl for her "fiery passion." Laoise included.

The duster floated back down and she grabbed it, determined to get out of the room before he started making demands. The duster tugged back as it headed for the next clock. She tugged on it again, but the duster continued to strain forward. She let go, giving up on it and heading out of the room. Three steps from the door he spoke up again.

"Is that you making all that noise?"

"What noise?" All she heard was the clocks.

"That banging noise. Go find it and quiet it down. And throw another log on the fire before you go. It's getting chilly." He shifted, resting a hand against the side of his face. "If you can't even serve my porridge hot the least you can do is warm the damned house."

There was no telling how long it'd taken him to get out of bed once she'd delivered his breakfast.

"Yes, sir. Of course, sir," she said, grabbing a log from the woodpile. The temptation to bash his head in with the log was great, but she gritted her teeth and tossed it onto the fire. She glanced back, making sure he'd shut his eyes before she reached for the nearest clock. She held onto the second hand for several seconds before letting go. As the hand resumed ticking, it did so out of time with the other clocks.

She was still smiling when she found the source of the banging. A noise she never would have noticed herself until she'd gone back upstairs. Another enchanted duster banged against a closed door, knocking against the wood as it failed to get in. Undeterred, it tried over and over again. A bedroom, she guessed. One of the family bedrooms since guests stayed in the opposite wing. Nothing marked this one as any different from the rest, except for small scratch marks at the bottom.

While magic helped speed up work for the servants at the Steepe residence in London and helped shorten their work days, this was why they couldn't rely on magic alone. Enchantments came with limitations and didn't always work as expected. Without someone to help the tools along they tended to get stuck on obstacles just like this one.

"Are you going to take care of that?"

She jumped as Mr. Steepe stepped up behind her, looking more stern-faced than ever. Much more like his uncle, on the rare times she'd actually seen him, than himself.

"Once it dusts the room it'll stop." She twisted the doorknob, finding the door locked. She jiggled the handle. Odd. None of the other bedrooms were locked.

"Stop that." He knocked her hand away. "You aren't allowed in that room."

"If the room doesn't get cleaned the duster will keep banging against the room. It's an easy fix."

"The room doesn't need dusted." He grabbed the duster and mumbled under his breath as he ran a thumb over the runes. The runes glowed once before blinking out. He shoved the duster at her. "There. Fixed."

"What did you do?"

"I erased the enchantment."

Her nostrils flared. "I can't do all the dusting myself, sir. This place is too big." She'd rather let it get dusty. Then it would be the problem of whoever came after her.

He shrugged. "You'll have to find a way."

"Or I can go inside and clean one room instead."

"No. We aren't discussing the room again," he said, his voice low. He then leaned back and straightened his cuffs. "I'll be downstairs. Try not to burn my dinner today. Remember: Simple fare."

He tromped off, his footsteps thudding down the hall despite the carpeting. Bertram Steepe hiding secrets shouldn't surprise her. Not after he tried to burn down a warehouse, blow up a shipment of his cousin's tea, stole exhibits at The Great Exhibition to frame his cousin and fiancée, and God only knew what else. All to bring down his cousin's tea business and keep him from marrying a baker's daughter.

He'd even kissed Charlotte at a party. A despicable thing to kiss your cousin's fiancée, and it'd confirmed to Laoise that Bertram Steepe's good looks couldn't make up for the rest of him. Underneath that chiseled jaw and muscular physique he was rotten to the core. An awful kisser too as Charlotte told it.

If he was plotting again, she wouldn't let him get away with it. He'd given Charlotte enough trouble already. Whatever he was hiding she'd find out. There had to be a way to get into the locked room to get proof of his misdeeds. She'd wait to expose him until after she'd received her first paycheck, enough to pay for her brother's next round of medicine. Giving Bertram his comeuppance would be the icing on the cake.

The fantasy energized her as she made her way to the kitchen. It'd be porridge for dinner. Simple fare indeed. And if he complained, she'd just remind him of all the dusting she now had to do by hand. With the now disenchanted duster still in hand, a wicked smile crept across her face. She shook the duster over the pot, letting a few gray particles fall into the porridge.

His just desserts would come later. For now, just porridge.

Chapter 4

For once, Mr. Steepe woke up bright and early, ruining her plan to go snooping around the locked room some more. So far, she'd made no progress. Three weeks ago she tried to pick the lock to no avail. Then she waited in the hallway to catch him coming out. Except he never seemed to go in. Even the servants' back passages stopped short of the room. Had Bertram blocked them off? Perhaps that was how he was getting inside.

While her attempts to get into the room had proven fruitless, she did have plenty of time to spy on Mr. Steepe as she worked. Last week he'd wandered around the perimeter of the estate's grounds, his hand running along the fence. On the other side of the fence, a black horse galloped to meet him.

She thought that perhaps he'd leap over the fence and ride the horse off into the countryside, but she thought better of expecting a spoiled brat like him to survive on his own outside of a comfortable manor. Instead, he simply fed it an apple and stroked its mane before heading back inside. Whatever he was planning, he wasn't ready to make his move. Not yet, at least.

The last remaining enchanted duster left her little time to unravel his scheming. It kept knocking against the door, forcing her to keep an eye on it and lead it away lest he wipe the enchantment from it. Thanks to the enchanted brooms, the floors didn't need swept, but she leaned against a broom pretending to sweep anyway as she stood near the door to the patio. The break gave her a much needed respite. The skin on her hands was still wrinkled from doing laundry.

Outside, Mr. Steepe practiced his fencing on an overgrown shrub. It'd been an hour now, and he showed no signs of stopping. He stepped back and then forward as he struck the shrub, his moves graceful. Without his fencing helmet on, his look of somber concentration was on full display. His back and arms tensed as he struck again, his muscles bunching and flexing as he moved. Watching him was hypnotizing.

At her feet, there wasn't a speck of dirt. She sighed, more in frustration at herself than anything. Feeling sorry over her failure to get into the room wouldn't help her mood. "Stop lookin'," she admonished herself. "He isn't worth the attention." And yet she couldn't peel her eyes away from him. His perfect form was like a work of art with each precise, calculated thrust.

Thrust... thrust... thrust...

The broom gave way beneath her and she stumbled. She hadn't realized she was leaning on it as she stared. Nor had she realized her jaw was hanging open. Thank goodness his back had been turned. Collecting herself, she reached down to her feet for the duster, but her hand found nothing but empty air. She finally pulled herself away from Bertram's form. The duster was gone. She spun in a circle, searching the floor. She sighed.

"Must've floated off again." That was the trouble with using enchanted tools. If the magic sensed more dirt elsewhere, off they went. As if responding to her accusation, the duster bumped into the side of her head. She stepped out of the way as it headed into the dining room off to her left. The long table fit up to twenty people. Every time she looked at it, memories of the hectic London parties came back to haunt her.

Mrs. Steepe loved to host ladies over for tea parties full of gossip and critiques of the latest fashions. And of course Martin always made sure to provide plenty of Steepe brand tea. Laoise was never quite sure whether it was his good business sense in marketing his tea to the wealthy families of London or whether he was just looking for an excuse to share his love of tea with others.

In the past, the family would retire here to the country estate for the winter, giving the London servants a break. Montgomery Steepe or his son Martin would sometimes show up to handle business matters, but their business dinners were small, simple, and over quickly. The staff always held a small celebration in the kitchens the day after the family left for the country estate. The only holiday that outdid that party was Christmas. Laoise sighed. Another party she'd miss trapped out here.

A sparkle to the right caught her eye. A golden bird flitted toward the patio. Bertram paused, watching the bird as it flew wide circles around his head. He lowered his sword. His eyes closed, his head tilted up toward the sky. Laoise couldn't tear her gaze away. He looked like a different man when he wasn't brooding and snapping at her. A veil of melancholy still clung to his features, making her wonder if he felt the same loneliness she did in this empty manor.

Then the bird swooped down and pecked the top of his head before making another circle. Bertram's eyes opened. With one quick flick of his sword, Bertram speared the bird through the chest. Laoise gasped and dropped the broom. Free of her, the broom righted itself, only to float toward the dining room to join the duster. Laoise yanked the broom back as Bertram pulled out a handkerchief to wipe the sweat from his face before yanking the bird off his sword.

He sheathed his blade and then headed for the door. As he stepped inside, his gaze landed on her. "Get me some water. I'll be in the parlor."

"Jesus! Did you just kill a wee bird?" The shock of the sight made Laoise's accent slip briefly back to her Irish brogue.

"Oh, calm yourself," he said, opening his hand to reveal a mess of gears and springs. "It's not real."

Her shoulders relaxed, and she breathed a sigh of relief. The mechanical bird in Bertram's hand looked similar to the honey dispensers flittering about the London house. "Is that one of your cousin's hummingbirds?"

"Yes. Somehow he's turned these abominations into messenger birds, too." He yanked off the little black box tied to the bird's left foot. "I will have to remind him that the postal service already exists." He stomped off.

The broom tried to pull her toward the dining room. This time she let it go to fetch the water. In the parlor he sat with an arm slung over the back of his arm chair, glaring at the family portrait above the fireplace. His cousin looked a few years older compared to the portrait at the London residence. The room's position at the front of the house kept the noise of the clocks at bay.

"Finally," Bertram groused when she offered him the water. He took a big swig before opening the package. Bertram opened the little box, only for it to fold out into a bigger box. He did that several more times, his sneer deepening each time the box grew in size. Finally, the box opened.

Laoise lingered, bewildered at the sight before her. Bertram, after the events of the Great Exhibition, where he'd brandished a pistol at both Martin and Charlotte and tried to frame them both for his own thefts, was sitting in a comfortable chair in a spacious mansion rather than the cold prison cell he deserved. That much she could accept. The Steepe Family had their reputation to manage, after all, and really the only victim of his antics had been Bertram himself.

But now he was getting care packages from home as well. Not only that, but here he sat like a petulant child opening an unwanted present. What could Martin have possibly sent his ungrateful cousin? Martin didn't have the disposition of a prankster, but Laoise held out hope that Charlotte had in some way tampered with the package. She snickered to herself at all the sorts of vile things she would have sent him given the chance.

To her disappointment, however, all he pulled out a letter from his mother followed by a small burlap bag of coffee. For the first time since she'd arrived at the house, he smiled. "God save my mother," he said as he inspected the contents of the bag emblazoned with the Remojo Coffee brand. "What a beautiful roast. And the aroma..." Bertram closed his eyes and drew a long, deep breath through his nose, savoring the scent. Laoise joined in, albeit with more subtlety. After working so long without it, a cup of coffee sounded like just the thing to keep her from going mad. If she was quick about it, she could steal a cup for herself when he'd inevitably demand a pot be made for him.

On cue, he turned to her, shoving the box at her, more like an excited child than a bratty one. "Go make me a cup of coffee. I've gone far too long without." For a brief moment, his air of aloof disdain cleared, and Laoise thought she heard genuine happiness in his words. But just as quickly, his mood changed back, his smile dropping. "I don't need the tea Martin sent. You can toss it." He leaned back, holding the metal bird up to the sunlight pouring in through the window. The light hit his face just right, making him look ready for a painting. The angle highlighted his perfect jaw and eyes.

Laoise grabbed the box and looked over the contents. Aside from the coffee bag, there was a tea tin and a few papers in the box, along with some odd looking green fruits which she didn't recognize.

"What are those?"

"Chili peppers from the Americas. Jalapeños if I'm not mistaken," he answered, not looking up as he read his mother's letter. His informative tone changed to a scolding one, adding, "They're beyond your culinary capabilities. Don't touch them."

Laoise looked closer at the mottled pepper in the middle. It seemed to shudder even though she was holding the box somewhat steadily. "...are they supposed to be moving?"

"What?"

Suddenly a pepper zipped out of the box. It circled the table a few times with a loud buzzing sound. It seemed Laoise was mistaken about Martin. Somewhere in that forgetful head of his lurked a prankster after all.

The pepper stopped and hovered in midair, buzzing like a bee. Now that it had stopped flitting around in midair, Laoise could see that it wasn't a pepper at all, but a very small bird.

"Not another one," Bertram groaned as he reached for the bird. It dodged him with a graceful swerve to the right. Bertram muttered under his breath in annoyance and drew his blade.

"A bit more colorful than usual, this one," remarked Laoise. Rather than the usual brass body and glassy thin wings, this bird was jewel green and had a white underbelly. "Goodness, is it real?" She'd never seen a live hummingbird before. All she had to compare it to was the mechanical honey dispensers, and this little bird zipped about just as nimbly. She held out a finger as it flew around her, but it wouldn't perch.

"I should hope not. Martin ought to know better than to mail a live bird." As before, he held the sword steady, following the flitting movements of the bird with the thin tip of his blade. Laoise had no doubt that he'd be able to strike this bird just as swiftly as the last, but as he watched, his mouth fell agape and he lowered his weapon. "My God, it is real. That fool sent a real hummingbird."

With hurried, frustrated movements so unlike his graceful fencing, he sheathed his blade and tried to grab the bird again. It flew right over his head, and as he tilted back to reach for it, the back of his legs hit his armchair. His arms swung as he fought to keep his balance.

She giggled at the sight. Watching him struggle never got old.

He scowled at her. "Stop laughing and do something!"

The bird flew at the window, bumping repeatedly against the glass. She pushed against the window, but it didn't budge. She tried to unlock the latch, but it took some fiddling before it gave way. The window creaked and groaned as she lifted it. Spooked, the bird darted away.

"Not that!" Mr. Steepe placed his hands over hers and shoved the window back down. For that brief moment, they felt warm and strong.

"I was trying to get it outside." What else had he expected?

"Are you simple, woman? It will die outside. A hummingbird can't survive an English winter, and it's too far from its home to start its migration."

For such a rude man, she'd never thought him one to care about a bird's fate. Particularly not with his penchant for going out of his way to break the mechanical birds back in London. "Then it seems we'll have a new guest 'til spring."

"I think not." Bertram huffed. "I'm sending it right back to that doorknob of a cousin of mine. Now find a way to catch it."

"Me? I don't know a thing about birds!"

"I don't expect you would," he said, his words dripping with their usual smugness. If only she could open the window back up and throw him out. "So it's time for you to learn. You can start with the orchids in the greenhouse. It should recognize some of the varieties."

"Forgive my boldness, sir," Laoise said, painting a smile on her face. It did little to hide her growing frustration. "But perhaps you would be better suited to the task? You know what it is, what it likes, and you clearly have the skills to catch it." She gestured to the pile of scrap that had once been a mechanical bird.

Bertram stepped back, more shocked than she'd ever seen him. "Are you suggesting that I stab the poor thing?"

"No no, not at all, sir. But if you're as quick with a net as with your little sword, you'd surely be able to catch it."

"Firstly, this 'little sword' is my great grandfather's colichemarde. It saw combat in the Americas, so try to show a bit of respect. Secondly, pest control is not the duty of a gentleman. It is a task for the help. Now quit complaining and get to work."

"Right away, sir. I'll go control the pests. And then I'll cook your dinner, wash the dishes, finish darning your socks, build a fire in your room, and fold the laundry." She ticked each item off her fingers. "Oh! And I'll be needing to brew your coffee as well, won't I?"

"Are you still here? I thought I told you to get to work!"

"Apologies, sir. Just finishing up with one pest before moving on to the next."

"Don't smart mouth me, Lisa." They stared one another down. Her hands balled as he mispronounced her name. It was becoming a habit of his, and as she stared daggers into his eyes, she increasingly felt compelled to remedy the problem with her fists. After a tense moment, Bertram let out a frustrated sigh. "Oh fine. I'll figure out how to catch the bird since you clearly can't. This is far too important to leave to a lowly maid anyway. Just go make my coffee."

"Right away, sir." She hissed the word 'sir' like a snake and stormed off, letting her shoulder hit him as she passed by.

"And bring extra sugar. For the bird."

"Damn brat," she grumbled as she plopped the box onto the kitchen table. He might not want the tea, but there was no reason to waste it. She pulled the little tin of tea out, finding a thick envelope attached with a strand of yarn. Her name was emblazoned across the front of the letter. Charlotte's writing. Her writing had always been cleaner than Laoise's quick, messy scrawl.

She pried the thick pile of paper out of the envelope. A letter in Charlotte's neat handwriting greeted her, followed by a page titled Chapter One. She was ready to share her latest project then. Laoise smiled, glad for good news at last. Even if Charlotte's last story never got published, she'd read it and enjoyed every page. She'd enjoyed the cutthroat vengeance and murders.

Chapter two and three followed the first. She scanned the letter.

Dear Laoise,

I hope this finds you well. The countryside should be beautiful this time of year, even if Bertram is there ruining your view.

That was exactly the problem, she thought. Bertram wasn't ruining the view. If anything, he was the most appealing sight in the whole manor. It was everything else about him that was infuriating.

The tea is for you. It's a new acquisition, a breakfast blend which Martin assures me is bold and energizing. I know you'll just love it.

I've also spent the last week writing like a woman possessed. My latest story, Calamity in a Coffee Pot, is already halfway done. The first three chapters are enclosed. I hope to have the next few chapters to you soon once I finish incorporating Mary's editing notes. This has to be the one. I'm crossing my fingers that readers will like it as much as Hawke Publishing does!

Are you well? When I'm not writing, I find myself imagining all of the gruesome ways you might rid Bertram of a finger or two. Honestly, I've drawn quite a deal of inspiration for my writing from the idea, but please do try not to get carried away with him. Or rather, not when I'm not around to join in!

I won't be able to stop worrying about you until you come home.

Ever your affectionate friend,

Charlotte Steepe

It was strange seeing Charlotte's new surname. Laoise read it a second time, and then a third. It was such a small thing, but she'd always been Charlotte Graham, and it felt strange to call her by a different name. Her new name meant she'd also be Mrs. Steepe. Laoise shivered at that. Mrs. Steepe was what she had always called Martin's mother. Her employer. And now technically, Charlotte was her employer too. She didn't want anything to change in their friendship, but it was hard to believe everything would stay the same.

Her eyebrow was also raised in concern as she read that Charlotte was writing like a "woman possessed." She hoped she didn't mean it literally. Maybe Charlotte had been spending too much time with her friend Mary. Between Mary's fiancé, a spiritual medium, and his brother, a vampire-hunting priest, Laoise could only imagine what sort of supernatural problems she'd have to fend off. Dealing with the living was trouble enough.

She set the letter and chapters on the table with a huff. Reading the story would have to wait, no matter how badly she wanted to sit in front of the fire and tear into the new chapters. She'd taken it as a small victory in convincing Mr. Steepe to handle the hummingbird. Best not to spoil it by keeping him waiting for coffee. Distant cursing drifted in from somewhere in the house. She smirked, taking it as a sign his hummingbird chase wasn't going well.

She opened up the small burlap bag and inhaled the aroma. The coffee beans smelled like heaven. She'd never admit it to Martin, but

Laoise much preferred the smell of coffee to tea. Walking into the kitchen with that scent hanging around the room was almost as good as walking into Charlotte's bakery.

For many years, that bakery had felt like her second home. A place to get away from all the noise and cramped quarters of her family's home. Charlotte always had a new book to tell her about and some sort of freshly baked sweet treat she'd saved for her. Other locals weren't as accepting of Laoise's Irish heritage, but Charlotte, her parents, and even clumsy Claude were always so happy to open their doors to her. They were like family.

Laoise got to work preparing the coffee just as she had back in London, but she noticed there was no dedicated grinder for the coffee beans. No matter. The pepper mill would do. She dropped the beans in, taking no care to clean out the specks of pepper still in the mill. Little victories like this got her through the day.

The coffee pot hadn't been over the fire long before a chiseled jaw came peering around the corner. Mr. Steepe sniffed the air like a bloodhound. "Where is it?"

She startled. Even Martin knew better than to come barging into the kitchen. For the most part, at least. "You needn't come to the kitchen, sir. I'll bring it out to you when it's ready."

"Convention be damned. I'm not waiting a moment longer than necessary to get my coffee."

"It'll be a minute yet." His intrusion felt too loud compared to the silent kitchen. If he'd really smelled the coffee brewing all the way upstairs from the kitchen, she'd have to be careful about making herself a cup in the morning. "How goes the hunt?"

"Fine, fine," he said dismissively. It was very clearly not going fine. "Are you brewing it strong? I like it strong."

"Yes. I ought to know how you like your coffee by now."

"You haven't made me coffee yet." He moved to the table and sat, watching as she pulled the pot off the fire.

"You ask for it when you visit your cousin all the time. If it's not hot enough or strong enough for you, you send it back and I have to bring you a fresh cup." Ever since Martin decided he liked the way she arranged his tea trays, she'd become his favorite maid when he wanted tea. Consequently, she ended up serving all of his guests at tea time as well. Most especially his cousin, who visited nearly every day.

She poured his coffee and set the mug down in front of him. As he sat there, he seemed so much more personable. She was starting to regret putting the pepper in the coffee. She held her breath as he took a sip.

"Oh, that's wonderful," he said, closing his eyes as if tasting a fine wine. "A bit more of a bite to this one. Is that pepper I'm tasting?"

"Don't know, sir," Laoise feigned ignorance. "The bag doesn't say."

"That's wonderfully pleasant. I'll need to get another bag of this." He took his cup and walked with a newfound determination in his stride. He turned and tilted his head to Laoise before leaving. "Thank you."

It was the first time he'd thanked her since coming to the manor. It might have been the first time he had ever thanked her. She held onto it, knowing better than to hope he'd ever utter it again. Bertram had been an ass from the moment she arrived, but somehow that little bit of appreciation still warmed her heart. She poured herself a small cup of the peppery coffee and took a sip. The instant it touched her tongue, she spat it back out and started coughing. Little victories. And sometimes little defeats.

"Lisa!" Mr. Steepe cried as he burst into her room, startling her awake. Her door slammed into the wall with a bang.

"What is it, sir?" She stood from the chair she'd fallen asleep in, her sore muscles sluggish as though she were wading through a pool of thick pudding.

"Being a lazy layabout as usual I see." He sneered.

"Lazy? Don't you know what I've been doing since I got to this god-forsaken manor?" Her temper finally got the better of her. She made her way over to him, her stiff muscles needing far too much power to jab him in the chest. "Why, I've been cooking your meals, laundering your clothes, and keeping your house clean." She aimed to slap his chest for good measure, her slow arm making her growl in frustration. This time her hand connected to skin instead of material. Odd. She remembered him wearing a shirt.

"Where did your shirt—" She forced her gaze onto his face, refusing to let herself admire the demon. Her hand betrayed her. It pressed against his chest, splaying out all five fingers.

"I thought you'd like it, my little coffee bean."

"Coffee bean?" She stepped away. "Do you know who you're talking to?"

He tilted his head as he regarded her, and then he barked, the same way Oolong barked for table scraps.

"What?"

He tackled her without warning. He scooped her right up off her feet as if she weighed no more than a pillow. He then jumped right through the open window and it exploded behind them in a cacophony of shattered glass and splintered wood. They landed on the hill outside. She could have sworn that hadn't been there the day before. Together they rolled down the hill, him barking the whole way down. His body seeming to grow longer with each roll, and his ears too.

She tried to break out of his grasp, but his hold was too tight. All she could do was scream as she rolled endlessly down the hill.

BANG

Laoise woke up. This time, she rubbed her eyes to make sure she was actually awake. The pages of Charlotte's story crinkled beneath her in the bed. She'd fallen asleep reading. The constant running about the manor while playing both maid and cook kept her too exhausted to have any time to herself in the evening. She didn't even remember climbing into the bed, only reading in the chair.

Great. Her frustrations with serving Bertram were mixing with her usual Oolong nightmares. Work always had a way of invading her dreams, making all too many of her nights as restless as her days.

Another loud bang echoed through the manor from somewhere above her head. She stumbled from her bed. Moonlight streamed in through the window. It had to be the middle of the night.

A thud sent her sprinting to the closet at the end of the hall. A burglar. One who thought the Steepes were all in London and saw this as the opportune time to strike. That had to be what all that banging was. If the house got burgled during her stay, would she be blamed? Or worse, not receive her extra promised pay? She could barely stomach this job as is.

"I'll be damned if I'm letting some burglar ruin this for me," she muttered brandishing the broom like an axe as she crept to the entry room. The banging grew louder with each step. Flickering light played across the walls by the top of the stairs.

"Come back here!" Mr. Steepe cried before another thud sent him cursing.

She rushed up the stairs, her hands clenching the broom tightly. If the burglar was fighting Mr. Steepe, maybe the man would rough him up and get a punch or two in. Lucky burglar. Upstairs she skipped to a stop at the threshold to his room.

Magical candles were lit on the desk and mantle, and the low fire in the hearth made the room too warm. A perilous pile of books sat at the bottom of the bed. A bird cage sat on the desk. What looked like metal flower garden decorations sat beside it. A bowl of sugar water sat inside the cage.

"Mr. Steepe? Are you alright?" She spun in a circle, the broom pointed in front of her, but there was no sign of him. Had the burglar knocked him out? Or better yet, kidnapped him? That would almost be worth losing wages over.

"What are you doing here?"

She jumped and whirled around, the end of the broom whacking against his hip. "Sorry! I heard loud noises and thought there was a thief. Is there?" She righted the broom and peered over his shoulder into the darkness of the hallway. A scarf dangled from his right hand.

"No. Only an irritating little bird fluttering about. I can't concentrate with it flying around the house." He stalked into his room, throwing the scarf onto the pile of other discarded tools on the desk. Dark bruises beneath his eyes attested to his lack of sleep.

"Where'd you get that cage?" As far as she knew, he wasn't supposed to leave the grounds.

"The garden of course. Aunt Gertie always used to keep song birds."

"She does have an awful lot of birdhouses in London" At least half a dozen. The birds woke everyone up first thing in the morning with their songs.

He ran a hand through his hair, mussing it. "The bird is too fast for me to catch." He grumbled to himself and in her half-asleep state she didn't understand the rest.

Laoise yawned. "Do you know what time it is? You should get some sleep, sir."

"Later." He flapped a hand at her as he studied the cage.

"Then if there's no burglar, I'm going back to bed.

"Coffee." He said, looking up from the cage. His right hand stroked the five o'clock shadow on his chin.

"Coffee?"

"Yes. Cup. Now," he said, his voice a cold, low, aggravated staccato.

"Don't have any left. You already drank it all today."

He tapped a hand against his desk. "You're sure?"

"Quite sure." Her hand tightened on the broom as she watched him, afraid he might start barking like in her dream. "Good night, sir."

She started to turn toward the door, but his hand shot out and grabbed the broom, stopping her. He lifted a finger to his mouth, telling her to be quiet. Laoise froze in place, half in shock, half in anger. Her nightmare was coming true. Then he slowly brought his finger down from his lips and pointed to the end of the broom. There the hummingbird was perched, puffing out its chest as it looked around the room. "Slowly," he murmured. "Let's get it in the cage." He stepped up alongside her, their shoulders brushing. The warmth of him was jarring in the chilly night air. He still smelled like coffee.

Together they held the broom steady while they crept toward the cage. An agonizing minute later the end of the broom rested in the cage. "I'm going to close the door," he whispered. "On the count of three, pull the broom out."

She nodded. Her palms sweat around the handle as he reached for the cage door. With his thumb and forefinger, he gingerly grabbed the door's handle and gently pulled. The door's hinges let out a high-pitched squeak, and before he could react, the hummingbird shot out of the cage. Bertram's face turned red, and he tried to yank the broom away.

"Don't you touch the broom!" Laoise yanked it away from him. She'd already lost one duster and couldn't stand to lose any more cleaning tools.

He huffed. "The bird got away."

"I know. I saw. I'm going back to bed now." She turned and marched out, ignoring his grumbling. He could stay up all night chasing after a wee birdie for all she cared, but she was going to get some much needed sleep.

And he wasn't allowed back in her dreams. No matter how warm his shoulders felt.

Chapter 5

The ringing of the little silver bell echoed into the kitchen long before it arrived. Laoise ignored it while she waited for the porridge to finish cooking. Over the past week she'd given up trying to make anything else for breakfast. Cooking took too long, and there was never enough time to get all her work done.

To save some herself some time, Laoise tried to fix the enchantment on the duster Mr. Steepe had ruined. She didn't know much about magic. Her knowledge covered only one spell along with the basics of glamour that any girl was familiar with. Still, she had to try. One duster wasn't enough to keep the house clean.

She carefully copied the runic inscription from the still-functioning duster to the ruined one, making sure to keep the spacing between the runes as uniform as possible. With magic, a small error could lead to a completely unpredictable and frequently messy outcome. Then again, how much havoc could a feather duster cause? Once she finished, she recalled a spell she'd heard the butler use when fixing tools for the housekeeper. She quietly muttered it into the duster, breathing life into the runes.

Instead of floating off to get to work, the duster spun in a circle. Fast. It kept going faster and faster, buffeting the air and blowing papers off of the table. A small tornado started to form as Laoise struggled against the gale force winds. It took several tries after being knocked away before she got close enough to throw herself over the duster. She wrestled it down to the floor and quickly wiped the enchantment off. The tornado blew itself out against the table, tipping one chair over and blowing the other across the room.

She tossed the duster onto the counter. Clearly her Latin wasn't as good as the butler's, if indeed the words she had said were Latin. Why couldn't magic be in plain English? It was always Greek or Aramaic or some other ancient language she'd never heard of. It was as if the magicians wanted to make magic as difficult and as inaccessible as possible. Which she supposed they did.

The whistling winds abated, and the sound of the bell grew louder as it neared the kitchen. "I hear ye," she shouted at the bell. "You can shut up."

The bell of course didn't listen. It never did. The ringing continued as she plated up Mr. Steepe's breakfast, and it followed after her as she made her way to the dining room where his latest experiments covered the table. Floating metal flowers hovered over the table, with pockets of sugar water in the center. Mixed amongst them were real flowers. Tropical ones she supposed, judging by their enormous size. Or maybe not. They certainly would have looked out of place in any traditional English garden. Any garden but the Steepes', that is.

"Would you open the window?" he demanded as soon as she stepped into the room. "The blasted messenger bird won't stop tapping at the window."

She sucked in a breath to keep in the insult which was eager to escape her mouth. "Right away, sir. Wouldn't want to interrupt your important flower arranging," she said as she dropped the porridge tray down beside him with a loud inelegant thud.

"I'm not arranging flowers," he snapped. He furrowed his brow as he continued tinkering with one of the flowers. "These are to lure our little friend into a trap. Now I just need something to drop the cage quickly enough to capture it..."

She let the messenger bird in. It perched on the dining room table.

"Check it for coffee," he demanded, barely glancing up from his work as Laoise took the little package from the bird's leg and opened the series of impossibly sized boxes that grew bigger as she pulled them out of the small delivery box.

"Only letters and some fruit," she said, peering into the last box. A few oranges and grapefruits rolled around on top of the pile of papers. She shook the box with suspicion, fully prepared for one of the fruits to suddenly sprout wings and throw the manor into even more disarray.

Wedged in the corner behind one of the fruits was a small burlap bag she hadn't seen before. It bore the distinctive Remojo brand coffee logo. With a careful sideways glance, she shook the box once more to cover it up, lest she be ordered to stop everything and brew another pot of coffee.

"Damn." He grabbed the mechanical bird, raising his hand to dash it against the table. Then he paused, rubbing his chin as his gaze turned distant. He began muttering like a man gone mad. "A new lure, yes. This might work."

Laoise paid him no mind and strolled out of the room, sorting out the letters in the box as she walked. The thickest was addressed to her in Charlotte's neat handwriting. More chapters. She patted the thick envelope and headed back to the kitchen to eat her breakfast.

She was greeted by the buzzing of the real humming bird as it fluttered around the ceiling of the kitchen.

"You tired of 'im too, huh?" she asked as she settled into her place at the table. Unlike the fancy dining room table, this one sported plenty of scratches and scuffs. The bird hovered about the bowl of sugar water on the counter. "I suppose I'm lucky. I'm at least getting paid to be here."

She watched for a moment as the bird perched and sipped at the water. It glanced around the room and puffed up its feathers, then started preening itself. She was mesmerized by its rapid jerky movements, so similar to those of the honey dispensers back in London, and yet so much more...alive.

Unanticipated as this guest may have been, Laoise found it soothing to watch as it flitted in a circle and returned to the bowl to drink. It made her wonder why a bird that would surely die if it ever got out of the house was sent to the manor without a cage to contain it. "Don't know how you drew the short straw to be sent here, little fella. Do you suppose he sent ye on purpose? Or was it all just an accident? Lord knows that Martin isn't the most observant man." She snorted.

He was naïve sometimes, but Charlotte wasn't. Her carefulness would balance him out. She used to do the same for Laoise when they were kids. One time a boy had tried to steal her muffin on a dare, and it was only because of Charlotte's intervention that the poor boy had been spared having his face pushed into a mud puddle.

Still, not even she wasn't able to save him from the tirade of curse words that Laoise slung at the boy as he ran. Over the years, her temper had mellowed a bit. Her old self wouldn't have been able to resist strangling Mr. Steepe with her bare hands. Nowadays, she only fantasized about doing so.

But she wasn't here for herself. It was for her brother's sake, and giving up would let her whole family down. The very thought of leaving before she made enough to cover her brother's medication made her stomach clench. "I won't," she promised herself. She wouldn't quit. And she wouldn't strangle Mr. Steepe to death. Not yet anyway.

She shook her head to clear it and then pulled out Charlotte's next several chapters from the envelope. If she was quick, she might find time to read today. She deserved a long enough break to do some reading, a fact her poor aching feet attested to.

The door knocker interrupted her thoughts. She sighed. Asking for a few minutes alone was impossible these days. The mail carrier greeted her at the door.

"Morning, miss." He tilted his hat to her before handing over a single letter. Charlotte's handwriting again. There had hardly been any mail at all since her arrival, only the letters Bertram sent. And now she had two letters in one day. What was going on?

"Thank you." She shut the door behind her and ripped the letter open.

Dear Laoise,

Marty and I are staying in the village for the next few days. Please come by for afternoon tea tomorrow. I want to hear all about how things are going. Martin is worried because his cousin hasn't written back. I've tried to reassure him that you haven't strangled Bertram to death. Merely broken his wrist, perhaps?

Laoise snorted. Charlotte knew her disdain for him all too well. The letter was followed by directions to the little shop where they were to meet. Finally, something to look forward to. A chance to see someone other than Bertram! Even better, she'd have a chance to talk to her friend about books just like they used to in London. Not just any book either, but a story Charlotte had written herself. After the last few miserable weeks in the manor, Laoise was giddy with excitement. Mr. Steepe wouldn't ruin this for her. If his dinner had to be late today while she got caught up on reading the new chapters she'd received, then so be it.

The little silver bell started ringing. She groaned. If he'd forgotten to eat his porridge before it got cold again, she swore she'd pour it over his head. As soon as the bell bumped into her shoulder, she grabbed it out of the air and yanked the clapper out. The little bell hung in the air, shaking without sound.

Much better.

Laoise waited outside for the carriage, sitting on the stairs as her left foot tapped against the ground. Mr. Steepe hadn't come looking for her yet. She planned to be in the village by the time he did.

The carriage she'd hired from the village was late. She looked at the summon stone, still glowing from when she'd first tapped the rune almost an hour ago. She eyed the driveway, wondering if she should just start walking. She was accustomed to being able to walk to most places she needed to get to in the city. Then again, the places she needed to get to in the city had never been so far outside of a reasonable walking distance. It would take her ages to walk to the village. Not an inviting prospect in the cold, but better than waiting outside for one of the bells to come find her. Just as she stood to get started on the walk, the carriage pulled up the driveway.

The same man who'd brought her to the estate greeted her with a tip of his hat. "To the train station, I assume?"

"No. I'm meeting with a friend." She didn't wait for him to climb down to open the door for her. She did it herself while she rattled off the address Charlotte had given her.

"Yer really stayin'?" The driver squinted at the house. "Hell. That's goin' to cost me."

"You made a bet on me?" She paused, peering over the top of the door at him.

"Aye. Once the servants started leavin' in droves, bettin' against any new ones was always an easy way to get a free drink. Although ye still have a few days to change your mind and leave. I'd bet ye'd be gone by the end of October."

It hadn't even been a full month yet, and it already felt like three. "Looks like you're losin' this one." She ducked into the carriage.

"Oh I don't know. Plenty of time for ye to go stormin' out."

"Buy me a drink and I'll consider it. Now get goin'."

The driver chuckled in response as he cracked the reins. Laoise glued herself to the window to watch the beautiful scenery go by. There'd been no time to sit and admire it since her arrival. A few stubborn leaves clung to their branches in highlights of bright yellow and deep reddish brown. Snow would start any day now, hiding the fallen leaves and charming country roads.

Charlotte liked to read stories of the unusual hiding in plain sight. Seeing the beauty of this place made Laoise understand why. There was a charm to the gloomy gray skies and fog over the rolling hills that made it feel like a fairy tale. The moors made it easy to imagine the roads disappearing into another realm on the other side of the hills, or for there to be a secret door in the ruined old castle they passed.

Oh no. She was starting to sound like Charlotte. Laoise sighed. She didn't have time to get lost in her own imagination. Never did. Creativity wasn't particularly useful for a maid, except perhaps when dodging Oolong. The dog was a virtuoso at tripping her up, which demanded the same level of inspiration to avoid falling flat on her face.

She thought for a moment about Charlotte's imagination and, with a chuckle to herself, wondered if she really had time for it herself. Her friend had always been a prolific writer, but not a particularly creative one. Her first big story had seemed to overlap considerably with *The String of Pearls*, and her most recent story, *Calamity in a Coffeepot*, was essentially a retelling of the events she had lived through earlier this year since her engagement to Martin.

She had changed the names of course, and made a few small changes to the story. The main character, rather than a baker's daughter, was a maid, a change which Laoise liked to think she had inspired. Even though she already knew the real story, it made for a satisfying read whenever the heroine would thwart the bumbling yet sinister Barnaby, the obvious stand-in for Bertram in the story.

The carriage slowed as they entered the small town. The shop they pulled up to perfectly matched the town. It was a little place that looked like it had once been a cottage. Fall flowers filled the window boxes and provided a pop of color against the stone of the building. Above the door hung the brand new Steepe Tea sign.

As soon as she stepped out of the carriage the door to the shop opened. Charlotte rushed out to wrap her friend up in a tight hug. "It's so good to see you Laoise!"

"Jesus, you're going to squeeze the life out of me!" she said with a laugh, squeezing her back. The hoop beneath Charlotte's dress made her skirts wider than Laoise's. Pale green silk peeked out from beneath her fur-lined cloak. Ribbons bedecked her skirts. The outfit was a far cry from the plainer clothes Charlotte used to wear, let alone the flour coated aprons of the bakery. Laoise shoved down the sour bite of envy.

Charlotte's grip loosened, and she pulled back, keeping a hold of Laoise's hand. "Just say the word and we'll bring you right back home to London. You don't need to spend a single minute longer dealing with that awful man."

"It's not so bad," she said, patting her friend's hand dismissively. She glanced around to make sure Martin wasn't in earshot before continuing, lowering her voice. "I get to keep the bastard in line. He gets stuck eating nothing but cold porridge with dust in it. And I'm getting double my wages to do it!"

The two giggled. "You deserve ten times as much. I'm afraid all I can offer you until you get back is what we can fit into those care packages. Have they been reaching you?"

"They have. Thanks for sending the tea. And those letters from my Ma."

"How is your mother, by the way? I confess I've been so busy lately I haven't gotten a chance to visit." She hesitated a moment. "...is Sean well?"

"Oh he's fine." Laoise bit her tongue. She couldn't tell her the truth. That he wasn't well, and that the medicine was getting more and more expensive with every bottle, and that the whole reason she'd taken this job in the first place was to help pay for it. If she did, it would only make Charlotte anxious on this one day Laoise had to relax. Or worse, she'd offer to pay for the medicine. The Hughes family had always managed to get by on its own without begging for charity off of friends. Laoise wasn't about to start. "And my Ma is just fine as well last I heard."

"Oh good," said Charlotte, giving a relieved smile. "I'd hate to think of your family missing you for *his* sake." Her voice oozed with bile as she gestured vaguely in the direction of the manor. "Martin seems to think that exile will do that rotten cousin of his some good. I think it's far too good for him, but you know Martin. He's too sweet to hold a grudge against someone he loves, no matter how unappreciative of that love they may be." She glanced over her shoulder at the shop.

Through the window they saw Martin pointing at shelves and holding up Oolong as if to show the shop to the dog. He turned and noticed the two of them, then waved one of the dog's paws at them.

Charlotte smiled and waved back. "Can you believe he even bought him a gift for when he returns? A hummingbird from America. A real one."

Laoise scoffed. "You mean he sent that thing on purpose? I thought it was some sort of mistake."

"Sent it? No, no. He hasn't sent it yet."Charlotte's head turned slowly to Laoise, raising her brow sheepishly. "Has he?"

Laoise nodded with a smirk.

Charlotte hid her face in her hand. "I'm so sorry."

"Sorry? What for?" She placed a hand on her friend's shoulder. "Bertram has been chasing that thing all over trying to catch it. It's kept him up late making all kinds of noise. He's gone half mad. It's really a sight to see."

Charlotte chewed on her bottom lip, glancing back one more time at Martin in the tea shop before taking Laoise by the arm and steering her down the road. "Tell me all about it. I want to know everything."

Laoise did, from the carriage driver's bet against the servants to the mysterious locked room. They spoke in hushed whispers as they walked down the main road of the town and then back up it. When the train pulled in, a small flood of people dispersed through the town, heading toward the inn and shops.

She wished she had more time to herself. Wandering through the little shops would make for a lovely morning alone, but she couldn't abandon Bertram too long.

"I had a feeling he wouldn't learn. Martin is determined to give him a chance, and he'll be devastated if this doesn't work."

"There's trouble a-brewin' in that room, but whatever he's plannin', I'll find it. One way or another I'm going to get into that room. I won't give him a chance to do anything else."

"Thank you so much, Laoise. Please tell me the moment you find out what he's up to. I'll help Martin handle him. If he doesn't reform, I don't want him getting his hands on anything important. We are lucky that his previous attempts were too incompetent to do any real damage."

Laoise cracked a wry smile. "If he is some sort of criminal mastermind, he's doing a good job of hiding it. He spends too much time wallowing and obsessing over the hummingbird to be doing much villainy. It at least keeps him occupied long enough for me to read your new story."

"Oh, you got the chapters? That's good. What are your thoughts on the new story?"

Laoise chuckled. "I can tell where you got your inspiration from. Only got a chance to skim it though. The second batch of chapters only came in yesterday."

"Only yesterday?" Charlotte frowned as she looked up at the cloudy sky. "I expected them to arrive a week ago. Martin said the bad weather might slow them down, but I never imagined it would be so much."

"I suppose you'll have to use the post like a regular person."

"Martin? A regular person?" Charlotte gave Laoise an incredulous look. The two laughed.

She'd missed this. It was nice to shop with her friend even if they hadn't gone in any stores. Seeing no one except Bertram was lonely. But things had changed, and she couldn't help but feel uneasy. She was used to seeing Charlotte in a simple frock covered with flour, at least when her nose wasn't buried in the latest penny blood. She spoke and laughed the same as she always had, but seeing her now dressed up in a fancy dress made her seem like a different person. Like her employer.

Serving her friend would be awkward. Charlotte wasn't the type to be embarrassed to be seen with Laoise, but she couldn't shake the feeling she was on the cusp of losing her best friend to her fancy new life. Maybe it would be best if she sought employment elsewhere. Charlotte would be alright. She already had a new, more respectable friend in Mary Hawke.

But those were problems for another time. Once Bertram had been dealt with, she might give it some more thought. For now, Laoise pushed aside the worries, wanting to enjoy herself.

Charlotte smiled. "It's just as well I suppose. I won't be able to send you more chapters for a while. I'm afraid I'm a bit stumped on where to take the story. And Mary wants to see how well the first chapters perform with readers."

"Oh? What's got you all held up?"

"Well I'm trying to show how at first Bertr—" Charlotte caught herself with a chuckle. "I mean Barnaby seems so charming to Cathy, but I need the readers to know what an awful person he ends up being. Maybe some sort of vision? Or a dream sequence..."

"No!" Laoise interrupted Charlotte's musings, her loud protest drawing titters from a group of elderly women fussing over apples at a market stand.

Charlotte's eyebrows rose. "I didn't expect you to have such intense emotions on the topic."

"Just never cared for them is all." Her eyes glazed over as she stared off in the distance. The image of a long shirtless Bertram holding her in his arms and barking had seared itself into Laoise's memory. She shuddered. It wasn't an entirely unpleasant memory, and that was what disturbed her most of all. "Maybe just have him kick a puppy or an orphan or something."

"Careful now," tutted Charlotte. "I can't have him be too much like the real one."

"I'm sure you'll think something up with that big ol' brain of yours." Laoise went to elbow her friend in the ribs, but stopped. It somehow seemed inappropriate now. "Any word on when the story's getting published?"

"Mary told me she'll be publishing the first chapter soon. I'm just crossing my fingers that *Calamity in a Coffee Pot* will do well."

"It will. I'm happy to see your work published at long last. And you've already got one loyal reader." Laoise shot Charlotte a smile. "I at least need to see Barnaby get his comeuppance."

"Of course. The villains always get what's coming to them in my stories. And they don't even get a cozy exile in the countryside once they're beaten. That's the perk of being the writer. "Charlotte giggled and tugged on Laoise's arm, steering her back to the shop. "Come inside for a bit. I have a gift for you."

"A gift? I didn't bring anything for you."

"Oh hush. With all you're doing for me you never need to get me a gift again. I just found something by the seaside that I thought would be perfect for you." Charlotte took her through the shop and into the back room. There she grabbed a wrapped package sitting on a set of shelves and dumped it into Laoise's arms. "Open it!"

Laoise opened the package, finding a new pair of gloves and a warm winter cloak. She stared, open-mouthed, at the gift. Both were too expensive for her to buy on her own. The quality far nicer than anything she owned, from the perfectly lined stitching to the warm velvety fabric to the soft fur trim. As a child she wore hand-me-downs from her mother and cousins. She didn't get new clothes until she started working as a maid and could buy them herself, and even then she had grown accustomed to shoddy quality.

"This is too much," Laoise said, tongue tripping over the words. "I can't accept this." She tried to hand them back, but Charlotte pushed her hands away.

"Please, they are a thank you gift. Without you supporting me, I wouldn't have gone through with the engagement. I would have ended it and never fought back against Bertram. Without you, I wouldn't have even gone to that party in the first place!" She held up the fur trimmed edge of the green cloak. "Since you will be in the countryside for a bit, I thought warm clothes would come in handy. When I saw the green of this cloak I knew it would be striking against your hair. I hope it will keep you warm this winter."

Laoise managed to choke back her tears. "It will. Thank you." She pulled Charlotte into another hug. Once they pulled away she slid the gloves on. They were soft and warm. Oh so warm. "I want to hear about your honeymoon. What was staying by the sea like? And how is your Da doing? I thought he was going to cry at your wedding."

"We are not talking about my 'Da.'" Charlotte's eyes narrowed. "That's what I need to get you next time. A good man to keep your pent up frustrations away from my father."

"You'll have to look hard to find as handsome or strong as your Da." A cloak and gloves were easy to find, but a man like him couldn't just be bought off a store shelf. A real shame too. He was incredibly dependable, almost never missing a day's work while still finding time to spend taking care of his family. And watching him make bread with his big muscular forearms made Laoise envy the dough.

"Moving on," Charlotte rolled her eyes. "Do let me know the moment you're back in London. I will try to send more care packages, but Martin said the mail is slow out here in the winter. The snow storms interfere. Is there anything you want me to send?"

"A cook would be nice. And another maid." Laoise scratched the back of her neck. "But I don't know if you can pay anyone enough to make the trip."

"I will talk to the Queen. Maybe she can offer title to anyone who comes to help you."

Laoise laughed. Even with everything that had changed, she was fairly confident her friend didn't have that kind of power. Not yet at least. "It'll take more than that. He is a living nightmare."

"A wise woman once told me to not let him have his way. To fight back." Charlotte grinned, patting her friend's arm. "Maybe you should heed her advice."

"Ha! Fighting back I can do, but I doubt I'll get paid if I bring him back to London in a pine box."

"Don't you dare. If anyone gets to do him in, it's me." Charlotte wagged her finger with a grin. "In the meantime, please try not to strain yourself for his sake. I wouldn't do anything beyond the bare minimum to keep him alive. I wouldn't even cook."

"He'd surely starve to death if I stopped cooking. There is no way the man knows how to feed himself. I'm shocked he's even managed to dress himself without a valet."

"A true mystery. Can you imagine the first day he had to put on his own clothes? I bet he was a mess."

She giggled. "Trousers on backwards, shirt unbuttoned…" Although that might be a step up. If he was going to make her miserable, he might as well give her something good to look at while he did it. "I'd better get back before he somehow manages to burn the place to the ground."

"Have some tea before you leave. What flavor would you like? I believe we have every Steepe tea available. The shop opens tomorrow, and I'd be honored if you had the very first cup."

Laoise grinned. "Something strong. I'm going to need it."

Chapter 6

I t was dark outside by the time Laoise returned. As soon as she walked through the doorway of the manor, her mouth fell open at the messy chaos that greeted her. Each new scene of destruction she passed fed her frustration. It looked as though a storm had gone through the manor. Knowing how capable Bertram was with magic, that may very well have been the case. All the paintings were crooked. Toppled furniture and a broken ottoman added to the disorder. Plants lay on their sides, leaving piles of dirt strewn across the hallway along with a shattered vase.

She found Bertram in the ballroom and marched on in. He sat in a chair with a half finished bottle of brandy in one hand in front of a roaring fire that was far larger than it needed to be. He sang a jaunty sea chanty while he drank.

"Ah! There you are," he said, words slurring. "Where've you been?"

"Cleaning. In the kitchen." She answered quickly. It was a plausible enough lie to explain her trip to the village. This was about him. Not her. She gestured to the chaotic scene in the hallway. "What in God's name did you do?"

"Oh, that?" He turned to glance back, fumbling with the bottle as he attempted to wave his hand dismissively. "I rang the bells. What more do you want?"

She stood, hands on her hips like she was a governess about to discipline a naughty child. But he deserved worse than a lecture or a slap on the wrist. For a brat this spoiled, more drastic measures were required. She balled her fists and stormed forward, her arms trembling with anticipation, eager to cave Bertram's face in.

She stood towering over the man as he slouched in his chair, but then he looked up at her with a disarming gaze. His eyes narrowed. "You haven't answered any of my bells. Why?"

She took a step back. Suddenly, she felt like she was the one in trouble. She'd already ripped the clappers out of most of the bells. They couldn't give her absences away if she always ignored their silent ringing. Before she could blurt out an excuse, a flitting shadow caught the corner of her eye. Now that her eyes had adjusted to the flickering light, she could see the bird cage on the table in front of him. Inside sat two hummingbirds, the real one along with the mechanical one. Her anger turned to bewilderment. "What is that?"

"I caught the hummingbird." He held up the bottle triumphantly as if to give a toast. He leaned forward and pointed at the copy of *Moby Dick* sitting on the table beside the cage. "You see that Ahab? That's how you catch a beast!"

"And did this Ahab destroy his entire house while he was at it?"

Bertram scoffed. "Of course not! He's a ship captain. A whale hunter." He took another long swig from the bottle, adding, "What he destroyed was his ship."

"I might as well be watching a child." Laoise threw her arms up in frustration. Her eyes turned to the bird cage. "And if you want to act like a child, you don't get to keep pets. Or take terrible lessons from books."

She reached for the cage, but Bertram stood up on wobbly legs, puffing out his chest to block her. "Don't hurt her. It's not her fault. You can't take revenge on nature. That's the entire point of the story."

"I'm not blaming the wee bird for the damage. I'm blaming you." She pointed at his face, grazing his chest. Even through his shirt, she could feel how firm and muscular he was. She shook her head. "And I don't care about the damn story!"

"Of course you don't. You wouldn't even understand it, would you? But how could you understand?" His voice turned sullen, leaning forward to peer into the cage, running a finger over it. "This bird and I...we're both prisoners. Locked in a gilded cage. So far from home."

Ugh, it was like listening to Charlotte discuss the themes and imagery in the books she was reading. Often books Laoise had never heard of before or didn't have time to read.

"Oh shut your mouth, you drunk. You want a prison? Heaven help me, I'll lock you in your room. That ought to keep you from tearing this whole damn house apart."

He glared. "Don't you raise your voice at me. You're the maid. I give the orders and the reprimands." He rolled his eyes as he tilted the bottle back, letting the last few droplets fall into his open mouth.

"Right you are, *sir*," she said, drawing out the sir. "Since I'm just a maid, I'll do the maid's job. I'll spend my evening cleaning up after you since you can't be left alone. And since I'm not the cook, I won't be doing any of the cooking tonight."

"Like hell you won't. I expected dinner to be served an hour ago."

"Sorry, sir. That's not a maid's job. Try talking to the cook about it." She turned and stomped out of the room, ignoring his protests. A prison. Only someone who had servants waiting on him hand and foot his whole life would think this manor a prison.

Laoise ground her teeth as she stormed off. A growl escaped her stomach, reminding her that she hadn't eaten dinner either. She'd make herself something to eat later, but right now she was too angry to eat.

She got started tidying up in the parlor. As distant a possibility as it was, it was the room likeliest to see any visitors to the manor. She got to work re-shelving the books, mumbling every insult she thought of against Bertram. It would all be worth it when she exposed whatever secrets he kept locked away in the upstairs bedroom. It was time to redouble her efforts on getting into that room.

A fallen book weighed down one of the enchanted dustpans, a small broom feebly brushing against its cover. The two items must have been trying to clean this book off of the floor for a few hours now based on the tiny scratch marks on the cover. Laoise huffed and yanked the book out of the dustpan.

"*Rookwood* by William Harrison Ainsworth." The title page depicted a sketching St. James's Square in London. That alone looked more exciting than chasing a whale. She tucked it into her apron pocket for later. The cleaning tools, no longer distracted by the book, floated off in search of a new mess to clean. The enchantments weren't as good as another maid helping, but at least they were doing something. Which was a lot more than could be said of the manor's other resident.

A prison. She imagined him being tossed into prison. A real one. Or being exiled to a small faraway village where he'd be forced to dig ditches. And her favorite, being forced to be the footman or valet for a man just like himself. That'd teach him how good he had it in his "gilded prison."

"Lisa!" Bertram called out.

Laoise groaned into her pillow. Her shoulders and back ached from staying up late getting the manor back in order. The sort of ache that burrowed itself deep between her shoulder blades and throbbed every time she moved wrong. She wasn't sure how long she'd been asleep for, but it wasn't nearly long enough.

"Lisa?" He knocked on the door across from hers before moving on to the next. "Where are you?"

The morning sun peeked around the edges of the curtain. What did he want at this hour? How was he even up at this hour? With as drunk as he'd been, she'd fully expected him to sleep late into the afternoon. She climbed out of bed, stretching her stiff muscles. To be sure it wasn't a dream this time, she pinched her cheeks. Unfortunately, it was all very real.

By the time he made it down the hallway and back up her side, never missing a single door, she was already dressed and ready to face him. The same couldn't be said for her long, curly hair, which hung loose over her shoulders.

She opened the door before his fist landed. "What do you want? Do you realize how early it is? Or how noisy you are?"

"There you are," he said, blinking in surprise, his fist still raised in the air to knock on the now open door. His jaw was still unshaven from the previous night, and his breath still reeked of alcohol. "Being a lazy layabout as usual, I see."

"Lazy?" She crossed her arms. "I stayed up 'til all hours cleaning up the mess you and that bird made and here you are waking me up early. There had better be a damn good reason."

"Don't take that tone with me, thief." He lifted the burlap bag of coffee from the most recent package Martin had sent. "Just how long did you plan on hiding it from me?"

She rolled her eyes. "I didn't hide it from you. I opened that box in front of you a couple of days ago."

"Oh yes," he said, "and you just so happened to neglect to inform me of the bag of coffee, which you hid underneath a pile of citrus!"

"My apologies, sir." Laoise curtsied, matching Bertram's mocking tone. "Next time we get a bag of coffee, I know where I'll shove it. Won't lose it then, now will you?"

He huffed. "Well, forget about the coffee. We have work to do. We need to make preparations for Pepper."

"Pepper?" Laoise asked, utterly dumbfounded. What could they possibly be doing with pepper? And how could it be so important it would make Bertram forget about the coffee? Perhaps that was it. He wanted her to grind up some more peppercorns to add to his coffee. Or maybe he'd grown some pepper plants himself. If he kept his hands busy outside, she might actually make some progress in keeping the manor looking orderly.

He scowled. "Yes. Pepper. The hummingbird. I've figured out what to do with her." Great. He'd named the bird.

She leaned against the doorway and let out a yawn. "You woke me up early to tell me about your new pet?"

He looked away with a glower. "We need to prepare the greenhouse for her. I'm not keeping her caged up in the house a moment longer."

"Her?" Laoise snickered. "I don't want to know how you figured out she was a lady."

"Don't be crass." He puffed out his chest. "Pepper is a ruby-throated hummingbird. They are native to North America. The greenhouse is a more suitable environment for her than the cage."

"Fascinating," she said, not meaning it at all. "Odd name for a creature with no red on its throat."

"The females of the species don't have red throats. Only the males do. They use it to attract their mates during—"

"I don't need all the details." She pushed away with a groan. "Let me eat first before you run me ragged again."

"You can eat afterwards. The sooner we get her into the greenhouse the better. There are some panels on the roof of the greenhouse I need you to shut before I can release her. I'll go fetch Pepper while you do that."

He walked away, leaving her groaning at the thought of getting back to work. She needed a day off. No, she needed a whole week. A week to do nothing but sleep.

Laoise headed for the greenhouse, following the covered outdoor walkway. Dead leaves swirled about her feet, making satisfying crunches whenever she stepped on them. The frosty air warned her that winter would come any day now. She sucked in another deep breath, enjoying how fresh and crisp the air smelled compared to the city. For a moment, she wished her brother could be here to enjoy the fresh air and wide open grounds to play in. Except then he'd be trapped with Bertram just like she was. She shook her head. Not a fate to wish on anyone.

The chill of the wind reminded her she'd be stuck here all winter without her family. No laughter around the dinner table. No hot tea while huddled around the fireplace. No Christmas. Her chest tightened at the thought of a quiet, lonely Christmas morning with only Bertram Steepe for company.

She turned her attention back to the greenhouse to fight off the growing melancholy fighting to blanket her. Compared to the dead landscape, the greenhouse was a pop of color when there shouldn't be any. No wonder Mrs. Steepe enjoyed spending winter out here. She opened the door to the greenhouse and a shimmering golden barrier rippled like water across the threshold. Passing through the magic barrier banished the wintery cold and replaced it with a summer humidity. The familiar tickle of Steepe magic filled the greenhouse.

She'd once read Charlotte's copy of *Robinson Crusoe*, and now surrounded by the overgrown vegetation and sweltering heat, she felt like she too was on a deserted tropical island. Large pink flowers surrounded by bright orange blossoms sat off to her right. Above a shallow pond, vines climbed over a statue of a stag. To her left, a cluster of orchids waited beside large ferns that hid the rest of the greenhouse from view.

She looked up to see the two glass panels swinging open at the top of the greenhouse. She hated to admit that Bertram was right, but unless those panels were shut, Pepper would almost certainly find her way out and be consumed by the cold.

She'd need a ladder to reach the panels. Looking out of the glass walls, she spotted the gardener's shed tucked in under a copse of trees. She headed out back out into the chilly air, already missing the greenhouse's warmth. The door to the shed stuck as she tugged on it, forcing her to put her shoulder into opening it. The door gave way with a screech from the hinges. Gardening equipment filled the small space, and there at the very back hung two ladders. She grabbed the biggest one and hauled it over to the greenhouse.

The ladder gave her just enough rungs to reach the slanted glass roof. She stared up at the greenhouse, debating on the best angle to approach from. Her eye caught on the manor window above her. Hadn't that been the window to the locked room? She counted the number of windows from the side of the house to check, and a smile crept across her face. There was no mistaking it. That was the room. She'd tried every trick she could think of to open the door, but the open panel was the perfect excuse she needed to climb up there and snoop through the window.

Laoise let out a mischievous chuckle as she started the climb. She imagined Bertram's humiliation when his plot was revealed, and when he learned that the one who defeated him was the lowly maid he always talked down to. She felt like the maid Louise foiling the schemes of the villainous Barnaby in *Calamity in a Coffeepot* alongside Cathy.

Halfway up the ladder, her climbing grew slower. She kept her attention aimed on the window. She'd often wondered what he was hiding, but being this close, her mind started to race. He might be planning to blow up more of the Steepe Company's merchant ships. Or Martin's tea shops this time. Whatever his scheme was, it was right on the other side of that window, and Laoise wasn't going to let it happen.

The greenhouse butted up against the back corner of the manor, blocking her path to the window, but giving the room a great view of the greenery below. When she reached the last rung of the ladder, the window was a hair too far out of reach. If she took one step down she'd be standing on the slanted roof of the greenhouse. But the little ledge running across the manor beneath the windows was wide enough for her to traverse if she held on.

She hesitated. She'd survive a fall from this height, but she might break her leg if she landed wrong. Even worse, she might come crashing through the glass into the greenhouse. But weeks of trying had given her no other way into the room. This could be her last chance to get inside.

Her spite against Bertram overcame her fear, and she drove her right foot off the ladder, easing herself onto the narrow ledge. She sidled her way across inch by inch, moving in small, careful steps.

When she reached the window, she had to bend down to peer in. Thick blue curtains blocked most of the window, and the narrow gap between them offered a dark, obscured view of the room. She pressed her face against the glass, but nothing emerged from the darkness. What looked like a shadowy bed filled the crack between the curtains, but she couldn't be sure with how gloomy the room was. She'd need to get inside to find his secrets.

It took a few precarious seconds to move both hands to the window and keep her balance. Then she tried to shove the window up. The window creaked but didn't budge. The second try sent her foot sliding off the ledge. Her stomach plummeted as she grabbed for the window sill, holding on until her fluttering heart calmed.

This was taking too long, and she couldn't afford for Bertram to get too suspicious of her actions. She inched back toward the ladder and the open panel. Maybe she could close the panel and try for the window once again.

She reached for the open glass panel, having to twist to the side to brush the edge with her fingertips. She pushed down, but the panel didn't budge either. From her position she couldn't get enough leverage. She tried once more, the panel finally giving way under her hand.

But it gave faster than expected. With a squeak of shock, she tumbled into the panel. It clicked closed, leaving her staring down into the greenhouse. There was no time to appreciate the scenery as she slid down the angled roof.

Her hands scrabbled for traction, but the smooth glass panels offered none. She kicked her right foot hoping to catch the ledge. Her knee whacked against the glass and she hissed in pain. Then a loud crack made her freeze. In front of her face, a single crack spread through the center of the panel. Smaller cracks branched off, zigzagging through the panel.

Laoise sucked in a breath, trying to remain motionless. The hammering of her heart drowned out the cracking of the glass. If she yelled for Bertram, would he hear her? Even if he did, would he bother to come check on her? She opened her mouth to yell, but a loud crack shot through the glass. She froze, her cry for help coming out as a quiet squeak.

The glass gave way, and she fell with a shout. She plummeted through the barrier, leaves and thin branches snagging on her arms, tearing her sleeves and scratching her skin. Her eyes opened just in time to see the surface of the pond before slamming through it.

Warm water rushed over her with a splash. Astonishingly, she didn't hit the bottom, but rather kept sinking. How deep was this pond? The rays of sunlight filtering through the plants and water dissipated into darkness beneath her. She kicked, but no matter how fast she thrashed, her head didn't break the surface. Bubbles burst around her head. The light only got farther away as she fought against the water.

In her panic she sucked in a gulp of water that sent her lungs burning. Her heavy boots dragged her down, but they were too tight to kick off. The water grew colder and colder as she fell. Something brushed against her left leg and she kicked at it, meeting nothing but water.

A firm hand clamped around her left arm. Water rushed past her ears as it hauled her to the surface. Then her head was free, and she sucked in a breath of air through her burning nose and throat. A gust of magic swept aside the shattered glass in their way as Bertram pulled her away from the water.

"Are you all right? Can you breathe?" His eyes were wide as he knelt down beside her.

In response, she rolled onto her side and vomited up a great gush of water. Right across his shoes. He wrinkled his nose, disgust replacing the concern his face had been wearing. He straightened back up and shook the water off his shoes.

"Are you trying to drown yourself?" He demanded, his anger sending his voice up a notch.

Her chest burned and felt too tight all at once. Her throat ached as she coughed and gasped for air. "I can't swim." Her voice came out hoarse.

"Then why did you throw yourself into the pond?"

"I didn't mean to." She lifted her head to glare at him. She felt like a drowned rat. Her soggy clothes were heavy with cold water. The cold water coating her made her shiver, her teeth clacking together as she spoke. "I was trying to close the panels like you ordered."

In one fluid motion, he took off his jacket and wrapped it around her shoulders. The jacket was warm, even compared to the heat of the greenhouse. His gaze fell to the shattered glass, and then drifted up to the ceiling. "And how the hell did you manage to break the ceiling?"

"It was an accident!" Laoise had sometimes fantasized about what it would be like to be rescued from danger by a mysterious handsome man. In none of her fantasies did the man then proceed to berate her. She eyed up the vine hanging off the stag statue beside Bertram and considered wrapping it around his neck a few times. She decided it would be poor manners to strangle the man who just saved her from drowning. At least for now.

"Oh for God's sake..." He rubbed a hand over his face. "Please tell me you didn't climb onto the roof to close the panels."

"Yes. How else am I supposed to close them?" She climbed onto her feet, water dripping from her clothes.

"By using the crank." He reached for a circular metal wheel hidden between two plants. He cranked it and the open panels above closed.

"Well, I didn't know about the crank because I've never been in here before. I'm not your damned gardener." She climbed onto wobbly legs and stepped away from the water. Large fish swam around far beneath the surface where the clear water turned into murky depths impossibly deep for a greenhouse pond. "How deep is that water?"

"As deep as it needs to be for the fish. My uncle likes to fish in here." As he spoke, a large fish broke the surface, its scaled golden back glinting in the sunlight before disappearing back under. The fish was almost as big as her. Bertram turned his attention back to the roof and groused as he stared up at the panel she'd fallen through. A few jagged shards of glass clung to the edges. "I can't believe you broke the roof."

"You know magic." Laoise bit her tongue. It was far too generous to say that Bertram "knew" magic, but now wasn't the best time to insult the man's magical abilities. "Can't you just fix it?"

"Glass is...difficult to work with." The embarrassed look on his face told her that by "difficult," what he meant was "impossible." At least for him.

He bent down to cup some of the pond water in his left hand. Then he pushed his way to the wall of the greenhouse, shoving past unruly plants. With one hand against the wall, he mumbled a long string of archaic words she couldn't understand.

Water from the pond spiraled up toward the roof. A silvery fish the size of her head got caught in the stream of water. With a flop to the side, it fell out of the spiral and crashed back into the pond below. The splash soaked Laoise's skirt again.

"Damn it all," she grumbled.

The spiraling water stopped at the ceiling, spreading out to seal the gap in the roof. By the time the spiral stopped, the water looked clear as glass. At a glance she wouldn't have been able to tell the glass panel was gone. That was until a moment later when the new roof panel started to drip, ruining the effect. The drops landed on the large fern at the edge of the pond.

"There. Fixed." Bertram declared. He rubbed his hands together, his palms smacking together as he dusted his hands of lingering magic. "Let's get back to work."

"You can't be serious. I'm soaking wet. Not to mention I almost drowned." She tossed an arm out, flicking water from her sleeves at him. "And I still haven't eaten. I'm in no condition to do any work."

"Then get changed." In another smooth and elegant motion, he took his jacket back from her shoulders. He rifled through the pockets while casting an accusatory look at Laoise. Evidently satisfied that she hadn't stolen anything from him in the few minutes she had been wearing it, he put the jacket back on.

He then tilted his head toward the pond, a finger tapping against his chin. "And as long as you're back there, I want a cup of coffee too. A quick break, then back to cleaning." He marched off toward the door and she regretted her choice to not strangle him with the vine when she had the chance.

Chapter 7

With all the magic clinging to the greenhouse, she didn't understand why the place couldn't clean itself. As for her, weeding was out of the question. She didn't know what to pull and what to leave alone. She smacked the wet sponge in her hand against the glass and let go, but no magic took over. The sponge flopped to the ground, landing at the base of a short lemon tree.

She balled her hands, fighting the urge to scream. Cleaning all these panels by herself would take days.

"Have you forgotten how to clean?" Bertram asked, barely looking up from his book, an anthology of ancient Greek tragedies. Bertram reclined in a luxurious green chair in the small sitting area, which sat at the far end of the greenhouse. Even among the fragrant flowers, she could still smell the sweet aroma from the cup of coffee on the table beside him. "Throwing sponges at the wall won't do anything."

She rested a hand on her right hip. "How about you come over here and show me how to clean?"

"Ha! As if I'd leave my reading for that. You're the maid. I'm sure you can figure it out." He shot a knowing smile to her. "You maids are always figuring things out, aren't you?"

Laoise wasn't quite sure what to make of that. She shrugged and leaned her forehead against the glass, staring out at the bare trees beyond. Where the lawn behind the property gave way to the forest, she thought she caught sight of a rider on horseback passing through. Must be the neighbors, since there weren't any horses at the manor stables.

She bet that horse had more than one servant. A whole crew of servants to attend to all of its horsely desires. "Better a horse for a master than this horse's ass," Laoise mumbled to herself. Never in her life had she been so envious of a stable hand.

As of last week she'd earned enough to cover several months' worth of medicine for her brother. There was no need to keep putting up with Bertram. She wouldn't be able to afford both the medicine and updating her wardrobe, but at least she had the beautiful cloak from Charlotte to console her.

She sighed. That was still a problem to deal with on her return. Now that Mrs. Charlotte Steepe was technically her employer, Laoise would be in service to her oldest friend. The growing social gap between them only made Laoise more embarrassed about her standing and more afraid to lose their friendship. But where else could she go? Mrs. Hammond might take her back as a maid, but dealing with Oolong was trouble enough. Dodging and dancing around Mrs. Hammond's dachshunds again would be a nightmare. As long as she stayed here she could avoid dealing with the issue.

"Don't just stand there or the cleaning will never get done," he said, flipping a page of his book with a condescending chuckle. "With the windows this filthy, the sun can't possibly recharge the barrier. I'm surprised the enchantments are still holding together after all this neglect."

She picked up the sponge and turned, debating on whether or not to lob it at his head next. The open bird cage sat near his feet. The hummingbird hovered around one of the colorful flowers near the pond. For the little bird's sake, Laoise held her tongue.

"For God's sake..." grumbled Bertram as he turned another page. Each snort and snicker he let out as he read echoed in the greenhouse, making Laoise grind her teeth so hard she thought they might shatter in her mouth.

"A compelling read I take it?" Laoise spoke through a forced smile. "Perhaps you would be less distracted at the other end of the damn manor?"

"Oh no, I'm right where I want to be. It's quite funny actually. The villain in this story made a critical mistake. He didn't keep a close enough eye on the help. He should have known better than to trust a maid."

"My word, sir!" she said with a mocking gasp. "You aren't suggesting anything about me, I hope."

He looked between her and his reading. "Now that you mention it, I'm noticing quite a few similarities between you and the disrespectful little maid in this story. I believe her name is..." He paused, setting the book down on the table and tapping his finger on the page. He looked up and shot an accusatory glance at Laoise. "Ah yes. Louise."

She froze. She looked down at the book to see that a stack of loose papers was strewn across its open pages. Even from a distance, Laoise could recognize it as her copy of *Calamity in a Coffee Pot*. "Is that my book? Did you steal my book?"

"I'd hardly call this drivel a book. It's little more than a biased and inaccurate portrayal of real life events. I don't think the phrase 'write what you know' was meant to be taken quite so literally."

"Inaccurate? How do you figure? Ol' Barnaby tried his hardest to interfere with his cousin's business *and* his marriage. And both blew up in his face. Spectacularly. Sounds pretty accurate to me. And not to spoil the upcoming chapters, but I've heard he ends up locked away somewhere."

"Oh please. She made me"—he cleared his throat—"She made Barnaby literally twirl his mustache. The only part she got right was that the maid was in fact scheming behind his back the whole time.

"It's clear the villain is fashioned after me. And he's right about the maid hiding things too. The most ridiculous thing is her assumption I wanted to marry her. I didn't even like her." He sipped at his coffee. "No wonder this isn't published."

"It is though. Hawke is publishing it. That's an early copy Charlotte sent me."

He almost dropped his cup. The deep brown liquid sloshed over the side, narrowly missing his left leg. "What? This rubbish? When is it getting published?"

She shrugged. "You'd have to ask Hawke. Or better yet, you could ask Charlotte."

"I refuse to ever talk to that wretched woman. I'd sooner speak with the Devil himself." He set his cup down and inspected his trouser leg for any stray drops of coffee.

"And why is that? She is your family now," Laoise teased.

"She is not family." Bertram grimaced. "I know for a fact that she and that Hawke girl were just using Martin to save that failing publishing house. Those two are no different from Martin's first fiancée. She was hoping she could marry into our family's money. I put an end to that, and I'll put an end to this sham of a marriage too."

"You'll put an end to it, will you? By stealing kisses from any girl your cousin takes a liking to? You disgusting cad."

He slapped the pages down onto the small table beside him. "Don't you dare question my integrity, maid. The first fiancée kissed me, not the other way around. I knew she didn't want to marry Martin. I think he knew as well, but he was too afraid of disappointing his father to turn her away. As Chaucer once wrote, 'Patience is a conquering virtue,' and I waited patiently for her to show her true colors. Once she asked to marry me instead, I simply capitalized on it."

"Never one to pass up an opportunity to capitalize on a woman, I see. I suppose that's the same line you used to justify kissing Charlotte, isn't it?"

"He had fallen under her spell. I swallowed my pride and kissed that awful woman because I thought that might finally make him see her for the fickle and money-hungry trollop she is. I didn't want to hurt my cousin, but he doesn't deserve to have some woman manipulating him.

"Better you manipulate him, then?" Laoise snorted. "I say he deserves a better cousin than you."

He spluttered, starting his sentence three times before getting out a "How dare you."

"You tried to destroy his business too. Don't try to hide it."

"Of course I did! To save him from ruining himself when his tea business failed."

"Oh, I hadn't heard it failed. I must have missed that news when I heard he opened a new shop near the train station in the village."

"Failure takes many forms, as *you* are no doubt well aware." He sneered. "Martin has a brilliant mind for business, and this little foray into tea is a complete waste of his talent."

"Doesn't seem a waste to me."

"These things are clearly beyond your comprehension." He sighed and relaxed back into the chair, picking up the pages to hide behind them. "I don't expect you to understand."

"You're the one who doesn't understand." She ripped the papers out of his hands. "And you have no right to go snooping through my personal things. Master of this house or no, it doesn't matter. Those are my things."

"Now that is rich." He stood and grabbed the papers back. "First you steal my coffee, then you presume to lecture me on respecting one's personal things? And that's to say nothing of all the other things you've stolen."

She crossed her arms and stared up at him, refusing to let his height intimidate her. "I didn't steal your damn coffee and I haven't taken anything else either. I don't want anything to do with you or your things" She couldn't think of anything she'd taken. The last thing she wanted was something of his as a token. She'd rather forget he existed when he wasn't in sight.

"Then explain this!" He pulled three bells out of his pocket. "You stole the clappers, which is why they weren't working whenever I rang for you. Did you think I wouldn't find out? I bet you planned to sell them."

"Sell them for what? No one wants bell clappers. I stole them because your bells are annoying when they are ringing in my ear every hour with your constant demands."

"Without them I can't summon you." He waved his hand and all three bells rang at once while they floated toward her.

"That's the idea." She plucked the bells out of the air and ripped the clappers out again. "Good job on figuring it out, sir."

He growled. "Do not touch my bells."

"You mean like this?" She poked each bell. As childish as it felt, the look of fury as his face turned red filled her with glee.

He spluttered. "Stop that."

One by one she poked them again. "Oops, sorry, sir," she said, sarcasm dripping from her words. "I just can't seem to help meself."

He waved a hand in frustration. "You are the most impertinent maid I've ever had the displeasure of meeting."

"Well, I wouldn't be here if you hadn't driven off all the other maids and servants." She threw the bells at his head. They caught themselves halfway, finishing the journey by gently floating toward him before shaking as if ringing. He batted them away from his face.

"Perhaps I should endeavor to do the same to you."

"Look at you and your big, fancy words. No need to try any harder because I'm happy to leave today!" She threw the bell clappers into the pond. "You can cook your own meals and wash your own laundry from now on, you horrid man."

His eyes widened at her words. She froze. No going back now that she'd gone and insulted him.

He reached toward the pond, his mouth going slack as he realized the clappers were gone.

"I quit."

He threw back his shoulders, fixing her with a harsh look. "Unacceptable. You can leave once someone comes to replace you."

"That's not how quitting works. I doubt your cousin can convince anyone else to come put up with you. At least not until the holidays are over." She headed for the door.

"I'll be sure my cousin and uncle both hear about your disgusting behavior."

She detoured to one of the windows connected to the house, grabbing one of the floating flower feeders as she went. She opened the window.

"What are you doing?"

"Keeping you busy." She chucked the flower feeder through the opening. Pepper followed after it and into the house. She slammed the window shut, trapping both in the house.

"How dare you?" He spluttered again, ending by pointing at her. "Once I find that bird you are finished!"

Laoise laughed. "I already quit." She headed for the door, doing a spin on her way there as if she were dancing. The thought of waking up tomorrow morning and not having to feed Bertram earned a giggle of joy.

She got to work packing her things while he stormed through the house on his quest to recapture the bird. He hadn't learned a thing in his exile. Letting him fend for himself might get the lesson of humility through his thick skull. Or starve him. Both options struck her as agreeable.

She sent a summons to the carriage driver before leaving her room, tapping the summon stone twice in her impatience to escape. A fresh blanket of snow already covered the ground when she stepped outside. She blinked in surprise at how white the world had turned. When had the snow started? There'd been plenty of gray in the sky during her adventure on the roof, but no snow.

Winter always sneaked up on her. No matter how cold the days got, she never felt ready. And yet this surprise storm felt ridiculous with its sudden onslaught. The snowfall grew heavier by the minute while she waited, dashing any hope of it going away soon.

After twenty minutes, she sat down on the stairs, clearing the snow off with a gloved hand before sitting. Her legs bounced as she tried to keep warm.

She summoned the driver again. "Where are you?" She grumbled as she braced her shoulders against the wind. The snow had already filled in her footprints. A shiver tore through her. The temperature had dropped along with the snow. Her last hopes for the storm blowing over faded.

Behind her, the door creaked open. "Are you finished with your tantrum now?" Bertram's snide voice made her grit her teeth.

"No." She kept her gaze forward to avoid looking at him. Her shoulders were stiff from the cold as much as from defiance.

He snorted. "No one is coming in this weather. I can't even see the road from here."

He was right. If the carriage did come, she wouldn't be able to see it until it was upon her. No driver would want to risk his neck in this weather.

He huffed. "Come inside. This weather is only going to get worse."

She crossed her arms and refused to answer.

"Fine then. Freeze to death if you like." He shut the door with a bang.

She hugged herself, but it did nothing to stop the shivers. She didn't want him to win. The very idea of going back inside with her tail tucked between her legs lit a fire in the pit of her stomach. But it was hopeless. Even if she somehow made it to the station, the train wouldn't arrive in this weather.

Pure spite had her half convinced to take Bertram up on his offer to freeze to death. To leave him one final mess she wouldn't have to clean up. It was only her memories of Sean, her sole reason for going through this entire ordeal, that dragged her out of her fantasy. Her cheeks turned numb, telling her it was time to go inside. She toddled back up the stairs on stiff legs, pausing at the door.

No. This wasn't defeat. Charlotte had her own setbacks with handling Bertram, but she still came out victorious. Laoise would do the same. She kicked at the snow, sending a cloud of it flying down the stairs. The weather wasn't willing to cooperate, but that didn't mean she would march back inside to play dutiful maid again.

She stepped inside, a gust of wind sending a dusting of snow flying in around her.

"There you are." Bertram sat on a chair he'd dragged into the entryway. He shut the book on his lap. In the other hand, he held a teacup, which could only mean one thing: with their coffee stash gone he'd grown desperate for something hot to drink. "I was beginning to think I'd have to come drag you inside."

Her cheeks puffed. "I refuse to work for you."

"Dereliction of your duties?" Bertram tutted, sarcasm dripping from his words. "What a surprise coming from you."

"There's no dereliction. I quit, remember?" She dropped her bag and considered kicking it at his head. "You're not seriously trying to bribe me back with tea?"

"Of course not. You were set on leaving." He changed his voice, imitating hers. "Remember?" He took a sip, his face twisting up from disgust. "Revolting. And over steeped."

She snorted. "Can't do anything for yourself, can ye?" She headed past him to the sitting room. Warmth poured from the fire. Pins and needles poked her feet and hands as warmth seeped back into them.

Bertram stood up and leaned against the doorway. "Now look here, Lisa—"

She whirled on him. "My name is Laoise. Laoise! Not Lisa." She tore her thick gloves off and pocketed them. How much would Martin dock her pay if she punched Bertram right in his smug, handsome face? "Say it with me, Lee-sha," she said, sounding it out for him. "L-A-O-I-S-E! Get it right."

"Do you hear yourself?" He squinted at her. "None of those letters match those sounds. Gaelic is an utter nonsense language."

She threw her hands up. "I can handle you speakin' ill of me, but you say one more word about my heritage and I swear to Jesus I'll smash that pretty face of yours in."

"Yes, it is a pretty face, isn't it?" He smirked as he stroke his chin. He clearly wasn't taking her seriously. "Well, rest assured that I can't think of a worse insult to your heritage than to say that it produced someone as stubborn and unpleasant as you."

A mop headed for her, following the trail of melting snow she'd left behind. She grabbed the mop and jabbed him with it. "And I can't think of a worse insult to your entire family than you! You might be breathtakingly handsome, but you are also full of yourself and a spoiled brat that needs servants to keep you from starving to death."

He took a step back to avoid the mop. His expression darkened. His nostrils flared. "You will not insult my family."

"Not your family. Just you. There's not a one of them as spoiled or rude or selfish as you." She jabbed at him again. "It's no wonder you aren't married yet. I've only been here a few months, and I'd already rather jump off a bridge than spend even one more minute with you."

He grabbed the end of the mop to stop her and lowered his voice, carefully enunciating every word. "Then it's a good thing that a lowly maid like you is so far below my station that she need not concern herself with marrying me."

And with that, Laoise snapped. She bared her teeth at Bertram and smacked him in the side with the soggy wet head of the mop, making him yelp in surprise. Taking a firm grip with both hands, she pressed the shaft against his chest and pushed Bertram back against the wall. A painting hanging on the wall came loose and fell to the floor.

But after the initial shock, Bertram grabbed a hold of the mop as well. He quickly began to overpower Laoise as they wrestled for control, pushing himself off of the wall and pressing the shaft like a fighting staff back against Laoise. He laughed. "Have you gone mad? Have you forgotten who you're dealing with?"

Laoise grunted in response. He was strong, that was for sure, forcing her to backpedal until her back was against a large cushioned chair near the fireplace. She could tell he was toying as he mashed the shaft into her breasts. He leered at her, his face illuminated by the blazing fire in the room. A gasp escaped her.

"Give up already. I was undefeated when I wrestled back in my college days."

"Oh yeah? My brothers taught me to not fight fair." With a quick tug on the mop, she flung herself backward over the ottoman and onto the floor, dragging Bertram with her. His momentum worked against him as she pressed her heel into his stomach, kicking and flipping him over her head. His back hit the carpeted floor with a thud, and the force of the impact knocked a small statue off of the mantel of the fireplace.

The smashing of the ceramic statue against the floor almost covered up the sound of Bertram's groan. In a fluid motion she'd practiced from years of roughhousing with her brothers as children, she continued rolling through the flip, ending by straddling Bertram's chest. She pressed the shaft under his chin and against his throat. Victory sang through her veins.

"Get off," Bertram groaned, having had the wind knocked out of him. He grabbed Laoise by the hips and pushed her off of his chest. Her legs slid down his body, anger and desire mixing in her core as his warmth seeped into her. He had been a nuisance to deal with ever since she first walked in the front door of the manor, but now that he was underneath her, the urge she'd had to see him suffer was disappearing. It was replaced by a more primal urge. The urge to conquer him.

Worse, whenever she got mad like this and couldn't think straight, the Irish brogue she kept so carefully hidden from her employers would come out. Emotions always made it harder to hide.

"'Lowly maid,' am I? Well if I'm so lowly, what's that make you when I'm on top o' ye?" she spat out, breathing heavily. Looking down at a vulnerable Bertram was more gratifying than she could have dreamed. She couldn't stop staring at his face, highlighted by the light of the blazing fire. His tousled hair. The hard set of his jaw. The heaving of his panting chest. Her fury wasn't enough to chase away the attraction she felt. The two only fueled each other as they melded together, one driving the other until she could no longer tell them apart.

"Impatient is what it makes me." He grunted, reaching up to grab her wrists and wrestle the mop away from his throat. "Now get off of me. Or I'll get angry."

Her thoughts were in disarray as the insult that rested on the tip of her tongue melted away. She tightened her grip and pressed her weight against the handle. "Not 'til ye apologize."

His fight grew more frantic, finally pressing the mop over his head. Laoise let go of the handle and lost her leverage, collapsing forward and pressing her chest against his. She felt his panting hot breath on her neck. The bulge pressing against her thigh grew.

"Off," he stammered, face souring from his own anger. "Before you regret this."

"Ye mean before I lose me senses and do somethin' mad like this?" She grinned as she swooped down and kissed him, eager to fuel the flames of his anger. He froze under her. For a tense moment he did nothing as Laoise pressed her lips against his. His hands released her wrists and worked their way around her waist. She ran her fingers through his hair as he kissed her back.

"You're a demon," he growled, pulling away for only a moment before kissing her once more. One of his hands wandered up her leg, starting at her calf and working its way up her skirts to her thigh. Her leg twitched, teasing a moan out of her. Goose bumps spread away from his fingertips.

His warmth felt like an inviting oasis after the freezing cold of the storm. She wanted to nestle closer and soak it in. The scents of the greenhouse clung to him, reminding her of summer, the floral notes mixing with the sweet smell of coffee still clinging to him.

The last of her thoughts fled as she kissed him back. She focused on nothing but his warmth and the tingles of pleasure shooting through her wherever his fingers touched. After her weeks of frustration and stress, this felt like a sweet release.

"Laoise..." he murmured, pronouncing it correctly for the very first time, and her legs squeezed him in response. He kissed her with desperation, like a man starved for affection. She wiggled her hips to urge his hand higher.

The storm rattled the window, but she was already too focused on the growing heat between them to remember the snow or the carriage that would never come.

Chapter 8

Laoise stretched like a contented cat. The wind whistled outside, the dark sky making it look as though night had arrived early. A layer of snow coated the outside windowsill, frost clinging to the glass. Despite the crackling fire dying down, the storm outside made the room feel cozy and warm. She could lie there for hours in front of the fire while watching the snow pile up.

Bertram lay behind her, an arm draped over her waist and a leg entwined between hers. Her eyes fluttered as sleep threatened to creep over her. The rug beneath them wasn't particularly thick or soft, but she couldn't remember a time she felt more comfortable since she'd arrived at the manor. She nestled back into his embrace and nodded off.

She had a brief and blissful moment of peace until Bertram pulled away. A rush of cold air ghosted over her skin, waking her up. She rolled back and reached over to lazily trace his spine. She couldn't remember when he'd lost the shirt, but she liked him better without it. All his time spent fencing showed in his toned muscles.

His mussed hair was an invitation that made her want to climb onto his lap to kiss him some more. But she couldn't. Not yet. Her legs still felt like jelly from the intense release he'd given her. Laoise had known other lovers before, but she'd never known any like this. The shy neighbor boy who had who stolen her heart before running away with a different girl. The driver for the Hammonds, who'd been so nervous he'd nearly fallen down the stairs leading to her room. And the boastful amateur boxer whose capabilities fell far short of his confidence.

Bertram blew them all away. He had been surprisingly unselfish, more excited by her cries of pleasure than his own desires. Unlike her previous lovers who'd left her wondering why she'd bothered with them at all, he had her wanting more and more.

She ran a finger over his back.

He shivered. "That tickles."

"I'd like to find out where you're ticklish." Her voice came out husky with longing. All she wanted was to lure him back down. To wrap herself back up in his arms and lose herself to ecstasy all over again.

He turned to watch the fire. She sat up and followed the contours of his jawline next, wanting to get rid of his deepening frown. He reached for her hand, stopping her.

"We shouldn't have done that." He let go of her hand to fix his pants. He searched for his shirt, turning this way and that. "My jacket. Where is my jacket?"

And there went his mouth ruining everything. As it always did. He was far more handsome when he was silent. Her brief respite was over, and she was right back to being his maid. She smoothed down her skirt and fixed her top. He avoided looking at her as he climbed to his feet.

"Are you about to run away from me?" Her nails dug into the rug.

"There is no sense lingering here. It was a mistake." He kept his gaze on the doorway. "No good can come from this. I shouldn't be dallying with my maid."

She rolled her eyes. "I see. Just another task for your maid to do. You're as bad as the Cavendish boy." The boy in question was the young master of the Cavendish household, who had been notorious for bedding the maids in exchange for money. There had even been a rumor that one maid had such an affair, and when her pregnancy was discovered, she was sacked. Laoise was grateful that she'd never been desperate enough to accept such an offer.

"I am nothing like that repugnant little—" He cleared his throat and continued gathering his clothes. "That man is a disgrace to himself and to his family. A gentleman keeps his distance from the help so as not to take advantage."

She laughed, the sound biting and unforgiving. "Take advantage? Of me? You were the one on your back while I did the hard work. Quite the 'gentleman' indeed." She'd rather liked the rush of having power over him instead of being at his beck and call. "As you may have noticed, I'm not some shy, naïve little girl. I'm a grown woman and can make my own decisions."

He took a step toward the door. "Look, I don't want you getting the wrong idea. This encounter was a moment of weakness is all. I'm not looking for a mistress."

"Oh, please. As if I'd want to be your mistress. You're easy on the eyes, sir, but that's about it." He was also well versed in carnal knowledge, but she wasn't going to tell him that. She climbed onto her feet.

"I simply need you to realize that I don't want to make a habit of …this." He stammered, struggling to find the words to politely articulate his sentiments. "And I…there won't be any additional…erm…that is to say…compensation for…"

"What do you take me for? One of Madame Beaumont's girls?" She poked a finger into his bare chest. There were many things Laoise was willing to do for extra money, but employment at one of Beaumont's houses of ill repute was a line she dared not cross.

"You don't understand," he said, shifting on his feet as he looked toward the door. "There's a difference in our station that—"

"To hell with you and to hell with your precious station." She crossed her arms. "If you're so ashamed, then you can forget about this ever happening again."

"Yes. Good." He put on a nervous smile and nodded. "Your…discretion in this matter is appreciated."

She looked him in the eyes, her expression icy. He looked away almost sheepishly. "Shut your mouth and go before I get the mop again."

He raised a finger to say something, but thinking better of it, turned and scurried out without another word. She headed for the woodpile to put another log on the fire. If she was going to be stuck inside, she would at least stay warm. Her gaze snagged on the jacket dangling from the far side of the ottoman, nestled between the ottoman and armchair.

"Sir, you forgot your jacket," she grumbled in a mocking tone. "Please allow me, your lowly maid, to clean up after you. Nothing makes my day brighter."

She picked up the jacket. A weight in the pocket drew her attention. She fished out a heavy key.

"Did you say something?" A moment later, he reappeared in the doorway.

She scowled. "You forgot this." She slid the key into her own pocket. Then she threw the jacket at him, but the fabric only made it halfway before plopping onto the floor between them. She threw up her hands in frustration. "Please, let me get that for ye, sir." She marched up to the jacket and grabbed it off the floor.

He shifted in discomfort as she approached him. She handed him the jacket and then curtsied with a dramatic flourish. "So very glad to be of service," she said in a high-pitched voice.

"Erm..." his mouth hung open as he searched for a response. "Yes. Thank you. Good... work." He backed away. A few steps later he turned and fled, running back up to his room.

She felt for the heavy key in her pocket, hating the way her chest tightened. Her mother had warned her to not get herself in trouble with her employers, especially the men. Laoise liked to enjoy herself, but this time she'd crossed a line, even by her own standards. She'd meant to hurt Bertram's pride, and from the way he talked it seemed as though she had. Except she hadn't expected her own pride to be hurt too.

Her heart felt hollow. Was this all she'd ever have to look forward to, temporary affairs and regrets? Bertram wasn't wrong either. As a maid her prospects for marriage were limited. And if she didn't find a new position soon, she'd be serving her best friend in the new year. Then she'd be nothing but Charlotte's maid too.

Her eyes burned as tears welled up. Now wasn't the time to stand around wallowing. That wasn't her way. She'd save the tears for later when she crawled into bed alone. Right now, she had the key. There was only one key he could possibly be so worried about that he'd keep it on his person, and Laoise had tried picking the lock enough times to realize the door this key opened.

It was time to find out what Bertram was hiding in that locked room.

Luckily for her, Bertram had hidden away in his room with the door closed. She'd thought their dalliance might leave him embarrassed, but she hadn't expected him to be too embarrassed to leave his room. He was clearly intent on avoiding her until the snow cleared and a carriage took her back to London.

As much as she hated to admit it, his reaction hurt. No one had ever called intimacy with her a mistake before. She was used to her partners begging for more, not running away like a frightened schoolboy. Her jaw clenched.

If he was waiting on her to leave, then she saw no better time than to test out her new key. She'd find out his dark secrets, and then tell Charlotte everything. Maybe then he'd finally get locked up in the deepest darkest cell of the Tower of London like he deserved. She'd relish destroying whatever foul plans he was making. And no matter what, she wouldn't cry over him. He didn't deserve any more of her time or her emotions.

She tiptoed past his door to get to the locked room, shoving her lit candle behind her back to hide the light. Her heart rate picked up the closer she got to the door. The key weighed down her pocket, bumping against her with each step.

Did he have weapons hidden in there? She recalled hearing a rumor about Bertram's dealings with foreign weapon makers prior to the Great Exhibition. Or perhaps it was another bomb to blow up Martin's shipments of tea. It was a distinct and deadly possibility considering how often Bertram's magic blew up in his face.

Idea after idea passed through her imagination, each growing more frightening than the last. She shuddered as she imagined a room full of taxidermied dachshunds he planned to mail to Martin as a threat. With the deranged way she'd found him her first day in the clock room, anything seemed possible.

She held her breath as she slid the key into the keyhole. She turned it and the lock clicked. Her heart jumped. She pushed the door open slowly. But not slow enough. The hinges let out a high-pitched squeak. She froze. Her heart beat hammered in her ears as she stared down the hallway, watching Bertram's door. A tense moment passed, but his door didn't open. She opened the door another notch, just wide enough to slip inside.

The closed curtains let no light in from outside, forcing her to rely on her dim candle. She took a step deeper into the room. The candlelight spilled over a dusty, but neat bed. A child's drawings dangled from a string strung between the posts of the headboard, the edges of the paper yellow from age. A pile of extra blankets sat at the bottom of the bed. Beside the bed sat a wardrobe decorated in drawings that grew better the higher up they were.

The scene made goosebumps prickle up the back of her neck. She felt like she'd entered a memorial room for a child. The thick layer of dust coated everything. Everything except for the armchair nestled in the corner, giving it a good view of the bed. It was the only tidy corner in the room. The thought of someone siting in that chair and staring at the empty bed made her throat close up. She'd be in the same position soon if her brother didn't improve. It was too easy to picture it. She let out a shaky breath as a sob stuck in her throat.

Across from the bed, a desk sat tucked against the wall. The bookshelf beside it was full of books ranging from fairy tales to histories of England, France, and magic. At first glance, she didn't find anything villainous lurking in the corners. Several pictures hanging on the string over the bed depicted a long dog. One showed two wobbly stick figures, one labeled "Bertie" and the other "Me."

She let out a relieved sigh. It wasn't the resting place of a dead Steepe child. It was only Martin's childhood room. Still, her relief didn't shake the clammy fingers of unease creeping down her spine.

On closer inspection, there were notebooks and old school work on the bookshelves. French writing mingled with English. Mechanical hummingbirds lay among an odd collection of gears and pieces on the desk next to a drawing of a real hummingbird beside the fake one.

She'd heard Martin had been sick as a child. His mother still worried incessantly over his health. He'd had nothing but a single cold once since she joined their household, but that had been enough for his mother to beg him to return to the countryside to rest. This must be where he'd stayed during his early years of poor health.

There was a crushing loneliness to the room. The books on the shelves and all the drawings spoke of dreams and travels that may never come to pass. But Mr. Martin Steepe was doing fine, she reminded herself. He had Charlotte to look after him now. For the young Martin sick in his bed, there was a happy ending to his story.

Unlike Bertram, Martin never yelled. Whenever she brought his tea, he always made sure to thank her. Sure, he always called her Shannon, but he didn't get most people's names right. It was never malicious, and in some ways quite charming. She appreciated that he at least tried to learn her name. For her employers, she'd always been called "maid." A nameless, faceless servant who didn't matter until something wasn't to their liking.

"What are you doing?" A harsh voice asked.

Laoise jumped. Bertram stood in the doorway, jacket back on and buttoned. He'd even fixed his hair. He spread his arms, resting his hands on the doorway, blocking her exit. "Out. Now," he snapped.

"No." She threw her shoulders back, refusing to let him intimidate her. "Not 'til I know what you are hiding in here."

"What the hell are you talking about?" His surprise leeched some of the anger from his voice.

"You wouldn't let me in to clean. You've kept the door locked the whole time I've been here. It's because you're plotting something, I know it!" She gestured to the pieces strewn about the desk. "Exploding hummingbirds! That's it, isn't it?"

"Wha..." His anger melted into a bewildered stare. "Exploding hummingbirds?"

"To blow up your cousin's shipments of tea. I'll bet that's why you were intent on saving Pepper. You wanted to study her."

"You read too many stories," he said, rubbing the bridge of his nose. "If you were hoping for a great mystery, here it is: This was Martin's room when he was sick. It is a sad place, and no one goes in here. Not you. Not me. Not the bloody brooms and dusters."

She took a step away from him. "There's more to it than that. I know it. I can tell you've been sitting in the chair." She reached for the desk drawers. He grabbed both her hands, keeping her away from the desk.

"Don't. Touch. Martin's. Things." He said, spitting each word out. His grip tightened around her wrists, making Laoise wince. This time wasn't like their playful fighting earlier. This time he was hurting her.

"I won't be frightened by you," she said, grunting defiantly. "I'll get to the truth."

"I've told you the truth. It's more than you deserve. Now get out." He tugged hard on her arms, and spun her towards the door. She dug in her heels, but it was no good. She lost her footing and stumbled.

Bertram followed behind her, setting his hands on her shoulders and shoving her out of the room.

"Don't touch me!" She tried to fight against him, but she could barely stand up straight with the force of him shoving her. It took all her focus to keep from falling over. Once they reached the hallway, he pushed her away from the door. She regained her footing and wheeled on him.

He shut the door and turned to her, holding his hand out, his expression that of a stern school teacher. "Give it back."

"Give what back?"

"The key. Give it back to me now."

She scoffed. "I don't know what key you—"

"Now, Laoise," he interrupted, his face set like stone and his hand motionless. "I'm in no mood for games."

He'd remembered her name, but hearing him say it so sternly sent a chill through her spine. Seeing no way out of her predicament, she handed the key over. She didn't make it easy on him though. He had to pry the metal from her fingers one by one.

"I suppose you're expecting me to forget about all this and go back to being your maid?"

"I honestly don't care what you do." He waved a hand in a shooing motion. "Just stay out of Martin's room and stay out of my sight." He stood in front of Martin's door to keep her away. When she reached the stairs, she glanced back. He hadn't budged.

Maybe she did read too many stories. Maybe there was no secret. Maybe he was just a sad, lonely man trapped in this manor. Good. A man that unpleasant deserved to be sad and lonely. And Laoise had been personally dismissed by him, so she saw no further reason to remain here.

She headed for the front door. Her stomach dropped when she opened it. A thick blanket of snow coated the land as far as she could see. The drift of snow at the threshold was up to her knees. There'd be no carriage getting to the manor any time soon. Not for days. Or weeks seeing as how there were no other servants to help dig them out.

Walking away was out of the question. The walk to the train station would be a risk in this weather. Even if she made it, the train might not show. She slammed the door shut and let out a string of curses. She'd been so close to freedom only for it to slip between her fingers. If she didn't get out soon, she'd be trapped here for Christmas after all.

Stuck with Bertram for the holidays. She couldn't think of a worse fate.

Chapter 9

The next few days, she crept around the house like a frightened mouse. She peered around every corner to make sure she wouldn't run into Bertram. Whether she liked it or not he was still the master of the house, and until the snow cleared up she remained trapped in the manor with him.

Being stuck didn't mean she would take back her resignation though. She didn't bother with his laundry. Or cleaning. She slept in late each day, not caring about how much time she wasted. Once her cooking was done, she would sit and stare out at the snow while she read Charlotte's story or mended her clothes. By day three, she moved on to reading *Moby Dick*, which Bertram had left lying in the sitting room.

In all of her years working as a maid, Laoise never had an easier assignment. It was nice to sleep in and finally have some free time, but she still couldn't bring herself to enjoy it. She'd rather be working her usual hours back in London if it meant she could see her family. Between her childhood home and all the small bedrooms she shared with other maids, she wasn't used to this loneliness. She wanted other people around. People that weren't Bertram.

"Get a new hobby," she grumbled at Ishmael before shutting the book to check on her bread. It was a newly published book, and curiosity had tugged at her when she found it lying around. After hearing Bertram ramble about it, she wanted to understand the story.

However, she just couldn't bring herself to care about a bunch of sailors hunting a whale. Charlotte would probably talk about how much she appreciated the themes or metaphors or whatever. Bertram would do the same while being condescending about it. No matter. She preferred the detective novel she'd found in the parlor.

Once the bread was out, she checked on the pantry. Supplies were sparse, but with only two of them they wouldn't need to leave the manor to stock back up for at least two more weeks. Food was one worry she checked off her list. Plenty of oats to go around for both of them.

She'd made nothing but porridge and sandwiches since quitting. She left them outside Bertram's room to keep him from poking around in the kitchen. Loathe though she was to feed him, it kept him away.

The yeasty scent of fresh bread filled the kitchen. She breathed it in as she pulled the bread from the oven. The aroma sent a stab of longing through her. She missed Charlotte. And Charlotte's Da. Sure he didn't have a perfect chin. Plus he'd grown a bit portly around his waist, and she'd never seen him wearing anything but his flour-covered work clothes, but at least she knew what to expect with him.

He was gruff, but reliable and kind-hearted. She wanted a man like him. Someone she wouldn't have to look after like a child. Someone who wouldn't call a night of passion with her a "mistake." Oh but what a night...

What was it about Bertram that twisted up her thoughts? She couldn't stand to be around him, and yet whenever she couldn't avoid him she found herself staring. She wanted to punch him square in his perfect jaw as much as she longed to plant kisses on his lips. "Shame all men aren't like Charlotte's Da," she said aloud, trying to clear her thoughts.

She pulled her oven mitts off and headed for the front door for her daily check, hoping the carriage would appear today. The snow remained too deep for easy travel with fresh snowfall every day. So far it had been a fruitless endeavor, but she checked anyway. The hope kept her sane.

A low tapping filled the air when she reached the hallway. Hope spread through her chest and she picked up the pace, jogging to the door as she envisioned all the apologies and excuses the carriage driver would give her. But nothing waited on the other side of the door. Nothing but snow, a fresh round of flurries, and cold air. She huffed. "Living with him is driving me mad."

She shut the door, but the tapping continued. She followed the sound to the dining room. There a metal hummingbird tapped against the glass. She let the bird inside and a gust of frigid wind as well. Laoise shivered as she slid the window shut. The bird perched on the dining room table, one wing frozen to its side as it made an odd clicking noise.

The box was the same as the previous ones. A small bag of coffee for Bertram, some jam and fresh fruit, and a letter for Laoise. The handwriting on the envelope made her pause. It wasn't Charlotte's. It was messier, like Laoise's own writing. Her mother's then.

Her heart skipped a beat. Bad news, her gut told her. Why else would her mother go through all the trouble of getting a letter through the Steepes?

Dear Laoise,

I hope all is well. Doctor Hoffman says the price of the medicine has risen again. At this point we won't be able to afford it. Your brother is—

Water smeared the ink and left the paper wrinkled. Letters ran into each other, creating long, inky smears. She held the paper up in front of the window, but the extra light didn't help her to read the smudged ink writing.

Her brother was what? Worse? Better? Dying? All while she was stuck here and unable to help. She leaned against the table. The mechanical hummingbird froze as it toppled onto its side.

There was no hope of getting a carriage through the snow. And there were no horses in the stables. If she got herself to the train station there might be magicians clearing the tracks. Then again, the village might be too small to expect that level of care for the railroad. There had to be some way to get to the city. So far her only connection to the outside world had been this hummingbird.

The hummingbird. Maybe she couldn't get back to London, but the little metal birds had already made the journey. Maybe she could send word back home. Or money for the medicine. She picked up the frozen bird, trying to find any sort of writing or address. Any rune she recognized and could try to activate. But there was nothing. It was another dead end. Tears welled up in the corners of her eyes. Her chest tightened at the onslaught of emotions.

She closed her eyes and took a deep breath. "No use cryin' about it," was what her Ma would say in times like these. There was always too much work to be done and not enough time. But maybe Bertram knew how to use the birds.

Ugh. Bertram. She shoved away from the table and stomped her way to the kitchen, the new package under one arm. Her ego smarted at the plan to warm Bertram back up to her. But for her brother, she'd do anything.

A fresh pot of coffee would be a good start.

Martin had gone through a remarkable improvement since Bertram's last visit. Bertram didn't doubt why. He'd dumped out the last batch of medicine and replaced it himself. Martin's good health proved the suspicion he'd had for quite some time. The doctor was a fraud and his medicine was poison. He wouldn't let a single drop pass Martin's lips again if he could help it.

This time Martin wasn't in bed, but wandering about the greenhouse. The room not only gave Bertram's aunt a garden for the exotic plants she so loved, but it gave Martin a warm place to visit during the cold months. A gold hummingbird flew in circles above Martin's head. Martin turned, his face breaking into a grin. "Bertie! I knew you'd come for my birthday."

"I've never missed it and I'm not about to start." The bird drifted his way, making a few laps over his head. "Looks like you fixed the bird."

"Yes. I made a few tweaks to it. I have to keep it flying high because Oolong loves to chase it until he wears himself out."

Hearing his name, the dachshund lying beside the pond lifted its head. His tongue lolled out of his mouth. He let out a low woof before laying his head back down.

"Is that my birthday present?" Martin pointed to the package under Bertram's arm.

"It is. Do you want it now or at your birthday dinner?"

Martin clapped his hands together. "Now! Now!"

Bertram handed over the package. Martin wasted no time in tearing off the string and brown paper. He gasped in delight. "A new book!"

"It is the one you mentioned. The Classic of Tea by Lu Yu."

Martin let out another delighted gasp. "I can't believe you found it." Only Martin could face months of sickness spent in bed and come out cheerful. He didn't let the dark cloud of illness shadowing him dampen his mood.

"I can't believe that out of everything you could have asked for, you wanted an old Chinese book." Bertram smiled. He'd gone to every bookshop in London in his search for it. It would have been much easier to send out servants to do it, but Bertram insisted on doing it himself. "Why did you want it so badly?"

"Because it's all about tea and how to make it properly. I will learn to make Mum tea like she makes for me. I'll make you some too." He excitedly flipped through the pages.

Bertram grimaced. "I'm sorry to say the only copy I found was in Chinese."

"No matter. Then we'll simply have to learn Chinese together," Martin said, not looking up from the page. He traced a line of characters down the page with his finger. "What do you suppose that says?"

"I haven't a clue." It shouldn't have been surprising, but Bertram was taken aback by Martin's sudden decision to take on yet another language. "But what about your French lessons?"

"I can make time for both." Martin waved a hand at him as he continued studying the characters. "Look. This one keeps repeating. Does that mean 'tea?'"

"I doubt you'll learn anything that way, but I will try to keep up with you." He smiled, knowing very well that he couldn't. His world was wider than Martin's. All Martin had was the greenhouse and manor. Bertram had London. Friends. Sisters. School. They kept him too busy to bury his nose in books as often as Martin did. Bertram longed to take his cousin back to the city. To get rid of the little bubble he lived in.

His aunt stepped into the greenhouse. "Bertram, your room is ready for you. I had the maids air it out for you while you were gone." She aired the house out often, afraid of Martin's sickness spreading.

"Thank you."

"Dinner is in an hour you two. Don't be late. The cook is making a cake, and the doctor brought more medicine. Make sure you take it before dinner, Marty."

Bertram pressed his hands together. "Auntie, are you sure he needs the medicine? He is doing fine without it."

"Oh, Bertram. It's because he's been taking his medicine that he is feeling so much better. Why, it's been weeks since his last relapse." She plucked a stray leaf out of Martin's hair. She gave him another worried once over that included pressing her palm to his forehead. "Enjoy playing, but not too rough." Finally satisfied, she left.

Bertram bit his tongue. He'd nearly let slip that Martin hadn't had the doctor's "medicine" in weeks. He fidgeted while Martin flipped through the book. Martin always relapsed when he started taking the medicine again. He'd be fine the week before the doctor's visits. Then a day or two after he'd be back in bed. Why did no one else see it?

"Keep looking through the book. I'll be right back. I just want to...grab my jacket."

Martin nodded and made his way to the chair at the water's edge.

Bertram snuck off to the kitchens. He'd had his suspicions about Martin's doctor for some time now. He wondered why the supposedly renowned Italian doctor, a man named Giovanni Speranza, seemed unable to speak or understand a word of Italian. Granted Bertram's own understanding of the language was only barely conversational thanks to a classmate's help, but attempts to get the doctor to speak with him for his language studies were met with flowery Italian-sounding gibberish and an assurance, in a crude, almost French-sounding accent, that his language skills were "a-coming along a-nicely."

No one else seemed to notice. Aunt Gertie was too distraught with Martin's condition to pay attention to the minutia of the doctor's accent. Uncle Monty might have noticed if he were ever around. Martin, the smart boy that he is, had realized something was wrong almost immediately, but was assured by the doctor that he spoke a rural regional dialect. It seems that only Bertram could see the doctor was a fraud, and therefore only he could expose him. While the issue with his language skills was circumstantial evidence at best, medicine wasn't. Neither was poison.

At his last visit, Bertram had filled a small glass with the bottle of Martin's medicine from his bedside. Later that night he crept down to the kitchen and found a hole in the wall where rats had been making their way inside. He left a few crumbs of cheese soaked in the medicine out for them, and when he returned early in the morning before anyone else had awakened, he found the rats dead. His medicine was poison. Arsenic perhaps, the favored poison in crime books for having no taste or smell.

He'd dumped the medicine out behind the manor and refilled the dark bottle with water and a hint of lemon juice to match the smell of the doctor's concoction. Evidently, the plan was working as no one had noticed in the past few weeks. If the adults wouldn't listen, Bertram would continue getting rid of the problem by himself. Once Martin stayed healthy long enough, there would be no need for the doctor's visits anymore.

He crept into the kitchens, being careful not to be seen. The staff wasn't malicious, but they'd tell his aunt if they found him, particularly if he had Martin's medicine in hand. Satisfied that he was alone, Bertram swiped the bottle and once more made his way to the back of the manor. He emptied the bottle onto the same patch of grass as last time. He could tell because it was brown and withered even after all this time.

"What are you doing?" a voice asked from behind him.

He froze at the sound of his uncle's voice. The man appeared behind him, as he always did, as if from thin air. To the best of his knowledge, his uncle didn't use magic to achieve this feat. He simply had the un-canny ability to move silently when he walked. And he would always stand far too close, towering menacingly over him.

Bertram quickly slipped the empty bottle into his pocket. "Uncle Monty, what are you doing home?" He hadn't seen the man in months. Whenever he did come home, he sent for Bertram in order to give him his own lessons on how to run a business.

"It's Martin's birthday," his uncle said, his voice cold.

Bertram stood slowly. He was almost as tall as his uncle now, but still the man's frigid demeanor made it seem as though he towered over Bertram. Uncle Monty was quiet, never quick to praise, and his face rarely betrayed his emotions. A face perfect for business negotiations.

"What's in your pocket?" He tapped Bertram's jacket with his cane.

Sweat beaded on the back of Bertram's neck. His feet shuffled. "It's nothing, Uncle."

"A gentleman does not keep secrets from his family." He didn't bother asking a second time. He reached into Bertram's pocket and pulled out the empty bottle. "What did you do with the medicine?"

"That medicine—"

"Boy," snapped his uncle. "Why is this bottle empty?" He shook the bottle.

"The doctor is a fraud! He's poisoning Martin!"

"That doctor is the best that money can buy."

"Please let me explain," Bertram stammered. He seldom found himself at a loss for words, but looking up at his uncle was like looking at a castle battlement. He struggled to find a way to articulate everything that he had discovered to his uncle. "It's exactly like in a story I read. The medicine is actually arsenic and—"

"A story," his uncle interrupted, his expression darkening. "You read too many stories."

"It's the truth! I tested it myself, and if you keep giving it to him, Martin will die."

His uncle let out a growl. His face reddened as a vein throbbed in his forehead. The end of his cane slammed hard onto the patio, cracking the cane into several pieces. Without a word, his valet stepped out from behind him, chanted a few words, and pressed a finger against a rune on the cane. The shattered pieces floated in midair and came together, reforming as if nothing had happened. "You are going back to London."

"But Martin's party—"

"It would be un-gentlemanly to strike a child, so you are going back to London. Now. Stay there until you quit believing in your stories and start respecting your elders. Martin's health isn't for you to trifle with." He snapped his fingers and the valet stood at attention.

"But Uncle—"

"Enough. It is out of respect for your father that I will forgive you talking back to me," he snapped, turning to his valet. "Escort my nephew to the train station. Make sure he gets on."

"Yes, sir."

"Uncle, you can't do this! It's killing him. I can prove it!"

His uncle turned and went into the kitchen, refusing to give him so much as another glance.

"Come on," the valet said. "I don't want to miss dinner."

Chapter 10

Laoise watched as Bertram crept out of Martin's old room and made his way to the greenhouse. Yesterday, he'd locked himself away and refused to come out or touch the porridge she left for him.

She returned to the kitchen to put together lunch to take to him. A food offering other than porridge might butter him up. The lunch spread was small, but hearty. Toast, sausages, cheese, and a sliced apple. An odd combination perhaps, but it was the best she could do with what they had in the pantry.

Inside the greenhouse, he sat by the water with a book in his hand. His jacket hung over the back of his chair and he wore his shirt sleeves rolled up. A pile of weeds sat by the garden path next to a dirty trowel.

"Are you gardening?" she blurted out in disbelief. Bertram doing anything useful at all was too much of a shock to her system to remember why she'd come.

His head jerked up. He scowled at her before returning to his book. Great. His bad moods were never fun to deal with. She didn't want to grovel to make peace with him to get her pay. Based on the letters that had come in from home today, she'd have no other choice if it came to that. Damn her and damn her big mouth for acting out the other day.

"I brought you your lunch, sir," she said in her sweetest voice.

He harrumphed.

Her grip on the tray tightened. "And a cup of coffee."

His head jerked up again. This time he sniffed at the air like a bloodhound. He set down his book and motioned her forward.

She set the food tray down on the little table beside him. "A letter from your cousin, too." She pulled the letter out of her pocket and laid it on the edge of the tray. "He sent the coffee." She took a step back to give him space.

He reached for the coffee first. His eyes closed as he took a long whiff. Then he sipped at it, a noise of approval vibrating in his throat. "A bit of a weak brew." Those were the first words he'd said to her in days. Despite the supposed weakness of the brew, he took another sip, giving a heavy contented sigh. He sat for another minute, eyes shut.

After a long moment, his eyes opened and he noticed her standing there. He huffed. "You're still here," he said, returning his attention to his coffee. On the other end of the room, Pepper hovered near one of the more impressive looking orchids.

"I'm terribly sorry to bother your reading, sir," she said, curtseying for effect. It would be rude to come right out and ask for money. She looked around, struggling to find something to comment on. "Your work on the greenhouse is looking very nice, sir."

"Spare me your faux niceties." He set the cup down and poked at the food offerings. "You want something."

"Right." She bit her lip. "It's about my pay. You see, I'd like to request that...perhaps..."

"No."

"B-but sir," she stammered, "I'm not asking for anything extra. I just need to—"

"No." He interrupted, punctuating the answer by biting into a piece of toast.

She squeezed her hands together. "I'm sorry about the other day. I hope—"

He raised a hand to silence her as he finished chewing. "I'm not going to give you any money."

"Why not?"

"Because I don't have any."

Laoise stood dumbfounded. "But you're a Steepe. You have lots of money. Unless... They haven't disowned you, have they?"

"No, you foolish—" He rubbed his temple, his exasperation clear. "I mean, I don't have any here. Technically I don't have any money at all. It's all in the bank."

"The bank! Yes." Laoise smiled, and her voice cracked. Finally there was hope. "Then can we go to the bank? Or get word to the bank? Please, sir?"

"Have you looked outside lately?"

Beyond the glass walls, the snow continued to pile up. Anyone with sense wouldn't want to travel in the storm.

"Of course, sir." Her patience frayed. She fiddled with her sleeve, running her thumb over the recent mending job she'd done. Her breathing hitched as hope was once again snatched away from her. "Then if I can't get my pay, can I please request that you send a message back to London for me?"

He gave her an incredulous look and repeated himself, slower this time. "I'll ask again. Have you looked outside?"

"I... no I mean with the hummingbirds. Can you send one of them back to London with a message?" Her voice trembled. Her mother's words echoed in her mind and she tried her hardest not to lose her composure.

"No." He scoffed and took another long sip of his coffee.

Tears welled up in the corners of her eyes. She slammed her hands down on the table. "Why not? Because you can't be bothered?" Her lower lip trembled as she gritted her teeth.

"Because I don't know how." He put down his coffee. "There are a number of locating and flying spells Martin could be using. He's always been better at making the birds than me. Any I send would fall apart in the storm and never arrive." He stabbed his fork into a sausage. "Assuming the bird held together at all."

He had a point there. His magic failed enough times for her to know better than to trust it. Every option was exhausted. Every path a dead end. Her sight went blurry as a tear rolled down her cheek. "Please. My brother is sick. My family needs my pay to get his medicine. If I can't get it to them in time, he won't get any."

"What's wrong with him? Other than—" he waggled one hand at her—"being related to you."

"Consumption." That was all she could say without losing her composure. To say any more than that would have made her start sobbing uncontrollably.

He looked up at her and took a bite of sausage, chewing it as he thought. For a long moment he sat and stroked his chin, watching Laoise as she trembled on the verge of tears. He put the food down and headed for the door.

"Is that all?" She dried her tears with her apron. "You are just going to walk away?"

He stopped. "No. You are supposed to follow." He motioned with his hands. "You see, this is why I need my bells. How else am I supposed to summon you?"

She sniffed and rolled her eyes. "You could try speaking like a normal person."

He cleared his throat. "Maid, follow me."

"Yes, sir. Of course, sir." She dipped into a curtsy for good measure.

"For God's sake..." He turned away in disgust. "No need to be dramatic."

"Can you at least tell me where we are going?"

"I have something to show you." Outside, he led her around to the far side of the greenhouse. The deep snow made trudging through it exhausting work.

"Are you showing me the snow?" She asked, sniffling as she fought to get her emotions under control. The anguish in her voice was slowly being replaced with raw frustration. "I promise you I already noticed it."

He ignored her jab. "The Barclay stables." He pointed at the neighbor's land. "My uncle boards our horses with the Barclays when we aren't using this manor. If you can go over there and free my horse, there might be a way I can get us to London."

"Us?"

"Yes. Us. Once everything is ready, I'm going to London with you. That is non-negotiable if you want my help."

"Not a chance. I may be desperate for the money, but I'm not stupid." Laoise turned her back to him and started to walk away.

"What?" He reached out to grab her shoulder. "But you said your brother—"

"Another word about him and I'll throttle you myself. Don't you dare use his life to help you bargain." She grabbed his wrist and pulled it off of her shoulder, turning to stare him down. "I know you're not going to pay me. You're going to sneak off the moment we get back to London and you'll put whatever wicked scheme you have into action. Well I won't let you. We can both rot in this damned manor."

"I can't get your money from the bank without going to the bank." Bertram pulled back his hand and straightened his jacket, his tone a calm contrast to Laoise's anger. "Yes, it's true that I am eager to get out of here. I am using you to help me escape. But for the moment, we need one another to achieve our respective goals. So let's set aside our squabbles and work together, shall we?"

She considered the offer. She knew him too well to expect any kindness without a catch. To be stuck with him would be a high enough price to pay. Not to mention she'd be helping to subject Charlotte and Martin to whatever terrible plans he may have in store. Then again, this was for her brother... "How do I know you'll hold up your end of this bargain?"

"As a gentleman, my word is my bond. On my word, you will have all the pay you're due." He gave her a sideways glance. "And not a penny more."

"Your word as a gentleman? That's not worth much. How about this. If you so much as try to cheat me, I'll gut you like a fish." She poked him in the gut to punctuate her statement.

"I believe you would too." A strangled noise came from his throat. "So do we have a deal?"

"All right. Suppose I did decide to help you. How would we get there in this weather?"

"First you get my horse. Then I'll tell you the next step. We aren't getting anywhere without my horse. That is non-negotiable as well."

"I hadn't figured there'd be so much negotiating," she said snidely. If fetching a horse gave her a chance to go home, she'd put up with his antics a little longer. "Which horse is yours?"

He turned his attention toward the Barclay stable. "Her name is Bess. She's black with a white mark on her forehead. You are going to have to sneak past the workers to get into the stable. Once inside, wait until nightfall. You'll need to sneak Bess out and back here. Oh, and be sure to take an apple. That should get her comfortable with you. As for the snow..." He rubbed the stubble on his chin as he considered his plan. "We can't be certain the snow will hide your tracks, so be sure to cover them when you leave. A tree branch will do the trick. That way they won't know who stole the horse."

"Right... Anything else?" She hugged herself, the cold already seeping beneath her coat. She'd need to wear the gift from Charlotte to stay warm in this weather. Like hell she was going to spend any more time than she needed to outside in the cold covering up her footprints or stealing a horse.

"Make sure no one sees you. If they do, tell them you're a new maid working for Master Rupert James Barclay and you got lost. Remember that name precisely. Master Rupert James Barclay. He's very particular about his name. If you get it wrong they'll know you're lying."

"Why can't you go get your horse? I doubt old Mr. Berkley would turn away a Steepe from his own horse."

"Master Rupert James Barclay. Get it right or this whole plan is ruined. And he's not old." He rolled up his left sleeve and pointed to the tight bracelet on his wrist. "As for me, I can't leave the grounds so long as this thing is shackled to my wrist. Furthermore, my uncle is keeping my reasons for being here quiet, so I don't know what he told the neighbors. It'll be easier for you to sneak in and just take Bess."

"I'll go get an apple then." She pumped her arm in faux excitement. "There's nothin' I like more than robbing the neighbors."

"That's the spirit." He suddenly turned and pointed. "A hobby horse! Of course!"

Laoise looked at him, utterly baffled.

"Yes yes. I'll find you one of Martin's old hobby horses. You can place it in Bess's stable when you take her. A crude replacement to be sure, but it should buy us a little more time before they realize she's gone."

Laoise shifted in her shoes. "I'll... see if I can procure a hobby horse on site. I'm sure the young master will have one. It'll give me something to do while I'm waiting for an opening."

He nodded, satisfied. "Very well. Just don't get caught. Meet me inside once you get her in my stables. I'm going to go get rid of this tracker." He headed back into the greenhouse. She took a brief detour to the pantry to get an apple since that was the only part of his plan that made any sense.. Then off to fetch Bess.

The short walk to the neighbors would have been nothing in the spring or summer, but the snow made it exhausting. The distance felt twice as long. Despite the exercise warming her up, her nose insisted on running from the cold, especially once it went numb. At least in the city the Steepes kept their homes warm to make the dreadful weather more bearable.

She went straight up the front drive. Hiding in this weather would be impossible. With how much the green of her cloak stuck out against the backdrop of white, she could forget about avoiding being seen. Let alone hiding a big black horse.

The rich always felt a bit out of touch with reality to her, but only Bertram could make a job as simple as fetching a horse and turn it into such a convoluted scheme. It was hardly any wonder his plots against Martin and Charlotte had so often blown up in his own face. Literally at times. He was a villain to be sure, but he wasn't a good one. Barely even a competent one. That at least was good news for his cousin.

She made her way around the back of the Barclay manor and walked towards the stables, waving down the first stable hand she spotted.

"Can I help you, miss?" he asked as she wheezed her way up to him. A stitch in her side throbbed as she struggled through the deep snow.

She took a moment to catch her breath. "I'm a maid for the Steepe family. We got snowed in and we need a horse to get supplies from town. Could you prepare Mr. Steepe's horse for me? I think her name was Bess?"

"Ah good ol' Black Bess!" said the man, waving her towards the stables. "She's a fine filly. Odd thing to name a horse though."

"It's from a book I think." The name rang a bell in her head, but she couldn't recall where she'd heard it before. "Just another way Mr. Steepe likes to show off how learned he is, the bastard."

"Bit of a surprise the dandy didn't come to fetch the horse himself. Seems like the type who wouldn't want anyone touching his things."

"You know how these people are. He can no more be bothered to do anything on his own than Master Rupert James Barclay, his grand royal exquisite excellence, beg pardon." She gave a mocking flourish as she enunciated the young master's name and titles.

"Jesus woman. Don't tell the boy he has any more titles. He'll demand we say them all whenever we so much as look at him." The man laughed. "Wait right here. I'll bring Bess to you." He stepped into the stables and returned a few minutes later with a black horse in tow.

"Thank you," she said as she took the reins from him.

He tipped his hat to her. "Be careful out there. And good luck dealin' with the dandy."

"Same to you!" With her previous path already forged through the snow, the return trip was easier. Bess gave her no trouble as she got the horse settled into one of the empty stalls. Then again, Bess must have patience to put up with the likes of her master.

"Black Bess, huh?" She said as she rubbed Bess's side. "I wonder what book that's from."

Bess neighed and returned to her hay. Laoise headed back to the greenhouse. The chairs were empty. The only movement came from Pepper buzzing about the flowers. Some of the plants looked tidier with the weeds they'd been choking on gone. She took her sweet time, soaking in the warmth before heading to the house. No wonder he'd been spending his time here. Compared to the snow outside, the greenhouse felt like paradise.

Back inside the manor, she didn't need a bell to call him. All she had to do was follow the muffled cursing to his room. He stood near the balcony, holding the bracelet up to the sunlight as he fiddled with it.

Laoise's hand wandered to her pocket where the apple still rested. She pulled it out and took a bite. The crunch and sweet juices came as a satisfying change after living off sandwiches and oatmeal for several days. Bertram mumbled under his breath, and then the runes on the bracelet glowed. Bertram yelped and pawed at the bracelet.

"What'd you do?" she asked, mouth full of apple.

"Accidentally tightened it." He grit his teeth and mumbled another string of Latin. The bracelet glowed again, but this time he relaxed. He rubbed at his wrist. "Did you get my horse?"

"Yeah. She's in the stable."

"Did you give her an apple?"

"Yes, of course, sir." She'd give the horse one later. Not for Bertram, but out of pity the horse had to put up with him too. The poor thing deserved a whole bag of apples.

"And the hobby horse?"

"It's in place," she said, doing her best to keep a straight face. She took another bite of the apple, chewing loudly as she spoke. "No one will suspect a thing."

"Please don't talk with your mouth full. It's bad manners."

She waved the apple in the air. "I want to know the next step. I got your horse, so spit it out."

He shook his arm. "The next step is getting this off. Then I'll pull the sled out. It'll get us to the village." He sighed. "Unfortunately, all my attempts with the bracelet so far have failed."

"What happens if you try to walk away from the manor?"

"This stops me at the property boundary." He shook his wrist. "It's like an invisible wall appears and I can't get past it. Believe me, the spell is very thorough. I've walked the whole boundary more than once. There are no gaps. The spell is too good to be anything but Martin's work. He's always had a knack for magic." His expression softened. "I don't think I can beat him."

"Have you tried using something other than magic to get that off?"

"Like what?"

"Come to the kitchen and let me show you. Maids have our own tricks."

His eyes went wide. "Are you planning on chopping off my hand?"

She gave him a wicked grin. "Only if I need to."

Chapter 11

He watched her with the same suspicion she'd given him earlier as she stepped out of the pantry. His gaze fell to the container of lard in her hands. "You aren't going to put that on me, are you?"

"Sure am." She scooped up a spoonful, and gave him a wide smile.

Bertram's face screwed up as she brought the spoon closer. He almost looked at home in the kitchen. The scruff on his face proved he'd forgotten to shave after their fight. He'd even mis-buttoned the top of his shirt. The steaming cup of coffee sitting in front of him gave the impression of early morning disarray about him, despite the afternoon hour.

"This will help the bracelet slip right off. I watched the cook at my last position use it to get a ring off Mrs. Hammond once."

"But it smells." He pulled his arm away. His nose twitched, and he scrunched up his face.

She rested her free hand on her hip and shook the spoon at him. "You know, your idea of loppin' your hand off is soundin' better by the moment."

His eyes narrowed. "You wouldn't."

"I would. Gladly in fact. Now, bracelet on or off?"

He sighed. "Fine." He rested his hand back on the table. "Make it fast."

She got to work. Bertram gagged as soon as the first spoonful plopped onto his arm. He squirmed. Glee rushed through her.

"Don't gag. You eat this stuff all the time."

"Well, yes, but good God not by the spoonful—" he gagged again.

Her grin grew. She smeared the lard over his wrist and hand and under the bracelet. The silver bracelet looked loose enough to slip off with a little help.

She paused. "On second thought, it may not have been lard that the cook used to get the ring off. It might have been cooking oil." Laoise had only seen the issue because of all the commotion the sobbing Mrs. Hammond caused. The boisterous woman had been under the impression she'd be stuck with "the gaudy ring" on for the rest of her life. Ironically, the ring was perhaps the least gaudy thing she had been wearing at the time.

A sound of indignation escaped him. "You're enjoying this too much. I'll see your pay docked for this."

"Oh, don't you worry, sir. I'll have this off before you know it." She waved the spoon at him again. A small glob of lard flew off and landed on his cheek.

He gagged and brushed his cheek, smearing the oily lard all over his face.

"Sorry about that." She wiped it off while his free hand gripped the edge of the table, his face turning red.

Once she put twice as much lard on him as she thought they needed, she put the spoon down. "That should do the trick. I'm going to tug the bracelet off now."

"Hurry up."

She grabbed the bracelet and tugged it down. It got stuck on the widest part of his hand. She tugged again. Then again. Finally, the bracelet came free, sliding right off. She dropped it onto the table. "There. Told you I'd get it off. No need to do fancy magic when a wee bit of grease will do."

"Magic would have been preferable," he said dryly without so much as a drop of appreciation. "Now, how am I supposed to get all this off?" He held up his arm and stuck his tongue out in disgust.

"That is going to need some hot water and lots of soap." The bracelet vibrated, clacking against the table. She frowned. "Is it supposed to do that?"

"I don't know. I didn't make the thing." He eyed the bracelet with caution, poking a finger at it. "I can't begin to guess at the runes used on it. They're in a language I don't recognize."

The bracelet flew off the table, heading right for Bertram. He jumped out of his chair and swatted at the bracelet, but it continued its course despite his interference. The bracelet clicked itself back into place on his wrist. He let out a curse, his free hand slapping the tabletop.

"That's one clever spell." Laoise crossed her arms. For as naïve and forgetful Martin was with names and social graces, he didn't miss a thing when it came to magic. "I don't suppose you have any ideas on how to keep it off?"

Bertram rubbed his temple, eyes closing. "I have one last idea. I was trying to avoid it, but I suppose I have no other choice." He wrinkled his nose. "First, I need to get this...gunk off of me."

"I'll get you some hot water and soap. Shall I put on the kettle while I'm at it? I want tea."

"Coffee."

"Suit yourself. More for me." The day's events had her nerves frazzled. She couldn't handle anything as strong as a cup of coffee. Particularly not the light roast she'd prepared for Bertram this morning. She swore it made her eye twitch when she took a sip earlier.

On the other hand, the scent of vanilla and orange arising from her cup of tea soothed Laoise's spirits. She'd managed to set aside just enough boiling water for herself and gave the rest to Bertram for cleaning his arm. She sat and sipped on her tea as he scrubbed himself. This time he didn't gag, only growled and cursed.

"I'll never get rid of this stench, will I?" Even once he'd scrubbed his skin pink, the pungent stench of the lard lingered. While it had been repulsive to pile great clumps of the stuff onto Bertram's arm, it had made her a little hungry if she was being honest with herself. She missed eating someone else's cooking.

"Wash up a few more times today and use cologne or something nice smelling."

He shuddered. "I'll have no skin left if I keep washing like this. I can't believe I let you put that filth on me." He tossed the rag into the bowl of hot water.

"It almost worked. If not for that fancy spell, you'd be a free man right now."

"But I'm not free." He took a long swig of his coffee, taking a moment to savor it. Then he blew out a long sigh. "All right. Let's get this over with. If we get out of here soon enough, there's still time to catch the last train."

"What's your plan?" She finished her tea and then rushed to catch up to his long strides.

"I need to remove the magic altogether." He headed back upstairs, stopping outside the door to Martin's old room.

He stared at the door but made no move to go in. His blank expression was unreadable. Laoise crossed her arms in impatience. He was right about the train, which meant they shouldn't dawdle.

"Well, go in already. You won't get free by staring at the door."

"I know what I'm doing."

"Doesn't seem like it."

He scoffed and pulled the key from his pocket. "Not that I expect you to understand, but this room is full of bad memories. No one who can't appreciate that deserves to see it. Least of all a nosy maid."

"I understand plenty. You're just upset that your misdeeds got you exiled. You don't want any reminders of how your cousin bested you."

That got him moving. He stepped inside and tried to close the door on her. She shoved her foot in the way, stopping him. "Touched a nerve I see. So it is because of Martin."

"Would you please stop talking," he said waving a dismissive hand at her and stalked into the room. "You're an awful maid, but you'd make a much worse detective."

"Well then enlighten this humble maid, yer grace," she crowed with faux sincerity, shoving the door open to join him.

He began searching the desk, methodically working his way from one end to the other. She looked away, not wanting to remember how his hands had been as thorough on her.

"Why should I bother? No one ever listens when I try to explain anything. If my uncle had listened, Martin never would have been engaged to his first fiancée. It was obvious she didn't like him and that her family just wanted our money.

"If Martin had listened, he wouldn't have rushed into his second engagement with a woman he'd only just met that day. And don't get me started on that awful..." he trailed off. His hands stopped searching and his eyes stared off at nothing In particular. After a brief moment, he shook his head, cleared his throat and resumed his search of the desk, "...that awful Dr. Speranza."

"His engagement worked out, don't forget. Charlotte and Martin are quite happy. Deliriously so based on what I've heard from Charlotte." Martin liked to make her tea and take it to her himself while she wrote. Laoise knew because he'd asked for her help in arranging the tray in a way he thought Charlotte would like, complete with snacks. It made Charlotte get all teary-eyed whenever Martin brought her a tray.

He paused and narrowed his eyes at her. "Would you want your brother proposing to a woman before he so much as asked her name?"

She pondered a moment. "Fair enough I suppose." When her eldest brother, Callum had first started courting a young woman he'd met in a park, Laoise had her suspicions about her. It wasn't until the two married that Laoise started to trust that they might be a decent match. It would have been very jarring to have only one day to come to terms with her brother's engagement. Still, the two had been happily married for quite some time now. It was hard to imagine one without the other, and it was just as difficult to imagine Martin without Charlotte. She turned back to Bertram, a bit more sincerity in her voice. "If you'd care to tell me, sir, I promise I'll listen to every word."

"If it shuts you up." He let out a sigh and resumed searching. "When Martin was a child, he spent several years in poor health. At his worst, he had consumption and there were several months where everyone feared he..." He cleared his throat. "That he wouldn't survive."

Laoise put a hand to her mouth. She recalled in her time back in London how Martin's mother had always been so protective of her son. She'd fret over airing out the house and making sure that every foul smell was immediately perfumed. She'd never seen the woman so distraught as when Martin caught a cold that kept him from his magical tinkering for a day.

Bertram waved his hand, indicating the room and continued. "He stayed here when he was sick. I'd come visit every month for a few days at a time. The first doctor saved his life, but then he retired. A few months later, Aunt Gertie employed a new doctor. The best money could buy. His name was Doctor Speranza, and he was a despicable fraud."

Laoise didn't know Sean's doctor well. Her work with the Steepes kept her away from home too often to get more involved in supporting him. This nightmare of a job included. The idea of a doctor lying to her family or hurting her brother brought her blood to a boil. She pulled herself back to Bertram's story to distract herself from her worries over Sean. "You visited even though you didn't like him?"

"I never said I didn't like him. Clearly you haven't listened to me either." He yanked a drawer out too hard, sending a stack of envelopes and paper spilling across the floor. He heaved a heavy sigh before bending down to pick up the mess.

She peeked down at the desk. A piece of paper sat in the corner, with a single address for Bertram Steepe written on it. Below were several doodles of a dachshund. Martin had always been a saint the way he dealt with Bertram on his grumpy days. If Bertram had once been his only visitor, no wonder Martin had learned to put up with him.

She already knew what Martin looked like as a child thanks to the family portraits that decorated the London home, but when it came to Bertram, she imagined him as a scowling child who wanted to discuss taxes and profits instead of marbles. Not the best playmate for a sick child.

"There were visits when the next month felt too far away. I thought I wouldn't see him again. The rest of the extended family wrote him off and decided I would be my uncle's heir. They never gave Martin a chance to survive, and they never bothered to visit him. Now they wonder why he grew up so..." Bertram paused, struggling to find the right word. "...odd. The boy only had his mother, dog, books, and tutor for company most days. I mean, really, what did they expect to happen? He can read runes and perform magic in multiple languages, but he can't remember names."

"True, but once you get to understand him, he makes a lot more sense." Martin didn't grasp social niceties as well as someone like Bertram, but she thought he had his priorities in order. His family always came first over business. And he took delight in every cup of tea. Those were the things important to him. Silly etiquette matters weren't worth stressing over in Martin's world. She envied him for that. "What are you lookin' for? I can help."

"Don't you touch anything." He pointed at her, his face stern. "Don't even think about it."

She held her hands up. "I won't. I'll stay right here." She wasn't going to risk angering him and losing the rest of the story. She'd spent too many days wondering about the room.

He closed the desk drawer. "Because of Martin's illness, we all hate this room. It's full of terrible memories. Once he recovered, Martin moved to a room with a better view. The greenhouse roof blocks too much of the scenery in here. Honestly, I don't understand why my aunt doesn't clean this one out and let it be a guest room." He moved to the nightstand next.

"So that's why you don't like Martin. You expected to inherit the family business. Is that it?"

He slapped the palm of his hand against the desk. "For the last time, I never said I don't like Martin. Imply anything of the sort again and I cannot be held responsible for my actions. I don't know how you got that in your head. "

"Silly me, sir. You're right." She clapped her hands to her cheeks in faux surprise." It couldn't have been you trying to frame him for all those thefts at The Great Exhibition that gave me that idea. Or you blowing up his ship. Or setting fire to your shared warehouse. It is truly a mystery as to how I got the impression you don't like your cousin."

"You have no proof I did any of that," he said curtly, a tinge of embarrassment in his voice. The nightstand rattled as he yanked open the stuck drawer. "And it seems you conveniently left out how I'm the only one trying to keep him from that Graham girl's clutches."

"There is no Graham girl, sir. Her last name is Steepe now."

He harrumphed. "That girl. A Steepe. A little more than kin but less than kind..."

"Beg your pardon, sir?" asked Laoise, raising an eyebrow.

"From *Hamlet*," he said, frustration seeping out of his words, "I should have known better than to expect you to understand."

"Well, I understand that Charlotte loves Martin. No matter what ol' Shakespeare says."

"I bet she's full of love. Love for all the wealth and status that comes with being a Steepe. Ladies looking for a husband love the idea of our family's fortune. That's all any of them ever want." He pinched the bridge of his nose and huffed. "All I wanted was to encourage Martin to use his talents. He has a great mind for business. A mind that could be working for the family. Instead, he's lost playing with his teapots and fawning over that...harpy."

"Just how much more money does the man need to make before you'll be happy? Your cousin is right about you. You spend too much time worrying about work." She'd rather be more like Martin, but having enough money to treat her family to luxury was a mere dream for her. "No wonder you're so grumpy all the time. You need to sit down with a cup of tea and relax for a change."

Bertram gave her an exasperated roll of the eyes. "Good lord now you're sounding like Martin. Some of us don't have the luxury of being able to simply sit down and relax with a cup of tea." He emptied the bedside drawer, finding nothing but a single book. "So it's still here after all this time."

Laoise peeked over his shoulder. "Is that Chinese?" She snatched up the book and squinted at the first page. "Could he even read this as a child?"

"A little. Martin insisted on learning to read Lu Yu's *The Classic of Tea* any way he could. I struggled with Chinese too much to keep up."

"Lu Yu? You mean like the teapot? Louie?" Louie the teapot had been enchanted to speak, as it so often liked to proclaim, by the ancient Chinese tea master Lu Yu. Martin was the only one who enjoyed its long droning stories which delved into the minutia of every possible detail. A poor conversation partner for most, but the teapot had also been the key witness in Bertram's arrest at the Great Exhibition.

"Don't speak to me about that damned pot." He ripped the book out of her hands.

"I didn't think you'd bother with learning how to read some old book about tea."

"I bought him the book." He returned the book to its drawer. "Years later when he found that damned talking teapot, he was so excited you would have thought he was having tea with the queen." He turned to the shelves.

"If Martin likes tea so much, why don't you?" She slid a finger over the bed covers. A thick layer of dust stuck to her skin. No wonder the enchanted cleaning tools were so desperate to get inside.

"Martin likes his tea. I like my coffee. He likes to sit back and relax. I like to rise early and get things done rather than dawdling." Laoise snorted at the notion of Bertram waking up early based on how many bowls of porridge he'd left untouched until noon. His voice softened as he continued. "My father always drank coffee in the mornings. The smell reminds me of him."

Laoise leaned over the desk, inspecting the dachshund drawings. "I don't think I've met your father. Is he as grumpy as you are?"

Bertram stopped and leaned against the desk. "He died when I was a child. A long time ago," he said in a voice soft enough she strained to hear him. "An accident at the warehouse after a shipment came in."

"I'm sorry. I didn't know." She reached a hand out as if on instinct, wanting to rest it on his shoulder. For a moment she wanted to wrap her arms around him, but she quickly snapped out of it. She pulled back short of grazing his jacket and leaned against the desk chair.

Bertram turned, snapping his fingers when he saw. "Hands off. I'm not letting your sticky fingers steal anything."

"Sticky fingers?" She balked at that. "Excuse me, but I'm not a thief. What gives you the right of accusin' me?"

"The bell clappers for one thing. And the coffee for another."

"Oh for God's sake..."

"That's to say nothing of how you stole the key to this room. My horse as well"

"You told me to steal your horse!" She threw up her hands. "And as for your key, I found it and planned to return it. Eventually."

"I doubt that."

"I was only looking for the truth, not to steal anything."

"The key counts." His hand swept over the top shelf, pausing. He smiled. "Ah ha!" He held up a small tool that looked a bit like a misshapen pen to her, but too thick with a flat, wide point. He sat down on the bed.

"What is that thing?"

"Just a little tool Martin and I made when we were children. We used it to break magical locks and sneak around the manor. It should still have enough power to break the bracelet." He held up his arm to inspect the bracelet. "Get the curtain."

"I can't."

"What do you mean you can't?" He looked up, settling his displeased gaze back on her.

"I promised not to touch anything. I'd hate to make you think I'm trying to make off with the curtains."

His nostrils flared in frustration as he sucked in a breath. "You have my permission to touch the curtains."

"As you say, sir." She opened them. "Maybe if you spent less time thinking about money, you wouldn't always think the worst about others."

"Everything is about money. It's the only reason you're helping me now. And it always brings out the worst in people." He shifted to get the bracelet in a sunbeam. "Your thieving, for instance."

"I'm not a thief," Laoise huffed. The dust of the curtain tickled her nose, and she sneezed.

"There's plenty of evidence to the contrary." He jabbed the tool at the other side of the room. "Can't you do that over there?"

"When I first came here," Laoise started, wondering if saying anything would be futile. "I worried my brother would worsen while I was gone. That I was wasting time I should spend with him instead. But without my pay, my family can't afford his medicine or doctor visits. For all I know, I could be too late by the time I make it back to London." Her throat tightened. Her mouth went dry. "You aren't the only person in the world who's ever worried about losing someone."

Bertram stared at her, eyebrows raised in surprise. His gaze roved her face. She met his eyes and squared her shoulders, refusing to feel small under his attention. "It would have been easy to be a thief. Could've robbed you blind back in London. But I didn't. I wanted to do it right. I wanted to earn money the honest way. That's why I came out here to deal with you. That's why I'm still here dealing with you."

He looked away, hiding the shame creeping over his face. "'The miserable have no other medicine. But only hope.'"

"Just what the hell does that mean? And don't you give me snark because I don't know my Shakespeare as well as you," snapped Laoise. "I've been cleaning while you've been studying up on all those old plays."

"You know, you're not the first servant to come to me with a sad story about her family and her finances. Usually it's a sick mother or a nefarious landlord or—"

"I see," she interrupted, her blood boiling. "It's not enough to call me a thief. You think I'm a liar now too?"

"On the contrary. You are one of the few I actually believe. I've seen you lie, so I know you're being sincere now." He fiddled with the strange tool. "It's how I know I can trust you."

He had said it so casually, not even looking up from his bracelet. It was as though he was remarking on the weather. Such a simple thing, yet the sincerity in his voice melted her anger away. He turned back to the bracelet. Little sparks of magic popped midair as he used the odd tool. A minute later, the sparks died away. Bertram held his arm up in triumph. "I'm free!"

"What did you do? Is the magic in that thing gone?"

"Not quite. Only Martin could possibly understand the runes keeping this bracelet from leaving the grounds, but I recognize the locking runes. With those gone, it won't come flying back to my wrist anymore. I can leave!"

She struggled to contain her smirk, lips twitching. "Are you keeping the bracelet as a souvenir?"

"Of course not." He clawed at the bracelet, but the clasp refused to give.

She let him struggle for a few seconds before interrupting. "What's wrong with it?"

"It won't come off." He yanked on the bracelet. "The clasp is stuck."

"I guess you'll have to keep it on then."

He rose from the bed to put the tool back on the shelves. Then he paused in front of the window, staring out at the snow. "Laoise."

"Yes, sir?"

"Get the lard."

She smiled. "Right away, sir."

Chapter 12

The waltz began, giving them a break from the Christmas music the band had been playing all evening for the Steepe's annual charity ball. The waltz gave Bertram a chance to dance with Eloise, Martin's fiancée. He hadn't missed the looks and smiles she'd been casting his way.

She smiled up at him. It was a genuine smile, and not the usual painted on smile she wore when talking with Martin or his mother. That practiced look was common among all the young ladies of noble title. It was no secret that her family's land holdings had shrunk in recent years and that their business ventures were in dire straits, yet she smiled up at Bertram as if the comfortable lifestyle she had grown accustomed to wasn't in jeopardy. And why wouldn't she? As far as she was concerned, her worries were over. Her marriage would fix her family's problems.

Young ladies dancing next to them stole glances at Bertram. The news of Martin's engagement seemed to encourage the single women, reminding them that Bertram was still available. All the fortune hunters cornered him every chance they got. Like Eloise's family, hard times saddled many of the old nobility with debts they hoped to pay off with the right marriage. Uncle Monty hadn't known about her family's financial woes when he'd arranged the marriage. Nor did he seem to care. Her noble title was enough to win his blessing. To him it was just another business transaction.

"Your aunt and uncle invited me to the country retreat for Christmas," Eloise said, breaking the ice. Of course they'd invited her. With her innocent eyes, blonde curls, and polite manners, she'd easily

charmed them. Bertram knew better. He caught the looks of disgust and frustration she gave Martin. The sharp remarks when she thought no one else was listening. The way she talked over him whenever he spoke at their dinners. Her visits always put Martin in a gloomy mood, and he seemed to take her unhappiness as a failing on his end.

Put plainly, she needed to go. Bertram wouldn't let a cruel woman trap Martin in a loveless marriage. His cousin deserved far better. But Martin was too gentle and innocent to escape the engagement on his own. He was too meek to turn Eloise away, and too afraid of disappointing his father to refuse the bride being provided to him. Once again, it fell to Bertram to protect his cousin. Just as he had with Dr. Speranza all those years ago, though hopefully not in quite such a violent manner this time...

He smiled at her. "How wonderful. Christmas is always beautiful in the countryside. I'm sure you'll enjoy the visit." He gave her a wink. As he'd expected, she blushed.

"I should hope that we might get to go sleigh riding together."

"Would you like that? Just you and I alone on a sleigh with hot cocoa?"

She nodded. "Yes! Very much. I..." She bit her bottom lip. "I think you'd be better company than your cousin." She lowered her voice to a whisper. "And I'd rather spend Christmas with you."

"You little devil," he said, pulling back to flash her a smile.

"A pity you're not the young Master Steepe I'm to wed."

"If I'm honest," he said, as he leaned closer. "I'd rather you not marry Martin either."

She giggled. "Well there's no reason we can't find a way to both be happy, is there?"

She tilted her head up, giving him easy access to her lips. Perfect. He'd had a feeling things would wind up this way. She'd made her attempts to cross paths with him as often as possible all too obvious. She spent too much time batting those pretty lashes at him while turning a scowl Martin's way. The last few months had been building to this moment.

He pulled her closer. And then he leaned toward her, pausing halfway as his conscience threatened to ruin his plan. Whether the engagement continued or ended, Martin would wind up hurt. Bertram would have to explain things later in private to him.

Eloise proved more eager than he expected and rushed to close the gap, pressing her red lips against his. Someone gasped behind them. Perfect. They'd been seen. Gossip would do the rest of the work for him.

He pushed Eloise away. "No," he said, loud enough for those nearby to hear him. "You're my cousin's betrothed. I can't be with you. I would never betray my cousin that way. Never speak to me again." He turned and stormed off the dance floor. He didn't smile. Not until he was alone in his aunt's garden.

Next time, he would help find Martin a better fiancée. Someone who could accept his quirks and eccentricities. It would not be an easy task, but Martin's happiness was too important.

Once Martin's future was settled, he would consider his own marriage prospects. As a handsome young socialite and a Steepe, Bertram knew he could have any woman he wanted. And when the time come, that is precisely who he would marry. A woman he wanted. Not a woman whose family was hungry for money or power. Not someone picked by his uncle because of her noble title. He'd find an honest woman. One he could trust and one who respected him for more than his family's name.

Until then, he'd keep his title as the most eligible bachelor in London. That should be enough to attract young ladies for his cousin and young bachelors for his sisters.

And if another Eloise showed up, he'd crush her too.

"We're going in that?" The sleigh looked old and full of splinters. No roof or doors meant it wouldn't keep the wind off of them like a carriage would. The afternoon sky threatened more snow any minute, and the weak sunlight filtering through the wispy clouds offered little warmth. It would be a long, freezing ride.

"Come now. This is the best way to get around in this weather. My horse can handle the snow, but wheels can't." Even bundled up and freshly washed, the scent of lard lingered on him. "It's our only way to make the journey."

"There's just one problem with this plan. Neither of us has any money with us. How are we going to get train tickets?"

"We'll stop at the bank first. Plenty of time before the last train." He held out an apple for his horse. "You'll get us there, won't you, girl?" He cooed to the horse while she ate, showing more affection for Bess than she'd ever seen him give another person. Barring of course, the husky-voiced compliments he'd given her the other day while squeezing certain parts of her and kissing his way down her neck. She refused to think about those, despite the memory warming her middle against her better judgment.

"I'll go get blankets for the ride. If I'm riding in that, I'm going to need a lot of them."

"Check on Pepper and make sure the greenhouse is locked," he called after her.

She stopped at the greenhouse first. Pepper darted around a feeder and headed for a large flower. "Well, there you are. I guess that counts as checking on you." She didn't know what he expected her to do about the bird. The birdie had flowers and feeders, and the magical barrier kept the room tropically warm. What more could a bird want? She locked the door, wishing she'd been sent to serve in the summer instead. The brief respite of the greenhouse made the cold feel worse. Especially the wind.

Her bag already waited for her by the front door. All she needed were the blankets, and they'd be on their way. And hot tea to keep her warm. She'd never been on a sleigh ride before, but she'd overheard Bertram's sisters excited giggling whenever the subject came up. It was one of their favorite winter activities when they visited this manor. It was a shame that her first ride would be such a stressful one, but she supposed there were worse traveling companions than Bertram. Not much worse, but still.

By the time she loaded everything into the sleigh, Bess was ready to go. Laoise climbed in, arranging a blanket around her shoulders and a second across her lap. She cupped the hot tea in her hands. At least there were clear skies ahead of them.

They turned onto the road and he settled in. "Did you get me a drink?"

"Of course." She handed him the cup of tea.

He took a sip and wrinkled his nose. "What is this? Where's my coffee?"

"It's tea. It was easier to make and it'll keep you warm just as well."

He harrumphed but argued no more on the matter. She kept a nervous eye on the sky. Sunset wasn't far away. They'd be cutting it close to reaching the train station in time.

Bertram broke their silence. "You did check on Pepper, right?"

"Yes, sir."

"Was she all right?"

"Yes?" She sipped at her tea.

"What was she doing when you checked on her?"

"She was flying. What else would she be doing? She's a bird."

"How was she flying? Was she calm or panicked?"

"The bird was...she was just flying!" She flapped an arm in imitation. "Like birds do. She is a happy birdie, all right? She is fine."

"Then describe the way she was flying."

"What do you mean?" Her tea was disappearing too fast. The biting wind found every inch of exposed skin and battered at her clothes.

"Was she flying in circles or zigzagging?"

"Uh, circles?" Laoise hadn't paid any attention to the bird's flying pattern. She hoped she'd picked the right option.

He shook his head. She'd guessed wrong. "She might be stressed. I should go back and check on her myself."

She lunged to grab the back of his coat. "You are not! The bird will be fine without you for a few days. We don't have time."

"She's all alone in there! What if she dies while I'm gone?"

"She won't, and I'm not missing the train."

He glanced between the sleigh and the greenhouse. "I'll only be a moment." He pulled out of her grip and turned the sleigh around. As soon as they returned to their starting point he jumped out and ran.

"If we miss the train, it's your fault!" She yelled after him. She turned her attention to the reins and considered leaving without him. But that wasn't an option. She would have no way to buy a train ticket on her own.

He returned a few minutes later. She crossed her arms over her chest and refused to look at him. He said nothing to her as he snapped the reins. They rode in silence. It would have been a calming, scenic trip if not for the constant feeling of dread she had about her brother. Bertram wasn't much comfort, either.

The sleigh sailed through a fork in the road. She twisted around to peer at the other road. "Weren't we supposed to take that turn?"

"What turn?"

"The road forked back there. Shouldn't we have gone right?"

He scratched at his chin. "This way should let us skip the closest village. They're incorrigible gossips. I don't need any of them alerting my uncle to my escape."

"I doubt they'd get word to him faster than we could get to the city."

"Try to have a little faith. This road is the long way around, but it will still get us to the train station. It's too late to turn back away." This road was narrower than the main one they'd left. They had to duck beneath a branch hanging over the road. There would be no way to maneuver the sleigh around.

"Is this even a road?" With everything bathed in white, the outlines of roads were hard to spot. "Or is it a path?"

"It's a road. I know where I'm going," he said, indignant.

"You missed our turn, didn't you?" She huddled under her pile of blankets, pulling them up higher around her neck.

"If you'd have done a better job checking on Pepper, we wouldn't be so tight on time."

"Well you'll excuse me if my brother's condition had me a bit distracted." She hugged herself, determined not to lean against him for warmth. "How am I supposed to know how a hummingbird flies? I've never seen one before her."

He adjusted the blanket around his shoulders. If he'd been kinder, she may have considered sharing one of her three with him.

"I'll bet if she were a cute little dog instead, you'd have paid closer attention. No one ever ignores Oolong like this."

"No one *can* ignore Oolong if they value their life. If you do, he'll get underfoot and send you crashing to the floor." She eyed the horizon. "Are you sure this route will get us to the station in time? The sun is setting."

"Yes, yes. Quit asking."

The white world around them grew monotonous. Nothing but farms and trees and hills. In the distance, a pair of horses pranced about in one of the fields, one following closely behind the other. They weaved back and forth across the hillside.

Desperate to break the silence that had fallen on the sleigh, Laoise pointed to the horses. "Never seen horses dance like that."

Bertram nodded. "Huddling for warmth I suppose."

The silence crept back in as she watched the horses. Against the monotonous backdrop of white, their weaving movements were almost hypnotic. She was drawn in by their dance, but its purpose became quite clear as one horse suddenly mounted the other.

Laoise snorted. "Looks like they're doin' a bit more than huddlin'!"

"Oh for God's sake..." Bertram averted his gaze. "Stop looking. That's revolting."

"Of course sir, but..." Laoise struggled to maintain her composure. "...do you suppose Bess will get distracted by the show?"

Bertram gave a disgusted look to Laoise. "She will not."

Then as quickly as it had begun, it was over. The stallion dismounted and stood looking around as if he were embarrassed by the act. Laosie couldn't contain her laughter as they rode past the field.

Laoise wiped away a tear. "Well you were right. It ended up not being much of a show after all,"

"Must you be so vulgar?" chastised Bertram.

"My apologies, sir." After a moment, she snorted and elbowed him. "Not very gentlemanly of the stallion, now was it?"

"Stop." Bertram tried to hold back a snorting laugh, but failed.

The sound of their laughter slowly subsided, returning to the quiet crunching of the snow beneath Bess's hooves. "You really care about your animals, don't you, sir?"

"Hmm?" He glanced over at her. "What do you mean?"

"I mean with Bess. Pepper too. With the way you treat us servants, I didn't think there was a kind bone in your body."

Bertram chuckled. "Well of course I care about them. Animals are easy to trust. They never lie or scheme behind your back. They just want food and shelter and affection, and they'll never pretend otherwise. They're not a thing like people."

"Is that how you see people? You really think everyone is scheming against you?"

"For a man in my position everyone *is* scheming against me. Everyone wants something, and they'll lie to your face to get it. Whether it's money, influence, or social recognition." He looked down. "And some just want to spend a night with the eligible and handsome young Master Steepe."

She wrinkled her nose. "You aren't very humble, are you?"

"I'm simply aware of my reputation. I know how women see me. Ladies young and old gather around to engage me in conversation. The new maids especially tend to fawn all over me. It can be exhausting."

"For someone so well loved, you certainly seem to take great pleasure in being cruel to the help."

"I'd hardly call that love." He scoffed. "And I don't take pleasure in it. Cruel though it may seem, it's much less cruel than if I were to give them hope. Far better to douse their passions early on than to string them along with hopes of courtship."

"Money and courtship. That's all anything is to you. Some people are just trying to be nice. They're not all hoping to bed you."

"Our...little rendezvous wasn't you trying to be nice. And it clearly wasn't about money. What else could it have been?"

It was the first time they'd talked about their dallying since the day it had happened, and he couldn't possibly have put his sentiments more bluntly. "You want to know my grand scheme? I was furious with you and I wanted to make you as upset as I was."

"An odd decision." He side-eyed her. "Why would you possibly think sleeping with me would upset me?"

"Because you think you're so much better than the rest of us. You reminded me yourself about the difference between our stations. I thought a romp with someone as far 'below your station' as me would make you feel like you'd lowered yourself." Spite was a powerful motivator for Laoise, and out of spite she had been prepared to grit her teeth and endure another incompetent bedfellow. She hadn't quite been prepared for his hands to be so very good at winding her up.

He kept his attention on the road as he thought her words over. "You were mistaken. Regardless of your station, a night with a beautiful woman wouldn't hurt my pride."

His answer shocked her. Her thoughts ground to a halt. Beside the sleigh, an old stone wall appeared alongside the narrow road. "Did you just call me beautiful?"

He quickly turned to look at the old church they passed by. "Would you look at that. The original church for the village. Can't imagine how old it is. Sometimes we go to the Christmas service there. The whole family comes along."

"You're avoiding my question, aren't you?"

"Absolutely." He gestured at the road. "And here's the second fork. We'll be at the station before you know it." They turned right.

They lapsed back into silence. She snuck glances at him, not missing his troubled look. Under happier circumstances and with a different man, the sleigh ride would have felt romantic. It'd almost been pleasant while she had a warm drink to help keep the cold at bay. But with her tea long gone, the cold wormed its way through her layers.

The sun started to sink and with it, the shadows lengthened. A few turns later, they passed the church again. "It's the same church. You've gotten us lost, haven't you?" She pointed.

"I'm not lost." He stood up as if it'd give him a better view of the road despite the trees in the way. "The roads just look a little different with all this snow."

Laoise's teeth chattered. "Can you at least find us an inn or something? We aren't going to make the train at this rate, but we could at least warm up."

The shadows grew deeper by the minute. It wouldn't be long before night fell and without lanterns there'd be no way to see.

"This way I think," he mumbled at the next turn. Ahead of them was nothing but trees and farm land with no end in sight. He scratched at his jaw, frowning. "We'll just head back to the manor and try again at dawn tomorrow. With better light the roads will be easier to see."

"Are you daft? Get us to an inn! We'll freeze before we make it back." Her stomach growled. "If we don't starve first, that is."

He stopped the sleigh without warning.

"What are you doing?" She shivered as a gust of wind blew down the road.

"We have no money for dinner or a room." He pulled a rifle out of the back of the sleigh. "We will have to fend for ourselves if you don't want to return."

"And so you are going to do what, exactly?"

"I'll get us something to eat," he said, pointing to the woods. "Make yourself useful and start us a fire."

"A fire?" Her voice rose in disbelief. "How do you expect me to do that?"

"You do it all the time when you cook, don't you? Gather some wood and make a fire. Someone's going to need to cook our dinner. And you are technically still my maid."

She shook her head in disbelief. "I can't possibly cook out here!"

Bertram huffed. "You can't cook in a kitchen either, but we do what we must to survive."

"We're not going to survive at all out in this! We'll be buried in a blizzard and we'll freeze to death."

"Not if there's fire we won't. Now if you'll excuse me, I haven't gotten a chance to hunt all year. I'll be back shortly with fresh pheasant." He pointed at the pheasant tracks in the snow and then marched off into the woods.

"You can't be serious. You've gone mad," she called after him, but he didn't respond.

She grumbled as she climbed out of the sleigh. His confidence in his wild plans bothered her more than the idea of camping out in the snow. Especially with his track record of schemes blowing up in his face.

"Just build a fire," she mumbled in a terrible impersonation of Bertram. The tone all wrong. "A fire will fix everything, you silly little maid." Not knowing what else to do, she worked on gathering an armload of sticks as she wandered the side of the road. At the very least, jabbing him with a stick when he returned would help her let off some steam.

"I should have known better. Damn fool can't get himself back to London. Let alone me." She stopped to lean against the side of a tree, sheltering herself from a gust of wind whipping up loose snow.

"Sean will be fine. He always is." She'd been telling herself that for months now. It no longer made her feel any better. The lie was getting harder and harder to believe, too. Every time a medication didn't work, or the price went up, a ragged piece of her hope was chipped away. The little chunk of hope left was getting harder to hang on to.

The wind died down, and she trudged on, wanting to keep herself busy. That way her mind had less time to dwell on all the things she couldn't do anything about.

Suddenly, her left foot sank deeper into the snow than her right and she stumbled forward, dropping all the sticks. "Damn it all!" She threw her hands in the air. "Nothing can go right today, can it?"

Ahead, between the trees, a light flickered. She lowered her hands, watching the light. She headed for it. Her calves burned from fighting her way through the snow. Some of it working its way into the tops of her boots and melting.

One window came into view, and then two. Then the sign for the inn. "Of course it'd be right there." She laughed, the sound rueful, and turned to head back to the sleigh. "Only Bertram could decide to set up camp right at the edge of town."

Just as she reached the sleigh, a gunshot went off, followed by a second. She climbed back in, curling up under the pile of blankets, and waited. A few minutes later, Bertram came out of the forest, his rifle slung over his shoulders and a pheasant dangling from each hand.

He gave her a grin of triumph and held them up. "Dinner." He shook the bird in his right hand. "And breakfast."

"Very nice."

His smile fell as he surveyed their lack of campsite. "Where's the fire?"

"Over that way." She pointed down the road.

He turned, following the direction. "Why exactly did you build a fire all the way down there?"

She let out a breath of exasperation. "No. The fire is over there inside a nice, warm hearth that is probably full of food."

"You found a farmer's house?"

"No! The inn. I found the inn. You're going to get back in this sleigh and drive us there." She patted the seat beside her. "Aren't you, sir? Or you can stay out here all by yourself tonight because I'm not going to."

"I told you we don't have money for a room," he said, pointing a finger at her, pheasant still in hand.

"Offer them the birds. I don't care if I have to sleep in the stables, it's better than staying out in this cold."

"Since you couldn't be trusted to make a fire, I suppose we have no choice." He sighed. "A decent cook might be a welcome change as well..."

"Oh hush," she said, elbowing his ribs through her many layers of blankets.

The inn was the most beautiful thing she'd seen all day. It didn't matter that the crooked sign was so weathered it was impossible to read. Inside, two men sat with pint glasses at one end of the bar. A man stood behind the bar reading a penny blood. He looked up over the pages when he spotted them.

"Evenin'," he said, setting down the book. "Here for a room or board?"

Laoise put on her brightest smile and held Bertram by the arm. "My fiancé and I would like a room please. Some supper would be lovely as well, wouldn't it, dear?"

"Yes. It would," said Bertram mechanically. His eyes went wide as he plastered a smile onto his own face. "But let's not get ahead of ourselves... darling. How much for two rooms and supper?"

The man named his price. Laoise looked to Bertram, who was still looking alarmed by his sudden engagement.

"Unfortunately, thanks to the storm, all I have is this." He laid a single coin on the bar followed by the two pheasants.

The man scratched his head.

"Jesus, Tommy, let the poor couple eat," a woman said as she leaned her broom against the bar. "We were out of meat anyway. These will cook up nice tonight." She grabbed the pheasants and headed into the kitchen.

The man pointed to an open table. "Have a seat and she'll bring supper out to ye."

"And our rooms?" Bertram asked.

"Can't give ye a room." Tommy shook his head. He pointed to the hearth. "But ye can wait in front of the fire til mornin'."

"Thank you kindly," Laoise shot him a bright smile. She turned to look up at Bertram, batting her eyelashes. "Much better than camping outside dear, isn't it?"

"Pardon me," said Bertram, no longer able to maintain the facade of an eager young fiancé. Without another word, he turned and walked out of the inn. Laoise shifted uncomfortably, unsure if she should follow. After a moment, he returned, brandishing his rifle.

"D-darling!" Laoise stammered. "There's no need to—"

Bertram strutted over and set the rifle down on the bar in front of the man. "This is my prized hunting rifle, and I shall wish to have it back none the worse for wear. May I..." He breathed in sharply and closed his eyes, pain in his voice, "put it up as collateral for lodging tonight?"

"Now that's a fine bit o' work." Tommy whistled as he admired the elaborate engravings on the side of the firearm. "Ye can have the nice room. Upstairs, last room on the left," the man said.

"We need two rooms. To give my..." Bertram gestured to Laoise and grimaced as he continued, "...beloved some privacy."

"Terribly sorry, sir, but we've only one room to offer."

Bertram looked around. "Come now, this place is empty. Surely you can spare a second room."

"Afraid that's the very last room, sir. Ye and yer bride-to-be will just have to share tonight." The man winked at Bertram. "Terribly sorry for the inconvenience."

"Thank you for your generosity," Laoise said, stifling a giggle as she pretended not to notice the wink. She tugged Bertram toward the table near the fire. "Come let's warm up and wait for dinner, dearest."

"Congratulations on your engagement," Betram said once they were out of earshot of the innkeeper. Maintaining a bright and convincing smile, he hissed his words through his teeth. "I should have known you had some ulterior motive in all of this."

"Don't flatter yourself. People are nicer to a young couple in love." She kept a wide smile on her own face as she set a hand on Bertram's and threw her head back, pretending to laugh. While she put on the show of a blushing bride, her words dripped with contempt as she spoke. "No one would let a wealthy businessman and his maid get away with paying for shelter and a meal with two smelly pheasants and an old rifle. We're lucky they aren't demanding a fortune."

"Did you hear the price for a room? They *are* demanding a fortune." He rubbed his hands together and blew into them to warm them. "You could have at least told me your plan first."

"And lose the chance to see that look on your face? Never!"

"Then it seems you've finally achieved your goal of upsetting me. Well done." He rubbed his temples. "I spend one day outside the manor and I find myself in a surprise engagement. I wonder if this is how that Graham girl felt. Perhaps that's why she was so ornery."

"Quit your whining, would you? It's not like you're going to see these people ever again."

"I most certainly will see them again. Once I have access to my money, I'm buying my rifle back before that man finds a way to ruin it."

"If it's so important to you why give it away in the first place? I was content to sleep on the floor in front of the fire."

"As you may recall, you and I rested together in front of a fire once, and we agreed we wouldn't repeat that." He smirked. "Most certainly not in public."

"Now, now, dearest," She kicked his shin under the table. "Save it for the honeymoon."

He stepped on her foot. "Of course, darling."

Chapter 13

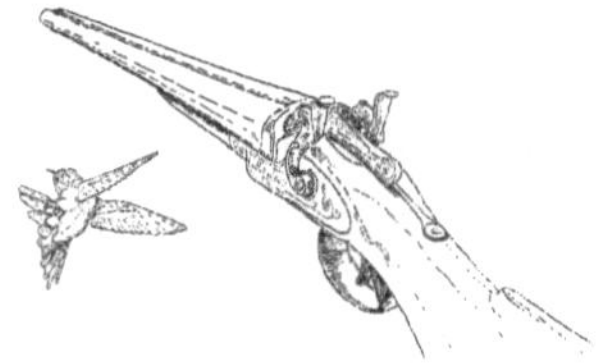

"This room is cozy," Laoise said as she added a log to the fire. The "nice" room as the host had called it had nothing but a bed, fireplace, and armchair. Their window looked over the road and the endless snow and trees.

Bertram sniffed. "There are many words I'd use to describe this room, and 'cozy' isn't one of them. 'Nice' isn't one either." His expression soured as he scanned the room. "A more appropriate term would be 'shambles' I think."

"Well, it's hardly luxury fit for a lofty Steepe," Laoise teased, "but the room is warm and that's what matters. Better than sleeping outside or in the stables."

"If you say so." He dropped their bags beside the door.

"Dare I ask if you know where we are? Or are we well and truly lost?"

"I know exactly where we are. It isn't my fault the snow made the roads a maze." He flopped onto the chair. "The train station isn't far from here. If we leave at first light, we'll easily make the earliest train back to London."

"Good news at last." She curled up on the rug, happy to stay close to the fire. As she rubbed her full belly, it was the first time she'd felt content all day. Perhaps all week." That roast pheasant was lovely. Tea was nice too. Not bad for shambles, I think."

"The coffee was decent," he said, giving a reluctant nod. "A bit burnt, but decent. And it was nice to eat something that wasn't oatmeal or a sandwich.'

She grinned. "Those are my specialties."

The corners of his mouth twitched as he tried to hold back a smile. "I'll remember to never drive another cook away. Wouldn't want to get stuck with your cuisine again."

"Let that be a lesson to you. Treat your staff poorly and I'll come serve you cold oatmeal." Light, fluffy snowflakes drifted against the window. "We better not be getting more snow. I don't want to miss the train tomorrow."

When he didn't respond, she turned to him, finding him watching her. "So all this work you're doing is to afford your brother's medicine?"

She turned her attention to the fire. His gaze felt too intimate in the small room. "Yes. It doesn't help that the medicine gets more expensive each month."

There was a long pause before Bertram broke the silence, his voice soft. "I could put in a good word for you with the Steepe Foundation, you know. A case like yours—"

"No," Laoise interjected.

"What? What do you mean no?" He was taken aback, sounding almost offended. "The Foundation was made specifically to—"

"I said no. We don't need any pity and we don't need charity." She glanced up at the cloak and gloves Charlotte had given her. An inexplicable feeling of shame burned in the pit of her stomach, and she felt determined to pay Charlotte back for it. One way or another.

"There's no shame in accepting a little help now and then, you know." He held up the wrist that the bracelet had been on, still pink from where he had scrubbed it. A faint scent of lard wafted around the room.

She covered her smile with her hand. "I do appreciate the offer, but we're perfectly capable of getting what we need ourselves." She turned her attention back to the fire. "That's why I accepted the position at the manor to serve you. Your cousin offered me extra pay while I'm in the countryside. I thought it was a stroke of good luck. Then I discovered you were driving everyone else off. No wonder he's paying so much." Her self-pity refused to stay away. Shannon had warned her, and yet she'd been too bullheaded to listen.

"Ah, I see. No charity, but a bribe is perfectly acceptable." Bertram rubbed his chin. "I had no idea Martin was paying so much for my sake. He never mentioned it in any of his letters."

"He thinks about you a great deal. Charlotte says he has been worrying because you aren't answering his letters. Lord knows why he cares so much. I certainly wouldn't if you tried to get me thrown in prison at The Great Exhibition."

"Oh please. Martin wouldn't have gone to prison. He'd have been exiled to the manor just as I was." He glared out the window, resting his head on his hand. "He actually might have enjoyed it. Plenty of time alone to work on his magic and drink his tea. And I certainly wouldn't need to bribe the help."

She slid her knees up to her chest and hugged them. "I know you don't hate Martin, but I don't see how you could have been doing anything else but getting your cousin out of the way to make yourself heir to the family business."

He balked. "That's absurd! I have no intention of harming Martin. Nor of replacing him in any capacity."

"Then why? Why go through all that trouble to get him sent away?"

He shifted in the chair. "Ideally, it would have been that Graham girl who got sent away. I know for a fact she was after Martin's money the whole time. If I'd been able to pry her away from him even for a moment, perhaps he'd see that himself."

"Her name is Charlotte, and she loves him." She said, wagging a finger at him. She continued, mocking Bertram's intonation. "If you'd listened to her even for a moment, perhaps *you'd* see *that* yourself."

"I refuse to believe she loves him. I mean, he proposed to her based on which tea his teapot gave her. What woman would be seduced by that?"

"Believe it or not, but some women like good men regardless of their eccentricities. She was nervous about the engagement, but Martin won her over."

"I can see I won't be convincing you." He cast his eyes towards Laoise's new cloak and gloves. "Perhaps your loyalty has already been bought and paid for."

"And exactly what do you mean by that?" She raised an eyebrow, clenching her fist.

He gave a smug and knowing smile. It slowly faded from his lips as he continued. "It wasn't all about the girl, however. I also wanted to wake Martin up from the fantasy world he's been living in. Show him that he is wasting his time playing around with tea instead of spending his efforts on diversifying his business ventures.

"Playing around? Everyone has Steepe tea in their pantries. Even this 'shambles' of a wee inn has it. I'd call that a serious business."

"Because you don't understand! Look, it's no secret that Martin is a bit of an odd fellow, but anyone would be if they grew up as he did." He stood up and looked out the window. A gentle curtain of fluffy flakes drifted down.

"He's brilliant, you know. He understands absolutely everything in the world. Everything except people. He places his trust so blindly, and even when he knows he's being taken advantage of, he won't speak up about it. He thinks he can just sell tea without diversifying his assets and everything will be just fine, but once this tea business fails, he'll have nothing else to fall back on. He'll be devastated. Emotionally and financially. Then no one will want to do business with him again."

"You're not making any sense. Steepe tea is a success. None of that bad stuff has happened at all."

"Not yet." He shook his head. "The business world is a fickle one. One shift in the markets, or one underhanded business partner, and suddenly all his success is swept away. What then, hmm?"

"I may not know much about the markets, but I do understand being over protective. I've always felt that way about my middle brother Rian, but I learned to let him make his own mistakes. He's a teenager now, and he's made plenty of decisions. Some good. Some bad. But he's learned from each one."

"I see. And did any of his decisions threaten the future of your family's business empire?"

"No, but we've gotten along just fine without having any business empire at all. Maybe it's not worth fretting too much over."

Bertram harrumphed.

Laoise smiled and continued. "I watched him make decisions I disagreed with that hurt him in the end. It was hard to watch, but he would have been angry at me if I'd interfered. He needed to learn for himself. And sometimes it turned out I worried over nothing."

"He sounds like a resilient young man," said Bertram, "and every bit as stubborn as his big sister."

"Watch it," she said with a smile.

"Martin, however, isn't quite so resilient. He needs a bit more protection."

"You can't protect everyone from everything, you know." She hugged her legs. The smile fell from her lips as her voice softened. "I wish I could protect Sean from his illness, but I can't." She lowered her voice. The pit in her stomach returned. It was an awful feeling she wouldn't wish on anyone, not even Bertram on his worst days back at the manor. "I'd give anything to be able to heal him."

"I know exactly how you feel." He dragged the chair closer to Laoise. As he sat back down, he rested a hand on her shoulder. "But with you to stand by him, he will get better. I promise."

"Thank you." She leaned back and rested her head on his arm. His touch helped soothe the pit in her stomach just a bit. She could hardly believe this was the same man she once wished had been locked up in a deep dark prison cell. "I'm sorry to put you through all of this again. It must have been hard for you when Martin got sick."

"I don't remember much about Martin before he fell ill. Most of the family wrote him off. I had to step up for his sake. And then my father was gone, and I had to step up to look after my mother and sisters too. Uncle Monty wasn't going to do it. No, he became busier than ever with work. I felt alone with the weight of everyone's well-being on my shoulders." His brow furrowed as he watched the fire. "It was a lot of responsibility at a young age."

"You're making more sense to me." She reached over to poke his leg. Imagining a stern young teenage Bertram with that same furrowed brow brought a smile to Laoise's face. "You aren't trying to get rid of Martin. No, you are more like an overprotective father. You are trying to coddle him instead of letting him fly free."

"I am not overprotective!"

"You are. Martin already has a father. He doesn't need you to be his second one."

Bertram scoffed. "Uncle Monty barely counts as a father. He's always away on meetings and business ventures."

"Either way, Martin's a grown man now." She poked his leg playfully again. "Consider yourself instead. Why stay locked up in that manor instead of traveling? Go anywhere you wanted." She sighed. "I wish I could travel. Or learn magic."

He swatted her hand away. "Are you going to sit on the floor all night? I can have them fetch a second chair."

Laoise plopped onto her side and stretched. "Oh I don't know. Lying in front of the fireplace brings back memories, don't you agree?"

"There's no audience to show off in front of this time 'dear,'" he said mockingly, sinking into his chair. "But in here, you're not my fiancée. You're my maid. And I'm still your employer."

"Right. That makes it your duty to look after all your workers, doesn't it?"

"It does." He cast her a look of suspicion. "What are you trying to get at?"

"It's just that it's so cold, sir." She ran a hand down her side, grinning as he squirmed. Desire ignited in his eyes as his gaze followed her hands. As infuriating as he was, he'd been good with his hands. And his mouth. And other certain parts of him. "Isn't it a gentleman's duty to care for his charges?"

"You're quite right." He stood and shuffled toward the door, his movements stiff.

"Where are you going?"

He reached for the door handle. "To check on Bess. She might need me to get her a blanket. As you said, it's cold tonight."

Laoise grabbed a pillow off the bed and threw it at him. "You know what I meant!"

He smiled as he caught the pillow. "Are you trying to tell me you need another blanket too?"

"Now you are spoiling the mood."

"I would hate to ruin the mood of this...cozy room as you called it." He pointed at the moth-eaten curtains. "I can see how you find the ambiance irresistible."

"Ha, ha." She crossed her arms. "Sorry that I don't have fancy tastes like you."

"Yes, well—" His gaze stopped in the back corner of the room near the window. He froze.

"Sir?"

His left eye twitched. Then he squealed and darted for the bed. He stood on top of it, his back against the wall.

"Is that you trying to get the mood back? It's not exactly seductive." She wrinkled her nose.

"M-mouse." He pointed at the corner.

Laoise climbed onto her feet, disappointment heavy in her chest. "I had no idea you were afraid of mice. They won't hurt you."

He blanched. "They are vermin. Full of diseases!"

"I'll shoo the poor creature out for you." She started around the bottom of the bed, stopping when she spotted the furry mass in the corner. Two beady eyes stared back at her, illuminated by the fire. They belonged to a creature much too large to be called a mouse. She screamed before jumping onto the bed to join him.

"I had no idea you were afraid of mice," he said, mimicking her accent. "They won't hurt you!"

"That's no mouse." She stood on the bed, keeping her back against Bertram for balance. "That's a bloody rat! The little demons will gnaw you in half as quick as look at you!"

"I don't care what it is, just get rid of it!"

"How?"

"I don't know. Don't you have some sort of maid trick for this sort of thing?"

"No. You have a gun. Can't you shoot it?"

"Had a gun." He corrected, huffing. "And I'd have to get past it to get the gun, anyway."

"I thought you were a hunter." She sniffed as she leaned against the headboard. "Can't sneak past a rat?"

"Shut up," he sniped. "How about the curtain rod?"

Laoise glanced up at the curtain rod. The ends were not pointed as she had hoped, but were flat and rounded like doorknobs. "It's better than nothin'. You're the tall, strong man. You reach up there and pull it down." She was taller than all the other Steepe maids, but even standing on the bed, the rod was just a bit too far out of reach.

"Playing to my ego. You're the real demon here." He took a deep breath before jumping back to the floor. He reached up and tugged on the curtains, yanking the curtain rod down with a metallic clang.

"Quick! He's coming for you," Laoise warned.

Bertram jabbed at the rat, the worn curtains flopping about. She yelped at the flurry of action. The rat scurried into a hole in the corner.

"Did you get him?"

"Of course not! I can't spear a rat with a blunt object."

"Well, shove the curtains into the hole to block his way. I don't want a rat running around while I sleep. He'll nibble my nose!" She pressed her back against the headboard, keeping herself as far away from them as possible.

He tugged at the curtains, sliding them off the rod. Before he finished a loud, impatient knock thudded against the door.

"You get it. I'm not getting off this bed until that hole is blocked," said Laoise, sitting on the bed and hugging her knees.

Another knock, this one rattling the door with its force. Bertram opened the door a crack. The innkeeper stood on the other side, his expression sheepish and his gaze averted. "How is the happy couple? Enjoyin' the evenin'?"

Bertram's eyes darted back to the rat hole, continuing to kick the curtains into it. "Yes. Fine. What is it?"

"Sorry to interrupt, but do ye suppose ye could keep the noise down while yer uhh..." He stammered a moment while he thought of the correct euphemism. "...makin' merry?"

"We weren't—" Bertram cut himself off, opening the door a bit more. "Did you know you have rats?"

The man turned his gaze to Bertram, evidently surprised to see him fully clothed. "Of course we do. The buggers are impossible to get rid of."

'There is a gigantic one in our room." He cast a nervous glance toward the rat hole.

"I'll put out some more traps. Consider it an early weddin' present." The man chuckled. "Just do try to keep a bit more quiet, if ye please."

The innkeeper clomped his way back down the hall. Bertram shut the door. He turned his back to it, gaze landing on Laoise. He widened his eyes, pleading. "Can I share the bed with you tonight? You did need me to keep you warm, didn't you?" He fluttered his eyelashes at her.

She let out a long, suffering sigh to hide her amusement. "I suppose I'll let you. Can't have the rats eating you in the middle of the night."

Laoise slept with her head under the sheet and the blanket tucked in around her to keep the rats out. Curling up to Bertram's back kept her warm despite the draft from the window. The creaking and scurrying of rats kept her on edge.

Bertram slept right through the noise, sometimes softly snoring. She didn't mind since his snores drowned out the rustling in the walls. She preferred him asleep. There was his warmth, the muscles of his back and chest she explored in peace, and best of all, there was no risk of him opening his mouth and ruining the moment. She fell asleep that way, cuddled up against his back until morning.

"Get off, Oolong."

Laoise yawned and popped her head out. Bertram's grumbling continued.

"You're at an inn. Oolong isn't here," she whispered.

His eyes opened, staring frozen at the ceiling. Then he sat up, crawling toward the headboard. A rat scurried out from under the blanket. Laoise clapped a hand over her mouth to hold in her scream.

"Grab the ash scoop." He jumped off the bed and pushed the window open. The icy blast pushed Laoise into motion. As soon as she had the scoop she rushed over to him, handing it over.

The rat scurried along the edge of the wall. He attacked, his fast movement reminding Laoise of his fencing practice. He scooped the rat up and tossed it out the window. The rat landed on the windowsill and turned to head back inside. Bertram used the scoop to shove it out.

"Get it, get it, get it!" Laoise chanted, too fast to be understood, shaking her fists in time to her chanting. She ran to the other side of the window, recoiling at the rat's advance.

When he yanked the scoop back in, the handle whacked against the outside of the glass, cracking the window. Laoise slammed the window shut with enough force that the crack widened into an angry, jagged line through the center of the window, too big to miss.

He swore.

"Can't you fix it with magic? Do that thing you did with the greenhouse panel?"

He scratched his chin. "I can try, I suppose. Grab me the pitcher of water." He traced runes into the fog on the glass as he spoke the spell. The runes glowed and water flowed from the pitcher to the window.

Then all at once, the glass blew out of the frame and into the snow below.

"What was that?"

"I don't know!" Bertram rested both hands on top of his head. He chewed on his bottom lip. "I'll do it again. There's enough water left."

Laoise swept the hair that had escaped her braid out of her face. "I don't see what it can hurt. Can't break the window any worse."

This time the water stuck to the frame and became a thick sheet of ice.

"We should leave," Bertram said as he grabbed his bag.

"Good idea. Wouldn't want to miss the morning train."

"Exactly." He nodded frantically.

The dining room was empty when they crept down the stairs. They walked on tiptoes to the front door. They were steps from the door when Bertram stopped, spotting a man sitting by the fire. The man's face was buried in a newspaper. "One moment." He strode across the room. Laoise crept over to the fire to warm up, keeping an eye on the door to the kitchen.

Bertram ripped the man's newspaper away. Laoise covered her mouth to silence her gasp of surprise. "Roger," Bertram said, jaw tense. Roger blinked up at him. Laoise recognized him. He was the same private detective Bertram once hired to follow Charlotte when he was determined to ruin Martin's engagement. She never would have spotted him.

"I should have known my uncle had you watching me."

Roger opened his mouth to respond, but Bertram held up a finger, silencing him. "I don't want to hear your excuses. You always have too many of them. But I can't have you running right off to my uncle about what's happened. So take this." He set his pocket watch on the table in front of Roger. "It's the best watch I own. And it cost more than I like to admit to spending on a watch. Keep it or sell it, but let's not tell my uncle about this."

Roger opened his mouth again, but Bertram shushed him. "Consider the consequences. I'd hate to have to use this instead." He opened the left side of his coat and tapped something inside. Roger blanched. "I hope we have an understanding."

Roger nodded.

Bertram headed for the door.

The woman called out from the kitchen. "Don't you want to stay for breakfast? It's hash today. Fresh meat! The first batch will be ready soon."

The thought of food tossed aside all of Laoise's worries over the broken window. "That sounds lovely—"

"We don't have time." Bertram steered Laoise the rest of the way to the door. "We have a train to catch and can't be late."

"Too bad. Take care you two!" She stepped back into the kitchen.

"What was that?" Laoise demanded once they were outside. "I'd like some breakfast. They won't notice the window until they go up to clean."

"You mean you want that fresh meat? Don't you remember saying he'd put out some rat traps? And when we came here, he said they were out of meat. So tell me, what do you think that meat is? I don't smell a pheasant roasting, but go ahead, take a guess."

Laoise stuck out her tongue in disgust. "He wouldn't feed his guests rats, would he?" She followed him, her stomach gurgling in complaint.

"Today I'd believe anything. I'd also rather leave before someone notices the damage we caused. I've spent my rifle and my watch already. I'll not be able to pay for much more." He got to work hooking Bess back up to the sleigh while she searched through the meager supplies they'd brought. Finding the right bag, she pulled out an apple.

Bertram grabbed her arm, his touch gentle. "Those are for Bess, not you."

"She got delicious hay all night. She won't miss an apple. Besides, you won't like me when I'm hungry."

"I don't like you when you're full either." He let go of her arm. A long stretch of silence passed between them as he got them back on the road.

Finally, after several minutes, he spoke again. "Save me an apple."

"Here we are," Bertram said as he pulled the sleigh up to the bank. The small building sat wedged between an apothecary and a grocer. Like everything else, a thick layer of white coated it. Hardly anyone else braved the snow-covered streets, making the village appear deserted. "A quick stop to get money for our tickets and then on to London."

"It looks closed." A snow drift blocked the lower half of the front door. The windows were dark with no movement inside. "In fact, it doesn't look like anyone has touched this place since the storm hit."

"They have to be open. If not, we have no way of getting money. I'm about out of things I can use to barter."

"You could always trade Bess," Laoise offered with a smile. She perused the flyers hanging in the window of the grocer. At least there was a fire in the hearth. In fact, it was the only hint of life on the street.

"I'd trade you away first." He trudged through the snow, leaning over the drift to knock on the door. No answer. He peered into the window.

As she peered into the window, she noticed the shopkeeper was behind the counter. She rushed to the door and threw it open. "Excuse me sir!"

"Damn it all, woman, close the door," the man snapped.

"Sorry!" She pulled the door shut behind her. "Do you know when the bank next door will be opening?"

The man rubbed the grey stubble of his chin. "I think Ralph was visiting family when the storm hit. If he's snowed in, he won't be back for another day or two."

Bertram met her outside the grocer. "No good news, I take it?"

She repeated what the man had told her. Bertram leaned against the window, head down.

"There, there. All hope isn't lost. We have another way to to get money for our tickets." She pointed to a wrinkled flyer in the window, grinning.

"What's this?"

"It caught my eye as I was lookin' inside." The flyer advertised an amateur boxing ring in a nearby pub. Two small, hand-drawn pugilists animated by magic dodged and blocked one another's punches in an endless loop. Above them was what had really caught her attention. In bold letters the flyer proclaimed that Tank Engine Frank, the favorite boxer of both her and her brothers, was going to be fighting in the ring.

"I wasn't sure if we'd have time, but without the bank, we need more money for our train tickets." It was as good an excuse as any to get to see Tank Engine Frank fight. She hadn't seen one of his matches in months. She couldn't think of a better gift on her way home. It'd give her something to tell Sean all about too when she got home. He'd enjoy hearing about the matches.

"Boxing?" His jaw hung slack. "You were in such a hurry before, and now you want to stop and watch a few fights?"

"Not just watch. Bet." Laoise grabbed his arm, excitement in her voice. "I don't have enough for the train, but I do have a little coin on me. With a few well-placed bets, we'll have more than enough to get back to London."

He raised an eyebrow. "And just how long were you going to keep that money hidden?"

Laoise rolled her eyes. "It was in case of an emergency. And this qualifies."

Bertram harrumphed, but as he surveyed the details on the flyer, he began stroking his chin. "Open bouts, eh? Then maybe there's another way to get the money we need."

Laoise shot Bertram a look halfway between laughter and shock. "You're not going to fight are you?"

"Of course I am." He rolled his shoulders. "I've been a student of Daniel Mendoza my whole life."

Laoise wracked her brain. She'd been to plenty of fights with her brothers and seen more fighters than she could count, but that particular name didn't stir any memories. "Can't say I've heard of him."

"I don't expect you would," said Bertram, as smugly as ever, "But he quite literally wrote the book on pugilism, and I've read it cover to cover. I believe I still have my copy of *The Art of Boxing* back at the manor."

"Fat lot of good it'll do you there." As much as she had fantasized about punching Bertram in that smug face, she felt strangely anxious imagining him being pummeled in the ring. "You'll be up against experienced fighters, you know. They didn't read some fancy book to get where they are."

"Then it seems I'll need to educate them."

She bit her bottom lip to hold back her smile. "As you say, sir."

"Besides, it might feel good to work out my anger."

"Anger at what?"

"At my family preferring to abandon me in the countryside rather than talk about what's happened. Uncle never has time for me unless money is involved." He ticked off his reasons on his fingers. "Martin is married, but my sisters still need suitable matches. With me gone, who will watch over them? I bet none of them have given me a second thought. I should go home, grab my things, and go to Italy for a few months. Getting rid of me would make them happy."

"Stop with the pity party. Your family is doing fine when they aren't worrying about you. Your aunt has been fussing over what to give you for Christmas for two months. Martin is looking after all the business nonsense they made you sign over to him. He wants to make sure everything is in good standing when you return. You can work out your grievances when you return to London. For now, boxing!" She turned to march down the street, and then paused. "Do you really plan to fight?"

"Yes," he said with the foolish confidence of a man who didn't know any better.

The address on the flyer wound up being the basement of a seedy pub down the road. People milled in and out as Bertram and Laoise rode past. A stark contrast to the rest of the town. If the snow kept any customers away, it didn't show in the dense crowd.

"Now listen," said Bertram as he climbed down from the sleigh, keeping his head down. "If you're going to be betting on me, we can't be seen talking to one another. If anyone thinks these fights are fixed, we'll be in trouble."

Laoise nodded. For once his scheming made sense. "I'll go in ahead of you to get a feel for the crowd. Maybe find out something about the other fighters."

"We'll also need disguises." Bertram stroked his chin. "Roger is already in pursuit. Who knows who else my uncle sent after us."

"Oh please." Laoise waved a dismissive hand. "Your uncle wouldn't be able to pick me out of his soup. Maids are used to blending into the background."

"I'm used to being noticed. Particularly by people I'd rather not have notice me." Bertram stopped in front of a particularly shiny window. He pulled a pen and ink from his pocket. With his attention riveted to his reflection, he wrote tiny runes above his upper lip. One mumbled spell under his breath later and a glamoured mustache appeared. He tweaked the glamour, shaping it with his skilled hands. He gave the ends one final twirl.

"Do you do this often? You seem rather...experienced with it." The mustache didn't suit him. She preferred him clean shaven.

Bertram frowned. "I've never been able to grow a mustache well. The hair is always too patchy. This one will help disguise me."

"The only thing that mustache is disguising is your upper lip." With his prominent chin and jaw line, it was obvious who he was. No one looking for him would be fooled.

He struck a pose. "I think it looks rather manly. I daresay I give off the air of a proper boxer."

"I suppose," she said, more to end the conversation than to agree.

Laoise went in ahead of Bertram into the basement. Based on the blood stains and scuff marks on the floor, this was far from the first fight the pub had seen. Nothing but chalk marked the fighting ring. Despite the early hour, a surprising amount of men had shown for the fight, along with more than a few working women.

Bertram strolled in a minute later, surveying the room. Nonchalantly, he approached Laoise, whispering to her. "Where do I sign up to fight?"

Laoise was already milling about the room, her back to Bertram pretending not to hear his request. With a subtle gesture, she cleared her throat and pointed to a man sitting behind a small, worn desk. She'd heard enough chatter to know he was the organizer of the fights.

"Excellent. We'll be out of here in time to catch the train and with full pockets too."

The man looked up as Bertram swaggered forward.

"Name?" asked the man, writing things down on a messy pile of papers.

"Bertram."

Laoise's palm struck her own forehead. Just what was the point of a disguise if he was just going to give his real name?

The organizer gave him an incredulous look. "Just Bertram then? Not very exciting."

"Very well then, something flashy..." Bertram stroked his mustache. "Bertram the Great."

"The great?" came a voice from behind him. "Ye, the great big pain in the arse, he is!"

Bertram turned to face the man who was now laughing at his own taunt. He had a patchy beard and a smile missing more than a few teeth. His forearms were stout and sported yet more scraggly patches of hair. In fact, the man seemed to have hair everywhere but the very top of his head.

"Is there a problem?" Bertram spoke softly, but his gaze was intense as he stared the man down.

"Yes, there's a problem. You're a bit lost, ya toff," said the man, seemingly undeterred. He pushed past Bertram, landing a sudden punch to his gut, doubling him over. "Yer tea shops are that way." He pointed to the front door of the pub.

The organizer laughed, reaching out a hand to shake the man's hand. "Back for more, are ya Danny Boy? I was worried you wouldn't show."

"And miss my cut of the money? Not a chance, ya old codger!" Danny bellowed. "I've been itchin' for a fight all day."

"If it's a fight you want, it's a fight you'll get, you coward." A hand gripped Danny's shoulder and spun him around. If Bertram had felt the punch to his stomach, his face wasn't showing it. "That is, unless you'd like to apologize."

"Don't know when yer beat do ye?" As he stared Bertram down, he called out to the organizer. "Gimme the toff. I'd like to 'apologize' to his graces."

The two men locked eyes for a long moment before Danny turned and wandered off to the tap. Laoise had fantasized about punching Bertram in the gut for almost as long as she'd known the man. Now more than anything, she so badly wanted to rush over to his side and tell Danny off. Bertram was hers to injure, not his. But the hard set of his gaze told her he didn't need any comforting, and she had work to do.

She slid her hand into her pocket, grabbing the handful of coins she had managed to gather snooping around the manor and the inn. The total wasn't more than two pence, but if she was smart with her bets, she would earn enough to get two tickets to London.

She surveyed Bertram's back and shoulders. How much did a man of his station know how to handle himself with fists? She'd watched Bertram practice his fencing, but a good fencer didn't necessarily make a good pugilist. She'd been to enough matches with her brothers to know looks could be deceiving, and to not make uniformed bets. Not when it came to money. If she lost the first bet, they'd have no way to get train tickets for both of them.

Laoise roamed about the pub, chatting with the locals and gleaning what information she could. Her years of eavesdropping on the wealthy had prepared her to gather information from a room without being obvious about it. Everyone spoke in excited murmurs as she roamed, giving up bits of gossip here and there.

"Did ya see ol' Handsome Danny's back?" said one man, pointing over to the patchy-faced man who had punched Bertram.

"Is he?" asked another man. "Didn't think he'd show after the thrashing Jack gave him last week."

"I'd say he deserved it after trying to gouge out the man's eyes. I'm surprised he wasn't killed."

"It looks like he'll have an easy fight against that genteel one." The second man gestured towards Bertram, who was shadowboxing outside of the circle. "I hope the toff's wearin' his monocles. Otherwise ol' Danny'll pop his eyes out like a pair of plums!"

The two men laughed. Laoise stuck her tongue out in revulsion. Even at his cruelest, Laoise hadn't envisioned something so grisly befalling Bertram. He could be insufferable, but a handsome face didn't deserve to be maimed. Being careful not to be seen, she weaved her way over to Bertram and reported the gossip.

"Dirty fighter, huh." Bertram patted his stomach."I knew that much from his little surprise attack."

"He likes to go for the eyes, so be careful out there. And keep an eye out for erm... him trying to put your eye out." Laoise slipped back into the crowd, aware of the scornful looks Bertram was receiving. He brushed back his hair with his fingers and rolled up his sleeves. Her gaze lingered on his forearms. He cut a dashing figure, but looked wildly out of place and seemed to be the only person in the room who didn't notice.

A burly man took to the center of the ring, wielding a bell and mallet. He struck the bell, quieting the crowded basement. "Alright you lot, get ready for our next bout! Let's welcome back to the ring, Handsome Danny!"

The man who struck Bertram strolled into the ring with a pint of ale in hand. The crowd cheered and booed in equal measure as he raised his fist.

"And his opponent, a newcomer to the ring." The man motioned for Bertram, then put on as posh an accent as he could muster. "A warm welcome to his grace, his excellency, his highness, Bertie the Toff!" Bertram scowled, none too pleased with his new titles. The crowd booed and laughed, and Laoise couldn't help but join in.

Before the match started, she made her way back to the desk to place her first bet. None of the fighters on the card were familiar to her, except of course for Frank. But after sneaking off to enough boxing matches, she'd learned to tell who was and wasn't a seasoned fighter. Cocky new fighters like Bertram came swaggering in expecting to be the new champion, only to be humbled time and time again.

The bookie frowned. "Are you sure you want to place it on him, miss?"

She sighed, trying to convince herself she was making the right decision. "I'm sure."

Laoise worked her way to the edge of the circle near Handsome Danny, getting a good view of the men as they sized up one another.

Danny puffed out his chest, finishing his pint and slamming the glass down triumphantly onto a table.

"Ladies! How 'bout a kiss from good ol' Danny boy? For luck!" As he walked around the chalk circle, the women either blew mocking kisses to the man or shifted away from him. By the time Laoise realized what was happening, the man was already upon her. He wrapped an arm around the small of her waist. "Come here, love!"

She tried to push against his chest as he pulled her in closer. A mix of groans and whooping came from the crowd.

"Come on now, dearie. It's your lucky day!" As he dipped her, Laoise slipped out of his grip and wheeled on him, slapping him across the cheek. The crowd erupted in laughter at the strike. Danny rubbed his cheek, a big grin on his face. "A fiery one, isn't she?"

She wound up for another slap, but the announcer pulled her away. She had half a mind to step right out into the circle and beat the man to a bloody pulp, but as she breathed in and straightened her skirts, she thought better of it. To do any more than she already had would invalidate her bet and might make her lose all of her money. She'd have to leave the rest to Bertram.

She looked over to see him rolling his neck and shoulders nonchalantly. Had he cared at all that his opponent had accosted her? Though his posture gave nothing away, the calm, focused intensity in his eyes told her that he wouldn't let Danny's actions go unpunished. Had she made the right bet after all?

As the men squared up, anticipation, excitement, and anxiety all swirled about in her stomach. She held her breath. The announcer rang the bell and the fight began.

Danny threw the first punches. Even for an amateur, Laoise recognized that the man had poor form, but plenty of power behind his attacks. Bertram however, was undaunted, effortlessly dodging and weaving around every strike. His movements were as graceful as when he had been fencing back at the manor. Laoise was mesmerized, but the crowd was unimpressed, booing and calling out insults to him.

"Quit runnin' and take it like a man, ya toff!" a woman called out.

"Get lost on yer way to the opery?" jeered another man.

Bertram appeared undeterred by the taunting, his eyes focused on his opponent. Danny grit his teeth, stomping forwards with every punch. Laoise recognized that he was trying to step on Bertram's feet, an underhanded move in most fights. But these too he dodged effortlessly. Bertram's almost elegant footwork really did make the fight seem more like a dance. It wasn't until he had lured Danny into an awkward stance that she remembered it was a boxing match at all. As the man stumbled to regain his footing, he lowered his guard, and Bertram caught him with a right hook to the nose.

Danny backpedaled, a thin trickle of blood pouring out of his nose. With a furious yell, he lunged at Bertram, the man's thumbs poised to reach for an eye gouge. Laoise's heart leapt, and she grabbed a fistful of her skirts to try to steady it. But Bertram's gaze was unwavering, like that of a hunter. He dodged to the left and landed a strike to Danny's stomach. The man doubled over with a wheeze, and Bertram capitalized with an uppercut to his chin. Danny's face contorted as he fell to the ground in a heap. With a ring of the bell, the announcer stepped in to declare Bertie the Toff as the victor.

"Apology accepted," Bertram said to the fallen Danny. He raised his arms in victory, but was greeted not by applause, but by the booing and hissing of the crowd. Confused, he made his way back to a free table. Laosie took a seat at an open table next to his. With their backs to one another, they could speak without appearing too conspicuous.

"Why are they booing?" he asked, still panting heavily. "I put that dirty fighter in his place."

"You were dodging and bobbing all about. It looked more like a ballet than a fist fight." Laoise smirked. "Like the way some rich toff would fight."

He scoffed. "Clearly these people haven't seen a real rich toff fight before."

"For what it's worth, I think you did a marvelous job setting that bastard straight." Laoise glanced over at Danny, who was finally starting to stumble around on his own without support from the other pub goers. "I'm just sorry I didn't help you bash his face in."

"I'm sorry I didn't let you. A brute like that has no business laying a finger on you," he said, leaning back in his chair.

Her breath hitched. She smoothed out her skirts as she got herself under control. She wasn't going to let him of all men make her swoon. "Right you are, sir."

"By the way, you should stop calling me 'sir' for now. Bertram is fine."

"Alright then." Laoise grinned. "Bertie." It was Martin's nickname for him.

"Oh don't you start now." He rapped his knuckles on the table and stood up. "That's why they're all booing. It's that awful moniker they've given me. I'm going to speak to the announcer at once."

"No, no, this is a good thing." She reached a hand to stop him from leaving, grabbing his forearm and squeezing his tense muscles. "The more people hate you, the more they'll bet against you, and the bigger the pot I can win off of you. Don't want to work against all that good ill will now, do you?"

Bertram raised an eyebrow. "So what you're saying is... that I should play the villain?"

Laoise giggled. "Unfamiliar territory for you, I know." She grinned at his huff.

"Hmm. Very well. But only this once." He grabbed his mustache and twirled it, giving Laoise a devious smile. "It seems Bertie the Toff still has some work to do."

Chapter 15

H e stood up and made his way to the tap. Laoise worked her way back through the crowd as another fight was announced. She didn't recognize either of the boxers, so rather than risk her small earnings on the fight, she gathered more information on Bertram's next opponent.

"They call 'im Jagged Jack, and 'e's tough as they come, 'e is," an older man told Laoise, pointing to a man standing in the corner of the room. He was a full head taller than anyone else in the pub, with broad shoulders to match his frame. His undershirt did little to hide his muscles, hewn from hard labor as a stable hand. Most remarkable of all however, was his face, looking far too young to belong to his body. His soft cheeks looked as though they'd never seen a razor, or even needed one for that matter.

"And why do they call him that?" asked Laoise, taking a sip of the pint the man had bought her.

"Reckon it's 'cause it sounds scary," said the man with a laugh. "And like a ferocious beast, 'e is! I've never seen 'im take more than a round to win."

Laoise stood up from her stool. "The Toff going down in the first round sounds like easy money to me. Thanks for the tip!"

She made her way back to the bookkeeper's table, passing by the side of the circle where Bertram was warming up. She pointed out his next opponent and recounted all that she had heard about Jagged Jack. "Think you can handle him?"

Bertram surveyed the tremendous, baby-faced pugilist. With his typical cocksure smirk, he responded, "Bet everything you've got on me."

It was all Laoise could do to not turn and shake some sense into Bertram. "Have you gone mad? Look at the size of him." Laoise had seen enough bouts to know what a tremendous advantage the man's height and reach afforded him.

"Don't look at his size. Look at his face. No broken nose. No missing teeth. Not a scratch on it."

"Because he wins before his opponents have a chance to fight back." Laoise kept her voice to a hushed whisper, but her frustration made her voice rise a notch. "Haven't you been listening?"

"No. It means he can throw a punch, but he doesn't know how to take one. He'll explode in a flurry of punches in the first round, and he won't know what to do with himself in the second. Mark my words." He took a gulp of his water and poured the rest on his own head before weaving through the crowd to the ring.

His arrogance was infuriating, but Laoise knew he was probably right about Jack. In the first few boxing matches she'd seen with her brothers, she'd cheered for plenty of young, energetic men only to be disappointed when they lost their momentum early in the match and were defeated by more practiced fighters. But could Bertram really capitalize on Jack's weaknesses? There was a clear gulf of capability between Jagged Jack and Handsome Danny.

When she made it to the betting table, she found herself swayed. Not merely by Bertram's absolute confidence either, but by the fact that she wanted Bertram to win. He'd be insufferable otherwise. More so than usual, that was. With a deep breath, she set her money on the table. "Put it all on the Toff."

A minute later the announcer stepped into the center of the circle once more, ringing the bell and announcing the fighters. Bertram smoothed down his hair, preening as he strolled into the center of the ring. The whole crowd booed him, but he simply puffed out his chest, strutting about like a rooster. Jagged Jack's entrance was a stark contrast, with the crowd erupting in cheers and applause as the man stood there, flushed and looking like a shy boy in a strongman's body.

The bell rang, and Bertram put on a show of not knowing how to hold his arms and fists, feigning injury and exhaustion from his previous bout. His ruse was too believable, making him look so new to the sport that Laoise started to regret her bet. It was growing too easy to believe the first match had been beginner's luck.

The crowd went wild for Jack as he threw the first flurry of punches. Bertram went on the defensive, dodging as deftly as before. Jack however, was not as clumsy as Handsome Danny. His fast punches left no time for Bertram to do anything but dodge and block. A few blows broke through Bertram's defense, striking him in the chest and the side of his head. Each hit was met with a roar from the crowd. After the first round, Bertram hadn't managed to land a single strike against his opponent, hobbling like a wounded animal to his stool.

Laoise squeezed her hands together, nerves making her want to chew on her thumbnail. Had she been wrong to bet on Bertram? She wormed her way through the jeering crowd to Bertram's side. Their eyes met, and she cast a worried expression, mouthing the words, "Are you alright?"

Bertram panted heavily, but the subtle smile on his face let Laoise know it was a ruse. He pointed to his opponent, whose haggard breathing matched his flushed face.

The start of the second round might as well have been a completely different match. Jack once more tried to open the round with a flurry of punches, but was clearly exhausted.

The previously stumbling Bertram on the other hand had found his footing and strength, landing a counter punch to Jack's gut. The man doubled over and stumbled back, but rather than capitalize on his advantage, Bertram preened and showboated to the crowd. With boos and jeers, the crowd recognized that the villain was winning. A few men called out to Jack to get back into the fight, while someone behind Laoise gasped. She smiled. There was hope yet.

Jack put up his guard, but he was too worn out from his earlier offensive to keep up with Bertram, who kept landing hit after hit to the man's sides. Clumsily, the man stepped back, and wound up for a wild right cross. With a villainous grin, Bertram ducked under the blow and caught Jack in the gut with a pair of wicked hooks. Jack once more doubled over, this time falling to his knees. No amount of goading from the crowd was able to coax Jack off the floor, and the announcer rang the bell, raising Bertram's hand in victory.

Shock rippled through the crowd. Then a chorus of boos broke the air. Someone from the crowd threw a pint glass at Bertram's head. In one fluid motion, he caught the glass, and made a show of swirling the remaining bit of ale like wine in a glass. He took a whiff, then held his nose and dumped out its contents, much to the fury of the crowd.

Excitement raced through Laoise. It was the rush of the fights kept her coming back to them. The exhilaration. It made her want more. Always more. But wasn't that the same dangerous feeling that convinced her to seduce Bertram in the first place? She pushed the thought aside, refusing to let it ruin her excitement.

Bertram caught her eye and winked. Her pulse raced. She loathed him, didn't she? And yet the excitement racing through her made her want to run over and kiss him. No, she couldn't. Watching men who treated boxing like an art always got Laoise riled up. She had to stay focused. Once they were on the train to London she could worry about addressing the tingling building inside of her.

She leaned against a table at the side of the ring, setting a cup of water down within Bertram's reach. "One last fight and then we'll be off to the train."

His chest heaved as he caught his breath. "Great." Noticing her staring, he paused with the cup to his lips. "What?"

"Nothing." She watched a bead of sweat fall down the side of his face. There was something rugged and sensual about watching his chest heave. A long moment passed before she realized she was staring again. She broke the silence, stammering as she spoke. "J-just wondering how you learned to fight like that. There's got to be more to it than your book."

He laughed. "I've been getting into scuffles my whole life, from primary school through university. I had enough good sense to not throw the first punch, though I always threw the last."

"I see." Laoise nodded. "So you've always been intolerable?"

He smirked. "Some are better at handling me than others."

Laoise blushed. She didn't have long to contemplate how well she had "handled" Bertram before the announcer stepped back into the ring.

"Ladies and gentlemen, it's the moment you've all been waiting for!"

The crowd parted as the next opponent made his way up to the side of the ring. The man was slightly shorter than Bertram, and his thick beard and brushed back hair were tidy, but unremarkable. His plain undershirt and trousers made him all the more forgettable. He might as well have been just another face in the crowd. Yet there could be no mistaking who it was, and Laoise's stomach fluttered with excitement. If there were any doubt about the man's identity, the chanting of the crowd put it to rest.

"Frank! Frank! Frank!"

"The famous Tank Engine Frank at last." Bertram rolled his shoulders. "Not much to look at, is he?"

"You mustn't underestimate him. Frank is an undefeated champion."

"He's never faced me," said Bertram, a cocksure smile on his face. "Still, a little luck can't hurt."

Suddenly, he grabbed Laoise by the waist and dipped her. "What are you doing?" She asked in a hushed whisper.

"Playing the villain." While she was still stunned, he leaned in and planted a kiss on her lips in full view of the crowd. In that moment, she didn't hear the outraged cries of the pub goers. All she could feel were Bertram's firm, strong muscles and his soft lips as she wrapped her arms around his shoulders and kissed him back.

Her head swam, briefly forgetting that she was supposed to be playing the role of a damsel being accosted by the fiendish Toff. Finally, he broke the kiss and allowed her to straighten up. As he preened for the crowd, she delivered a slap across his cheek, but with less force than the one she'd given Danny. A bright pink mark appeared on his cheek.

The crowd erupted in cheering, loud enough to drown out Bertram as he spoke. "Go now. Bet it all on me. I promise I won't lose." He rubbed his cheek. "Despite your little love tap."

"Good luck." She whispered before stepping back and weaving her way through the crowd. She rushed over to the bookie to make her last bet. After pulling out her money and counting it, Laoise paused. She'd already made enough to cover her own ticket back to London. For a brief moment she considered slipping out of the pub and making for the train station. Martin could get her the money she needed, couldn't he? All without all the trouble his cousin had put her through.

She shook her head. Bertram was out there fighting for her sake, and she wasn't going to let him down. With a deep breath, she placed her bet and made her way back to the circle just in time for the start of the first round.

The fight started slow, Frank testing the waters with a few quick jabs while Bertram took more time to regain his strength. Then the fight began to pick up steam.

Bertram had been able to easily dodge the wild punches of his first two opponents, but Frank's quick, controlled strikes caught him off guard more than once. Bertram blocked a punch and countered. The strike glanced off Frank's shoulder as he leaned back. Neither of them landed a clean blow as they kept circling one another, and at the end of the first round, neither had a clear advantage.

The second round was much like the first, a brutal dance between the two pugilists. Punch. Block. Punch. Bertram held his own, finally landing a solid strike to Frank's side. The man adjusted his guard, seemingly unfazed by the blow. The tension amplified the longer the battle went on, and the crowd erupted in cheers and insults.

"Run him right over, Frank!"

"Send him back to his mansion in pieces!"

"Frank! Frank!" a man called out from the crowd, more shrill and panicked than the other hecklers. "Train leaves in twenty!"

Frank looked to the source of the panicked voice, and Bertram capitalized on his momentary break in focus, lashing out with a flurry of blows. A hook slipped under Frank's guard and struck him hard in the stomach. Frank fell to one knee, wheezing.

"Hurry up, Frank!" called the voice once more.

This time Bertram turned and scanned the crowd, searching for the source of the complaints. "You can have him when I'm done with him!" He yelled to the mystery man, brushing his hair back and showing off for the crowd before turning to face his opponent.

Frank however, was no longer kneeling, and had taken full advantage of Bertram's distraction. He threw a quick shot to his opponent's gut, making him drop his guard, and followed up with an uppercut to his chin. Bertram's glamoured mustache flew high into the air as he stumbled back and fell to the floor in a heap

"He knocked his mustache clean off!" The announcer yelled, ringing the bell as it floated to the ground. The crowd went wild. Several people chased the mustache as it drifted across the floor and got lost among the crush of boots.

Laoise rushed to Bertram's side. He groaned as he rose onto his hands and knees. Frank on the other hand, had already stepped out of the ring and made for the door, walking swiftly with cold, rigid determination. A man walking next to him in a dusty suit, most likely the source of the panicked voice, handed him a stack of clothes as they walked out of the pub.

"Are you alright?"

"No." He rubbed his jaw. Dark bruises were already sprouting along his arms. His gaze gave him the haunted look of a man who'd seen his life flash before his eyes.

"Your lip is bleeding. And we need to get going. You heard the man. The train is leaving in twenty."

"No. You go." He shook his head with another groan, refusing to meet her eyes. He spoke, his soft voice morose. "I'm sorry I lost your winnings, but my prize money should be enough to cover a ticket for you."

"But—" Laoise started before Bertram interrupted her.

"No. I don't care how you feel about charity. Just take the ticket and go talk to Martin. He'll pay you everything you're owed and your brother will be safe." He rubbed his left shoulder. "I'll find my own way."

"Bertram..." There was a long silence as she helped him to his feet. Once he was up, she clapped a hand on his shoulder, ignoring his wince. "Stop bein' so damned dramatic. You're coming with me."

He cast her a confused look, his bruised face making him look even more bewildered. "But I lost. We can't possibly afford two tickets."

"You surely did lose." She patted his arm, earning another wince. "Oops. Sorry. Luckily for you, I bet on Frank. Now let's go catch our train."

His mouth opened as he stared at her. "You bet on Frank?" he asked with a mix of sadness and outrage. He rubbed at a bruise on his shoulder.

She didn't let the puppy eyes make her feel guilty. "I told you he's never been beaten." She pushed him toward the organizer's desk to collect their winnings. He mumbled something about feeling betrayed, but his words got lost beneath the hoots of the crowd celebrating another Frank victory. "Time to get a move on. The train leaves soon."

Chapter 16

By the time Laoise reached the ticket counter, she was the last one buying tickets. She bought two, just in case Bertram made it. He'd been too busy fussing about overpaying to have Bess taken care of when she sprinted into the station. He was free to dote on his horse all he wanted, but she wouldn't risk missing the train.

"Better hurry, miss," the man warned her as he handed two tickets over. "The train leaves in five minutes."

"I'll run."

His attention landed on something behind her. His eyebrows shot up in alarm. "Sir, are you alright?"

Bertram stood behind her, huffing and puffing. His bruises were becoming more obvious by the minute as they darkened. Paired with his outfit, which spoke of impeccable tailoring and an expensive taste in fashionable suits, he gave off the look of a rich man who'd just been mugged.

"Just a fall. A trip and fall," Bertram said curtly. "Not as bad as the other man."

The ticket seller's face wrinkled in bewilderment. "Another man fell?"

"Yes, and not a scratch on him!" Laoise giggled as Bertram harrumphed. "Don't wallow. We made it in time." She shoved his ticket into his hand and then rushed for the train. The platform had already emptied of travelers. Everyone was already on board, except for an elderly lady being helped into a train car by the conductor.

Laoise dashed towards a ticket collector at the door to one of the cars and handed both her and Bertram's tickets over. The man looked them over and frowned.

"Miss, these tickets are for tomorrow."

"What?" Laoise exclaimed, "Well there's been a mistake. I need to be on this train."

The man handed the tickets back and pointed to the ticket counter. "Take it up with him, miss."

"By the time I do all that, the train will have left! Can't you just let us on?"

"Afraid I can't miss. No boarding without a ticket." He stepped into the car. "Now excuse me, we're on a tight schedule."

Bertram hobbled forward and grabbed the man by the lapels, pinning him against the side of the train car. He spat his words through clenched teeth. "It's been a trying day today. Surely, good sir, you can find it in your heart to be a bit more accommodating, can't you?"

The man's voice went shrill as he stammered. "I suggest you unhand me, sir." He waved over to the conductor. A pair of footsteps drew closer behind Laoise. Bertram released the ticket taker and turned around, staring down a very familiar bearded face.

Tank Engine Frank looked equal parts dashing and imposing in his conductor's uniform. At a glance, she never would have guessed him to be such a skilled boxer. And from his spotless cap, vest, and coat, she certainly wouldn't have known that he'd rushed to work from a bout. At long last she knew how he got his moniker.

Bertram and Frank squared up to one another. For a long moment, the two stared each other down. As Bertram balled his hands into fists, it was Frank who finally broke the stalemate.

"You've read your Mendoza." His voice was deep and had an implacable accent.

Bertram nodded, relaxing his hands. "Extensively." Another tense moment passed, the men continuing their stare down.

Frank laughed and patted Bertram on the shoulder. "You look better without the mustache." He nodded to the ticket taker. Without a word, the shrill man took the tickets back from Laoise's hand and punched them.

"Thank you," said Bertram, nodding to the man, "But don't think I'll go easy on you next time."

"I'll look forward to it." With a smile, Frank tipped his hat to Laoise, then turned and walked to the front of the train. Not only had she learned Tank Engine Frank's secret identity, but he'd personally swooped in to save the day. That was a memory worth cherishing.

"Ahem," said the ticket taker. "We're running behind schedule. All aboard!"

The two climbed onto the train. Laoise turned one last time to see Frank climb onto the engine. Bertram nudged her. "You were staring," he hissed.

"It's not my fault he wears his uniform well."

The train whistle blared as they grabbed two empty seats facing each other by the aisle near the back of the car.

"When all of this is finished, I'm going to have that rematch," Bertram grumbled as he took his seat.

"Oh don't feel bad. Frank boxes all over the country and they say he's never been beaten. You can take pride in having landed any hits at all." She'd seen him fight a few times, each one a convincing victory. There was something enchanting about the way he'd pick apart his opponents. Or maybe it was just seeing his thick powerful forearms in action that made her swoon. Only Charlotte's Da's strong dough-kneading arms could rival them.

The woman in the seats in front of them glared at Bertram. She gathered up her three children. "Come now, let's move away from the rough man." She took the children to the last empty seats near the front of the car.

Bertram puffed out his chest. "Did you hear that? I'm a rough man. A real fighter."

"Don't be getting a swelled head now. The rest of you is swollen enough as is." She pulled out a handkerchief and dabbed at his bloody lip. He winced in pain as she brushed the bruise on his jaw.

"Stop that. I'm fine." Bertram flushed. "And I would have defeated him if I'd had breakfast. I've been sluggish all day. "

"Does your jaw hurt?"

"Of course it does." He pushed her hand away.

"You handled yourself pretty well, breakfast or no." She pocketed her handkerchief. "So why did you end up getting into so many fights growing up? I wouldn't have taken you for the type."

Bertram gazed out the window as the train left the station. "I didn't set out to be a fighter, but throughout my schooling, those from noble backgrounds looked down on the sons of business and tradesmen. My family's reputation didn't lesson their scorn any. They would insult me and my family every chance they got." A sly smile crept at the corner of his lips. "That was until I learned how to throw a punch. They never learned how to take one, but they did learn to keep their mouths shut."

After watching him fight, she believed every word. He'd fought with the patience and precision that came from experience. Just like after their fight back at the manor... No. She needed to stop thinking about that rendezvous.

"If you hate the nobility so much, why'd you want to get Martin and your sisters married off to them?"

"In a word, spite." He shifted in his seat as he settled in. "They've looked down on my family my whole life, so I relish any opportunity to humble them. I attend every ball invitation I receive just to watch them squirm when I arrive. It's even better when they want to do business with Steepe Shipping and have to come groveling, pretending to like me."

She nodded, immediately picturing of a few uppity nobles she'd served who she would enjoy to see humbled. If they knew all the dirty secrets she'd overheard, they'd be terrified of the maid they thought beneath them. There were multiple affairs, secret mistresses, and one woman who ruined an engagement with lies in order to marry her own daughter off to a wealthy gentleman.

All the snide remarks and poor treatment made it tempting somedays, but she'd never be able to find work again. Then there were the men who she feared would retaliate with violence to protect their false reputations. The maids were always whispering about which men to avoid. Which ones liked to get handsy with the servants and which ones had tempers. "I don't know whether to be impressed by your dedication, or tell you to find a new hobby."

"It's not all because of spite. I thought getting a step up would help Martin and my sisters. They all needed good matches and moving up would bring the family new opportunities. That way they wouldn't be looked down on, and they certainly wouldn't need to take up boxing." He chuckled, and turned from the window to look back at Laoise.

"What about you? I imagine you got into plenty of fights in your school days."

"No. I don't remember much from back then other than struggling to get my numbers right. I went into service as a maid by the time I was thirteen."

He gaped at her, horror written across his features. "Why so young? You should have had more schooling."

"I needed to help support my family. At least I can read and write. Plenty of maids can't." She was embarrassingly slow at reading, unlike Charlotte. Her work left her with little free time, and what time she did have was spent with family and friends rather than with books. Her heart ached with longing at the thought of seeing her family soon.

He shook his head. "A waste. With a mind and mouth like yours you'd make the scariest solicitor in all of London."

She shrugged, turning her head away to hide her smile at the compliment. Her smile faded as she considered that he might have been right. If things had been different, maybe she would have a more fulfilling career. Or at least a better paying one. But luxuries like education weren't meant for her class. She was already lucky to have gotten as much as she did before she had to go into service.

"I don't know about being a solicitor," she started as she considered a life spent serving no one but herself, "but if I had my way I'd be like Frank."

"You have an unhealthy obsession with that man," Bertram scoffed, shaking his head. "His form was sloppy too. You know boxing. Surely you saw it."

She giggled. "Oh I don't care about how well he boxes. It's more about how free he is. He gets to travel all over England, gettin' into brawls in front of cheering crowds. Big cities, small villages, the moors, the sea..." She trailed off. A wave of desolation rushed through her chest, filling every crack and crevice too fast for her to stop it. Her voice trembled. "I might never even see the sea."

As a child, Laoise had dreamed of traveling the world. That dream had always seemed so impossibly out of reach that it never bothered her. It was just something you read about in tales of swashbuckling adventures, nothing at all like reality. But now Charlotte, her childhood friend, the girl she'd known and confided in her whole life, was living that dream. When she'd heard Charlotte went to the seaside for her honeymoon, Laoise was consumed with jealousy. Thinking about a beautiful life just out of her grasp did nothing but threaten to drown her in sorrow.

"Oh please. You saw how quickly he dashed out of that pub when the train was leaving. You really think he's enjoying a carefree life of travel?" He patted Laoise's arm. "You can dream a little bigger than Tank Engine Frank."

"Did I hear you say Tank Engine Frank?" A man two rows up called as he twisted around to look back at them. "I fought him once."

Bertram's lips pressed into an angry, thin line at the interruption.

"Did you win?" Laoise asked.

"'Course I did, lass." He puffed up in his chair, the uneven whiskers on his face quivering. "The fight lasted ten minutes and by the end of it, the skies opened up on us with the fattest raindrops you've ever seen." He made an O with his thumb and index finger.

In the same row across the aisle, a man snorted from the window seat. His flat cap was pulled low as if he'd planned to sleep. He pushed the cap up. "No you didn't. I saw that fight. You went down like a sack of bricks as soon as Frank landed his second punch."

The man's expression soured. "The lass didn't ask you, Greg." He emphasized the man's name.

"She didn't ask for you to make up stories either, Eugene." Greg gave Eugene's name the same hissing emphasis he'd given him.

"Is it always like this in the public train compartments?" Bertram whispered.

"Yes. Talking is a good way to pass the time."

Bertram shuddered. "How awful. I'd rather sleep."

The two men bickered as Laoise pulled out a book from her bag. It'd been waiting in her apron pocket and then her bedside table until today. Laoise had no idea of what it was about, but anything had to be better than reading about a man obsessed with a whale. She didn't understand the appeal.

"What is that you're reading?" Bertram stiffened.

"*Rookwood* by some fella named Ainsworth. Have you read it?"

"I would never read such drivel." He looked toward the window, keeping his gaze away from her.

"That's odd, considering your name is written on the inside." She smiled as she read the note written on the back of the front cover. "'To

Ber-Tea from Mar-Tea. I hope you enjoy the story!' A present I take it? I hope you gave him one back."

"Of course I did. It was Christmas." His gaze went distant as he lost himself to the memory. "That was the year we were most worried about his health. I bought him some sort of new tea I'd found. It's really quite strange. He could barely even walk, but I'd never seen him smile as brightly as when he opened his presents that year." His mouth twitched as though he were holding in a smile.

"I would never expect you of all people to encourage him with tea. I thought you said tea was a waste of his talents."

"It is," quipped Bertram, "but back then tea comforted him. Who was I to deny him that comfort? Least of all at Christmas time."

"And Martin still managed to buy you something even when he was that sick?"

He nodded. "More accurately, his mother bought the gifts, but it was always Martin who picked them out. Usually a book he'd read that he thought we would like. Either that or some little magical contraption he'd put together."

"Was he right? Did you like the book he picked out for you?" Laoise prodded, relishing the opportunity to learn more about a young Bertram. "Or did you even bother to read it?"

He hesitated. "It would have been rude not to read it."

"So you did like it!" she teased, "and you kept it all this time. Then I'm certain I'll enjoy it as well."

Bertram's face heated. "I never gave you permission to borrow my book." He tried to snatch the book away from her, but she held tight. His eagerness to take his book back made her all the more determined to read it.

"Why are you embarrassed? It's just a book." An odd reaction, she thought, but the truth dawned on her as she turned to the title page. "It's a romance, isn't it?" Surely enough, under the title were the words "A romance." She grinned as his blush deepened. "How wonderful. I had no idea you were such a romantic!"

"It is far more than a simple romance. There is drama too. And action." Their tug of war continued, neither making any progress.

"You men always act ashamed about liking romance. It's popular for good reason. Everyone likes to feel loved." Their fingers touched as they both tugged at the book, each pull weaker than the last. "What kind of romance is it? Is there a lot of kissing?"

He let out a heavy sigh. "I have read that the genre is called gothic romance. Hardly a fitting description, since it's dark and brooding, and I assure you the romance is quite forgettable. A man who wants to force a woman who loves someone else into marriage? Unsympathetic. And I didn't care about who would inherit Rookwood Place in the end either. The only character worth reading about is Dick Turpin. That book made me want more stories about him."

"The highwayman?" Laoise had heard of Dick Turpin in passing, much the same way she'd heard of Robin Hood. She knew he robbed the wealthy at gunpoint, commanding them to stand and deliver, but she didn't know much beyond that.

Their tugging had stopped, but they still held the book between them, fingers pressed together. He held her gaze. Her heart sped up as he lazily brushed his index finger over hers. The train suddenly felt far warmer.

He cleared his throat. "He's the most memorable character. I'd even go as far as to say he made the book. Plenty of writers have written about highwaymen since, but *Rookwood* started the craze."

She swallowed, taking a second to get a hold of herself. "I didn't know about any of that. As much as I like reading, I rarely have the time for it." And during the rare times she did, she often found herself reading aloud so that the maids who didn't know how to read got to enjoy the stories as well.

His mouth pursed as if he'd tasted a lemon, and he finally let go of the book. "I suppose I have kept you a bit busier than usual these last few weeks."

Laoise smiled. "Is this your way of apologizing?"

His mouth pursed further at the words.

"Well then thank you, sir. I look forward to reading about Dick Turpin." She shook the book. "And the romance. I bet that's your favorite part."

Bertram opened his mouth to protest, but Eugene chimed in to interrupt him.

"Did you say Dick Turpin?" the man asked. "Why my grandfather was held up by him once. Barely escaped with his life he did!"

"Escaped with his life?" Greg laughed, slapping his knee for effect. "I'll tell ya what really happened. That old drunk got scared by a cow stumbling home one night, then he tossed his money at the beast and ran!"

"And how did you hear that story, hmm?" Eugene's hand slapped the back of his seat. "From your old liar of a grandfather?"

Greg snorted. "You don't get to call anyone a liar. No one's a bigger liar than you, Eugene. Or a bigger drunk."

"You're sour because I cleaned you out playing cards last week. Get over it before the next game."

"I only lost because you cheated."

"I did not."

Their bickering continued as Bertram slid down in his seat. "Next time, I want a private compartment. Better yet a whole private car."

"Ha! And I want a month-long vacation." He had a far better chance of getting his wish than she did hers. She didn't doubt that he always bought a private compartment. Even buying a whole private car didn't seem like much of an exaggeration.

"Doesn't this drive you mad?" He whispered, gesturing to Eugene.

"No. I've lived most of my life serving the well-to-do. They'll treat you like you're invisible until they want something. " And when they did want something, they were rude and treated her as though her very presence was a nuisance. She knew the sting of people snapping their fingers to get her attention as though she were a dog. The Steepes of course had treated her with some level of respect and decency, Bertram being the exception. But even they left her feeling inadequate. "People like Eugene might be too eager to chat, but at least they'll treat you like a person."

Bertram watched her, but didn't respond. His head tilted as his gaze shifted to the window, lost in thought. His habit of staring off into the distance made it easy for her to tell when he was thinking. She returned to her book, finally getting to open it and read a few pages. Highwaymen and romance. A better choice than hunting whales.

The train slowed and then stopped altogether.

"Now what?" Bertram straightened in his seat.

Laoise held in a groan.

"I'll bet it's those damned magicians causing trouble again," Eugene said. "This'll be the second time in a month they've stopped a train."

"This is why people shouldn't be dabbling about with magic," Greg said as he slid down in his seat and pulled his hat over his face. "It's all dangerous nonsense."

"He isn't wrong," Bertram muttered.

"What do you mean?" Laoise asked, widening her eyes in faux innocence. "Do you believe us poor lowly commoners shouldn't use magic?"

"Not if they aren't trained," Bertram said, falling right into her trap. "For instance, there's a young boy who works at that Graham girl's bakery who—"

"Mrs. Steepe, you mean," Laoise interjected.

"The boy somehow managed to curse himself in a way not even Martin could fix." Bertram said in exasperation. "Magic is dangerous. And not something to be trifled with."

"Baaaah," came a call from outside the windows. They both turned in unison. A sheep floated by the window. Another followed soon after, bouncing off the side of the train before drifting toward a pasture. Both of them needed a trimming. Their thick wool coats made them look spherical.

Bertram held out his hands toward the window. "See. Magic does not need to be wasted on sheep."

"You're right," Laoise said, fighting back a smile. "Commoners don't need magic. We'd just waste it on things like making tea."

Bertram chuckled, and then covered it up with a fake coughing fit.

"Are you all right? Should I get you some water?"

"I'm fine. It's dusty in here is all." He shifted in his seat, crossing one leg over the other. "I never said commoners shouldn't use magic. But those who aren't trained in it shouldn't, no matter their social standing. Like that cursed baker fellow."

"His name is Claude. He's clumsy, but sweet. He didn't curse himself, either. That was his father's mistake. If magic wasn't so well guarded, people wouldn't be fumbling in the dark using it."

"Best not to fumble around with it at all then. Not with something so dangerous." He gestured to the sheep. "Even at its most harmless, little mishaps like this are hard to avoid. And that goes for magicians who actually know what they're doing."

"Baaah," bleated a sheep.

"See? She agrees with me."

Laoise gave him a serious nod. "Indeed. You would know better than anyone, sir. What with all your magic mishaps."

Bertram crossed his arms. "I would most certainly know better than you. If you knew the first thing about magic, perhaps you'd understand what I'm talking about."

Laoise stuck out her chin proudly. "As it turns out, I *do* know a spell. So I do understand."

"Is that so." He scoffed. "Quite convenient that I've never seen you do it before. Perhaps you'll enlighten me about this spell."

"Oh I've used it plenty. It's just not something I prefer to do in public." She winked at him. "I might show you later when we're not in mixed company."

Bertram blinked and then furrowed his brow. "You're positively vulgar."

Outside, a shepherd tossed a rope around one of the floating sheep. Another followed behind, holding four lengths of rope, each one tied to a floating sheep. One sheep strained to reach the grass, its backside bobbing toward the sky. Two other sheep kept bouncing off of one another like marbles, forcing the shepherd to pull them back in. As soon as he did, one sheep would push off the other, causing the struggle all over again.

"I wonder what they were trying to do with the sheep." She didn't understand why a shepherd would want their sheep floating away.

"Trying to get more wool, I imagine."

"How can you tell that?" To Laoise's untrained eye, in regards to both magic and sheep, they appeared no more wooly than a normal sheep, though perhaps a little too round. Nothing else appeared out of the ordinary. Except for the floating, of course.

Bertram reached for a newspaper someone had left behind on a seat. "They are fatter than they should be, as if they tried to increase the amount of wool. Instead they put extra air in the wool, creating sheep balloons."

"You really think that's what happened?"

Bertram shrugged. "Call it an educated guess. Martin would know for certain. He's been studying magic ever since he learned to read. But as you've so kindly pointed out, magic isn't my strong suit. Or sheep really."

Laoise nudged him with her elbow. "Did you admit to not being good at something just now? I didn't know you were capable of admitting to a weakness."

"We all have a weakness. It's only human. Some of us simply have more than others." He nudged her back.

She raised an eyebrow. "And what is that supposed to mean?"

"Take me for instance. My mastery of magic could stand to see some improvement." His smile started to grow. "As for you, there's your cooking. And your temper. There's also your stubbornness, your—"

"Alright, alright." She gave his thigh a quick slap. "Keep it up. I'll show you how bad my temper can get." She scrunched her nose at him. Laoise toyed with a button on her shirt as she glanced back out at the sheep. "How long will this set us back?" The hold up would take them that much longer to reach her brother. He needed medicine. She couldn't shake the feeling that every hour counted. Her leg bounced in impatience.

"Your brother will be fine for a few extra hours," Bertram said. "Read your book and wake me up when we get there." He shifted in his seat, ignoring the bleating sheep as he closed your eyes.

"Aye. I'll read your little romance."

He opened one eye to glare at her, but said nothing.

"Does anyone else smell lard?" Eugene asked. "It's making me hungry."

Bertram closed his eyes and pretended to not hear. A minute later he sniffed his arm, nose wrinkling in disgust.

<h1 style="text-align:center">Chapter 17</h1>

Stretching her legs after the train ride felt good. She'd even made it to Dick Turpin's appearance under the name John Palmer in *Rookwood*. It was an exciting read, but the rest of the book would have to wait. There was no telling when she'd find time to read again.

Beside her, Bertram let out a yawn, his eyes bleary from his long nap. Other travelers streamed around them. As they left the train platform, she craned her neck to get one last peek of Tank Engine Frank as he helped travelers. Her gaze settled on his powerful forearms, perfectly framed by his rolled up shirt sleeves. She hoped if she wound back up on a train in the future, it would be Frank's.

"Stop leering at him."

"I'm not leering. I'm admiring. There's a difference." She turned her attention forward.

"There is a difference, and you're leering."

They left the station, and the bustle of the city felt welcoming and overwhelming all at once. After the quiet of the countryside, the city sounded louder than ever. How had she never noticed all the noise before? Or the foul smells. They made her want to run right back to the manor.

"I'd forgotten how awful the air is in the city," said Bertram, his face scrunching up. "Do we have enough money to pay for a ride to the bank?"

She swallowed down the bile rising in her throat. "Not much left. We'll have to walk." She'd rather save the money for better uses rather than waste it traveling a few blocks.

"Then we'd better get going. It's high time we both put our money woes behind us."

"Thank you," she said, barely loud enough to be heard over the noisy racket of carriages and cabs passing by.

He led the way, turning left at the corner. The bruises on his face sent a few women rushing to stay out of his way. She didn't blame them. The bruises accentuated his grumpiness, giving him the look of a man searching for another fight.

"I regret missing breakfast," he said as they dodged around two men loading crates onto a wagon. "I would even eat your oatmeal."

"I wouldn't," Laoise snorted. "I still haven't figured out how to make it like my Ma does. She makes the best of everything." Her mother's food was always comforting, no matter how simple the meal. Despite all the feasts the Steepe's kitchen churned out, she never stopped craving her mother's cooking. Her stomach growled as a gust of wind kicked soot covered snow into her face. First, she needed to get her brother's medicine, then she'd let herself think about food.

"What are you going to do once we get some money? Are you going to go pick a fight with your uncle for shipping you off to the manor?" Despite working in his house, Montgomery Steepe was always so busy that Laoise didn't see him often. And those few times she did see him, it was because he had appeared behind her as if from thin air, silent and intimidating.

"First," Bertram said as he held up one finger, "I'm going to have something to eat. Then I'm going to meet with Martin."

"Finally going to apologize about the Great Exhibition?"

He scowled at her. "No."

"I see." There was a long pause. "Well it ought to be an interesting reunion."

He offered nothing in response as he continued his march to the bank. She'd have to wait to get the gossip from Charlotte. Her breath hitched at the thought of seeing her friend again. Charlotte had seemed like her old, kind, innocent self when she saw her back at the village, but at the same time Laoise couldn't shake the fear that her marriage would change her. She would become just like the stuck up women Laoise served. Then her friend would be gone.

Bertram swore.

"What is it?" She lifted her head, squinting through the wind at the bank.

"Closed for the day already. Damned bankers' hours."

"Is it really past two already?"

Bertram fumbled around in his pocket. "Must be. The train delay put us behind schedule. If the whole world ran on banker's hours, nothing would ever get done." Bertram patted all of his pockets repeatedly. "Where the hell is it?"

"Where's what sir?"

"My pocket watch!" his search was now frantic, casting his gaze back towards their footprints in the snow. "I swear if one of those blathering old men on the train picked my pocket…"

Laoise held in a chuckle. "You gave it to Roger back at the inn, sir."

"Ah." He grimaced. "Damn. I really liked that one."

"Because it was expensive and fancy?"

He shook his head. "Expensive yes, but fancy no. I bought it from a struggling watchmaker in Cork who lost his wife to the potato famine. I paid three times its price, and it was worth every coin. It's the most reliable thing I've ever had. It gave the time, the date, and the runes rarely ever needed to be touched up. No winding necessary."

"Long way to go for a watch. My condolences for your loss. But what now? Should we go see your cousin?"

Bertram squinted. "What day is it today?"

"It's Thursday. What has that got to do with anything?"

"It seems I've lost track of time more than I realized. This weekend is the Steepe Foundation Charity Ball. It's always the last event the family does before retiring to the countryside manor for the holidays and winter."

"And?" she pressed, not understanding what that had to do with the closed bank. Personally, she'd been glad to miss working the event. Most Steepe events left her dead on her feet, and sometimes in tears depending on how rude the guests were. An event was never a success unless it ended with a maid hiding somewhere to cry.

"And that means I can't go see Martin. I won't be able to avoid Uncle Monty. They'll be preparing the house today, and if my uncle sees me, I'll get sent back to the countryside. He might actually have me shipped off to Italy this time. More importantly, you won't get your advance."

She doubted the amount she'd already sent was enough. She needed that money. "But I don't want to wait another day."

Bertram slapped his hand down on the door beside the closed sign. "Complain to them, not me."

"Do you know of any banks with longer hours?"

He shook his head. "They all have the same schedule."

"Can nothing go right?" She threw up her hands and blew the stray hairs out of her face. With no banker, there was no reason to stay. No use cryin' about it. She'd head for home. It was all she could do. "Then I'll meet you here tomorrow, first thing in the morning. Right when the bank opens."

"Meet you here?" He turned to her, widening his eyes. "I have no money, which means I have no where to stay the night. I'll be homeless." He lifted a hand to his heart, faux innocence painted on his face. "You wouldn't let me sleep on the streets, would you?"

"You're not homeless. You've got a nice big manor to sulk in."

"I don't sulk."

"Fine. To brood in then. And don't you have your own townhouse in the city?"

"I most certainly can't go there." He scrunched his nose in distaste. "It's much too far to walk, and I have no money for a carriage. And even if I made it home, someone would let my presence slip to my uncle by morning. He'll have me on a ship to Italy before nightfall."

She crossed her arms over her chest and made a show of looking him up and down. "I suppose I can find enough good will to help you out this one time." She wouldn't have believed herself a week ago, but she was actually looking forward to spending more time with him. Not that she would admit it to him.

He gave her a mock bow. "I'll be forever indebted to you. At least until I pay you in the morning."

She turned to hide her smile. "Come on then, let's get going. We have a bit of a walk ahead of us."

He groaned. "I did not wear the right boots for all this tromping."

"You said no to a carriage all so you could buy that?" Bertram asked as Laoise stepped out of the butcher's shop, the wrapped chicken cradled against her chest.

"We skipped breakfast. A hearty supper will do us some good."

"That skinny bird will hardly make for a hearty supper. I could have hunted something more substantial than that." He wrinkled his nose.

"I won't force you to eat any. More for me." She grinned.

He cleared his throat and shifted his bag, holding out his hands. "Allow me."

"How gentlemanly," she said as she handed the chicken to him. At least she wouldn't have to carry it the last two blocks. They continued on their way, hesitating outside of Clarke Bakery. Charlotte wouldn't be inside anymore whenever Laoise stopped by, something she already missed. It had always been her favorite place to visit, but it wasn't the same without her best friend.

"What is it?" Bertram glanced at the bakery. His expression soured. "This place. I never understood why Martin invited a baker's daughter to the party in the first place. I'd never heard of the Grahams before."

"He invited damn near every girl in London he had any connection to. As I understand, more young ladies meant the teapot's spell had a better chance of finding someone for him." She gave a sly smile. "And it seems it worked."

Bertram pointed an indignant finger at Laoise. "That's exactly what I'm talking about. He entrusted his future to a bloody teapot! He didn't take time to get to know her before asking her to marry him. He should have at least spent more time with her instead of proposing as soon as they met."

Martin had been quick on the proposal. Like an excited puppy. Or rather an excited dachshund. "An odd start for an engagement, yes, but it went better than his first arranged marriage, didn't it?"

"That Graham girl is every bit as wicked as his first fiancée. I know it." Bertram stepped around a frozen puddle. "Where are we going?"

"To my family's home. We need to take a right at this corner." The manicured storefronts gave way to crowded buildings and narrow alleys.

They crossed the road. Bertram's head swiveled this way and that as he took in the apartment buildings. "I can't remember the last time I went down this road."

"I wouldn't expect you to ever come this way. This road leads to the slums." Laoise's family had been lucky to escape the worst of the slums, but many families weren't. With each new factory that went up, the slums grew larger, the poor overflowing into the streets and alleyways. The owners of the factories called it progress, forgetting about those they sacrificed for their cheap products made with even cheaper labor. She'd only escaped factory work herself by going into service as a maid.

"The doctor we partner with at the Steepe Foundation comes this way all the time." The buildings grew more crowded as they walked. "The very first family we helped was on this road. I'd almost forgotten about that trip." His forehead wrinkled as he considered the memory.

"Magicians like this end of town. They all show up with big ideas on how to solve the hunger and poverty, but they've made little progress." The residents had long grown tired of all the young, starry-eyed magicians wanting to talk to them.

"Some magicians like to claim magic is the answer to everything, but there is still much we don't know about it. Every culture and language has their own magical intricacies. A spell performed in French doesn't always work the same when performed in English, for example."

"I thought it was all just runes."

"Not necessarily. Rune magic is common and allows the most control, but different languages and types of spells might require other spell casting methods. There are no easy answers to things like hunger or bad weather, even with magic."

"The Irish magicians have been focused on fighting the potato famine," Laoise said. Her family got news every few months from distant cousins who'd stayed. "They stopped the blight on the potato crops from spreading over the entire country, but not fast enough to stop the famine. Without magic..." It was a dire thought. Her foot sank into the edges of a snowbank and she yanked it out, shaking the snow off her boot.

"Is that why your family came to England?" His gaze fell on the strands of red hair peeking out of her hood. The color ran in her family, making it difficult to hide their origins. Plenty of places wouldn't hire her family or even rent to them. They saw the Irish immigrants as the cause of England's woes. Blaming them was easier than facing the harsh realities of all the hard issues facing the country.

"Not quite. When I was a little girl, my parents left in search of work. It didn't go as they'd hoped, but by the time they decided to go back, the blight had hit. Then the famine came, and so we stayed here." She pointed at a two-story town house up ahead. "Almost there."

"Good. One more block and my nose might freeze right off my face."

The narrow townhouse was meant for a single family, but between all her siblings and her married brother staying with his wife, the house was full to bursting. It took multiple incomes to afford a townhouse, even one as small as theirs. The house was crowded, but not as crowded as the tenement they used to live in. Even with the cramped quarters, the house always felt cozy when her family was around.

She stopped in front of the brick house. Two window box planters flanked the door, both covered in snow. Come spring, herbs would replace the snow, one of her mother's loves. Her mother's job gave her little time at home, but she always made the best of the time she had.

Laoise sucked in a deep breath, savoring the moment. Nothing beat the warmth of coming home. It was even better than curling up under a warm blanket in front of a fire on a cold winter's night. No matter what was going on elsewhere, there was always plenty of love waiting for her on the other side of the weather worn door.

Beside her, Bertram shifted the chicken. As she reached for the handle, the door swung open. Her mother let go of the door to wipe her hands on her apron.

"Ma!" Laoise set her valise down to wrap her mother in a tight hug.

"Laoise! Don't tell me you walked all the way here." She pulled away to pat Laoise's right cheek. "Look at ye, your cheeks are as red as apples. Come warm up by the fire." Her attention moved to Bertram, and she straightened up. "And who might this be?"

"Good evening, madam. My name is Bert—" Bertram's eyes want wide. He hesitated for a moment, stumbling over his own words. "—ler. The butler."

Laoise's mother raised an eyebrow. "Bertler the butler?"

"John. This is John Bertler. He's the butler. We work together," Laoise added in a rush. Laoise was no stranger to thinking on her feet, but doing so in front of her mother without sounding panicked was a challenge. "He's on his way home for Christmas too, but his lodgings for the night fell through. Think we can find room for him?"

"Pleased to make yer acquaintance, Mr. Bertler." Her mother stepped aside and waved them both in. "Everyone is welcome here. We'll make room for ye somewhere. Get inside before you freeze to death."

"Thank you, Mrs. Hughes." For once, he sounded humbled. Laoise was astonished he knew her last name.

Within minutes they were both sitting in front of the kitchen fire, a warm cup of tea between their cold hands and a slice of Irish soda bread balanced on small plates on their laps. The Steepes only ever had the fanciest and most elegant pastries for their meals. Never fare as simple as soda bread with a thick pad of butter. Her mother always had a loaf she'd made on hand, and in that moment she wouldn't have traded her slice for all the fancy cakes or gateaus or profiteroles in the world.

Bertram frowned at his tea. Thankfully, he kept any complaints to himself, though Laoise didn't doubt he was thinking plenty of them.

"A fat chicken like this? What's the occasion?" asked her mother as she inspected the bird.

"No occasion. I just thought we could have it for dinner."

Her mother nodded. "A grand idea. I'll get it roasting." She turned her back as she got to work at the table.

Bertram sipped his tea, his frown deepening. "This tea is rather strong."

"Steepe's Irish Breakfast blend. It's a bit more bold than what you may be used to," Laoise explained.

"Do you have any sweetener?"

"Your options are milk or whisky."

He grimaced. "I need it less Irish, not more. I'll take the milk."

She fetched it for him. He poured the milk himself, not stopping until his tea was almost white. What an odd sense of taste to favor strong coffee but weak tea.

Laoise winced. "Good thing your cousin isn't here to see that."

They sipped at their tea and nibbled on the bread, Bertram staying silent as Laoise watched her mother work. Unlike Laoise, she wasn't a woman to hesitate in the kitchen. She always knew exactly what she wanted and how to bring out the best of her ingredients.

"Need a hand in there, Ma?" Laoise called out.

Her mother waved a hand dismissively, barely looking up from her work "Not at all, dear."

Laoise's foot tapped impatiently. "Well I can't just sit here and watch you do all the work. Why don't you let me—"

"Laoise Ann Hughes, you stay right where you are. You brought the food and I'll be the one to cook it. I'll not hear another word on the matter."

Her talent as a cook was matched only by how set in her ways she could be. Her father always told Laoise she got her stubbornness from her mother. But how else could either of them make it in a country full of people who turned their noses up at them?

Bertram leaned over and whispered, "Perhaps it's best that you stay out of the kitchen, hmm?"

"Shush," she said, shooting him a dirty look. She turned back to her mother. "How's Sean?"

Her mother paused in her work, before resuming spatchcocking the chicken. Removing the backbone let the chicken lie flat, which shortened the cooking time. Laoise mangled the bird whenever she tried the technique.

"He was better last week, but he's been in bed all day today. I'd hoped the medicine had him on the mend, but lately he's been feeling worse. The doctor thinks he may need a stronger dosage."

"How is the price of the medicine?"

"Too high." She wiped her forehead with the inside of her arm. "At this rate, we won't be able to afford it next time. It'll either be the medicine, or the house."

Laoise's hand tightened on her teacup. Her mother would never deny Sean medicine, but the rising price would put them all back in the slums if they lost the house. Sean was the baby of the family, but besides Laoise, there was still Rian, only fifteen and too young to move out on his own. Callum was two years older than her, but his income alone wouldn't be enough to rent a respectable home for his wife and daughter. Not to mention the filth of the slums wouldn't do Sean's health any favors.

"Well, no use cryin' about it," her mother added, as she always did when things were dire. She then started to smile, as if forgetting the entire conversation up to that point. "The others should be here by dinner. And what a surprise you'll be. Everyone will be so glad to have you back for Christmas."

By the time they gathered around the table to eat over an hour later, Bertram had still barely said a word. Laoise's Ma gave him Sean's spot since the boy was too sick to join them. The table wasn't big enough to fit all of them, so her Da sat on a stool by the fire. Callum joined him.

Rian plopped down across from Bertram. Like Sean, his hair was more strawberry blond than red, a color Laoise used to wish she had as well.

"Did Mr. Steepe give you those bruises?" Rian pointed to his own face, indicating the spots.

"I hear he can be a brute," Laoise said, biting back a smirk. She would let him stay with her family. But she wouldn't take it easy on him.

"If he is beatin' his servants, you shouldn't be working for his family," Rian said, frowning.

Bertram set his cup down too hard. "He didn't beat me."

"Then what did happen?"

"I fell while carrying a bag of..." His mind came up blank. "Teapots."

"Teapots?" Rian's suspicion deepened. He tilted his head as he watched Bertram.

Laoise attempted her own look of concern, but had to use her hand to cover her smile.

"For his cousin."

"Why were the teapots in a bag?"

"I meant box. The bag was in a box with the teapots in the bag. In the box." He gestured wildly as he fumbled his way through his lie. "I tripped and couldn't catch my balance with all the weight."

Rian squinted one eye, mulling over whether to believe him. "Aye, I suppose you'd have to have a lot of teapots to run a tea company."

"Mr. Bertler here is just being modest," Laoise said, bumping her shoulder into his. "Tank Engine Frank gave him those bruises. Frank knocked him right down."

"Him? Fighting Frank?" Rian laughed. "The bag of teapots was more believable."

Bertram squirmed in his seat as Mrs. Hughes pulled the chicken out of the oven. Dinner was nothing but hard leftover rolls, chicken, and potatoes mashed with kale. Simple fare, far simpler than what was usually served at any of the Steepe households. The family said grace and started passing food around.

Callum chimed in. "If that Steepe fella does try to smack you around again, just give him a swift punch to the jaw. I doubt the ol' toff could handle it."

"Now, now," Mrs. Hughes said as she sat the chicken down on the table. "I'll hear no ill spoken of the Steepes. Not even of that spoiled one that got sent off to rot in the countryside."

Bertram shot Laoise a look. She pretended not to notice.

"Aye indeed," her father chimed in. "They gave Laoise decent work, and when the blight hit that Steepe Foundation even donated food to the people. I saw for myself that their ships refused to take any food out of Ireland."

"I never heard this story," Callum's wife chimed in, elbowing her husband. "Is that true?"

Laoise's father nodded. "Every word of it. I was loading a Steepe ship in Cork when the captain ordered a whole shipment of potatoes be left at the docks because they were 'unfit for the English market.' I inspected the crates myself. There wasn't anything wrong with them. The clever devil knew exactly what he was doin'."

"I remember seein' that man when your ship came back in. Awfully young fella for a captain. Handsome too. Very strong jawline," said Laoise's mother, looking Bertram up and down and smiling. "A bit like Mr. Bertler here."

"A bit." Laoise's father stared daggers at his wife. "Tough to say with all the bruises Mr. Steepe left on our guest."

"I wasn't beaten by Mr. Steepe I assure you." Bertram cleared his throat. "Besides, one typically gets sacked for tussling with one's employer." A smile crept at the corner of his mouth as Laoise shot him another dirty look. She felt her cheeks flush as she remembered the last time she and her employer had "tussled."

"Can't get sacked. Then you couldn't work as a butler." Rian nodded, unable to take his attention away from Bertram. "Are you from a family of butlers?"

"Excuse me?" Bertram looked up from the chicken Laoise's mother had served him.

"Your last name is Bertler. Is that because you come from a long line of butlers?"

"It does sound a bit like fate," Callum's wife added.

"That's not why our last name is Bertler. It's just a coincidence." Bertram waved his fork, eager to get the topic away from himself. "This is nice tableware that you have."

Rian puffed up, pleased with the compliment. "I fixed 'em all up myself. They were an old set. Mrs. Hammond got rid of 'em when Laoise was still working for her. I got rid of the rust and dents."

"You're a tinker?"

"For now. Callum is teaching me how to repair the machinery in factories so I can work alongside him someday."

"It's fine work." Bertram took a small bite of the potato and kale mash. Laoise recognized it as the same cautious way he ate her cooking back at the manor. No doubt the humble meal was not up to his high-class standards, but she doubted even he would criticize the food on such an empty stomach. To her surprise, he did more than take a few polite bites, instead practically shoveling the food into his mouth.

Laoise took a bite herself and was overwhelmed by the flavor. Despite the simple ingredients, it tasted like the best home cooked meal she'd had in a long time. Unlike the burnt goods she'd been making at the manor for the past few weeks, the perfectly seasoned fluffy potatoes melted on her tongue.

"This is amazing. After eating your daughter's cooking I didn't expect such a flavorful meal."

Mrs. Hughes smiled. "Our Laoise has many talents, but cooking was never one of them. I knew she'd never work as a cook like me."

Rian turned his attention back to Bertram, his gaze full of suspicion as his brow wrinkled. "Why are you eating Laoise's cooking? Are you two a-courting?"

Laoise smiled in delight at the question and leaned against Bertram's shoulder. "Not officially. I'm still waiting for him to ask."

Bertram's eyes widened. His water went down the wrong pipe, sending him into a coughing fit. In mirrored images of each other, Callum and Mr. Hughes stopped eating to assess Bertram.

"Oh! This must be that dashing butler you were telling us about!" Mrs. Hughes clapped her hands together. "Finally brought him home after all this time, did you?"

She coughed as the large bite of potatoes struggled to go down her throat. Laoise held up her hands. "Different butler, Ma! Different butler!"

Bertram smirked, seeming to relish making Laoise squirm for a change. "A different butler? You know I'm the only butler at the manor. To whom else could you be referring?"

Laoise couldn't think quickly enough on her feet. She shoved a large bite of potatoes into her mouth while she tried to avoid everyone's gaze.

"No need to be embarrassed, dear," Mrs. Hughes said. "Why I used to go to the docks for weeks to watch your father before getting the courage to talk to him."

"Well if you're not a-courtin' yet, then when are you gonna ask her?" Rian demanded around his own mouthful of potatoes, his eyes narrowed.

"I'll ask once I'm sure she'll say yes."

"John." Laoise rested a hand on his arm and smiled. "In that case, I have an important question for you."

"Yes?" He tensed. Laoise drew the moment out as the rest of the table watched the two of them in silent anticipation.

"Can you pass me the butter on your left?"

Rian groaned.

He passed the butter as the conversation turned to the latest snow storm. Laoise patted his knee, but it didn't calm his tension any. Bertram for his part remained charmingly polite throughout dinner, as though he were a completely different person. And in a way, he was. She much preferred dining with John Bertler than with Bertram Steepe.

Chapter 18

L aoise shook herself awake. A kink in her neck ached from falling asleep in the hard wooden chair. She shifted, the chair creaking beneath her as she stretched, trying to work out the aches. She would be sore all day after this.

Beside her, Sean slept soundly in bed. He looked too small when he was sick with the way he curled up. It always hurt to see him this way. On his healthy days he was full of energy. The days he was sick made him a shell of himself.

Seeing him like this made her ashamed that she'd wanted to quit. It'd been a selfish decision when the extra money would help with his care. She should never have risked losing that security, except she'd let her emotions get the best of her. She brushed a stray lock of hair out of his face, and then wiped the cold sweat off his forehead with a clean washcloth.

A gentle knock on the doorframe made her jump. She turned, clutching at her heart.

"Didn't mean to scare you," Bertram said. "Do you want to switch places? I can keep an eye on him while you get some sleep."

She chewed on her bottom lip. The thought of sleep somewhere that wasn't a chair was tempting, but to leave Bertram with Sean? After how helpless he'd been at the manor, she didn't trust him to be capable enough to look after her brother.

As if reading her thoughts, he added, "I used to sit with Martin at night when he was sick. This isn't new to me. Besides, I actually managed to get some rest on the train. You look about ready to fall out of your chair."

In truth, she didn't know how she hadn't fallen out already. She'd always been one to roll about in her sleep. Plus, Sean was fast asleep. He'd be fine until morning. "A few hours can't hurt." She stood and rolled her shoulders, working out the last of the kinks. "I've been wondering how you knew our last name. I never told you."

"No, but you work for Martin, and until recently you worked for me too. I make it a point of knowing the name of everyone who works under my roof."

"I suppose the makes one of you." She clamped a hand over her mouth to hold in her laugh. A snort escaped her.

"I checked into you a few months back," he admitted as he leaned against the doorframe. "Martin mentioned the redhead maid being his favorite. After I looked into your background. I feared his favoritism meant future problems ahead. I was afraid he'd get tangled up in a romance with a seductress eager to take advantage of his naivety."

Martin was always polite, but to be his favorite maid? It sounded like a stretch. "He's always been a perfect gentleman to me. I clean his study and make sure not to move anything. And I serve him his tea when the butler isn't about to do it. He likes the way I arrange his tea trays and I've learned how he takes all his favorites. That's the extent of our relationship. Plus he still calls me Shannon."

"It never hurts to be too careful. I don't doubt that a pretty girl with a little knowledge of tea would be able to take full advantage of his...eccentric personality." He crossed his arms and looked towards the window. "Like a certain person I won't name."

"You say that like you haven't seen him in a business meeting. He warms everyone up with tea, and then he is ruthless in negotiations. If I tried to take advantage of him, he'd see right through me." She slid past him, her side brushing against him in the small space. "Give your cousin more credit." She yawned as she stumbled out of the room.

"Wait," he said, grabbing her hand. Realizing what he'd done, he let go of her and moved away a step. "At dinner, your mother mentioned how you used to erm...carry a bit of a torch for Martin's butler." He shifted in the small space. "Did you two...?"

She groaned. Of course her mother had to bring up that old mistake. "No. We did not. I don't want to talk about that man or his odd fixation on being able to see himself in the silverware." Thank goodness he never caught onto the extra attention she used to show him, hoping to receive some in kind. Working for him and his impossibly high standards would douse any flame.

She glanced back at Sean. "Are you sure you'll be alright watching him?"

"We'll be fine." He settled onto the chair. "I'll take good care of him."

"Thank you, Mr. Bertler." She smiled, her eyes already drooping. "And I'm sorry about letting you get hit by...by the bag of teapots."

"Box of teapots," he said with a chuckle. "Now go get some sleep."

Laoise rubbed the crusty bits of sleep from her eyes. Another two hours of rest would have been nice. Or four. She would never dare sleep in with Bertram in her house. His voice drifted from Sean's room. She figured she should check on them first to make sure he wasn't causing trouble for her little brother. No doubt he'd end up complaining to poor Sean about the lack of luxuries in his lodgings.

"...and BAM! Just in that one moment when I was distracted, he caught me right on the chin with an uppercut," Bertram said, miming the punch while Sean gawked at him. "He punched me hard enough to knock my mustache off."

"Wow," Sean said, entranced by the story. "Did it hurt?"

"No, not a bit." he said, puffing out his chest. "And if it weren't for that little distraction, I would have won too."

"Nuh-uh." Sean shook his head. "You couldn't have beat Frank, could you?"

"Yes I could! His punches didn't hurt at all. In fact...and don't tell your sister this, but..." He glanced side to side, then he leaned in and added in a hushed voice, "It hurt way more when she slapped me."

Laoise knocked on the door frame, making Bertram jump. "What's that you're not supposed to be tellin' me, Sean?"

"Nothin'." Sean let out a giggle. "Nothin' at all!"

Laoise put her hands on her hips. "Well if you're done talkin' about nothin', then it's time for breakfast. Mr Bertler here had better eat fast before the bank closes."

"Right you are." Bertram stood up and turned to Sean. "Remember. Mum's the word." He held a finger to his lips and shot Sean a wink, and the boy returned the gesture.

Her mother had made porridge for breakfast. It was leagues above her own, dressed up with an apple and a touch of cinnamon. Bertram gave her mother nothing but praise as they finished and headed out into the cold. She'd expected plenty of grumbling and complaints from him, not polite smiles and compliments.

Worse, her mother gave her a look as Laoise put on her boots. A look that said they'd be discussing the butler she'd brought home on her return. She'd have no choice but to tell her mother the truth unless she wanted to be badgered about courting him.

"They can't be closed this time," Bertram said as they headed for the bank. "We'll not even be an hour past opening." Nervous energy radiated off him.

"I wouldn't be too sure. Bankers haven't come through for us yet." She stifled a yawn. The frigid morning air made her want to climb back into her warm bed with a pile of blankets on top.

"Third time's a charm, as they say." Bertram cleared his throat. "By the way Laoise, thank you. For inviting me to stay the night."

Laoise was dumbfounded. "You're never this polite. It's a refreshing change of pace, but it's a bit unsettling coming from you."

"I'm always polite." Bertram huffed. "So. Did your family like me?"

"Why are you worried about that?" She watched him closely and the way his fingers twitched. He refused to make eye contact. She was surprised he'd care about what her family thought. People like them were beneath him. Weren't they?

"I want to make sure I didn't overstay my welcome."

"They liked you just fine. They all agree it's a shame about Mr. Steepe beating you is all."

"I don't beat anyone!" His raised voice earned them a stare from a passing couple. Splotches of red climbed Bertram's neck.

"Especially not Frank." She cackled. "A bag of teapots, though? Was that the best you could think of?"

"In all fairness, a box of bags of teapots isn't too far from the truth with Martin." His pace quickened as the bank came into view. "Besides, I couldn't tell your mother and father that I was in a boxing match yesterday. They'd think me some sort of ruffian."

"Oh Ma wouldn't think any less of you. Hell, Da would probably like ya more if he knew it really was Frank who gave you that shiner."

"First impressions count, you know."

"I know for certain your first impression was a good one."

"I see. Did you hear something this morning from your family?"

"I'm not talking about last night. I meant your first impression."

"What do you mean?" Bertram raised an eyebrow.

Laoise gave a knowing smile. "I mean about a certain handsome-faced young ship's captain for the Steepe Company who docked in Cork. The same city where you just so happened to have bought your fancy watch from."

"I've no idea what you mean by that." He quickened his pace, and as they turned the street corner he waved at the bank ahead of them, letting out a heavy sigh of relief. "Here we are. It won't take but a few minutes for me to get you your pay."

"And then we can be done with this little adventure." She tried and failed to ignore the lump sitting in her throat. She'd been dying to escape him at the manor ever since she arrived. However, their trip together had almost been fun at times. They'd gotten lost on the sleigh ride, battled the rats at the inn, and gambled and won at the boxing match. And they'd done it all together.

Maybe it was the reunion with her family after such a long time, but dining at the same table with Bertram had filled her heart with a sense of warmth and comfort she hadn't known since childhood. Even more so when she saw the way Sean's eyes had sparkled looking up at Bertram as he recounted his stories to the boy.

Part of her wanted this "little adventure" to become a great big adventure like the ones she'd read about in books and penny bloods. But a greater part of her wanted to see Sean up and out of his bed, running around and playing as he used to, and with the money she was about to receive, it didn't seem like such a wild fantasy. At least her adventure would have a happy ending.

Bertram reached for the door, but as he did it flew open, forcing them both to step back.

A dark and imposing figure stood over them at the top step, appearing as if from thin air. Martin's father. Bertram's uncle. None other than the elusive Montgomery Steepe himself stepped forward, two men following him. One of the men was his valet, who seemed to constantly be plucking a fresh fallen hair, dust, or some other blemish off his employer's left shoulder. The other was Roger, the same private detective who had followed them back at the inn.

"Bertram." Disappointment punctuated his name like a lance. "I had thought I had made myself very clear that you were to stay out of the city."

Out of all the Steepe men, Bertram's uncle intimidated Laoise the most. Perhaps it was the way he chose his words with care in that stern voice of his, the way his wide shoulders made his frame look large and imposing despite being shorter than Bertram, or the fact that she'd never seen him smile. It was hard to believe he was the same man who'd fathered gentle, sweet Martin. Above all, he wasn't a man Laoise wanted to cross.

Bertram glanced at the man following his uncle. "So you had Roger watching me the whole time, didn't you?"

"Of course I did. Roger's services were the prudent choice to make sure you don't cause any more trouble. He's been keeping an eye on you since I sent you to the countryside. He took the same train you took to London and guessed you would show up at the bank first thing this morning. As usual, he was right."

Bertram shot a look of disgust at Roger. "You can't keep your mouth shut, can you, Roger? I should have known better than to expect you to keep a secret."

Roger opened his mouth, but Bertram's uncle cut him off. "I had hoped your stay in the countryside would have given you plenty of time to reflect on your actions at The Great Exhibition. I see now that I was wrong. It's clear to me you cannot be trusted with any degree of freedom or leniency. You can't imagine my disappointment in you."

Roger closed his mouth while Mr. Steepe's valet picked a piece of lint off his master's sleeve.

"How typical of you, uncle." Bertram practically spat the words as he stared down at the man. "I haven't seen so much as a letter from you in months, and the first thing you do is express your disappointment in me? You haven't bothered to ask why I've gone through all the trouble of escaping the manor to come to a bank."

"Frankly, I don't care what bullheaded idea you've gotten into your head to justify coming here." He frowned at Laoise, finally noticing her. "Nor does it matter what lie you've told this young lady to get her to follow you."

She wasn't surprised he didn't recognize her. He spent little time at home, and when he did, he was either locked up in his study or busy hosting a dinner. She'd never known the two men butted heads this much. Their conversations always happened behind closed doors or at Bertram's house. Nevertheless, she couldn't leave until she got her money, no matter how uncomfortable their fighting made her feel. "Please, sir. Let him get the money I'm owed, and we'll be on our way."

The elder Steepe furrowed his brow. "I dread to imagine why you owe this woman money. One of Madame Beaumont's girls, I presume?"

"Don't you dare insult her." Bertram stepped in front of Laoise, blocking her from his uncle's view. "If you would stop and listen for a moment—"

His uncle clicked his tongue. "There isn't time for this nonsense. The charity gala is this weekend, and it requires my full attention."

"I see," sneered Bertram, sarcasm dripping from his words. "Back from your business adventures to put on appearances for the London's social elites I see?"

"How dare you, boy." A crack appeared in Montgomery Steepe's countenance, and outrage began to creep into his words. "What I do, I do for the sake of our family"

"And who's there to care for the family when you're off on your business trips? Where were you when your son got engaged? Twice?" He pushed on. "You weren't even there to handle Dr. Speranza. I had to do it myself."

"I was cleaning up the mess you made. If you had put even a modicum of thought behind your actions, Speranza could have been dealt with in a court of law. Instead you very nearly compromised Martin's future as well as your own. As well as that of our entire family! Have you any idea..." Monty stopped himself and drew a deep breath, regaining his stern composure. "You've embarrassed the family enough already. Don't embarrass yourself any further." He yanked on his gloves and beckoned to someone behind Bertram. During their conversation, neither Bertram nor Laoise had noticed the pair of constables standing behind them. With Roger blocking them from the front, they were surrounded. "Take him away."

"I'm not going back," Bertram said, backing down the stairs and sliding one hand into his coat pocket.

"No. You're not," his uncle said curtly. The constables each laid a hand on Bertram's shoulders. "You'll be sent to jail this time. I'm not going to call in any more favors on your behalf."

"Stop." Bertram pulled a small metallic ball out of his pocket, and Roger froze, his eyes wide. The two constables looked to one another in confusion, but slowly began to match Roger's caution. "You know what this is, don't you? You are going to let me go or I'll set this off."

He took a few steps backward, inching his way towards a narrow alleyway. Bertram gestured for Laoise to stay behind him. Laoise frowned. "What are you doing?"

"Getting us an escape route."

"What are you imbeciles waiting for?" Bertram's uncle asked impatiently. Roger raised a finger and opened his mouth to respond, but was interrupted once more. "I said take him away. Now!"

"I tried warning you back at the inn, Roger." Bertram tossed the ball. It disappeared into the middle of a snow drift. The officers shielded their eyes, and Roger dove away.

Laoise waited for something to happen. Anything at all. A long moment of silence stretched between them. Then a thin plume of smoke drifted out of the snowbank. The tendrils curled up toward the roof of the bank.

"Run," Bertram hissed. He shot down the alleyway.

Laoise followed. "That little bit of smoke is supposed to save us?" Sarcasm dripped from her words.

"It was a bluff!"

"Get up! After them!" Montgomery demanded, punctuating his yells by cracking his cane against the stair. Roger had gotten back on his feet while Bertram's uncle barked orders to the dumbfounded officers.

Suddenly, the snow drift exploded, tossing the men off their feet. Laoise stumbled in surprise. A plume of green fire rose high into the air, reaching the very top of the alleyway and melting the snow on the nearby roofs. The melted snow poured down into the alley, missing the two officers, but completely soaking Roger.

Bertram let out an indecipherable string of curses.

"That was a bluff?" They turned out of the alley, putting the destruction out of sight. "Does your magic ever work right?"

He grunted. "Just run."

"Run where? You never told me where we are going."

"I haven't figured that out yet. First, we need to lose them."

They reached the end of the alleyway. Bertram grabbed her hand to pull her down the next road.

"I thought you paid him off at the inn!"

"Not well enough, it seems. Lost my pocket watch for nothing." He didn't let go of her hand, and she didn't pull away. "Ah, good. We're close."

They stepped out onto a busy road full of pedestrians window shopping about the various shops. Her left foot slid across a patch of ice, sending her tumbling forward. She fell against Bertram's back, and he twisted around in time to catch her before she went all the way down.

"Thanks," she mumbled as she steadied her feet.

"Quickly." He pointed to a coffee house across the street. "In there. We'll hide inside until they've gone."

They settled into an empty table a row away from the windows. The rich smell of coffee permeated the air. Under different circumstances, it might have been an inviting atmosphere. She wished she'd brought along some money to buy a cup to chase away the cold slithering its way beneath all her layers.

"Damn it all," Bertram grumbled. "I didn't expect Uncle to be on to us so quickly."

Laoise huffed. "Not one for discussion, is he?" She had to raise her voice to be heard over all the noise. Too many competing voices made it hard to be heard. Two men near the door were engaged in a heated argument over Prince Albert's plans to use the profits from The Great Exhibition to build museums. "What's the plan now?"

"There is no plan," Bertram whined. "I've lost."

"What? After all we've been through you're giving up?

"I am. My assets have no doubt been frozen, and Uncle will never let me close enough to Martin to speak with him. I can't return to my home or to the manor. I suppose I'll just have to keep running until…" He cast his gaze out the window and trailed off, finally whispering, "I don't know."

"We're not running from this." Laoise gritted her teeth. "That's not good enough. Not for Sean."

"No. We are not running. I am." He sighed and rubbed the bridge of his nose. "You will stay here."

Laoise's jaw hung slack. "I beg your pardon?"

"Uncle is after me, not you. I mean good Lord, you've been working for him all these years and he still thought you were some streetwalker." Bertram snorted. "You can return to Martin and he'll pay you what you've earned. And you can go back to work. No drama. No complications. Just take your money and go."

A cold tingle shot up Laoise's spine. He was absolutely right. There was no reason she needed to run. She could walk straight back to the Steepe household and get more than enough money to cover the cost of the medicine. But to do that she'd need to face Charlotte. To beg for money off of her friend. She shifted uncomfortably at the thought, but she was willing to swallow her pride for Sean's sake. No, there was something more. Something that kept her seated at the table. Her loyalty took her by surprise.

"No. There has to be more to it than that. You're Bertram Steepe. You always have some grand and wicked scheme at work."

"And those grand and wicked schemes have a tendency to blow up in my face. Quite spectacularly might I add." He stood up. "I'm getting a cup of coffee. Would you like one as well?"

"I don't have any money."

"It's my treat. Consider it my way of thanking you for getting me this far." He looked down sheepishly. "And my...apology for not getting you the money I promised you."

"That's very kind, but how are you planning on paying? You don't have money either." She looked up at him and raised an eyebrow. "Are you going to steal coffee?"

"I'm not above it at this point," he said with a shrug. "But they know me here. I'll have them send me the bill by mail."

"They know you?" Laoise turned to the window, watching the end of the alleyway for any sign of their pursuers. Roger appeared with the two constables in tow, his hat and hair looking half frozen. Each step was stiff as though his pants were trying to freeze him in place. "Will they tell your uncle you're here?"

Bertram remained nonchalant. "If they do, then at least I'll have a cup of warm coffee in me before I'm shipped off to prison. Might be my last for a while, so I plan on enjoying it." He headed to the front.

Laoise squinted at a man two tables over reading a penny blood. She recognized the cover from the early drafts Charlotte had sent her. Apparently the first chapters of Calamity in a Coffeepot had released while Laoise had been away at the manor. She smiled, remembering all the years of Charlotte writing and struggling to get herself published. She'd written story after story. It was gratifying to see her finally succeed. It was like seeing a piece of her old friend again. A sweet and innocent piece she'd grown up with, and one she feared wouldn't be around for much longer.

Laoise's blood went cold. What if that piece of Charlotte was truly gone? Sure she had seemed like her old self back in the village, but that was back when Bertram was safely locked away in the manor. Not only had Laoise helped Bertram escape, but she'd brought him right to the Steepes' doorstep. What if Charlotte refused to pay Laoise for dereliction of her duties? Worse, she'd be released from employment. By her own friend, no less. She squeezed her arm. There had to be another way.

Bertram returned with two coffee cups, steaming hot on their saucers. He glanced down at the book as he walked past the man. He was nearly back to the table when he shook his head and doubled back to him, leaning down and scowling at him.

"Barnaby tries to frame Cathy for burglarizing the Great Exhibition, but she outsmarts him using a talking coffee pot. He goes off to jail while she and Marshall get married and live happily ever after," Bertram said in a mocking tone. "Nyeeh."

The man grunted in disgust, and Bertram turned and sat back down at the table, placing a cup of coffee in front of her.

"Just what was that all about?" It was one of the most childish things she'd ever seen him do.

"I'm saving him the trouble of reading through that rubbish." He shook his head. "It was bad enough to see the drafts at the manor, but seeing this drivel get published is salt in the wound."

"Be nice. She's been working hard for years to make it as a writer. She deserves her success." She wrapped her hands around the cup with a sigh. She was ready for winter to be over.

"That's the result of years of hard work? Ha!" He gave a scornful laugh. "Cathy's character is flat and shallow, Marshall is a one-dimensional bumbling oaf, and don't get me started on how awful Barnaby is."

"I'm pretty sure he's supposed to be awful. He is the villain after all." Laoise took a sip of her coffee, feeling a brief moment of contentment as the warmth of the drink made its way through her body.

"Oh please. The man is no mere villain. He's hyperbolically evil." Bertram began counting off Barnaby's crimes on his fingers. "The man stole the ownership rights to an orphanage. Then he stole all the donations meant for the orphans. Then he burned down the orphanage for the insurance money. And on top of it all, he sold the orphans into indentured servitude."

"I believe she drew inspiration from some real villains she encountered in her life," she suggested innocently. "Can't imagine which one though."

"Clearly she didn't draw enough inspiration from real life. To hear her tell it, the man's actions make no sense beyond impeding Cathy. She probably didn't even consider the reasoning behind his actions."

"Of course, sir." Laoise rested her head on her hand. "I'm certain there was a perfectly good reason he burned down the orphanage."

He gave her a withering look, then turned from the window, resting his hand on his cheek to hide his face. Outside, Montgomery Steepe waved his arms this way and that as he spoke to Roger, who looked to be yelling something back. His scarf, soaked from the melted snow, had frozen stiff as he hunched over, making it stick out from his neck like a sail. He lifted his arm, fighting against the rapidly freezing wet fabric of his coat and pointed towards an alleyway. Whatever they were saying, the noise of the coffee house drowned it out.

"Suppose there was a good reason. A reason that compelled him into such wild acts of villainy in service of a greater good. Would anyone even bother to listen to his explanation? Or to even try to understand his motivations?"

Laoise reached out a hand and set it on his. "I'd listen."

His jaw clenched. "Not that it much matters. I doubt there's much hope for his redemption. No doubt he'll just be caught and sent to jail where he'll rot away out of everyone's sight. Yes, that would be 'happily ever after' for all involved, wouldn't it?"

"No it wouldn't." Laoise grabbed a hold of his hand. "There's still plenty of people here who need you. Your sisters. And Martin. And..."

She stopped just short of adding her own name to the list. "And Frank. He needs a good rival. I won't let them take you to jail."

"What?" Bertram blinked at her a moment. "I know how much I'm needed. I'm not going to just let them take me to jail."

"Uh, good." She was taken aback. "You sounded so defeated just now."

"Because Barnaby is awful! He's a poorly written, incomprehensibly evil villain and he's going to be written off in the most obvious way possible." He gestured at the man reading the book. "And these slack-jawed philistines are gobbling it up like biscuits."

The man looked up from his reading and shot him a dirty look, but Bertram didn't seem to notice.

"But I...but," Laoise stammered. "You were speaking awfully passionately about him I thought you were...talking about yourself"

"What? No! I was very clearly talking about Barnaby. Haven't you been listening to a word I said?" He sipped his coffee, incensed. His jaw twitched. "And frankly, I'm quite offended that you would make any comparisons to myself and any part of that dreadful gutter wash."

"As much as I'm enjoying our little book club, we can't spend all day here." She looked around, seeing that the man reading wasn't the only one casting them a sideways glance.

"I'm well aware. But I don't think my best laid schemes will be enough to get out of this one."

"Your schemes have gotten us this far, haven't they?"

He gave a begrudging nod.

"And that's because you had me to help you this time. Face it. Your plans are always far more complicated than they need to be."

"They are exactly as complicated as they need to be."

"Look," started Laoise, tapping the table. "You came all this way because you wanted to talk to Martin, right? Then let's go to him."

"Have you forgotten that the charity gala is tomorrow? The house will be a fortress."

"If you take the front door, maybe," she said, giving him a knowing smile. "But we servants have our own ways into these events."

"Sneak in through the servants' entrance? Hmm." He contemplated the idea, stroking his chin, but then shook his head. "No. It wouldn't work. The staff would recognize me. I confess my capacity for glamour is somewhat limited, and with my reputation, I doubt the others would be as eager to help me as you are. But..." A spark of inspiration seemed to light up behind his eyes. "But you could get in easily."

"Me? You won't even tell me what you want to talk to him about."

"I'm still working on that," he said. "Now we need somewhere to spend the night. I wouldn't want to impose on your family twice. Not with Roger on our trail."

"Oh I don't think Roger will be too much of a problem." Peering out the window, she saw that the cold had gotten the best of the man. He stood motionless with his arms outstretched, his waterlogged clothes now having completely frozen. The two constables lifted Roger up and carried him, stiff as a statue, down the alleyway. Bertram's uncle grumbled behind them with his valet, still fidgeting and brushing his masters coat as he walked. "Although I may have somewhere we can stay the night."

"You do? Where?"

"You have your secrets and I have mine."

"Very well. Lead the way then." He smiled. "And...thank you, Laoise."

"What for? You bought the coffee. Even served it to me." She finished her cup. It was nice to be on the receiving end of service for a change. "And if I might add, a job very well done, Mr. Bertler."

"A token for staying by my side through all of this," he said. "I don't have it figured out yet, but we may be able to get you your money as well."

Laoise's eyes lit up. "Really? How?"

Bertram sputtered. "Yes w-well it's only the start of an idea. The seed. The spark of a seed of the—"

"Out with it," interrupted Laoise, growing more concerned by the second.

"Well we..." He cleared his throat. "Borrow some of the uh... donations to the Steepe Foundation."

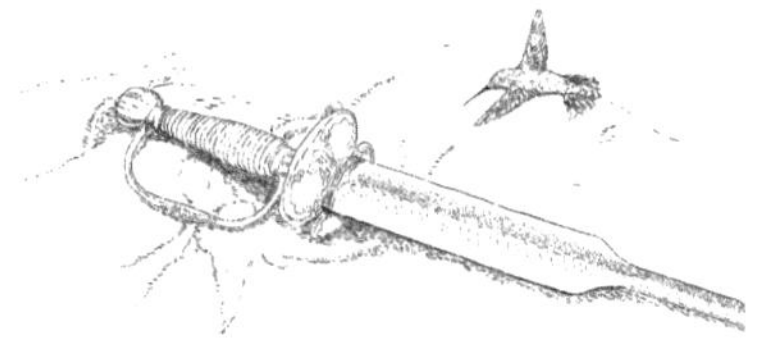

Chapter 19

Laoise turned and struck Bertram on the arm. "You want to rob a charity?"

"Keep your voice down!" He looked around in a panic and led the way to an alley beside the building.

"I will not keep quiet. You're as bad as Barnaby. No. You're worse!" She pounded her fists against his chest.

He caught her wrists. "The charity is for sick children from families who can't afford medical care. Your brother qualifies. It isn't stealing when the money is going for the exact cause it's meant for."

She pulled her hands back and folded her arms across her chest. "I told you we don't want charity."

"Then you can pay it back later." He threw his arms up in exasperation. "Pay back double for all I care. But that money isn't going to be of use to anyone just sitting in that box. You've already earned it, so you may as well have it."

"I'm not sure. This still seems wrong somehow."

"Look, it's perfectly fine. This wouldn't be the first time I've done this you know," said Bertram flatly. As though he were discussing the weather. As though it were perfectly commonplace to steal donations meant for children in need. She wheeled on him and raised her fists once more. He held out his hands. "Alright I know that sounds—"

"It sounds like every awful rumor I've heard about you is true." She glanced around. "I wonder if Roger is still nearby."

"Just listen," he pleaded, voice strained. "The Steepe Foundation is largely run by my mother and Aunt Gertie. They mean well of course, but I don't think they quite understand time is of the essence for many of the sick. They tend to use charity meetings as social events instead of getting anything useful done, and it can take weeks before the families in need see any money at all." He looked down sheepishly and kicked at a chunk of snow on the ground. "Sometimes I'll just circumvent the time-consuming bookkeeping and I'll reach into the coffers to fulfill the requests myself."

"I see." Laoise considered his claim. "It's a bit of a dodgy thing to do, but I suppose your heart's in the right place."

Bertram let out a sigh of relief. "You know, for as stubborn as you can be, you're very understanding. I wish Uncle would listen like you do."

"He did seem dismissive. Especially about that awful Dr. Speranza."

Bertram froze. His eyes went wide. "What about him?"

"Your uncle mentioned it at the bank. Something about dealing with him in a court of law. I know you told me hew was a fraud, but the man's not still giving you problems, is he?"

"No. No he—" He cleared his throat. "He's been dealt with. And he's nothing with which we need concern ourselves anymore."

Laoise chuckled. "Another one of your secrets? You make it sound like you killed him."

Bertram didn't respond. Instead his gaze went distant and vacant as he walked.

"You didn't..." A cold tingle shot up Laoise's spine. "Did you kill him?"

Bertram remained silent, chewing on his lower lip.

"Jesus, Mary, and Joseph," muttered Laoise. "First I hear you rob charities and now you tell me you're a murderer?"

Betram held a finger to his lips, looking around panicked. 'Keep your voice down. I'm not a murderer I just... Look if you'd let me explain—"

"Oh you'd damn well better explain. I'm not walking one more step with you until I hear the truth."

He glanced around, evidently satisfied that the streets were free of prying ears. With a heavy sigh, he began, "Well..."

When puberty hit Bertram, it had struck faster than he could keep up with. His lanky, uncoordinated limbs had given him plenty to trip over, even without a dachshund underfoot.

Taking up fencing had helped ease him into his new body. Conflicts with school bullies had taught him how to use his height to his advantage in a fight. Dodging Oolong during his visits to Martin kept him nimble on his feet. Keeping up with his cousin's insatiable appetite for learning magic had made him quite the capable young magician. His uncle's lengthy lectures on how to be a gentleman and how to run the family business had taught him to use his wits and his natural charisma to his advantage. He was developing all sorts of skills, and today he would need all of them.

All his research about Dr. Speranza had only proven his worries. The man was a fraud. He'd taken over the identity of a doctor who'd moved away, and his medicine was poison. The fraud made it himself and hawked it as a miracle cure all. None of his patients recovered under his care. Not until they quit using his services or were unable to afford his snake oil.

Bertram was still just a young teenager, closer to being a boy than a man, but he hoped his height would let him pass as someone older and more threatening. He wouldn't be playing the role of a businessman, but he wanted to exude the same confidence his uncle tried to hammer into him for contract negotiations. Having started training how to box, he wasn't afraid of throwing a few punches if necessary.

Martin had already come too close to death once. Bertram wouldn't let it happen again. He'd tried to talk to his aunt, his uncle, and his mother. They all dismissed him, at best as a boy with an overactive imagination, and at worst as seeking to replace Martin as heir to the Steepe shipping business. No matter. If no one wanted to listen to him, then he had no choice but to take matters into his own hands.

He tucked his favorite book away. Reading Rookwood had planted the seed of an idea. One he was now determined to see through to fruition. He would confront the so-called doctor, and force him to admit to his crimes. He patted his pocket to ensure the bundle of papers was still there.

Using his newfound knowledge of correspondence and contracts, Bertram had forged an official-looking letter, which he would pass off as proof that the doctor was not who he claimed to be. In truth,

Bertram wasn't certain what sorts of documents the police would use to prove a doctor was a fraud, but he was certain the doctor wouldn't know either. He might be able to use the letter to trick the man into a confession. It was a long shot, but with this forged blackmail in hand, he had a chance to defeat the doctor and save his cousin.

Sitting atop his new black horse Bess, he hid in the copse of trees as the last dregs of a thunderstorm passed by. The Thames had climbed its banks, but not enough to spill over. If his research was still correct, the doctor would visit a nearby village today to "tend" to a few patients. The storm had done a perfect job of clearing out road traffic. With another bout of dark clouds on the horizon, he didn't expect to see anyone else. No one except the doctor.

The creak of the gig alerted him to the doctor's presence. The man sat huddled under a wool blanket. Rain speckled his glasses. Bertram straightened as he did his best to ignore the pounding of his heart. For Martin, he reminded himself. He'd do anything if it kept his cousin safe. He adjusted his mask one last time.

Time seemed to slow as he waited to the tune of his own harsh breathing. He waited until the perfect moment before sending his horse flying out of the trees and onto the road. The doctor's horse whinnied in fright.

"Watch out!" the doctor startled, dropping his accent. His blanket slipped from his shoulders. "You're in the way."

Bertram took a deep breath. "Stand and deliver." The enchanted rune necklace hidden under his shirt deepened his voice, making it unrecognizable. He'd learned about the phrase in his readings on legendary highwayman Dick Turpin. Highwaymen were largely a thing of the past, but they were more popular than ever in books.

"What?" The man put his accent back on. "Eh... no a-delivery today, signore."

Bertram resisted slapping his hand against his face in exasperation. Did the man not see he was dressed as a highwayman? Who else would tromp around the roads in a mask? "I don't want a delivery. I'm robbing you. By deliver, I mean your money. Or your life. It's your decision." Since his outfit hadn't done the trick yet, he drew his great grandfather's colichemarde. No doubt he'd be scolded for stealing the sword off the wall mount, but he couldn't concern himself with that now. The blade was old, but still quite sharp, and very threatening in Bertram's capable hands.

The doctor's eyes widened as he finally understood that this was, in fact, a robbery and not a misunderstanding. He held out his hands in a plea. "I don't have a-no money on me. I am a humble-a doctor. Only some a-medicine for patients!"

"Except it isn't real medicine, is it?"

The doctor swallowed, his large Adam's apple bobbing. "I don't a-know what you mean."

"You're a fraud. The real Dr. Speranza is still in Milan, and the medicine you've been peddling is nothing but poison." His righteous anger chased the lingering fear away. The man was a criminal. Bertram wouldn't wait around for someone else to save Martin. "How many people have died because of your lies?"

"None!" the man cried out, his awful fake accent gone now. "No one's ever died from it."

Bertram trotted Bess to the side of the gig, now close enough to strike the doctor with his blade. "And how long until someone does?"

The doctor paled. His mouth opened and closed like a fish out of water. It took him a few tries before he got any words out. "What do you want from me?"

"You are going to turn yourself in to Scotland Yard. Understand?" He'd already tried Scotland Yard, but the officers refused to take a young boy seriously. The man's confession, however, would be impossible for them to ignore.

"Scotland Yard?" The doctor's face scrunched. "Wh-what kind of robbery is this?"

Bertram reached into his pocket, pulling out one of the forged letters, letting it unfold. "I have plenty of evidence of your misdeeds, but I'll offer you the dignity of turning yourself in. The bounty is mine either way."

The wind suddenly picked up, ripping the letter from Bertram's hand. It blew up into the air and then back down towards the steady current of the Thames.

"No!" Bertram yelled, his voice cracking, and unfortunately it seemed as though the voice-changing enchantment on his necklace had cracked as well. He cleared his throat and tried to speak with as deep a voice as he could muster. "I...I have more evidence."

"Wait a minute." The doctor stared down Bertram's now shaking blade.. "I know you."

Bertram froze, heart thumping. He tightened his grip on his sword, pointing it at the doctor's heart. "No you don't."

"Yes that's it!" He snapped his fingers. "You're the other Steepe boy. Bart, isn't it?"

"Bertra—" He blurted out, unable to stop himself from correcting the man. With an exasperated groan, he took off his mask. "Look it doesn't matter. Now turn yourself in or I'll run you through."

He held the blade to the man's neck. Was he capable of killing the man if it came down to it? As much as he wanted to believe he could do anything to save Martin's life, he didn't know if he had the courage to go that far. If the doctor would hurry up and confess, he wouldn't need to find out.

"Bloody hell, you really had me worried there for a moment, boy." The doctor let out a nervous laugh. He slowly raised his hand and pushed the tip of the blade away from his neck. "Now be a good lad and let me pass."

Bertram lowered the blade and hung his head in shame. The doctor smiled, and with a crack of his reins the gig lurched forwards.

"My thanks, young Master Steepe." He turned and waved. "Let's just keep this our little secret then, shall we? No need to tell your father about all this nastiness."

By "father" he no doubt meant his Uncle Monty, but it didn't matter. The loss of his father still burned within him, and the man's words had awakened a new sense of righteous fury deep within him. The doctor was too far away now to strike with his sword, but he still had one last backup plan. His hand sweat as he dug around in his pockets, looking for the ball tucked against his side.

"Wait!" Bertram called out.

The doctor paid him no heed, instead cracking the reins again and coaxing his horse into a gallop. Bertram gave chase, pulling his horse alongside the doctor. He finally managed to get a hold of the metal ball from his pocket, and pressing the rune with his finger, tossed it into the doctor's gig. After a moment, a thin, wispy plume of smoke burst forth from the ball.

Bertram cursed. He'd fumbled his magic once more. The smoke bomb was too small to disorient the doctor as he'd hoped. He'd need *to dash ahead of the doctor and force him to stop, letting the smoke accumulate. Then maybe Bertram could sneak up and climb into the back of the doctor's gig. He'd tackle the man right off and wrestle him down. While that all sounded good in theory, Bertram was no longer feeling confident in his plan.*

The doctor was a coward and a weakling, but even if Bertram managed to subdue him, the man would lie to his uncle. Uncle Monty hadn't listened to him about the doctor before, and he certainly wouldn't once the man tattled on him. Facing his uncle's disappointment made him feel small. Small and terrified and useless.

He needed to be stronger. To not let anyone hurt Martin like this again. Once more he drew his sword. He wouldn't let this fraud get away twice.

BANG!

A bright, loud explosion burst forth from the gig, followed by a massive plume of smoke. Rather than make the bomb too weak, it seemed Bertram had made it far too strong. He couldn't quite figure out how to get them to work, and he hadn't wanted to ask Martin for help, afraid he would realize something was wrong.

Bess reared, but Bertram quickly regained control of her. The doctor's horse whinnied, and dashed out of the smoke, galloping toward the river and dragging a cracked and wobbling gig behind it. The horse turned when it reached the edge of the riverbank, but the angle was too sharp and the banks of the river too muddy for the gig to follow the same path.

The gig's left wheel broke with a loud crack, and the carriage fell onto its side. The doctor tumbled from his seat onto the muddy bank, coating his back and right side in a smear of mud. He climbed onto his feet, slipping and sliding as he struggled to stay upright. He clawed at the ground, pulling clumps of mud out in his desperate attempt to avoid the river, but his fighting did nothing to stop his slow descent.

A gust of wind dragged the worst of the smoke away as the bomb continued to sputter puffs of fog. With another snap, the doctor's horse broke free of the broken gig and shot up the road.

Dumbfounded, Bertram dismounted and cautiously approached the bank, holding his sword aloft. A scar in the bank showed where the doctor had slid right down into the water. Thanks to all the storms, the fast river currents could test even a seasoned swimmer.

He surveyed the water, but saw no sign of the doctor. His right foot slid in the mud, and he jumped backward, landing on his behind. No way would he dare risk the dangerous currents to save such a despicable man. And after seeing the doctor's slide, he knew better than to assume he'd fare any better against the mud.

No. The man would meet his fate on his own.

Bertram rose on shaking legs and made his way back to Bess. He breathed a haggard sigh of relief. Dr. Speranza had been dealt with, and Martin was safe. Bertram still didn't know if he would have had the courage to take the man's life, but he was grateful that he didn't need to find out.

"Is that all?" Laoise blew out a puff of air, sending a stray piece of hair flying up. Her nose and cheeks had turned numb over the course of his story. Their walk proved to take longer than she'd hoped. They turned a corner onto the final stretch, a road full of fenced yards and houses bigger than anyone truly needed.

"What do you mean 'Is that all?' You're the first person other than Uncle Monty I've ever told about this." He rubbed the back of his neck. "I'm responsible for a man's death. I can't count how many nights it's kept me awake." His nose had turned red from the cold, but it wasn't dripping like hers.

"You're responsible for saving Martin's life. As for that bastard, I say it serves him right. You've nothing to feel ashamed of."

"So you don't think I'm a monster?"

"For that? Not at all." She nudged his side. "Plenty of other reasons to think you're a monster, though."

"Ha ha," he said flatly. "Where are you taking me exactly?"

She grinned. "Well, besides Oolong, how do you feel about dachshunds?"

"Oh no. Oh dear God no." His voice wavered as he looked up at the brick wall blocking the stately manor and yard from view of the busy road. "Not Auntie Hammond's."

Chapter 20

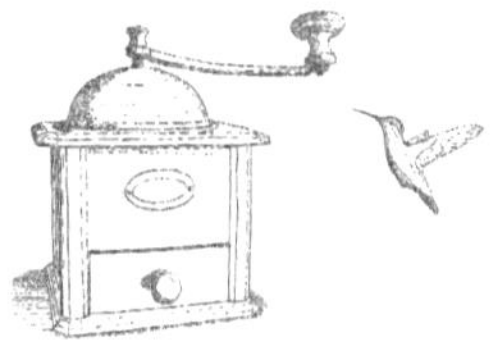

Laoise had to drag Bertram by the hand to get him to the wrought-iron gate of the Hammond household. "Please tell me you're joking," he said, pulling his hat lower as if he didn't want to be spotted. Not an uncommon reaction. Mrs. Hammond's guests always had the air of social hostages about them when they visited.

"Relax, she's not here. She'll be staying at her sister's house until after the new year."

"I know. There's a reason we always host the charity gala this time of year. We send her an invitation out of politeness since she always sends a donation, but she never comes. We've been very careful to thank her for her donation without implying that we wished she would attend." He turned his gaze on her. "How did you know she wouldn't be home?"

"I used to work for her right up until I joined your uncle's staff." She'd left for the slight pay increase, and to get away from Mrs. Hammond's herd of dachshunds. For creatures of such small stature, they always found ways to cause remarkable amounts of mayhem. Plus, after Charlotte's mortifying incident at one of the luncheons that briefly ruined her social life, it felt cruel to talk about the household and remind her of the embarrassment. "Since she always kept to the same schedule, I figured there's no reason she'd change it this year."

He scratched his chin. "I do remember one of Martin's maids coming with a letter of recommendation from the Hammond household. I should have remembered it was you. Still, that doesn't explain why you expect us to stay here."

"I have a few friends here. Since some of the staff goes with the Hammonds, there should be enough spare beds until the new year. That gives us a place to hide where no one would expect us."

"That is rather clever. Uncle would never look for me here. He wouldn't even come by the neighborhood unless his life depended on it."

"Exactly. Follow me."

They headed in through the back, passing an exasperated gardener chasing after two dachshunds. One dog ran with a hat in its mouth, making it a few more steps before stumbling over it and getting caught. The second dog scampered into the bushes, leaving nothing but shaking branches in its wake.

"To think I thought Oolong was bad." Bertram shuddered. "I can't imagine more than one of him."

"It's never a dull day at the Hammond household. Nothing keeps you fit like chasing dogs at every waking moment." Oolong was enough. She didn't miss the herd.

They met the cook first, a ruddy-faced woman busy rolling out crust for meat pies. She paused when she noticed them. "Laoise, what brings you here?"

"Came to ask for a favor. Is Eliza still head housekeeper?"

"Sure is. Not like anyone else would ever take the position." The cook spotted Bertram's bruises and frowned. "You haven't gotten yourself mixed up in trouble, have you?"

"Don't mind him," Laoise said. "Just a bit of a tussle in the boxing ring."

"Bit of a tussle, eh?" She arched an eyebrow. "I thought you weren't into the trouble making kind anymore?"

"It's not like that." She could feel Bertram's gaze burning into her. The attention made her cheeks heat, and she turned her head. She wouldn't let him see her blush on his account.

The kitchen door swung open. Eliza burst in, her hair in disarray as usual. Despite the attention to cleanliness and detail she gave the mansion, she herself always had a way of looking a mess. It was as if all her time went into managing the household, leaving none for herself. "The butler is missing. Don't tell me he went off to the pub again. Just because we get no visitors this time of year doesn't mean he can slack off every day."

"Don't know where he is," the cook said as she slapped a slab of dough onto a meat pie. She crimped the edges. "Laoise says she needs a favor."

"Laoise?" Eliza looked about the kitchen before finally spotting her. "What are you doing here?"

"I need a place to stay the night." She pointed at Bertram. "He got us in trouble with the Steepes and we can't go back until tomorrow."

"What'd he do? Wait, I don't want to know." She swiped the stringy hairs that had fallen out of her bun from her eyes. "Any chance I can convince you to stay more than the night?"

"Afraid not. At least not yet. I might be willing to reconsider in the new year."

"Wouldn't blame you if you didn't. We've gone through four maids since you left. The dogs scare 'em all off. We've got extra beds if you can be gone by lunchtime. A new girl is arriving tomorrow."

"That shouldn't be a problem. We'll be gone first thing in the morning."

"Then take any of the free beds in the servants' quarters."

"Any chance we can have something more...private?" Bertram asked.

Eliza grinned. "Need a bit of privacy for the two of you, do you?" She winked at him.

"Yes." He painted the same smile on his face that he had worn when speaking to the innkeeper. "Privacy, right my dear?"

"Ooh 'my dear,' he says." Eliza grinned and nudged Laoise. "Found yourself a romantic type, I see?"

"Indeed I have," said Laoise, holding her hand up in a conspiratorial whisper. "Why this one time in front of a fireplace—"

"Laoise!" Bertram pulled her away from Eliza.

"I don't need the details." Eliza giggled. "You can have Mrs. Hammond's second room. It was to be stripped tomorrow, anyway. Strip it and clean it yourself, and you can have it for tonight."

"Not a problem." Laoise elbowed Bertram in the side. "Just leave all the strippin' to us."

Bertram spluttered. Both women laughed heartily at his reaction. When her laughter abated, Eliza got back to business, turning her attention back to the cook. "As soon as the butler gets back, send him my way. If he shows up drunk, dump a bucket of water on his head first. We're going to lose another gardener if we don't keep the dogs rounded up." She left, her hurried footsteps tapping down the hallway.

The cook slapped down another ball of dough to roll out. "Going to lose the butler too, I bet. That'll be the second one this year."

Laoise shook her head. "I swear you and Eliza are the only ones mad enough to stay."

"It's not so bad for me. The snobs don't come down to bother me, and the beasties are on their best behavior when there's kitchen scraps to be had." The cook shook the rolling pin at her. "As for Eliza, she'd never land a position as head housekeeper elsewhere. Too young, she is. She only got the spot here because no one else will take it." She attacked the fresh dough. "So how's life with the Steepes?"

"Could be worse. Only one dachshund, and plenty of tea in the servant's quarters."

"And you're going to leave that to come join this madhouse in the new year?"

"I might." She gave a sad smile. "If I've gone as mad as the pair of you by then."

The cook nodded. "There'll be plenty to eat for supper. You can come back then."

Laoise recognized the cook's dismissal. "This way," she told Bertram as she headed into a passageway leading to the staircase. The narrow, dim space was still familiar to her. She remembered which stairs were uneven from wear, and when to turn at the dark corners to miss smacking into a wall. All things she hadn't put a thought to since leaving, but habits were hard to kill.

Bertram wasn't faring as well behind her. He tripped over an uneven stair and banged his shoulder off the wall. "Couldn't we use the main stairs instead?"

"No. Mrs. Hammond doesn't allow it. She prefers we keep out of sight as much as possible. So much as one errant stain on the carpeting and she'll have the whole staff sacked." She rounded a corner and ducked under a low ceiling. Below her Bertram cursed as he smacked his head off of a rafter. "Besides, these passages are better. They may be cramped, but the dachshunds can't get back here."

"This hardly seems worth it to avoid a few tripping hazards."

"Tripping hazard?" Laoise scoffed. "Oolong is a tripping hazard. These dogs are a coordinated team of assassins. I once saw a guest fall

down the stairs after tripping over three dogs in a row. And one time..."
Best not to tell him about Charlotte's incident with the dachshunds.
She didn't want to find out what he'd dare do with the information.

"You don't need to remind me. We all heard about the Dachshund
Incident. I wonder whatever happened to that poor girl."

Laoise bit her tongue. "I had to live in that chaos for several years.
The only time there was ever peace was when young Master Hammond would bring them to the countryside to hunt with them."

"Can you imagine Martin and Oolong trying to hunt together?"
Bertram snorted.

"Oolong would have to trip his prey to death." Laoise laughed.
"Watch out for the sharp right turn up here."

She pushed up the door. Like most of the doors to the servants'
passageways, it blended in with the surroundings. The same floral
wallpaper that covered the hallways covered the door, making all the
doors hard to find unless you knew where to look.

"Mrs. Hammond's room is over here." She crossed the hall and
barged right into the room.

"We aren't really going to stay in there, are we?" he asked, aghast as
he stepped into the room.

"It's either this or the servants' quarters." She gestured to the line
of wardrobes along one wall. "Besides, she doesn't even sleep in this
room. It's more of a giant wardrobe than anything else. She buys too
many clothes and decided she needed a full room dedicated to them."

Bertram backed towards the servant's door they had entered
through, running his hands against the wall, trying to find the seam.
"I can't stay here."

Laosie rolled her eyes. "You've got a comfortable room where no
one will bother us 'til morning, and all you need to do is help tidy it up
a bit. What exactly are you still complaining about?"

"What am I complaining about? Just look at all these mismatched
florals." He waved his arm at them. "I mean really. Who in their right
mind would pair these drapes with those bed covers? The purples
clash with that sickly shade of brown." He stuck out his tongue in
disgust.

"If you don't like the bed covers, you could strip em off." She waggled her eyebrows at him.

"Ever the seductress." He threw the nearest wardrobe doors open and began flipping through the dresses.

She flopped onto the chair resting near the door, draping her legs over the armrests. "What are you doing? Eliza said we could stay here, not go picking through Mrs. Hammond's clothes."

"Hush. I'm devising a plan." He made a disgusted grunt at each dress he looked over. "And I'm going to ignore for a moment just how easily you managed to talk your way into bringing a strange man with you to have free rein over this house. It's almost as though you've don't it before." He shot her an accusatory glance.

"Perhaps I have, and perhaps I haven't," said Laoise, smiling coyly.

Bertram shuddered. "The first thing I'm doing when I get back home is putting up wards to make sure no one can come trespassing like this into my rooms."

"Treat your servants well and you'll never need to worry about it. Between the dachshunds and Mrs. Hammond herself, it's hard to say who's more demanding. I've never known wages to go up or for any of the servant's requests to be answered. I doubt Eliza would have been so quick to offer the room if she wasn't already at the end of her rope."

"Hardly surprising. Auntie Hammond is difficult enough to handle in social functions. I can't imagine having to see her every day. But Mabel..." He shut the wardrobe and stroked his chin. "Her granddaughter Mabel has been staying here, hasn't she?"

Laoise raised an eyebrow. "She has. Why?"

He rubbed his hands together. "Excellent. All these dresses are too gaudy. No young lady of taste would be caught dead in one. Which room is hers?"

"Assuming she hasn't moved rooms, Miss Mabel's room is across the hall." She sat up in her chair. "Why are you asking?"

"I told you I'm devising a plan. Now let's go find you something more..." He looked her up and down. "More suitable for the event."

"You're not answering the question." She stood up and brushed her skirts, not liking the dread coiling itself into a tight ball in her middle.

He led her to the room across the hall. "I've been thinking about how we'll get into the donation box. You see, Uncle is always suspicious of the help, so a maid wouldn't be able to get close for long. Certainly not long enough to get past the magical seals Martin will have placed on it. However, a young lady from a wealthy family, like one of the

Hammonds for instance, could take her time socializing near all of that money without drawing any unwanted attention."

"You're not suggesting that I—"

"Yes. You will go to the gala disguised as Mabel Hammond. She's about your height, and she has an unassuming enough personality that no one will pay too much notice."

"Absolutely not. I haven't seen Miss Hammond in a year. I can't disguise myself as her. And I can't act like her." Laoise shook her head. "And what about Martin's magical seals? Even you couldn't beat them, and I only know one spell."

"Come now. I didn't think you were one to give up so easily," goaded Bertram, shooting her a devilish smirk.

Mabel Hammond's room was smaller and more plainly decorated in shades of ivory and pale blue. Bertram went straight to the wardrobe full of her old clothes. She always took her best clothes and new outfits with her when she traveled.

Laoise squirmed, looking for any excuse not to go forward with this plan. "But what about you and Martin? You still want to talk to him, don't you? I can't do that for you if I'm impersonating Miss Hammond."

"I believe I have the solution. I'll write a letter tonight and you can deliver it to him at the party. It's a long shot, but Martin's familiar enough with Mabel to not think hard about why she's handing him a letter. Just don't be surprised if he calls you Mary or Martha or something." He turned from rifling through the dresses. "Now come help me pick out a dress for you to wear."

She mumbled to herself when a pink dress caught her eye. She stopped Bertram and pulled it out to get a better look. "I like this one."

Bertram looked as though he'd sucked on a lemon. "Yes, well, your skin tone does not." He plucked the dress out of her hands and put it back, ignoring the disappointed expression she made at him. He chose an emerald dress and held it up to her, muttering in satisfaction. "Better. This one's a bit behind the current trends, but with some accessories you should blend in to the crowd. At least well enough to avoid the worst of the insecure socialites' mockery."

"Anyone who mocks me does it at her own risk." Laoise pumped her arm for emphasis. "How do you know so much about fashion anyway?"

He got to work undoing the buttons on the dress. "A gentleman always leaves the house looking his best. That means one must keep abreast of the latest trends in fashion. No washed out pastels. No floral patterns. And most certainly no orange."

"Orange is an awful color."

"Perhaps you have more fashion sense than I thought." He shook the dress. "Do you like it?"

"I'll ignore that remark." It was beautiful, but when it came to pretty dresses, she didn't know how to put an outfit together. She was used to having the same old drab dresses until she couldn't patch them anymore. She'd never had anything half as fine as Mabel Hammond's old clothes. "And yes. Yes I do like it."

"Good. Then take off that old dress."

"Can't help yourself, can you?" She took the dress from him and ran her hands over the silky fabric. It felt like a dream against her skin.

"You're going to need to learn to be a bit more demure if this plan is to work." He wagged a finger at her. "While you switch clothes, I'm going to see what jewelry I can find."

She felt like she should object. Staying in Mrs. Hammond's wardrobe room was bad enough, but stealing her granddaughter's clothes? And yet the dress was the finest thing she'd ever gotten the chance to wear. Mabel Hammond had always acted spoiled and rude to the servants, though she'd never yelled at them directly. Rather than speak to the servants, she'd communicate her demands to her parents. She once demanded they sack Laoise for getting the number of sugar cubes in her tea wrong. Eliza of course, ensured she wouldn't have to deal with the unpleasant young lady again lest they lose another maid.

After a very brief conflict of conscience, Laoise went behind the changing wall to put on the dress. All the while Bertram grumbled over the jewelry. She tilted her head at her reflection. She'd never expected to wear dresses like the women who bossed her about. Even so, she saw the appeal. The dress highlighted her features and flaunted more skin than she was accustomed to.

"I don't know if it's quite right." The top of the dress hugged her chest and dipped low. The skirts were wider than what she wore. They'd only get in the way if she worked, but maybe Bertram would like the dress. Her pulse jumped at the thought. What if he saw her as a lady in this dress instead of a maid? Did she want that? She smoothed out the skirts to keep her trembling hands busy. Why did thinking about him looking at her suddenly make her nervous?

"Put these on." He held out his hand around the changing wall. A pair of emerald earrings sat on his palm.

No. She wouldn't let him make her nervous. She slid the earrings on and then she stepped out, finding Bertram had moved a chair into the center of the room.

He leaned forward, resting an elbow on his thigh as he rubbed his chin. His rapt attention caused her to squeeze her hands together, her nerves trying their hardest to rattle her against her will.

"A slow spin, please." He made a circle with his pointer finger, directing her as though she were an actress in a play.

She spun, finding that his serious demeanor had deepened by the time she faced him again. After a long beat of silence, she swallowed. "What do you think?" She swished the skirts.

His mouth hung agape. "Incredible. Truly incredible."

Laoise's cheeks flushed, and a warm tingle rose up from her stomach and spread up her body. "You really think so?"

He rested his head on his hand, as if drinking in her figure. "Yes. I've never seen you look so stiff and uncomfortable."

And with that, the warm feeling drained out of her. She'd hoped to hear any number of words come out of his mouth. Ravishing. Beautiful. Some poetic Shakespearean verse. She would even have settled for being called pretty. Instead, his words struck her like a slap to the face. "Well you'll excuse me for not being able to pass as that spoiled brat on my first try."

He continued, unaware of the internal war he'd caused in her. "We'll need to work on that temper of yours if this is to work. The hair too."

"And what's wrong with my hair?" That pulled her out of her shocked stupor. "God help me if you call me a fiery redhead."

He snorted. "Fiery? Hardly. That takes passion. You're more stubborn. Like an ox." He pointed at his face. "I meant the color of your hair. We'll need to darken yours quite a bit. And as much of a shame it will be to cover them, we'll have no choice but to cover your freckles as well to make you look more like Mabel."

She pressed a hand to her right cheek. This plan sounded more difficult by the minute. "I can use makeup on my freckles, but not my hair. The maids share bits and pieces of magic here and there gathered from the women we work for, but I don't know how to change my hair color."

He stood. "I can take care of that. Come over to the mirror." He sat her at the vanity table and circled around her. "Miss Hammond's hair is almost black if I remember right."

"It is." She avoided touching anything on the table except to nudge the bottle of perfume away from the edge.

He released her hair, letting the curls cascade down her back. Then he brushed his fingers over her hair, fighting to get them free whenever a curl snagged him. As he uttered an incantation, black spread from his fingers and through her hair as if someone had spilled a bottle of ink all over her. Her scalp tingled from the magic, a tingle that made her squirm in her seat while remembering what this hands had done to her during their tumble in front of the fire.

"There. That is about the right shade."

"It's perfect. Why do you know her color so well?"

"Auntie Hammond is Aunt Gertie's aunt. Or at least that's what I always assumed. I've learned that everyone seems to call her Auntie, and to be quite honest, I'm not certain she has any blood relation to anyone. Oolong, however, is most definitely a relative as he is from one of the Hammond litters. Mabel would sometimes come over under the pretext of visiting the dog, but really it was our families hoping for a match between us."

The thought of him courting Mabel hit her like a cold bucket of water. He'd have to court eventually. His family would want him to marry. Whoever he courted would be on the Hammond's social level, not that of a maid. She swallowed, hating the emotions stirring in her chest. "You two...did you...?"

"Good God, No." He snorted. "I'm glad things never worked out between us. I could never be able to handle all those dachshunds. Or Auntie Hammond. "

She breathed a quiet sigh of relief. "How long will this hair last?" Sure, the dark hair would help her fit in with high society better, but she didn't care about their opinions anymore. She'd already twisted herself in enough knots in the past to fit in. If she covered up her freckles, she wouldn't even recognize herself.

"A few hours. Without runes controlling it, the spell should wear off on its own."

"Should?" Great. Knowing his magic, that would translate to a few minutes or a few weeks instead.

He stepped away to return to his chair. "Now I want to see your best Mabel Hammond act. Give me a curtsy and say, 'A pleasure to see you today.'"

She peeled her attention away from the mirror. "Good evening." She dropped into a low curtsy. "A pleasure to see you today." Nothing about the words sounded sincere. Emotions continued to roil inside her, making it difficult to control her tone.

"Try again, but more enthusiastic this time. And sweeter."

She held in her sigh and went back through the greeting.

"Your dialect is off."

She huffed. "Would you rather I try to sound more like a toff?" she asked, over enunciating each word. "Oh my dear Mr. Steepe. How lovely to see you today. I do hope the weather gave you no trouble."

He rubbed the bridge of his nose. "We've got one day to pull this off. Do try to take this seriously."

"I am taking this seriously!" She rested her hands on her hips, tired of this game. "And if you think I'm so bad at it, why don't you show me how it's done?"

He stood, making a show of dusting off his waistcoat. "I was afraid it would come to this. Let me show you how a true lady acts."

She had no good argument against him calling her bluff. If anything, she should have known better by now. And so, she sat in the chair while Bertram took a dark purple dress with him behind the changing wall. After a few minutes of cursing and the sound of seams being torn open, Bertram stepped out.

The sight of him was mortifying. The dress was tight across his broad shoulders, and hung low on his chest, exposing his chest hair. He was already tall, and the high heels he wore made him positively tower over Laoise.

"Now pay very close attention to both my movements and my mannerisms." He cleared his throat and curtsied before striding about the room in small, modest steps, all the while fanning himself gracefully. "Darling, good evening. So happy to be here. Just think of all those poor children in need of my help. How dreadful!" He snapped his fingers. "Oh I do wish Papa would tell the servants to bring a bowl of water for my dog." When he stopped, he stood to the side of a portrait of the Hammonds on the wall.

"Bravo!" Laoise laughed. He was more over dramatic than she'd been, but his mannerisms were a closer match.

He bowed. "A convincing impression I hope."

She pointed at the portrait, still giggling. "A convincing impression alright. Of dear old Auntie Hammond!"

"Oh, now you're just being..." He trailed off and his smile left, replaced with that same serious look he had earlier. "That is a good point. No one would look twice at Mrs. Hammond. They'd all be too busy trying to avoid her and the embarrassment she causes wherever she goes."

"Oh no. There's no way I'm pretending to be her." Mrs. Hammond had a sharp wit and a sharper tongue, and she wasn't afraid to use either. Most socialites spoke their biting remarks behind their targets' backs, but Auntie Hammond could loudly tear a person to shreds to their face, all the while maintaining a sweet and cheerful disposition. Even if she could disguise herself as Auntie Hammond, Laoise couldn't replicate her personality. She'd be unable to cut people down with her turns of phrase, and more likely to clobber them with her bare hands.

"You're right." Bertram rubbed his chin. "If you can't rise to the challenge, then you leave me no choice. Find me a wig."

Chapter 21

Bertram managed an uncanny disguise as Mrs. Hammond, right down to the clashing florals, his gray hair, and his over the top mannerisms. If someone looked close enough, they'd see the discrepancies, like the glistening edges where the glamour clung to his face, or the excessive amount of stuffing he'd used to fill out the top of his dress. He'd gotten carried away crafting the oversized bust. It made Laoise roll her eyes and mutter about men.

That was to say nothing of the fact that his shoulders were much too wide, or that his height put him a full head above the real Mrs. Hammond. If the woman's reputation held strong, Laoise expected everyone to be too busy trying to escape Auntie Hammond to linger long enough to notice anything peculiar about her. No one wanted to become her next target.

"Are you really planning to waltz in and resume your position as maid?" He tugged on his dress, readjusting the stuffing at his chest. "It seems a bit...simple."

"Not everything needs to be an elaborate scheme." At dinner Laoise had told the staff their plan, and after everyone at the table enjoyed a long and hearty laugh, it'd secured her the support she'd hoped for. The carriage driver offered to drop them off in Mrs. Hammond's spare carriage. Eliza even fetched Mrs. Hammond's invitation. Laoise doubted they'd need proof to get in, but it would be handy as a backup.

"And you don't think your sudden reappearance will cause us any trouble?"

"Trust me, the staff will be much too happy to have an extra pair of hands to question my return." She cast another weary eye up and down Bertram's disguise, growing less and less confident in their plan. "What about you? Are you sure you want to do this?"

"Your brother needs medicine. I need to talk to Martin. I admit that circumstances are hardly ideal, but we'll both get what we want this way. Right out from under my uncle's nose, too." He adjusted his wig. "Besides, it will give me a chance to brush up on my acting skills."

"Don't suppose you're accustomed to playing the role of an entitled lady, are you?"

He stuck out his chest proudly. "As a matter of fact, I am. We did a performance of The Scottish Play in my university days. None of the other boys were willing to step up, so I played Lady M herself. A fine performance as well if I do say so myself."

"The Scottish Play? Which Scottish play?"

"Come now, even you know this one," he said with a touch of exasperation, gesturing as he gave his clues. "Written by Shakespeare. Starts with an M. Brings bad luck to say the name out loud..."

Laoise tapped a finger on her chin. "Macbeth? If that's what you mean just say Mac—"

He clapped a hand over her mouth and leaned close. "I just told you it brings bad luck. Stop saying it," he said through gritted teeth. Under any other circumstance, his proximity would have been exciting. However, his striking resemblance to Mrs. Hammond made her pull away and shudder.

"Playing Lady Mac—" Laoise stopped herself and groaned. "Lady M is a wee bit different from playing Auntie Hammond. I hope you're bringing more than an amateur's experience to this performance."

"Amateur? Why I never! I'm wearing these horrendous florals for you, darling," he said in his best imitation of Mrs. Hammond. "Do these look perky enough?" He groped his chest. It was unsettling how believable his disguise worked despite the rushed plan. She was almost certain she'd heard Mrs. Hammond ask that exact question at tea once, too.

Laoise shivered. "I certainly have the urge to throw myself out of this carriage. Bravo, I suppose." She toyed with her bun as her nerves set in. The glamour Bertram had applied to her hair had faded back to her natural shade after a few hours as expected, but a few dark strands still streaked her hair. She hoped it wouldn't be too noticeable.

"Which means my disguise is working!" He said the last word in a sing-song voice that perfectly mimicked Mrs. Hammond's way of talking when she was especially excited about something.

"Indeed it is. Keep this up, and you have a bright future as a wealthy heiress ahead of you."

"I'd rather not abandon my business ventures, but if Uncle Monty refuses to give me back what's mine, perhaps I will consider finding a fabulously wealthy woman to look after me. It worked well enough for Mr. Hammond."

"Sure, if you don't count the fact that the two of them don't spend more than a month each year living in the same house. When I first started working for her, I thought Auntie Hammond was a widow." The carriage stopped. "I'll meet you inside. Let's get this awful day over with."

Bertram flounced out of the carriage, complimenting the footman who rushed to assist him with gusto. Laoise went in through the servants' entrance.

The kitchen was already in chaos. Maids rushed in and out, getting in the way of the cook. "If he can make 'em heat up faster, why can't he make the bloody things clean themselves?" a scullery maid grumbled as she cleaned teapot after teapot.

"Miss Hughes, back already?" The butler asked as he polished silverware until she was certain the shine could blind someone.

"I'm only here for the gala."

He jutted his chin toward the chaos. "Then get to work. There is food and tea ready to go out." And just like that, she was in. Guests milled through the parlor, library, dining room, and through the shimmering magical barrier that made being outside bearable despite the snow and cold. It reminded her of the greenhouse back in the countryside. Good thing there was no pond here for her to fall into.

She started into the yard, but backpedaled when she spotted Charlotte. She didn't feel ready to talk to her. Not in the middle of a party. Not when the difference in their stations was so obvious. As much as she wanted to rush over and talk with her friend, she was afraid she'd embarrass Charlotte in front of the socialites who were now her peers. At least that's what Laoise told herself.

In the parlor, spotting Bertram was easy. The crowd parted like the Red Sea wherever he went. Laoise made her way from room to room, scoping out the party while she poured tea. The guests were exactly who she'd expected, the local well-to-do businessmen sprinkled in with a few guests of noble birth and successful magicians. Like many other magicians, Martin's social circle included a blending of classes that the old-fashioned aristocracy scoffed at.

Overhead, mechanical hummingbirds flitted about, alighting on the guests' teacups to deposit honey on request. The guests packed into the house, making for some tight squeezes through a crowd who refused to move for a mere maid.

Charlotte would have her hands full helping Martin navigate all the names. While businessmen and magicians loved to visit him, his talents went unappreciated by everyone else, especially those who couldn't get past his struggle with names.

A woman with too much rouge on snapped her fingers at Laoise. "You. More tea. And don't keep me waiting."

Laoise poured tea for the lady, but another guest bumped into her back, jostling her forward. Tea sloshed over the teacup rim. The tea spilled over the saucer and onto the table. Laoise grabbed a napkin to sop up the tea before it dripped off the table.

"I expected better service than this," the woman groused. She squirmed in her chair, huffing and puffing her indignation.

"Sorry, ma'am. I'll have a fresh cup brought to you."

The woman's face soured as her gaze landed on Laoise's red hair. "An Irish girl?" she said, waving a dismissive hand to Laoise as she addressed another lady sitting across from her. "It's no wonder she's stumbling about. Back from one of those dreadful public houses still deep in her cups, no doubt. That's why I don't employ her kind. Plus that red hair is an eyesore."

"Why my dear Mrs. Johnston, surely you of all people ought to know a thing or two about intoxication," said Bertram, strolling over to the coffee table. Laoise tensed in dread, forgetting for a moment that he wasn't the real Mrs. Hammond. He gave a high-pitched giggle. "Why, who could forget the Dartford's fête? You must have finished off two whole bottles of sherry yourself!"

Mrs. Johnston leaned as far back as her chair let her, eyes as wide as teacup saucers. She winced and dropped her cup on the floor, proving that Bertram's arrow had found its mark. "M-Mrs. Hammond. I didn't see you there." Oolong popped out from under the woman's chair to lap at the spilled tea.

"And speaking of sherry, I was sharing a glass when I visited my cousin in Londonderry and she told me the most amusing thing. Oh how did it go... Ah yes! 'Better red hair than no hair!'" He let out a haughty laugh. "Hilarious, wouldn't you say?"

The woman was petrified, unable to muster a response. Instead, she gripped the back of her head, shifting the wig she was wearing. According to the whispers floating around the party, the wig had appeared after a mishap with a hair spell gone wrong. She wouldn't be the first to suffer the magical consequences of vanity. It seemed to happen to someone every social season. Among this crowd, only a fool would hope for sympathy.

"It was good to see you again, Mrs. Johnston! Give my regards to that handsome husband of yours, would you?" Bertram turned to Laoise. "A cup of tea, my dear. I'm absolutely parched."

"Of course si—ma'am." By the time she returned, another maid had already collected the fallen cup and shooed Oolong off.

"Thank you." Bertram accepted the tea from her. "What a darling party this is," he said as two women rushed past him. Once they were out of earshot, he lowered his voice. "I'm feeling a little faint from all of this excitement. Would you escort an old lady somewhere a little quieter?"

"Right away, ma'am." Even fully aware of who was behind the disguise, Laoise felt as though she was walking beside the real Mrs. Hammond. Her shoulders kept aching from tension while her ears strained to hear the herd of dachshunds coming, but the only dog wandering the party was Oolong, complete with a noisy bell on his collar to warn guests of his presence. The bell of course did little more than make Oolong's victims look around in confusion before tripping over him.

A woman bit into a scone, several crumbs falling to the ground. Oolong snatched them up, his sudden stop nearly tripping a gentleman who was busy craning his neck to leer at a young lady waving her fan his way.

This party would end the same way it always did for Oolong. Come evening he'd be in his favorite dog bed in Martin's study, lying on his back with his legs up and his tongue lolling out of his mouth. All the excitement of dropped food and extra pats on the head always tired him out. Meanwhile, there would be tears and shouting in the kitchen from the staff over the pressure to make everything run smoothly.

"The second floor of the library," Bertram said. He took her arm to lean against her. The second floor was more of a walkway than a floor. It wound around the room, giving access to a second row of bookshelves.

The library doubled as Montgomery Steepe's study. Before Charlotte's arrival, the shelves had been sparse, but she'd already filled an entire shelf with penny bloods on the second floor and was making quick work of the next shelf. Before long, the room would be a proper library.

Three men stood at the base of the narrow metal stairs, lost in conversation. She recognized the one in the middle. She didn't remember his name, but he was some distant cousin of the Steepes. The young man loved bragging about the connection, but as far as Laoise knew, he had yet to accomplish much of anything himself. Unless drama over his two mistresses meeting and fighting outside his house counted.

"They are waiting until the holidays are over to bring me into the business," he told his friends, his voice oozing confidence. "I'm certain of it. And since we're family, they practically owe me a spot."

Laoise rolled her eyes. It wasn't unusual for distant family to crawl out of the woodwork when they wanted something.

"My, my. Is that little Harry all grown up?" Bertram asked as they reached the stairs. He grabbed the man's biceps and winked. "Have you come all this way to see your Auntie Hammond?"

The other two men backed away, abandoning Harry.

"H-hello, Auntie," the man said, the confidence in his voice a ghost of what it had been a moment ago.

"Why, if you are looking for a job, you should come pay your dear Auntie a visit. There are a lot of things I could use a handsome, strapping young man for."

Laoise had almost forgotten Mrs. Hammond's way of flirting. Young, old, middle-aged—it didn't matter. She liked all men just the same. Or perhaps she simply enjoyed making them squirm.

"You're working now, aren't you? Why, I remember when you were little seeing how excited you were to drop your father's cheque into donation boxes." He hooked his arm under Harry's and patted his hand. "And now you can write your own cheques! How exciting! So have you made your donation yet?"

Harry swallowed, his prominent Adam's apple bobbing. "Not yet, Auntie."

"Then run along and do so. After all, we're all here for the children, aren't we?"

"Yes ma'am right away, ma'am." Harry's voice cracked as he scurried off.

"See to it that your friends donate as well!" Bertram called after him.

Laoise watched the young man scamper away like a wounded rabbit that had escaped a snare. "With you here, maybe the charity can make a new record in donations."

"You flatter me." Bertram patted her hand before heading up the stairs. Once they reached the top, he dropped his voice. "I didn't get a chance to apologize for Mrs. Johnston's behavior earlier. She isn't even drunk yet and she's already behaving like a beast."

"I'm fine. It's always this way with this lot. They all whine and make unreasonable demands the whole day. You adapt to it."

"You absolutely do not need to accept it," he said indignantly.

"Not accept. Adapt." She gave him a wicked smile. "May I refresh your beverage, ma'am?" The cup looked full of more milk than tea, just the way Bertram liked it. She traced her finger around the rim of the cup. "*Exspuo pro ultionem,*" she muttered, and a faint glow emanated from the teacup. She then spat into it, and the milky white beverage swirled. In a flash, the liquid shot up to the ceiling and positioned itself above Mrs. Johnston, then just as quickly, shot down onto her wig.

Below, the woman didn't notice the cold milky tea dripping down her hair right away. She reached up to rub the back of her neck and let out a cry of shock, standing and turning to try to identify whoever had spilled their drink on her. Harry happened to be walking behind the chair she was sitting in, which was evidence enough for her to loudly chide him before storming out of the room. Harry stood dumbfounded while his two friends poked fun at him.

Throughout the whole ordeal, Bertram's mouth hung slack. "I see why you don't use that one often."

"I use it plenty." She smirked. "Just not when people are lookin'."

"What do you mean by 'plenty?'" A look of horror dawned on Bertram's face. "Exactly how many times have you used that spell in this house? Or in my coffee?" His voice turned shrill on the last question.

"I've never been caught, so it's best you don't worry too much about it." Laoise stepped away from the railing to keep out of sight. "I'd be more worried about you being caught. Have you not caught anyone's suspicion?"

"Not at all." Bertram cleared his throat. He looked up from Mrs. Johnston, shaking himself out of his shocked daze and taking a step back. "I'm rather enjoying playing the role of Auntie Hammond."

Laoise grimaced. "It is rather disturbing how well you're taking to her."

"It's wonderful. No one argues with me or disturbs me in conversation. Everyone is too afraid of me to be even the slightest bit impolite. They'll do whatever I want to get me to go away." He brushed a piece of lint from his arm, his face smug. "I'd say Auntie has life figured out. I've gained a newfound respect for her after quite literally walking in her shoes."

"All the same, I'd rather you not make a habit of this. I much prefer Bertram Steepe to there being two Mrs. Hammonds in the world."

Laoise glanced to her left, where an evergreen tree decorated with candles stood. The tree was a new Christmas tradition Prince Albert brought with him from Germany. An odd one, Laoise thought. Trees didn't belong inside. All those falling needles would be more work for the maids, too. And to put candles on them for decoration felt downright foolish. Thank goodness Martin had lit the candles using a silvery magical flame that was cool to the touch and wouldn't cause any fires.

"Gaudy looking thing, isn't it?" she asked, tilting her head towards the tree.

"Hmm? The tree? I disagree. I find it quite beautiful. I confess I've always been rather envious of the German tradition of the Tannenbaum." He quietly sang a couple of lines of "*O Tannenbaum*."

"What was that, German?" The schoolgirl in Laoise was positively swooning hearing Bertram's singing voice. She'd always considered German a harsh language, but the words settled like a soft lullaby in her ears.

Bertram nodded. "Uncle Monty insisted that Martin and I learn Latin, French, and enough Italian to understand sheet music. We were also made to choose another language for study. I chose German while Martin"—he sighed—"chose ancient Sumerian of course."

"Sumerian? I'm not familiar with that one. I'm not even sure where Sumeria is."

"Sumer, you mean. Not 'Sumeria'. Though I'm not surprised you didn't know that considering it hasn't existed for about five thousand years." He let out an exasperated groan. "Hardly useful in a conversation, but apparently Sumerian cuneiform makes for very powerful runic magic."

Laoise smirked. "Then maybe you could learn a thing or two from those old Sumerians."

"Mhmm," Bertram finally answered after a long pause.

Laoise turned, finding him distracted by something on the other side of the room. She followed his gaze past the Christmas tree to Charlotte and her friend Mary Hawke. "You just can't leave those two alone, can you?"

He scoffed. His haughty demeanor gave way to the bitterness she was so familiar with back at the manor. "Those scheming conspirators? Not a chance. They're up to something. I know it."

"We're the ones who are up to something," she said, smacking Bertram on the arm. "They're just enjoying the party. Not conspiring against you."

"Why wouldn't they be plotting something? They already conspired to trick Martin into buying that failing Hawke Publishing House, and don't think your role in their little conspiracy escaped my notice."

Laoise balked. She had indeed stolen a guest list from under Bertram's nose, preventing him from learning Charlotte's background as a baker's daughter. Only Martin would invite ladies from all backgrounds to a tea party outside of the social season to find a wife.

Still, she refused to be intimidated, least of all by a scheming man disguised as an old woman. "As I recall, it was you who ended up buying Hawke. Martin sold the business back to the Hawkes and made you two investors after you got exiled. And now that they're successful, I've been told that investment is paying off handsomely. "

"Of course you'd cover for the Graham girl," said Bertram, huffing. "Has she bribed you with another set of gloves?"

"I ought to push you right over this edge." She pressed her hand against his shoulder, pushing him against the railing. They were almost intimately close, but anger burned in Laoise's chest as she spoke through her teeth. "Her name is Charlotte. Charlotte Steepe, not 'Graham girl.' And that cloak was a gift, not a bribe. The world isn't all just scheming and backstabbing."

"A gift?" Bertram repaid her anger with his usual cool smugness. "Sorry, but you don't seem the type to accept such gifts that easily."

"I'm not," said Laoise, backing up defensively. "And I'll pay her back for it. Eventually."

"On your salary? That might take a while." Bertram chuckled.

"That doesn't matter. What matters is that she's a good friend, and a good wife to Martin." Laoise took a deep breath. "I know you're only acting like this to protect Martin, but really, what more does she need to do before you'll accept that she actually loves him?"

"She needs to prove herself to you." He poked a finger at her. "After all, if she's innocent, then why are you avoiding her?"

Laoise froze. "What do you mean?"

"As soon as she enters a room, you leave. It's happened three times now," he said with a smirk, pushing himself up from the railing. "A guilty conscience, perhaps?"

Her hands sweat. "That has nothing to do with you."

"Laoise, you have a good sense of morality, and I admire that, but there's something you're not telling me. You know some secret about her, and I need to know it too. This plan is only going to work if you trust me as much as I trust you." He leered over her. Bertram she could stand tall against, but an extra tall Mrs. Hammond looming over her was too much to bear. "Now tell me."

"Hard to believe someone as clever as you could miss something so obvious," she said, turning and hanging her head. "She's a Steepe, and I'm still just a maid. How can she not be embarrassed to have me as a friend?"

"Oh." Bertram fanned himself. "Is that all?"

"What do you mean 'is that all?' She's been my best friend my whole life, and now I have to call her 'ma'am.' It's only a matter of time before she becomes too refined for the likes of me. Either that or she'll lose the respect of all these hoity-toity types. Then she'll blame me for ruining her new life." She hugged herself. "Just thinking about it makes me want to go hide in a hole."

"Let me assure you of one thing." He set a hand on her shoulder. "That Graham girl is a rube."

Laoise turned, her expression more confused than angry. "What did you say?"

"It's true. Those 'hoity-toity' types, as you so succinctly put it, will never accept her as one of their own. Martin and I are still considered too nouveau-riche to be their social equals. Even our considerable wealth can't buy their respect." He looked down with disdain on the other party-goers. "And frankly, I don't want it. I've never cared much what those vapid socialites think, and based on what I know about your Charlotte, I'd say she doesn't either."

Laoise knew she should have been angry with him for insulting her friend, yet somehow his words comforted her. "You really think so?"

"Even if she does, she has far bigger obstacles than being seen speaking friendly to a maid." He cast his gaze back to her. "For what it's worth, I'm not embarrassed to be seen talking to you either."

"I should be the one embarrassed to be seen with you," said Laoise, fighting back a giggle. "Well then, do we trust each other enough now to go forward with the plan?"

"About that," Bertram looked around the room, catching nervous glances from nearly everyone who rushed to look away from his gaze. "The plan is going to need to change slightly."

"Change? Change how?"

"I had planned on people avoiding me all night, but it seems I'm still drawing a bit too much attention."

"How are we supposed to get into the box to get the money?"

He shook his head. "I'm afraid there will be too many eyes on me if I attempt to break open the lockbox...."

She held her breath, afraid he was going where she thought he was.

"...which means you will need to get into it for us."

Her breath left her in a woosh. She held up her hands. "Not happening."

"You didn't hear the whole plan."

"Don't care. Getting caught stealing will not only ruin my employment with your cousin and uncle, but everywhere else, too. And then how am I going to pay for Sean's medicine? If that's your plan, I might as well give up and get back to work." Her arm knocked into a book sticking out of the shelf. She slammed the book the rest of the way in.

"Now if you'll excuse me, I'm sure there's hors d'oeuvres or something I need to be serving."

He held his arm out to block her exit. "You won't be caught. I promise. You said it yourself, you're used to blending in. I, on the other hand, plan on creating a distraction."

"Not even you can fool everyone," said Laoise, shaking her head.

Bertram sighed and produced a small envelope from between his breasts. "If you get into trouble, just use this. Do not lose it and do not open it."

Laoise's nose scrunched up as she took the letter with her thumb and forefinger. "I'm not certain I want to know what this is."

"It's a letter. The letter I intend to give to Martin tonight. If anyone catches you, just tell them this envelope contains Mrs. Hammond's donation and that you're having trouble getting it into the box. They'll either assume you're stupid or there's some issue with the runes. Either way, you'll have plenty of time to break in, take the money, and bring my letter back to me before anyone is the wiser."

It would be risky. But her brother's health was on the line. "Alright, but how do I open the lockbox?"

"I'm glad you asked." He pulled out something wrapped in a piece of paper he'd tucked into his fake chest.

Laoise cast a sideways glance at him. "Just how much do you have stuffed between those things?"

"I had a lot of time alone to think and prepare last night," he said defensively. He set the package down on the shelf and unwrapped it, revealing a handwritten note and the small tool he'd used to free himself from the bracelet back at the manor. He pointed to the symbols scrawled across the top of the sheet. "Look for these runes on the box. Then press the tool to them and read this incantation."

Laoise read the words written on the bottom of the page. "*Obsecro tu, domine, seram tuum apera.*"

"No, no. You pronounced it wrong." He corrected her, making her repeat it back.

Laoise said the line again, tripping over the last word. "What language is this?"

"It's Latin." Bertram looked at her in shock. "I thought you knew it."

"Of course I don't. Why would I know Latin?"

"But you were just speaking it! Don't you even know what the words of your little revenge spell mean?"

"Never much thought about it. Never much cared either so long as it works." She memorized the locking runes. There were only four of them, easy enough to remember. "I can hardly keep track of all these damned runes and incantations. Why can't magicians just wave around wands like in the stories?"

Bertram fixed her with a stern expression. "That would take hours of magical theory to answer." He reached up to adjust his hair. "Now, hurry downstairs to the lockbox. I'm going to create a distraction. Take whatever you can and I'll repay it back later."

"What is the distraction, exactly?"

Bertram slid his hand down the top of his dress once more and pulled out a small box. She recognized it as one of the impossibly sized boxes from the manor. He continued pulling out larger and larger boxes, stacking them on a low shelf. When he got to the final box, he reached in and took hold of a hummingbird. At first she thought it was one of the mechanical ones until it shook itself awake. She gasped. "You brought Pepper?"

"I couldn't just leave her all alone at the manor. She would have been lonely, and Sean wouldn't have had the chance to meet her." He ran a finger over Pepper's head. "Besides, I'm certain Oolong will appreciate a new playmate."

Laoise grabbed his wrist. "Don't you dare. What if he catches her?"

"Even if Oolong had the speed and prowess to catch Pepper, the worst he would do is lick her." He made a shooing motion with his free hand. "Now go to the lockbox."

Laoise shook her head and started down the stairs. Just as she hit the floor, Pepper zoomed off the balcony. A bark followed, and a woman cried out in surprise as Oolong barreled right between her legs to give chase. Someone whistled and a mechanical hummingbird joined Pepper. The dog wiggled in excitement, tail wagging hard enough Laoise feared he'd sprain it. Again.

As all eyes turned to watch the commotion, Laoise crept over to the lockbox nestled on one of the shelves. Pictures of some of the children the charity had helped stood on either side of it. Her stomach clenched as she searched for the right runes. Bile threatened to climb up her throat. There was little she wouldn't do for her brother, but that didn't make stealing from a charity feel any better.

"Is that a bird?" one of the guests shouted.

Laoise ignored the commotion and pressed the tool against the first rune.

Chapter 22

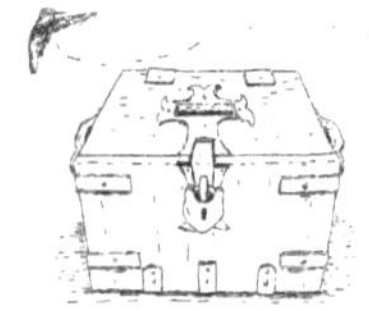

Laoise fumbled with the tool as she pressed it against the runes of the lockbox. The Latin felt thick in her mouth as she tripped over the words. She was no stranger to sneaking about and getting herself into trouble, but she couldn't recall a time she'd ever felt this nervous.

She kept looking over her shoulder, making sure that Bertram's distraction was working. All eyes were fortunately fixed on the parade of hummingbirds and all the chaos that they were causing. Partygoers tripped and cursed, showing where Oolong was dashing about as he chased the birds.

Pepper flitted about, then perched on a high branch of the tree. Several mechanical hummingbirds crashed into it behind her. While chasing the flying entourage of birds, Oolong had evidently been oblivious to the presence of the massive tree as he went skidding across the wooden floors, crashing into it. A few ladies shrieked as the tree tipped over.

"The Christmas tree!" A man yelled. A few candles came tumbling to the floor. The silvery flames licked at the carpeting, but the cold magical fire did not spread from their candlesticks. At least in all the chaos the house wouldn't burn down. Probably.

Laoise turned back to the lock, feeling her chance slipping away by the second. With a deep breath, she started over, focusing on the way Bertram had said the words, and the way the vowels rolled off his tongue.

The spell came smoother this time, and when the runes on the tool flared to life, the lock clicked open. Laoise grabbed a fistful of banknotes and stuffed them under her apron before hastily shutting the lid and scurrying away from the box. She pressed her back against the narrow staircase. Where had Bertram gone? He no longer stood on the balcony.

"No need to worry!" Martin called out to calm everyone as he approached the tree, which leaned threateningly over the crowd. Nothing visible held it in place, yet it didn't tip any farther. "It will right itself in a moment."

"You enchanted the tree?" A magician asked as he swished his glass of wine before taking a sip. He peered at the tree in interest. "Why, it's as though you anticipated this happenstance."

"One must always expect the unexpected with a dog in the house."

Oolong, for his part, sat under the tree, looking guilty. He trotted over to Martin to hide behind him, his tail tucked beneath his legs. Just as Martin had said, the tree righted itself, and even the fallen candles floated back into position amongst its branches.

Laoise stood on her tiptoes to get a better view of the rooms. Where had Bertram run off to? She'd gotten what she came for. It was time to leave before someone caught her with a pocketful of stolen money. She tried to keep her head low as she scanned the room for him. Instead, the butler caught her eye, and he tapped his watch. His way of saying get back to work.

She returned to the kitchen, the wad of bank notes feeling like it weighed a ton. She carried out more scones, putting on a smile as she served the partygoers, her eyes nervously darting from face to face looking for Bertram. Then she met perhaps the last face she hoped to see this evening.

Charlotte was seated beside Martin on a sofa next to the fireplace, and when her eyes met Laoise's, she wore an expression she hadn't seen her wear before. Her smile was bright and painted on smile, but her eyes belied a mixture of fear, disgust, and embarrassment. Laoise's heart sunk. Her friend was truly gone.

"Ch-Charlotte..." Her voice came out as barely a whisper.

"Well, well, look who it is!" said a singsong voice behind Laoise. She ducked to the side, turning her head to see Bertram. Charlotte's eyes remained transfixed on him, quaking in wide-eyed terror as he greeted her.

So she hadn't seen her after all. For anyone else, Laoise would be upset that her friend hadn't recognized her, but after the trauma of the incident with the Hammond dachshunds, she could understand if Charlotte wasn't aware of anything else in the room. She looked like a frightened animal, and Laoise was convinced the girl wouldn't react at all if she snapped her fingers in her face. With her gaze still focused, unblinking, on Bertram, Charlotte slowly reached over and tugged on Martin's arm.

Her husband turned his attention from his conversation, and the look of horror on his face matched Charlotte's. His voice came out strained and shaky. "Auntie Hammond. What a surprise. We truly weren't expecting you."

"Well 'one must expect the unexpected,' eh, Marty?" Bertram let out his haughtiest laugh. "I'm so glad to see Oolong bringing you as much joy as my dogs bring me."

Charlotte let out a muffled yelp at the mention of her dogs, her gaze darting about the room, no doubt looking for renegade dachshunds. She wasn't the only guest on alert, judging by all the shifting, nervous glances aimed at Bertram.

"This must be your lovely new bride. Why I've heard so much about you." He offered his hand to Charlotte. When she didn't take it, he gave her an awkward pat on the head much the same way Laoise had seen him do to Oolong.

Laoise stood off to the side, powerless to stop the uncomfortable scene unfolding before her. Suddenly, she remembered the envelope Bertram had given her. Balancing the tray in one hand, she tried to act nonchalant, rifling through the stolen money under her apron to find his letter.

Throughout the entire awkward encounter, one voice continued to speak, undaunted by the presence of Auntie Hammond. That voice came from a teapot sitting on the coffee table. It was the droning voice of Louie in the middle of another tale, "...to which the tax collector replied, 'What you say had been true this past winter, but according to the latest imperial decree...'"

Bertram looked down at the teapot, his face still wearing a smile, but fury clearly burning behind his eyes. "My, what a fascinating curiosity you have, little Marty! Of all the enchanted items I've seen in my day, I don't think I've ever seen a talking teapot before." He reached down and picked up Louie.

"Y-yes, he truly is one-of-a-kind." Martin grimaced, holding out his hands as though he feared Mrs. Hammond would drop the teapot. "Please do be careful. He is an antique."

Louie paused his story, steam rising from his spout as he addressed Bertram. "Though I am hesitant to interrupt my tale as it is reaching its climax, I feel it is necessary to clarify that this is not our first meeting. We have in fact met several times, for though you wear glamour and a wig, I recognize that beneath it all you—"

Bertram quickly pulled the lid of the teapot off, and Louie abruptly stopped talking. Evidently the teapot was able to see through his Auntie Hammond disguise. "Oh dear, I haven't broken it, have I?" Bertram asked, trying his hardest to sound innocent.

At last, Laoise managed to get a hold of the letter. She tried not to draw attention as she slipped it onto her tray of scones, then turned to present it to Bertram. "Scone, ma'am?"

"Hmm? Why yes, thank you." Wiggling his fingers as he perused the plate, Bertram plucked a scone from the tray, leaving the letter. Laoise tried to thrust the tray at him once more, but he had already turned his attention back to Martin. Charlotte, however, was no longer with him, having taken the momentary distraction to spring up from the sofa and quickly shuffle out of the room.

"Off to powder her nose, I presume," Bertram said, taking a bite of the scone. "These are simply divine! I shall have to borrow your baker at my next soirée."

"Ah yes, well, erm..." Martin took a nervous sip of his tea. "Actually, Charlotte baked those herself. We were thinking of serving them in some of the new tea shops."

Bertram chewed. For the first time that evening, he was at a loss for words. "I see."

Charlotte shuffled hurriedly back to the sofa. "Martin. Dearest. Do come along. It's nearly time to introduce the guest of honor."

Martin lifted an eyebrow and checked his pocket watch. "But that's not for another—"

"Come dear. Let's not keep the doctor waiting." She took a hold of Martin's hand and practically pulled him up from his seat. With a polite curtsy, she addressed Bertram for the first time. "Please excuse us, Mrs. Hammond."

Charlotte scurried out of the room once more, this time with Martin in tow. A few others who had been in the sitting area cleared out as well, leaving Bertram and Laoise alone with Louie.

"You know I've held that girl at gunpoint. Twice." Bertram turned to Laoise. "And neither time did she look as frightened as she did just now. Has Mrs. Hammond really had that much of an effect on her?"

"It's a bit of a long story." Laoise bit her tongue as she recalled Charlotte's humiliation at the hands, or rather paws of the Hammond Dachshunds.

Having finished his scone, Bertram idly replaced the teapot's lid, and Louie continued speaking right where he had left off. "—are in fact, Bertram Steepe."

Bertram pulled Louie close, dropping his impression of Mrs. Hammond as he spoke through his teeth. "That is a fact which you will keep to yourself unless you wish to end up smashed into a million pieces. Do I make myself clear?"

"I have been threatened with destruction a total of five thousand seven hundred and twenty-two times," said the teapot. His flat, droning voice made it hard to tell if he was intimidated by Bertram's threat. "The first of which..."

Bertram groaned as he set the teapot back down, letting it continue to prattle on.

"If you're finished threatening the pottery, I've got what I came for." Laoise patted the wad of bank notes under her apron. "Now quit stalling and give Martin your letter so we can get out of here."

"Ah yes. That whole business." Bertram took the letter from Laoise's tray. He strolled over to the fire and took one last look at the envelope before tossing it into the flames.

Laoise's mouth hung slack. "What in the hell are you doing?"

"What I should have done long ago."

"That doesn't explain what the hell you're doing!"

Bertram rested his hands on his hips. "Look, if you must know, I had planned on making one more appeal to Martin urging him to rid himself of that girl."

"You came all this way, went through all this trouble, and kept all these secrets just so you could tell Martin the same thing you've been saying since the start?" She considered throwing the tray at him.

"Not my most brilliant scheme, I confess," he said, nodding sheepishly, "But it hardly matters now. I see I may not have been entirely correct about her after all."

"In other words, you were wrong about her." Laoise nudged his side.

"I wasn't wrong. She was using him. In the beginning at least," he said, straightening his back. "But she's not just relying on the family's wealth and status. She's working with him to make his tea shops an even greater success."

Laoise rolled her eyes. "I could have told you that back at the manor and saved us both a great deal of trouble."

"Perhaps, but I saw something even more important. As terrified as she was of Auntie Hammond, she still came back to rescue Martin from my clutches. Courage like that is rare indeed." He snickered. "And if she's still doing the baking herself even with all the cooks and bakers we employ, I'd say she's not about to become one of those 'hoity-toity types.'"

"It's good that you're finally seeing things that way," she said with an exasperated smile. "Now, if you've done all you need to, I suggest we get out of here before anyone checks the lockbox."

"A fine idea. I shall excuse myself and meet you back at the carriage."

Laoise nodded and headed back to the kitchen. Her heart fluttered with excitement and it took all her strength to not break out into a sprint. Bertram's plan had actually worked. All she had to do was make her way out the servants' entrance and back to the carriage and her family's worries would be over. There was enough money stuffed in her apron to cover months of medicine, even if the doctor had to raise prices again. It would take a while to pay back all that she'd stolen, but it would be worth it to see Sean healthy again.

Laoise set her tray down on a counter in the kitchen and made her way past the flurry of cooks and maids.

"Miss Hughes," said a voice behind her. "Where on Earth are you going?"

She turned around. It was the butler. "Apologies, sir. Mrs. Hammond wanted me to—"

"Yes, yes. Mrs. Hammond this, Mrs. Hammond that," he said, furrowing his brow and waving a hand in frustration. "I know she's demanding, but she's only one guest. I can't have all of you serving her.

Now take this." He thrust a tray and teapot at her. "Earl Grey. It was meant to go out five minutes ago."

"But sir—"

"But nothing. I'll not have this night be spoiled on account of our service. Now go." With a look of disgust, he returned to his work of buffing out an imperceptible stain from one of the metal teapots.

Her face heated at the thought of blame falling at her feet if something went wrong. She should have known her sneaking out earlier wouldn't go unnoticed. Laoise accepted the tray and returned to the party.

She cursed Bertram's name under her breath. He was getting carried away with his performance as Auntie Hammond. Even at her worst, she'd only be an inconvenience for a few of the servants at most. Then again, she hadn't seen Bertram ordering the staff around too much. Perhaps some of the lazier maids were just using Auntie Hammond as an excuse. Laoise couldn't blame them. In any other situation, she'd likely be doing the same.

No matter. She'd continue serving for now. She was a Steepe maid after all. Shirking on her duties now might make things difficult when she properly returned from her shift at the manor. Even more so when it came time to seek new employment.

Still, she needed to let Bertram know that she would be delayed in meeting him at the carriage. Perhaps she could even have him hold on to the stolen money. She no longer felt as though eyes were being cast on her with suspicion, but the fear of bank notes falling out of her apron chilled her spine. Besides, Bertram clearly had plenty of storage space in his glamoured bust.

Luckily for her, Bertram still hadn't left the house yet. She spotted him in the dining room picking at the display of tea snacks piled onto the table while chatting with another lady.

She leaned over and whispered in his ear, "Looks like I can't leave yet. The staff is in an uproar over you."

"I beg your pardon!" Bertram's voice was different. A touch shriller. When he turned around to face her, she saw that it hadn't been Bertram at all, but Auntie Hammond. The real one.

Laoise froze. Her eyes went wide as she began stammering. "Sorry ma'am. I mistook you for someone else. Terribly sorry, ma'am." With a trembling hand she offered the teapot. "Earl grey, ma'am?"

The dress was almost exactly the same, but up close she could see that she stood substantially shorter than Bertram, much of her height coming from her ostentatious wig. The look of smug disdain on her face was also much more genuine.

"Irish girl, eh? Deep in your cups no doubt." She held out her teacup for Laoise to fill, turning her attention back to the other party guest. "I suppose it's just as my cousin in Londonderry once told me. How did it go..."

Laoise finished pouring and snuck out of the room, her search for Bertram now frantic. She searched the other rooms, finally finding Bertram back in the library. He cast smiles and flirtatious remarks to the other guests. No one showed any sign of noticing that there were two Mrs. Hammonds at the party. Yet.

"Earl grey, ma'am?" she asked, voice trembling. The other guests seized the opportunity to escape Bertram.

Bertram raised an eyebrow at her and lowered his voice. "I'm saying my farewells as quickly as I can. People will get suspicious if Mrs. Hammond leaves too suddenly."

She slammed the tray down on a nearby table and grabbed his hand. "They'll be even more suspicious when they see there's two of you here. It's time to go."

"What? But that's impossible. She never—" As if responding to him, Oolong ran past with two other dachshunds chasing after him in a neat line. All their ears flopped in perfect sync. Bertram jerked to attention. "Dear God."

"Let's go out the servants' door. We need to avoid the dining room." She led the way. When she reached the top of the stairs, a frazzled man ran into her, too busy looking over his shoulder to see where he was going. The man mumbled an apology, eyes widening when he saw Bertram.

"Auntie Hammond, you were just in the dining room," the man said, wilting under Bertram's attention.

"Don't be silly. Go to the parlor and sit down. All that tea must be going to your head."

The man scurried past, a harrowed look in his eyes. Laoise and Bertram pressed on down the stairs, when suddenly a ringing rang out. A trio of silver bells floated above the heads of the partygoers, quieting them down and leading them all towards the Christmas tree. There at the base were Martin and Charlotte, with Martin's mother at his side.

"Good evening ladies and gentlemen, and thank you all for gathering tonight," announced Martin. Laoise tried to continue down the stair, but Bertram took her arm and pulled her back into an alcove.

"Wait for the crowd to clear," whispered Bertram. Laoise tapped her foot impatiently.

Martin continued with his announcement, "...of course many of us have known Doctor Camden for years, and though he cannot be with us tonight, we wish him the very best in his retirement."

Bertram muttered to himself, "Camden retired? I hadn't heard of this..."

"...but tonight I'd like to introduce you all to our guest of honor. In Doctor Camden's absence, this man has proven himself to be an invaluable asset, not only to the Steepe Foundation, but to the sick children of London as well. Please join me in giving a warm welcome to Doctor Gustav Hartman!"

Charlotte leaned in and whispered something in Martin's ear.

"Hoffman. Doctor Gustav Hoffman!" Martin corrected. He waved forward a short, bald man with glasses and a pointed beard. Even from a distance, it was a face Laoise recognized.

"Hoffman? That's Sean's doctor." He had a calm, quiet demeanor that always made him seem careful about his work. It also made him intimidating, which wasn't helped by his refusal to negotiate prices. With all the increases in the cost of medicine lately, Laoise had been starting to worry that he had been extorting her family, but seeing him now put her mind at ease.

The Steepe Foundation was a reputable organization. With their support, perhaps the doctor could drop the price of his medicine. With a soft chuckle, she turned to Bertram. "If all the money's going to him anyway, I suppose there wasn't much reason for me to come here tonight either."

Bertram, however, looked as though he had seen a ghost. His eyes were wide, his mouth agape, and even through his glamour his face looked pale. He supported himself by gripping onto a bookshelf, his knuckles turning white from his grip.

"Something wrong?"

"Yes. That man. H-he can't be here. That's Doctor Speranza."

Chapter 23

Laoise turned her head in shock. "Speranza? But that is impossible. You killed him, didn't you?"

"Technically, I didn't kill him. He fell in on his own." Bertram bobbed head indecisively. Then he shook his head. "But that's not the point. Somehow he's still alive."

With an incredibly thick German accent, the doctor began his speech. "I vould like to sank all of you for your support zis evening. And ze children of London vould also like to sank you for..."

"And you're absolutely certain that's him?" she asked.

"There's no doubt about it. I'd never forget that face, no matter how he hides it," Bertram whispered, anger and confusion making his voice quiver. "And it seems he's back to his old tricks as well."

Laoise ground her teeth. "Which means he's poisoning Sean."

"Most likely."

"I'll kill him." Laoise started forward out of the alcove. "I swear to God I'm going to kill him."

"Wait," said Bertram, reaching out and grabbing her arm. "He's clever and resilient. We're going to need a plan."

Laoise hissed. "I have a plan. My plan is to kill the bastard, and make sure he'd actually dead this time."

"Laoise, listen. If we attack him now, he'll just slip away again. You'll be stopped before you can lay a finger on him. I don't think anyone will be willing to hear your side of the story if they catch you with a pocketful of stolen money."

Laoise's breath hitched. He was right, of course. She slammed her fist against the closest bookshelf in frustration. "Then what's the plan?"

Bertram shook his head. "I don't know."

"We'll tell Martin then," Laoise blurted out. "Or your uncle. They'll know him for the fraud he is."

"Uncle Monty's made it clear he's not interested in listening to me, and I'm not certain Martin will hear me out either."

Laoise groaned. Couldn't anything go right? She racked her brain for a solution, then snapped her fingers. "You got that coward to confess to his crimes when you were only a child. If we catch him outside of the gala, we can hold him up and do it again."

"It could work." Bertram tapped his chin. "But I'm unarmed at the moment. We'll need some sort of weapon if we're going to confront him."

"You mean you didn't bring along your collie-march between those things?" Laoise pantomimed a sword while pointing at Bertram's bosom.

"Colichemarde," corrected Bertram. "No, I did not bring it with me, but there must be something we can use." He looked down at his dress. "I should fetch a change of clothes as well. Mrs. Hammond isn't quite the right kind of intimidating for this task."

"Well, what are we waiting for? Let's get going."

The audience gave a polite round of applause, turning Laoise's attention back to the doctor. He held up a hand and concluded his speech, "...and as grateful as I am for zis gala and for your generosity, I must take my leave. I must return to my vork for ze sake of ze children. Sank you all!"

"He's leaving already?" Laoise burned with anger.

"Change of plans," said Bertram. "You go gather what you can. I'll try to stall him until we're ready to make our move."

Laoise lifted an eyebrow. "That might be difficult to do with the real Auntie Hammond roaming about."

"It will, but I have an idea. Give me the money you took from the box. The lock breaking tool as well."

"Of course. There's no chance I'd ever let that snake see a single penny of this money." She reached into her apron and pulled out the wad of banknotes. They felt filthy to the touch, and even though she'd worked all night to get a hold of them, she was glad to be rid of them.

"Then you won't like my plan," Bertram said with a smile. "If I can sneak these into his pockets, we might be able to frame him for our little theft. It's a long shot, but it might be enough to get him to start talking."

"It's worth a try. If it doesn't work, then I'll go find something to bludgeon him with." Laoise started out of the alcove before Bertram caught her arm once more.

"Wait. One more thing." He pressed a smooth ball into her hand. "If you find yourself in trouble and you have absolutely no other options, use this."

"Is it another one of your bombs?" Laoise held the thing at arm's length. "Jesus, Bertie, I'm not trying to burn the house down."

"Oh relax. I've fixed the issue with the bombs from before. These ones will release more smoke, and the fire burns cold, not hot." He pointed to the Christmas tree. "Just like those candles."

Laoise raised an eyebrow as she closed her hand around the ball, feeling its weight in her hand. Her thumb brushed over the inscribed runes. "Then why bother with fire at all? Why not just have smoke?"

Bertram sighed. "Because it's a great deal harder than one might think. I can't figure out how to get rid of the fire, and frankly I'm not even sure why there's fire at all. As long as it is there, however, it would be best if the fire doesn't burn everything to the ground. Now just take the thing."

Laoise grimaced and tucked it into her apron. With Bertram's signature craftsmanship, the bomb was as likely to do nothing at all as it was to blow the whole house to smithereens, but in a pinch it might be better than nothing at all. She desperately hoped she wouldn't have to put it to the test.

With the presentation of the guest of honor concluded, the partygoers once more talked amongst themselves. Bertram made his way through the crowd, giving a wide berth to the real Auntie Hammond. Laoise took off in the opposite direction, melting into the crowd as she made her way up the stairs to the Steepes' bedchambers.

She knew the perfect bedroom to get clothes from, the room tucked away in a back corner on the second floor. The wardrobe held all the random pieces of clothing left behind by guests, some of them long out of style. Some of the clothes were so old she was convinced they had to have come with the place when the Steepes bought it.

Her hunch proved correct. The odd mix of clothing hung in the wardrobe, free of moths thanks to the enchantment on the wood and the herbs the maids left in all the wardrobes each month to aid the magic. She dug through the offerings. There'd be no time to change Bertram out of his dress, so she'd need to find something large that he could wear overtop of it. Rifling through the various articles, she found a dark cloak a touch too long for him, an old tricorn hat that could replace his wig, and a silk scarf to hide the sloppy makeup and wrinkles of his glamoured face.

She bundled the scarf and hat up in the cloak before making her way to Martin's study. The Steepes didn't make a habit out of leaving weapons lying around, so a couple of fire pokers would have to do. She stepped into the room. Dim light from the fire guided her. As she approached the fireplace, she looked up and noticed a large ornamental shield with a pair of crossed swords hanging above the mantel.

"Laoise?"

She jumped and spun around. Charlotte was sitting on a large leather chair, hugging her knees by the fire. "Lottie? What are you doing in here?"

Charlotte jumped to her feet and yanked the curtains closed. "Hiding from Mrs. Hammond. We didn't expect her to come. She never does. My very first gala and she comes. What luck." She wrung her hands. "I must be going mad. I could swear I saw two of her."

Laoise bit her tongue. "Don't be silly. It's not as bad as all that."

Charlotte sank back into the chair. "What if her dogs find me again? My social life will be over for good this time. Martin couldn't possibly bear being seen with me. The Steepes will be ruined, and their business will fail and it will all be my fault."

"Now you're just being ridiculous. I'm sure no one even remembers what happened last time." Laoise winced at the white lie. "And even if they did, Martin wouldn't leave you over something like that."

"I hope you're right…" Her hands paused. She spun around to face Laoise. "I've been so distraught I didn't notice you'd come back from the manor. Is everything alright? Are you well?"

"I'm fine. Just fine." She held the bundle of items against her chest. "Listen, Lottie, I don't need to be rude, but this is a bit of an urgent matter." She reached up and tugged on the sword above the fireplace, but it wouldn't budge.

"Yes, of course. Anything—" Charlotte's hand covered her mouth. "But if you're here, where's Bertram? Is he still at the manor? Or has he escaped?"

"Well he—"

"He has escaped, hasn't he!"

Laoise grimaced. "Yes, but—"

"I knew it! That's why you need that sword. Say no more." With surprising speed and strength, Charlotte threw her chair to the fireplace and stood on it, yanking the shield and both swords to the ground with a force Laoise didn't know she was capable of. She muttered to herself as she pulled the swords loose from the display. "That cad. I'll bet he's the reason Auntie Hammond is here."

"That...never mind." Though she was missing many important details, Charlotte's assumptions had been surprisingly accurate. Laoise would have to clarify things eventually, but it was far too long and complicated a story to explain. Best to just let her go along with things for now. No doubt she'd lose her nerve and run when she saw Bertram's disguise once more.

"Never mind indeed." She handed one of the swords to Laoise, and like a soldier she marched to the door. "Now let's get him."

The door nudged open, letting more light into the room. The dachshunds raced each other into the room. Now there were four Hammond dachshunds. Oolong followed behind, tongue flopping out of his mouth in excitement.

Charlotte yelped and bumped into the chair, knocking it over.

"Get out of here!" Laoise chased the dogs out before shutting the door.

"It's too late. The dogs found me. They know where I am," Charlotte muttered as she wrung her hands in despair. She yanked the curtains apart and opened the window. "I'm sorry, but you'll have to handle Bertram on your own. Godspeed!" With that, Charlotte threw herself out the window.

"Lottie!" Laoise sprinted to the window and peered out. Below, Charlotte climbed off the pile of snow she'd landed on. At least she was alright. Charlotte wasn't normally one to overreact. Then again, after the dachshund incident at the Hammond's luncheon, perhaps her dramatic escape was somewhat justified. Laoise could still hear the ripping of fabric, the mortified gasps of the guests, and the excited barks of a tiny army of dachshunds...

A dog whined from the other side of the door. Oolong, no doubt. Laoise cursed and gathered up the sword, wrapping it in the cloak before running out. Oolong chased after her as she raced for the stairs.

Laoise rushed to the front door, ignoring requests for more tea as she dashed past guests. She was relieved to see that Bertram had accosted the doctor, his tall frame stopping the small man from walking out the door. The boisterous personality of Auntie Hammond did the rest.

Bertram held a hand to his chest, looking shocked. "Why *A Christmas Carol* has got to be Dickens's finest work. I think it will become a classic of the Christmas season. You mean to tell me you haven't read it?

The doctor shifted uncomfortably. "I have not."

"You simply must. It's about a greedy old man who's visited by three spirits which convince him to change his wicked ways." He spoke in a singsong voice and gave the doctor a knowing smile. "An intriguing concept, wouldn't you say?"

The doctor turned his gaze and nervously adjusted his glasses. "I'm afraid I much prefer ze vork of Zachery, ma'am. Now please excuse—"

"Zachary?" Bertram asked, raising his eyebrows in confusion. "Or do you mean Thackery, my dear?"

The doctor groaned and annunciated, briefly breaking his accent. "Thackery. Now if you vould kindly—"

As the two spoke, Laoise discreetly waved to Bertram, holding up her bundle of supplies. He nodded at her in acknowledgement. "Doctor, it was lovely seeing you this evening." He held out his hand for the man, who reluctantly took it and kissed it.

"You," said a voice behind Laoise. Her spine tingled from the imposing presence that had suddenly appeared as if from thin air. She turned to find Montgomery Steepe standing over her with his valet in tow. She gasped as his gaze met hers, terrified that she'd finally been caught. With a quivering hand she reached for the smoke bomb. The man, however, paid no mind to Laoise as he strode past her towards the doctor.

"I was hoping I'd get the chance to greet you personally before you left." He extended his hand to the doctor. Bertram's position in the doorway had obscured his presence from his uncle, as the man jumped when he looked up to see the smiling face of Auntie Hammond greeting him.

"Little Monty, is that you?" Bertram gushed as he took his uncle's hand and shook it. Laoise clasped a hand over her mouth as Bertram pinched the man's cheek. Uncle Monty frowned, but didn't dare pull away. "You're a hard man to find. It means so much that you made time for me!"

"Of course, Auntie Hammond," he said, clearing his throat.

"It's been such an enchanting evening. I can't believe I've been missing out on this event all these years. I shall have to make time in my schedule to come back every year!"

"Of course, Auntie Hammond," Monty repeated, speaking in the tone of a man resigned to his own death.

The doctor sneaked toward the door, but Bertram was back upon him. "Doctor, you must tell me one thing. My cousin from Stuttgart was writing to me, and she told me how to say 'Happy New Year' in German. Oh how did it go..." Bertram cleared his throat. "*Diese Möpse sind für dich!*" Even to Laoise's untrained ear, she could tell he was going out of his way to pronounce the words harshly. Much the way she expected German to sound. "So how is my pronunciation?"

The doctor adjusted his glasses and nodded shyly. "Yes, very good. Your skills are coming along nicely, madam. But please, I vill have to be going now."

Bertram looked to Laoise and tilted his head to the door, and she started down the stairs towards him. He then turned his attention back to his uncle. "I'm afraid I will need to be going as well, Monty. You will keep in touch, won't you, darling?"

"Of course, Auntie Hammond," he repeated once more. With a bow, he turned around and started out of the cramped hallway. He stopped as a figure appeared in the doorway before him. A squat figure with a tall wig. Montgomery let out an uncharacteristic gasp at the sight of the real Mrs. Hammond.

"Why little Monty, are you in here talking about your favorite Auntie? My ears have been positively burning all evening!" As she flounced into the hallway. She stopped, eyes widening as she caught sight of her imposter. Her mouth flopped open, and she covered it with a hand.

Bertram stood, stunned. With the two of them together, the differences were easier to spot. Bertram's proportions looked ridiculous compared to the real Mrs. Hammond. Montgomery's face snapped from one Mrs. Hammond to the other. "Just what in God's name—"

Mrs. Hammond squealed. It was the same squeal she made whenever her dachshunds did something especially cute. "What a lovely surprise. Oh Monty, you know just how to bring cheer to this lonely old soul." She pinched Mr. Steepe's cheek the same way Bertram had earlier.

"I've not quite been feeling myself lately. I'm always so sorry to miss this gala every year, but I had no idea you missed me enough to have someone stand in for me." She pinched Bertram's cheek this time. "Imitation is the highest form of flattery. And I must say, you got my figure perfect. And this dress! I love it. You must tell me where you bought it." She grinned as she slapped Bertram's rump. "I do have Viking ancestors, you know. It's what makes all the women in my family indomitable."

Montgomery collected himself and snapped his fingers, pointing to the doors of the cramped entryway. The valet directed the footmen to stand guard at the doorways, blocking the view of the hallway from the guests. Fortunately for them, no one was much interested in what was happening. Knowing Mrs. Hammond was involved was enough to keep them away. One of the footmen took up a position at the foot of the stairs, standing between Laoise and the scene unfolding before her.

"With my children all grown up and out on their own adventures, I always get melancholy this time of year." Auntie Hammond pressed a hand to her chest and blinked as though she were trying not to cry. "It brings me comfort to know there are others thinking of me. I couldn't have asked for a better Christmas gift."

"Yes, well," started Bertram, refusing to drop character. "Now that you are here, I'd best not overstay my welcome. I'm afraid I can't quite compare to the genuine article."

Mrs. Hammond gave a haughty laugh. "How right you are. Then I suppose I shall get back to the party before I am missed!" She pulled Bertram in and kissed him once on each cheek, then flounced back past the footmen into the party.

Bertram's eyes were wide as they followed her out of the room, then turned back to his uncle, grinning nervously. "Once again, I must thank you for an enchanting evening, but I must—"

"A moment," said Montgomery, snapping and pointing to Bertram. His valet seized him by the arm. "Just who in the hell are you?"

Laoise flashed the hilt of the sword to Bertram, ready to jump into action. He shot her a glance and subtly shook his head. "I'm no one of consequence. And now that my work is done, I'll be leaving."

"I think not," replied Montgomery coldly. "The locks on the donation box have been broken, and now I see a mysterious imposter in my midst. A gentleman does not jump to conclusions, but I hardly believe that to be a coincidence." With another snap of his fingers, the valet and another footman got to work searching Bertram.

"Unhand me!" Bertram said, his voice no longer wholly imitating Mrs. Hammond. He pushed his attackers back and assumed a boxing stance. The outrageous dress he was wearing had thrown off his balance, but he still kept his uncle's men at bay for a moment.

Suddenly, the bell around Oolong's neck rang out, and a parade of dachshunds shot between Bertram's feet. He stumbled and then tripped over the dogs as they came back for round two. Bertram twisted to the side, his wig flying off as he went down. His breasts popped like balloons, and the stolen money spilled across the floor.

"Bertram. I should have known," Montgomery said, spitting the words through his teeth as he spoke. "You continue to surprise me with how low you are willing to sink." The doctor, who had been hiding behind the elder Steepe during the fracas, looked pleased at Bertram's predicament.

Bertram stood, determination in every move as he prepared to square off with his uncle. "Uncle, listen. The money is for a sick boy who needs medicine."

His uncle's knuckles were white as he gripped his cane. "And just what do you suppose this charity is for then, hmm? Of all your lies, boy, this has got to be the most egregious."

"No. The most egregious liar in this room is that man." He pointed an accusatory finger at the doctor. "That's the man who poisoned Martin. That's Dr. Speranza! He's come back to swindle us again."

"That is quite impossible. You know that better than anyone else."

"Uncle, you're not listening! The man doesn't even speak German. He couldn't even tell the difference between 'Happy new year' and 'Look at my puppies.'" Bertram grabbed his chest for emphasis.

The doctor recoiled at the accusation, but Montgomery's eyes darkened, unconvinced. He turned to the doctor. "I'm terribly sorry, Doctor Hoffman. I didn't know my nephew planned to cause trouble. I'll see to it that he is punished for this."

"It is no trouble, Herr Steepe." His accent came out thick, thick enough Laoise struggled to understand him. "But if zis is all being taken care of, I vill take my leave."

With a nod, he motioned the doctor to the door. The footman allowed him to pass, and the doctor slunk away from the scene.

"Aren't you listening?" Bertram spat. "That man is a fraud! Don't just let him—"

"Be silent, boy. Your antics have already cost this family dearly. To think you would not only stoop to stealing from a charity, but slander a doctor's name to do it..." He drew in close to his nephew. "I had such hopes for you, Bertram, but I have never before been so ashamed to call you family."

Bertram was silent. He looked as though he'd been slapped.

Montgomery took a deep breath. "Hold him in the cellar and send for the police."

As the footmen pushed Bertram towards the cellar, he spoke at last, "Once again, uncle, your inaction has forced me to do something drastic. Luckily, I'm not alone this time." He looked to Laoise once more and winked. From his sleeve he produced the smoke bomb and threw it to the floor. The smoke came out in a thin, but powerful plume. It shrieked as the force of the smoke propelled the ball like a bullet, ricocheting about the room, and leaving wispy strands of smoke and silvery flame behind. The commotion was enough for Bertram to break from the footmen's grip and dash back into the party. With all the footmen giving chase, the front door was left unguarded.

Laoise looked down at the sword and cloak in her arms. He'd created the distraction, and now it was her turn to do something drastic. She dashed out the front door. It was up to her to go after the doctor now. She wouldn't betray Bertram's faith in her, and she would sooner die than let the doctor go free.

Chapter 24

She followed Doctor Hoffman down the line of carriages. There was no sign of the carriage she'd come in. It'd left, likely trying to avoid getting caught by the real Mrs. Hammond. She couldn't blame the driver. Had he been caught, his pay would have been cut. Or worse, he'd be forced to herd her dachshunds back into the carriage too. In his position, she'd have done the same.

A late hansom cab pulled up, which Laoise recognized as the Steepe's old cab. She couldn't recall the name of the distant Steepe relative who climbed out, but she instantly knew the driver from the rowdy dinners the staff would have together.

"Cyril! Hey, Cyril!"

"Laoise? Is that you?" The driver squinted at her in the darkness. "Didn't know you were back fro—"

"Back early," interrupted Laoise. "Listen. I need you to drive me. Now."

"Oh no," he said, casting her a sideways glance and shaking his head. "You're not roping me into whatever trouble you've gotten yourself into. Not again."

"This is an emergency. Please." She craned her neck to keep an eye on the doctor's gig as it headed down the main road.

"I'm not driving you, Laoise," he said sharply, "but..."

"But what?"

"I've been shuttling guests from all over London. But if this cab were to be stolen by a mysterious bandit, I'd have no way to perform my duties." A slow smile crept over his face as he stood up and gently set the reins on the seat. He climbed off of the cab and spoke in a deadpan voice. "No. Stop, thief. You'll never get away with this."

"Thank you!" Laoise quickly climbed up and grabbed the reins. She'd never driven a cab before, but she had ridden in enough of them to have a vague understanding of how they worked. With a crack of the reins, her horse took off into a gallop. There was hope of catching up to the doctor yet.

The road was a straight shot through fancy houses, but in a few minutes they would leave the neighborhood. Then the buildings would become crowded and the roads narrow. Best to catch up to him right away before they attracted an audience.

Steering the cab seemed intuitive enough. As she raced up the road, she proceeded with the rest of Bertram's plan, slipping the large cloak on and tying the scarf around the bottom half of her face. The drooping hood hid the rest. The sword rattled against the seat next to her as the cab bounced along the bumpy road. If she had Bertram's skill with a blade, she might have had a little more confidence in her ability to overpower the doctor. However, she'd never used a sword before in her life, so waving it around would have to be threatening enough.

Bertram... She ignored the way her heart sped up thinking about him. He'd taken the fall for the crime they committed together, and he'd given Laoise the chance to bring the doctor to justice. A few short days ago, she wouldn't have thought Bertram Steepe capable of any sort of self sacrifice, and it made her giddy that she was the one he was willing to sacrifice himself for.

She wouldn't waste the chance he'd given her. Everything else could wait. She'd prove to him she'd been worth it. And she'd prove it to herself as well.

With no other carriages coming, she moved to overtake the doctor. Another crack of the reins propelled the horse to run faster, and she pulled her cab right up alongside the doctor's. "Stop your horse!"

The doctor looked at her as though she were mad, which she supposed she probably was. "Not a chance!" With a whoop to his horse, his gig pulled ahead of hers.

"I said stop!" Laoise rushed to catch back up. She grabbed the sword and held it aloft, waving it around to appear more intimidating. The sword was heavy, and holding it above her head threw off her balance.

As she stumbled, she kept her hold of the reins, tugging the horse into an unexpectedly sharp turn. The right side of her cab hit a long patch of ice. The wheels lost traction and slid right into the side of the doctor's gig. Her cab shuddered at the contact, and the sudden sound of a sharp splintery crack told her something had broken. Her beginner's luck in driving had run out.

The noise spooked Hoffman's horse, and its pace quickened to a frantic run. Hoffman tugged on the reins, but the horse wouldn't listen. She didn't dare match the dangerous speed of Hoffman's, not with all the ice around. Her horse, as if sensing the damage to the cab, slowed down its pace just as the turn came into view.

Hoffman charged headlong into the turn. A narrow driveway continued straight ahead, surrounded on either side by a stone wall separating the thin patch of trees from the house's large front lawn.

His horse turned too late. The wheels of the gig caught on a large patch of ice and it skidded to the side, sliding right into the stone wall with a loud bang. The wagon tilted toward the fence, the smashed wheel unable to keep it righted. Hoffman tumbled right over the fence and into the snowbank on the other side.

The doctor's horse whinnied and reared up. Free of the broken gig, the horse took off again, this time alone. Laoise pulled clumsily on the reins, slowing her own horse to a stop, and boxing in the driveway and doctor. She climbed down, adjusting her hood and scarf to hide her face. Then she lifted the sword, struggling to hold its heavy weight it one hand.

The doctor pulled himself back onto his feet. What remained of his gig was wrapped around a now dented gas lamp post. Broken fragments and splinters of wood surrounded the wreck. Snow coated his trousers and coat as he pulled himself out of the snowbank to assess the damage to his gig. He muttered a string of curses under his breath, none of which were in German.

He stumbled away from the scene when he noticed Laoise blocking his path. She deepened her voice, trying to sound intimidating. "You should have stopped when you had the chance."

He paused and then backpedaled as he dug around in his pockets. She approached, her steps slow as she avoided the patches of ice. The doctor threw a handful of coins at her as he hunched against the gate. "Take my money. That's all I have on me. I swear it."

Not a trace of his earlier thick accent remained. He sounded English through and through. The revelation flamed her anger. Bertram was right. The man was a fraud. "I'm not here for money."

His brow furrowed. Then his eyes widened. "I swear I didn't know she was married. 'An eligible young maiden' is what she called herself. On my word!"

"Your word? Your word is worthless."

"I-It's true! I wouldn't dare lie to you I'm as much a victim here as you are, good sir." His voice grew a little more confident with every word, his panic ebbing away. He patted at his pockets wildly. "She seduced me in a moment of weakness. Please, won't you forgive me?"

"Your crimes are unforgivable." Laoise continued forward. She didn't have the slightest clue as to what he was going on about. What kind of woman would go out of her way to spend more time with a sniveling worm like him? The idea filled Laoise with disgust, but the pure, blind rage she felt looking at him overshadowed it.

She closed the distance and yanked him to his feet by his collar. The pounding of her heart thrummed in her ears as her anger surged through her, making it difficult to hear the man speak.

"Crimes? What crimes?" the doctor squeaked out. His gaze darted to his gig. "I don't know what you mean."

"You know exactly what I mean." She pressed the blunted edge of the blade to his throat and lowered her voice. "You've been poisoning your patients. You're a fraud."

He closed his eyes and whimpered, his Adam's apple bobbing as he swallowed. "What do you want from me?" Once more he stole glances at his broken gig.

"Everything." She pressed him back against the gate. No punishment would be enough. Her brother suffered through countless weeks because of one man's greed. Martin too. How many others had done the same? Bertram told Laoise about how he had hesitated in taking the man's life all those years ago. It was not a mistake she would repeat.

Still, Laoise was of sound enough mind to know that a dull sword wouldn't be able to do much, even pressed against his throat. The tip looked sharp enough to run the man through if she applied a little effort. Satisfied that this would be the easiest way to dispatch the doctor, she shifted her grip on both the man and her blade.

The sword proved too heavy to be wieldy. As she repositioned herself, the doctor seized the opportunity to duck out of her grip, falling to the ground. He scrambled backwards towards the wreckage.

"No more running, Doctor Hoffman. Or should I say Doctor Speranza?" She closed the distance between them again. "But it doesn't much matter what you call yourself. Your time is up."

"That's close enough." He had found what he was looking for, drawing a pistol from the wreckage and aiming it at her with an unsteady hand. Laoise stopped her advance, and he smiled through his panting. "I admit you did give me a fright, but I know exactly who you are now."

Her chest tightened. She'd relished in his fear too long and let him get the upper hand. But she'd only seen him once or twice back at her family's home. Did he truly recognize her from those interactions alone?

"Your father is going to be very upset with you, isn't he?" The doctor slowly pushed his way to his feet. "Mr. Bart Steepe!"

Laoise blinked, not quite able to process everything the man had gotten incorrect.

"Surprised I remember you after all these years? Don't be, boy. I'll never forget what you did to me," he taunted. "And I'll never forget that you didn't have it in you to finish the job yourself. But there's no flooded Thames to help you this time. Now drop the sword." He gestured with his gun to the sword.

"That's right. You prefer your victims defenseless, don't you?" She crept forward, sword still in hand. She knew it was a foolish move, but fury drove her on.

"Victims? What victims? I'm the victim here," sputtered the doctor. He cocked the hammer of his pistol. "I said drop that sword now!"

She complied, letting it fall to the floor with a heavy thud. Rage burned inside of her, but she had to remain calm. He'd gained the edge by letting her talk. Perhaps she could do the same. "Are you going to shoot me now that I'm unarmed?"

"Only if I need to," he said. "I'm content to hold you here and tell your father how you attacked me."

Her vision tunneled around the gun. "He's not my father." She slid a finger up her sleeve, struggling to get a grip on the smoke bomb Bertram had given her. If she could just activate the rune, maybe she could escape through the smokescreen. The more likely option was that the bomb would blow her arm off, but it might be a slight improvement on her current situation.

"Father, uncle, whatever. Either way, he'll see how you rammed your carriage into me, a poor helpless doctor just trying to do charitable work for the poor. I doubt he'll keep you out of prison after you not only stole from the Steepe Foundation, but tried to assassinate its guest of honor." He chuckled.

Her fingers closed on the smoke bomb. She needed to distract him long enough to throw it. A crunching noise drew both of their attention. A rider on horseback. She held onto the bomb for now. If help came, maybe she wouldn't need it.

"See, there comes your uncle now. He'll see what you've done here." Like an actor on a stage, the doctor threw himself on the ground in a dramatic pose, the gun still pointed at Laoise. He cupped a hand to his mouth. "Help! Von't somevone please help? I've been attacked by Bart Steepe!"

A horse stopped on the far side of the wagons. Snow crunched as the rider drew near. Hoffman's smirk grew.

"Who in the hell is Bart Steepe?" a voice answered.

Hoffman's head jerked toward the voice.

Bertram appeared at the back of the wagons, hiking up his skirts as he made to climb over the front seat of Laoise's carriage. Laoise felt a quick flash of relief, but seeing that Bertram was armed only with a lady's fan, she realized that she hadn't been rescued just yet.

"Zat vould be you," he stammered, taken by surprise, "vouldn't it?"

"Bertram. My name is Bertram Steepe." Bertram scoffed. "And you may drop the accent. You're not fooling anyone." He fanned himself with his right hand, the irony of him still enacting Mrs. Hammond's mannerisms evidently lost on him.

The doctor's mouth flopped open. He aimed his pistol back and forth between them before stopping on Laoise. "It doesn't matter! I've got the gun, and both you and your little accomplice are going to prison!"

"What accomplice?" Bertram looked about, his gaze finally settling on Laoise. His eyes went wide, and he jumped. "Who is that?"

She wasn't certain if he was setting up another scheme or if he truly didn't recognize her. Either way, she wouldn't get another opportunity to strike. Without a word, she tossed the bomb at her feet. A tremendous volume of smoke burst forth from the bomb, though it only rose to about the height of her ankles. It fanned out from her in a wide, low circle.

Once more, a smoke bomb made by Bertram had failed. She shouldn't have been surprised, but it took every bit of Laoise's self control to not yell at him. She considered raising her hands in surrender. But when she looked at the doctor, she only saw fear there.

Bits of of the wreck that the smoke touched lit up with silvery flames. Then the flames climbed the backs of her legs, quickly gaining height. She found herself engulfed in the shimmering silver flames, but as Bertram had promised, the fires were not the least bit hot. They felt freezing cold even compared to the cold winter air, biting into her skin unpleasantly.

"Demon! Wraith! Spectre!" Shouted Bertram, sidling up next to the doctor and pointing a shaky finger at Laoise. "It's come for us! Death itself has come for us!"

"No that's... that's nonsense! This is one of your tricks, isn't it?"

Laoise maintained her composure despite the flames. She saw them climbing the broken gas lamp from the corner of her eye. Despite the coldness of the flames, it felt as though they were starting to heat up.

"Look for yourself." Bertram slapped the doctor's shoulder and pointed once more. "We've got to run before it—"

A thunderous boom erupted around Laoise, shooting a blinding flash of silver into the sky. A great gust of wind blew past her, nearly knocking her off of her feet.

Chapter 25

Dots danced behind Laoise's eyelids. When she dared open her eyes a few seconds later, silver flames covered the entire alley. It seemed that somehow the magical flames had ignited the gas from the lamp post. The doctor cowered on his knees, covering his head to protect himself. Bertram huddled up next to him.

"Th-there's no escape!" Bertram cried out. His plain expression did not match his voice as he scanned the ground. Finally, his gaze fell upon the pistol the doctor had dropped in terror. He subtly kicked the firearm aside. "Confess your sins and maybe it will spare you."

Laoise lurched forward. As the flames grew warmer and warmer, her steps became more stiff. The bottom of the cloak was smoldering now, almost pleasantly warm in the cold air.

"B-but I've done nothing wrong! Spare me, please." Hoffman tipped over onto his behind as he gawked at Laoise. Behind him, Bertram looked up and gestured for her to press on.

"Confess, sinner, or face damnation," said Laoise, trying to conjure up the gravitas of a priest giving a fiery sermon. It was difficult to focus as the flames grew hotter and hotter. The edge of her smoldering cloak climbed higher and higher as the flames devoured it. Heat seeped through her boots, but the flames had yet to eat their way through the leather. Still, she had to remain calm. For Sean's sake.

"Fine, yes, I'll confess! I slept with Mrs. Carvey even though I knew she was married." The doctor cried out in a panic. "Mrs. Bennington too."

"Mrs. Bennington? But she's seventy. She's been married for fifty years." Bertram's lips curled in disgust, but he shook himself out of it.

"I meant the poison, not the affairs. You're no doctor at all. You've been poisoning the children of London, not saving them."

"It's true. But I only wanted to steal the Steepe Foundation's money this time. I swear I never wanted to kill anyone."

Bertram stared him down, fire burning in his eyes. "You poisoned Martin Steepe when he was a child, didn't you?"

"What? Yes. Probably," the doctor said, tripping over his words. "I can't remember all of my patients."

The doctor's confession was right on time, as Laoise's resolve finally broke. The fire was becoming too hot to ignore. She ripped the cloak off and tossed it into the snow. Then she dove into the snowbank, flailing about as she rolled. Bertram stood up and patted away the flames eating her skirts. The chill of the snow soothed her hot skin. No burns, but her sweaty skin made her clothes cling to her.

Seeing an opportunity to escape, the doctor scuttled backward like a crab, only to knock into a pair of legs none of them had noticed arriving. He stopped and peered up, meeting Montgomery Steepe's furious gaze. "What is going on here?"

"Herr Steepe!" said the doctor, once more donning his accent. "Sank goodness you're here! Zees two tried to kill me!"

Having smothered the flames on Laoise's clothes, Bertram stood up and stomped toward the doctor. "Don't you dare try to hide behind him again, you sniveling coward! I swear I'll—"

"Bertram," interrupted Uncle Monty, his voice sharp. "Do you have proof of your claim?"

"Uncle, you don't seriously believe—"

"I asked if you had proof."

He scoffed. "Two eyewitness accounts to his confession aren't enough for you?"

"For me, yes, but the police may not be so accommodating to a known criminal fugitive."

"Well if they won't listen to me..." Bertram reached into the top of his dress, pulling out a small teapot. "Perhaps they'll listen to him."

"Good evening," said the teapot. "I am an ancient teapot enchanted by Lu Yu, the author of *The Classic of Tea*, a book which includes a wealth of information—"

"Louie, please." Bertram sighed. "Just recount the doctor's confession, would you?"

Louie harrumphed. "It is only because it is so cold that I'll tolerate such a rude interruption. For you see, I am running out of steam." The teapot laughed at its own joke. Bertram groaned. As promised, Louie recited back the doctor's confession.

"Did I hear that correctly?" Montgomery gripped his walking cane, knuckles turning white as he set his sharp gaze upon the doctor. "Did you poison my son?"

The doctor's lower lip trembled. His shoulders hunched. Dropping his accent, he spoke at last. "There's a very good explanation—"

The whack that came next made everyone jump. Montgomery's cane slammed into the doctor's ribcage, sending him reeling into the snow. The cane cracked in half in the middle, the bottom dangling from a thin sliver of wood. Behind Montgomery, his valet climbed over the fence, sliding around on a patch of ice before righting himself against the wall.

"Fix this," Montgomery growled as he handed his broken cane to the valet. He turned his attention back to Bertram. "And you suppose the testimony of a talking teapot will be enough to get this despicable creature put away?"

Bertram gave a rueful smirk. "Believe me, Uncle. It's enough. It got me exiled, didn't it?"

One last wiggle of the valet's fingers and the cane straightened, becoming whole again. He handed it back to Montgomery. "A gentleman does not strike a helpless opponent, but in your case, I will make an exception." He raised the cane overhead, winding up to strike the doctor once more.

"Wait!" Laoise climbed out of the snowbank and staggered over.

He stopped himself mid swing, slowly setting the cane back on the ground, his face contorted through an array of emotions before settling into its usual stern mask. "My apologies, miss. I've let my emotions get the better of me. I hope you will forgive me for behaving in such an ungentlemanly—"

"I don't care about that," she said, delivering a hard kick to the doctor's stomach. "The rotten bastard poisoned my brother. I wanted a go at him."

"Of course. Ladies first." He took a couple steps back, an amused smirk on his face. Both Bertram and the valet shared a look, relieved to have him holding back from striking the doctor.

Then their expressions returned to horror as Laoise descended upon the doctor, delivering a flurry of violent strikes to his body. The doctor's groans and squeals punctuated her string of curses and profanities with each strike. She reached up and snatched the cane out from Montgomery's grasp, smashing it to pieces against the doctor's chest. She continued to bludgeon him with the broken pieces.

"Jesus Christ," the valet muttered.

"I think he's had enough." Bertram grabbed her and held her back, struggling to pull her away from the man. "The police will be here soon."

The doctor lay in the snow, curled up in a ball with his arms over his head. She gave him one last kick as Bertram pulled her away. "You'd better hope the bobbies come before I throttle the life out of ya myself!"

"Laoise please. We can't have the police seeing you hitting him." Bertram steered her away from Hoffman. He snatched the largest piece of the cane remaining away and tossed it to the valet, who caught it in one smooth flourish.

Her arms shook. "I don't feel any better." She'd drained her anger, but it hadn't fixed anything. Her brother was still sick and her family was none the wiser about the fraud.

Her foot met a bottle of the doctor's medicine that had rolled away from his wrecked gig. She stomped on the bottle, shattering it and spilling its contents. Her eyes burning with anger, she muttered, *"Exspuo pro ultionem,"* and spat into the spilled medicine. It rose into the air and splashed down onto the doctor's hair, trickling onto his face and mouth as he sputtered.

"Surely that made you feel a little bit better. Better than him at least." Bertram offered a smile to Laoise. Still huffing, she returned it.

It took a few breaths to clear her head. The winter cold creeped under her cloak. She looked around, seeing a few tongues of flame still burning around the alley. "You said the fire wouldn't burn anything."

"Oh right, the fire." Bertram inscribed a few runes on the snowbank, and thin strands of water rose up to douse the few small flames still clinging to the debris in the alley. Once the fires were out, the water froze into stringy icicles, which shattered under their own weight. "I didn't expect you to use it near a broken gas lamp. Or on yourself."

"Hadn't planned on it. I didn't think it would set off the gas so...violently." She leaned back against Bertram. He wrapped his arms around her, pulling her in close. He felt warm against the cold as it burrowed back in past her charred clothing.

"I don't quite understand it myself. Perhaps Martin can explain it all to us later." He pointed to her tattered cloak covered in silver scorch marks and holes. "Did it burn you?"

"No, but not for lack of trying."

The valet cleaned and polished the walking cane before handing it back to Bertram's uncle, who hovered over the doctor, whispering about what would happen next. The fury on his face would have terrified her to be on the other end of. But it was her who the doctor kept shrinking away from.

As soon as the officers arrived, the youngest one lit up when he spotted Louie. "Is that the talking teapot? Everyone at Scotland Yard talked about it for weeks. Is it a witness again?"

"It is a great honor to both myself and my creator to know that I have such a positive reputation among the enforcers of law in..." Louie continued to drone on in response.

"Great," said the other officer, his voice lacking enthusiasm. "Sam, you can take the teapot's statement."

"Lucky thing we had Louie here." Laoise hugged herself and leaned against Bertram's side. "Why did you bring him, anyway?"

"Serendipity I suppose. I certainly hadn't planned on smashing him."

"Right," she said, drawing the word out.

Sam bent down to get a better look at Louie. "Can it do impressions?"

"I have no idea. Here, have the teapot for questioning." Bertram dropped Louie into Sam's hands. "Keep him as long as you need."

"What happened to him?" The other officer asked as he pointed at the doctor lying curled up in the snow.

"A terrible wreck," Montgomery said. "Isn't that right?"

Hoffman cast a terrified look, first to Monty, then to Laoise. She crossed her arms and raised her eyebrows, silently daring him to disagree.

"Y-yes. A wreck. A terrible wreck!" He pointed a shaking finger at his broken gig.

"And it seems this man so feared for his soul that he confessed to some rather heinous crimes when we found him, including poisoning children."

"Wait a moment, a doctor poisoning children?" The officer asked, turning to face the doctor. "By chance are you Dr. Giovanni Speranza aka Dr. Gaston Espere aka Mr. George Hopewell?"

The doctor's nose bled as he nodded rapidly. "Aka Dr. Gustav Hoffman. I'm a quack and a fraud and I belong in prison. Please take me away now." He held out his wrists, ready to be clapped in irons. Or more likely ready to be taken away from Laoise.

"Bertram," said Montgomery. "A word."

Bertram shuffled over to his uncle. "I suppose you're going to have me taken away as well, then?"

"No, I..." The Elder Steepe trailed off, at a rare loss for words. "I believe I have made some rather poor judgements of late."

Bertram seemed taken aback. "It's not often you admit a fault, Uncle."

"Only a fool thinks his own actions beyond reproach." Montgomery scoffed. "And these past few days have given me time to reevaluate some of my decisions. I had thought that securing our family's finances would secure a happy future for you, your sisters, and for Martin." His shoulders slumped in defeat.

"Only now am I seeing just how much responsibility I had placed upon your shoulders while I was away. I think I shall spend more time at home to look after the family. I've been considering it ever since I sent you off to the countryside."

"I confess that I haven't been the most attentive to matters of family myself. Martin has become his own man, and I hardly think he needs either one of us watching over him like when he was a child."

His uncle gave him an incredulous look. "If you had seen how he reacted when Mr. Zhang told him he didn't care for that talking teapot, you'd know that he still needs someone to look after him." The two men shared a polite laugh.

Bertram rubbed at his jaw. "He does have someone. And I'm certain she'll take excellent care of him."

"Ah, yes, the Graham girl," said Monty. His right hand twitched. Without a cane to hold on to, he crammed his hands into his pockets. "I've only met with her briefly. Haven't had much time with all the traveling I've been doing, but I would like to learn more about her. You as well."

"Me?" Bertram's eyebrows shot up in surprise.

He nodded. "In my time abroad, I haven't been able to see things firsthand. I've allowed hearsay to cloud my judgement regarding you. A gentleman ought not be so quick to jump to conclusions."

"I'm afraid that in your absence I have not become the gentleman you hoped I would be."

His uncle smiled. "It's not often you admit a fault."

"Only a fool thinks his actions beyond reproach." Bertram smiled back.

"I may question your... methodology," he said, looking Bertram up and down in his dress. "But your actions speak for themselves. That fraud of a doctor had us all fooled, but you alone were able to sniff him out. Moreover, you were willing to go to any and all lengths to not only bring him to justice, but to support his victims as well. Selflessness like that is what exemplifies gentlemanly conduct."

Bertram's cheeks turned pink from the compliment. "So you're not still ashamed to call me family?"

"No, not in the least." Uncle Monty held out his hand. "I'm proud of the man you've become, Bertram, and I know that your father would be as well."

He shook his uncle's hand.

Monty then pulled Bertram in close and lowered his voice. "But the next time you pinch my cheek, you do so at your own peril, boy."

"Yes, sir," Bertram said, standing up straight. He bit his lip to keep from smiling.

After a moment, Monty cleared his throat. "Now then. I believe there are matters requiring your immediate attention." He pointed his cane to Laoise, who was hurling insults at the doctor as the young officer escorted him away. He shuffled away from his uncle to set a hand on her shoulder.

"Let's go get somewhere warmer." Bertram pressed a hand against the small of her back, urging her back toward her carriage. He looked at the officer. "We've done all we can for the good doctor, haven't we?"

"You have," he said, turning his frown on Bertram as he surveyed his outfit. "And there ought to be a law against whatever it is you're doing, but as far as I know there isn't. So go about your business." Under his breath he grumbled, "All those clashing florals. Just dreadful."

Bertram hurried past the man.

Laoise hugged herself. "Can you take me home? I need to tend to Sean and find a new doctor."

"I doubt you'll need one. If Sean quits taking the medicine, he should recover."

"If he doesn't, I'll be paying Doctor Hoffman a visit in jail."

"We'll be sure he makes it there. You tend to your family. We'll take care of everything else."

She settled onto the driver's bench of the carriage, but let him take the reins. "Thank you for coming. And for telling me about the doctor. I—" Her throat closed up. The edges of her eyes burned as she blinked back tears.

"You're welcome. I got close to being the hero this time, didn't I?" He gave her a sad smile. "I suppose the bar was too high for me."

She leaned her head against his shoulder. "For what it's worth to you, you were my hero today."

"No, you were the hero. You did what I never managed all those years ago." He leaned down and kissed the top of her head, earning a smile from her.

"Fine. I'll be the hero, and you can be my sidekick."

He made a noise of strangled disagreement against the top of her head. "We'll discuss that later."

Chapter 26

For Christmas, Charlotte had given Laoise a new dress. A fine green gown that came with an invitation to the Steepe New Year's party as Charlotte's guest. She hadn't been to the Steepe residence since the charity gala, and she told herself that was why her nerves were swooping and bouncing around her stomach. It wasn't at all because she'd be seeing Bertram for the first time since their encounter with Doctor Hoffman.

She missed him. Something she never would have thought possible a few weeks ago. But she did. Fiercely so, and if she was being completely honest with herself, that terrified her. She didn't expect anything else from him. Doctor Hoffman was in jail, and Bertram had paid the costs for the new doctor who helped Sean back to full health. All that was enough of a parting gift. She just wished it would be as easy for her to forget and move on as it would be for Bertram.

Charlotte had insisted on her taking a long break over the holidays to look after Sean. Laoise hadn't argued against it. With her little brother feeling better, and no longer needing to worry over him, she couldn't remember a better Christmas.

This year they'd also had quite the Christmas feast. Bertram had sent them a goose, a pheasant, and a Christmas cake to thank them for hosting him, much to Sean's delight. Laoise was certain the boy had eaten his own body weight in Christmas treats. Her mother, on the other hand, had drunk a little too much of the wine he'd sent. Some sort of fancy vintage Laoise hadn't given more than a sip.

Her mother grinned when she noticed Laoise standing in the kitchen. Her cheeks were still red from all the wine.

"Do you think I look alright for a Steepe party?" Despite Charlotte visiting multiple times over the holidays, Laoise hadn't worked up the courage to broach the topic of her quitting her position with the Steepes yet. Her throat closed up every time she tried. At this rate, she'd have to send a letter, and that felt cruel.

"There's not a fairer looking girl in the whole city," her mother said, nudging her. "That nice butler fellow won't be able to take his eyes off you."

"Ma," she groaned. "You're drunk." Avoiding her family's questions about Bertram was getting harder with each passing day.

"Aye, indeed I am." Her mother offered her a spoonful of stew. "I put some of the fancy wine in the stew. Have a taste, would you?"

Laoise tasted it. The wine played well with the meat and vegetables. It was the sort of balanced dish she would struggle to make on her own. "Delicious. Save me a bowl if you can."

"Can't promise Sean won't eat the lot. I've never known the boy to have such an appetite as he's had lately."

Laoise nodded. "He damn near ate the whole loaf of soda bread for breakfast. You'll have to start baking one for him and one for the rest of us."

A knock on the door made the nerves in her stomach lurch.

"Charlotte is here!" Sean called as he ran past them. Charlotte always brought something from her family's bakery with her, and now that he was up and out of bed, he always rushed to get first pick of the offerings.

"Have a good time." Her mother rested a hand on her shoulder. "Make sure to thank Mr. Bertler for us. He's a good lad."

"Will do." Someday she'd have to explain who he really was, but she wasn't ready for that. She left her mother to go greet Charlotte. Sean went scampering past her with a box of cinnamon buns and a grin that told Laoise there would be no survivors.

"He's doing much better," Charlotte said as she slipped her gloves off. "It's nice to see him get excited over the buns."

"The new doctor gave him medicine to flush out the poison. He's been gaining more and more energy since." Soon he would look as though he'd never been sick. "You wouldn't believe how much he's eaten."

"I'm glad. I forgot how energetic he can be." Charlotte ran a hand over Laoise's skirt. "This looks gorgeous on you."

"I appreciate the gift, but you don't have to dress me." Laoise had tried to be gracious in accepting the gift. She tried to tell herself it was just a nice thing her friend had given her. Deep down, however, she couldn't shake the insecurity telling her that Charlotte was trying to dress her up to hide her station as a lowly maid.

"My mother picked that one out, actually. It didn't look quite right on me and we both agreed it would suit you." She reached for Laoise's cloak. "Let's get going. There is so much to talk about. But perhaps not in front of your family." Her gaze drifted past Laoise to Rian chasing Sean and the cinnamon buns around the table.

Charlotte rushed her to the carriage. As soon as the driver shut the door, Charlotte's words came out in a rush. "Lately Bertram has been acting like a different person. He's being much more polite to Martin, to me, even to Oolong. He hasn't even smashed one of the mechanical hummingbirds since he got back. And out of the blue he gave me a signed Dickens book for Christmas, along with a whole pound of Lapsang Souchong. I've no idea what I'll do with it all." She rested a hand on Louise's knee. "Just what did you do to him?"

"That's a tricky question. I have no idea of where to even begin." She'd avoided asking after Bertram during Charlotte's visits. In fact, they'd avoided the topic of Bertram altogether. Until now. She would be a mere maid again, putting them back on different social levels in every way. He could easily pretend their adventure never happened and carry on with his life. She expected nothing less.

"You can begin at the manor. What happened after we met back in the village?"

"Well, not long after we last saw each other, I got fed up with him and quit, but we got snowed in. The driver couldn't get to me, so I was stuck there with him, and we got into a pretty nasty fight."

"That scoundrel! I swear if he so much as laid a finger on you…"

Laoise leaned back and grinned. "Believe me, he did a lot more than that."

Charlotte covered her mouth. "You did not."

"We did."

Charlotte grabbed Laoise's hands. "I'm so sorry I let you get sent out to that monster. Never did I think he'd take such liberties with you."

She pulled her hands back. "Please. If anyone took liberties, it was me." He certainly hadn't protested her wandering hands in front of the fireplace.

"You?" Charlotte's eyes were wide and her jaw hung slack. "With that selfish man?"

"He may be many things, but selfish in bed he is not. Downright gentlemanly even." Laoise wiggled her eyebrows. "Ladies first, as they say."

Charlotte's face scrunched in confusion. Then as the realization dawned, she gasped. "Laoise!"

Laoise giggled, but as she looked at Charlotte's stunned expression, she soon realized she was the only one laughing. She'd gotten so lost in schoolgirl bragging that she hadn't stopped to consider what her friend would think of her. The carriage rocked as silence descended, and the nerves in Laoise's stomach twisted this way and that.

Charlotte cleared her throat, breaking the silence. "I suppose that does explain a few things. Like why Bertram keeps asking Martin about you."

"He's been asking about me?" She pressed a hand against her stomach, wanting the little bubble of hope to go away.

"He has. Christmas Day he asked me if you were coming to the New Year's party. I thought it an odd question coming from him of all people. He even looked somewhat expectant, almost frightened when Martin told him that 'Laoise is right over there.'" Charlotte sighed. "Of course, he was just pointing to Shannon again. As usual."

She smiled. "I don't think he'll ever get our names straightened out."

"He'd better figure your name out. After all, you're the only guest this year. Without all the spare bedrooms their country retreat has, they opted to keep the party small this year."

Laoise blinked. "You mean to say that I'm the only guest? But what about your friend Mary?"

"Hmm? Her?" Charlotte peered out the window, distracted. "She'll be spending the Holiday at Hallow Manor."

"Hallow Manor?" Laoise lifted an eyebrow. "As in *Twilight at Hallow Manor*?"

"I said Hallow again, didn't I?" Charlotte sighed and shook her head. "Holiday Manor. Lucas Holiday. She'll be having her engagement party

in the spring. I ought to at least remember her fiancé's name by then."
She continued muttering the man's name to herself under her breath.

Laoise giggled. "Looks like Martin's little habit is rubbing off on you."

"Sorry, I can't seem to keep my thoughts straight. It's just that... you
and Bertram. I never once thought you may have..." She cleared her
throat. "You have to tell me how it happened."

"Oh no. I'm not one to kiss and tell," said Laoise, turning away coyly.

Charlotte gave her an incredulous look. "Yes, you most certainly are.
Now out with it."

Laoise gave her a condensed version. Her throat went dry as she
spoke, emotions threatening to finally catch up to her. She couldn't
find the right words to explain how her feelings for him had gone from
loathing to something else. But what exactly they'd become she wasn't
sure. Or perhaps the path they could send her down felt too daunting.
She didn't want to get her hopes up only to be crushed. And really... her
and Bertram? The look of astonishment on Charlotte matched Laoise's
own feelings on the matter.

They arrived before she could finish, and so they stood on the
walkway to the door, heads together as they whispered.

"What do you plan to do now?" Charlotte asked as soon as Laoise
finished.

"I haven't a clue. I'm still just a maid. The difference in our station
means things between us will have to end, won't they?"

"If you're just a maid, then I'm just a baker," Charlotte said with a
scoff. "Don't you remember what you said to me before I told Martin
I wasn't nobility?"

"Hard to say. I'm full of so many pearls of wisdom it's hard to keep
track of them all."

"You're full of something, all right," said Charlotte, elbowing her
friend in the arm. "You said to me, 'why shouldn't girls like us get a
chance with men like them?' Neither of us would be here today if we
worried about silly little things like station. It's all a bunch of nonsense."

"The world would be a much better place if more people thought
like you do," she said with a smile. She hoped that Bertram shared
Charlotte's sentiments.

"I know that whatever you decide will be the right decision. And if
that scoundrel hurts you, I'll make sure he regrets it."

Laoise's lips twitched into a smile. "If he so much as tries to hurt me, you can have whatever scraps of him are left once I'm done with him."

"I suppose if anyone could keep him in line, it would be you."

The butler opened the door and ushered them in. Piano music trickled out of the parlor.

"Hello," Bertram said as he stepped out of the shadows. Laoise and Charlotte both jumped.

"Bertram," Charlotte answered, tone icy.

"Charlotte," Bertram replied, looking uncomfortable as he shifted on his feet. "You look... nice today." His gaze flickered to Laoise. He gave her a stiff bow. "Miss Hughes."

"What are you doing skulking about the entryway?" Charlotte asked as she passed her cloak to the butler.

Laoise avoided meeting the butler's eyes. Serving the Steepes was awkward enough with Charlotte in the household. Being invited as a guest would earn her nothing but scorn from a few of the staff when she returned to her duties.

Bertram's shoulders stiffened in offense. "I wasn't skulking. I was passing by the door is all."

A brown blur shot out of the parlor and crashed into Bertram's legs. An unfamiliar dachshund puppy pawed at his legs.

Laoise gasped. "Oh no. Did Oolong... did he?"

"No, no. Mrs. Hammond decided to send her regards over Christmas. His gaze turned distant, lost in whatever Mrs. Hammond memories assailed him. He shook the memories off. "Thanks to her, I now have a dachshund of my very own." He reached down to scratch the dog's head. "She's an obstinate one. I was considering naming her Laoise."

"You'd better not." Laoise considered throwing her gloves at him.

He chuckled. "It's out of my hands anyway. I gave her to my sisters. Martin is helping them train her."

A whistle from the parlor sent the dog hurtling after the noise.

"Let's go get a hot drink." Charlotte wrapped an arm through Laoise's and steered her into the parlor. Her amused smile grew as she sneaked glances between Laoise and Bertram.

The oldest of Bertram's little sisters played the piano while the other two played with their new puppy. Both girls burst into applause as Martin got both Oolong and the puppy to sit at the same time.

"Bravo!"

"I do hope our dogs will be the very best of friends."

The girls were two years apart, but because of the way they always had matching outfits and hairstyles, Laoise thought they looked more like twins.

"I'm quite certain they will be, girls." Martin lit up when he spotted Charlotte. He gave his younger cousins a theatrical bow before handing the puppy over to them.

Charlotte practically pulled Laoise down onto the sofa. "Sit! Hot tea will warm you up after the drive. Your hands are like ice."

Her stomach swooped as Bertram settled into an armchair across from them. His attention kept darting between her and his sisters.

Shannon set a tea tray down on the coffee table. The tray included a pot of coffee for Bertram. Laoise grabbed the coffeepot and began pouring Bertram's cup.

"And just what do you think you're doing?" Shannon slapped her hand.

She blinked. It was second nature to do the serving. "I just—"

"You just nothing. You're a guest and I'll not have you doing any of the serving," said Shannon, snatching away the pot. "Now what'll it be Laoise?"

"Ahem," said Laoise, sitting up straight and striking a prim pose. "I believe you mean 'Miss Hughes.'"

"Apologies, miss," said Shannon with a wink.

Laoise winked back. "A cup of coffee, if you please."

Martin joined them, greeting Charlotte with a kiss to the back of her hand. He took the other armchair as Shannon poured his tea. "Ah, there you are, Laoise. I believe Bertram was looking for you." He pointed at Shannon.

Bertram let out a long, suffering sigh. "For the last time, that's Shannon. That's Laoise." Rubbing his temple, he indicated the correct names for the women.

Martin's face scrunched up in bewilderment. "But that can't be Laoise. That's Alice."

Shannon somehow remained stone faced as she finished serving them. Serving Martin made the staff accustomed to name mixups.

"Who's Alice?" Bertram raised an eyebrow. "Did you hire someone new while I was gone?"

Charlotte shook her head. "There is no Alice. That's Shannon, and that's Laoise. Laoise Hughes. My friend and guest for the evening."

Laoise waved nervously. "A pleasure to meet y— erm... see you again. Sir." She slowly lowered her hand, not quite sure what to do with it.

His bewilderment turned grim. "I'm terribly sorry, ladies." He stood, taking his teacup with him. "Please excuse me." He hurried out of the parlor.

"Forgive him," Charlotte said. "He's still struggling to get names right and is embarrassed about it. Let me check on him." She headed for the mantel first, pulling Louie off it. She shoved him at Bertram.

"What are you doing?" he asked, refusing to take the teapot.

"Someone ought to chaperone you two," she declared, setting Louie on his lap. "Louie, you're able to watch them in my stead, aren't you?"

"I have been a chaperone four times," Louie said. "The first time was for none other than the most esteemed student of Lu Yu himself, a young man by the name of..."

"Good enough for me," said Charlotte, rushing after Martin as the teapot continued droning on with the minutia of his story. Laoise covered her mouth to hide her smile at Bertram's look of defeat.

"Well then," said Bertram, "would you like to join me in the parlor?"

"I would."

He tucked Louie under one arm. In his other hand, he held his coffee cup. He wiggled his arms. "Forgive me for not being able to offer you an arm at the moment. I don't want to spill coffee on that lovely dress of yours."

She swished her skirts. "Do I still look stiff and uncomfortable?"

He smiled. "Only a little."

Louie rambled the whole way to the library. Bertram sat him down beside the door before leading her to the far side of the room.

"I've heard you've been talking to your uncle." Her throat tightened at the prospect of where their conversation might head. No doubt he was going to let her down. Gently of course, the way a gentleman would. He'd explain about why it would be best for her to forget about what happened between them. Maybe he'd even confess he already had his eye on some insufferable nobleman's daughter.

"I have. There's been years of topics to discuss." He cleared his throat. "But we've agreed it would be best for me to take a short trip elsewhere after the holidays. Apparently the police are still suspicious of me, so Mr. John Bertler will be traveling abroad for some time." He twirled an imaginary mustache and gave her a shy smile, and she returned it.

"Shipping off to Italy for real this time, then?" She squeezed her hands together as she fought to keep her voice even. She'd been fourteen the last time a boy twisted her feelings up like this, and she felt every bit as vulnerable now as she had back then.

"No, South America. You may recall my beloved Remojo brand coffee from our time together at the manor. I plan on doing some work for them while on my trip. I've become a partner in the business."

"I'm surprised you're not going into the family business."

"Take a wild guess as to who created Remojo," he said, smirking.

Laoise's face twisted in confusion. "Martin? But he hates coffee."

"It came as a surprise to me too. Then again, I ought to have been suspicious from the start considering the word remojo is Spanish for 'to steep.'" He took another sip of his coffee. "He got the idea to start a coffee brand to ensure I'd have a stable business when I returned, but he doesn't want to taste test any of the coffee himself. The duties of meeting and negotiating with suppliers will therefore fall to me. We're still discussing the official name. I think it might be a good idea to include it under the same umbrella as his tea business."

She gazed out the window, her hopes dashed. "Sounds like you've got a busy year ahead of you."

"It won't all be work. Some time away would probably do me some good. I don't feel quite ready to rejoin the family fully yet. Besides, it's been a long time since I took a vacation."

"I suppose the manor wasn't much of a vacation, was it?" Her own vacation would be over soon. She'd need to figure our her employment situation. Find somewhere new that wouldn't be as bad as her days working for Mrs. Hammond.

"You know that as well as I do," he said with a chuckle. "As I understand, you've been able to take an actual break yourself. How is Sean?"

"Better. Some days you'd never know how sick he'd been. He ate plenty of food at Christmas." She snapped her fingers. "That reminds me. My mother told me to send our regards to Mr. Bertler for his kindness. She made a very nice beef stew with the wine you sent."

He paused, fingers tightening on his cup. "She used an 1805 Bordeaux," he said, voice strained, "to make stew?"

"Oh yes. A very good stew, too."

He took a deep breath. "As long as it made her happy."

Her hands loosened. "She got drunk on the rest of it. Too many sips while she was cooking."

"Well I'm glad she was able to enjoy it as it was meant to be enjoyed. And I'm glad Sean is better. Hoffman is already in jail and will remain there for the foreseeable future. He won't get a chance to poison anyone else."

"Good. I hope he rots in there." She straightened her hands, turning her gaze to the floor. "I hope your time staying with my family wasn't too painful."

Louie continued talking near the door, unaware he'd lost his audience. "...and she would sneak off to the stables whenever the opportunity presented itself. However..."

Bertram paid the teapot no mind. "Not at all. Your family didn't know who I really was, and yet they still showed me kindness simply because they are good people." His voice softened. "I would be happy to eat at your mother's table again."

Laoise looked away, rubbing her side to get the butterflies in her stomach to settle down. They were dancing around discussing the future, yet she couldn't bring herself to bring it up first. "She'll be happy to hear you liked her cooking."

Silence passed between them. Bertram took another sip of his coffee before speaking again. "I've already informed my uncle I plan to take someone with me on my trip."

Her heart sped up. Her right hand squeezed the armrest.

"We agree that company would be good for me. And so..." he stopped to adjust himself, swinging one leg over the other.

She resisted the urge to rush him. The last thing she wanted was to come off as desperate.

"And so," he continued, "I was thinking about asking Charlotte to accompany me."

"Charlotte?" Her thoughts spluttered in disbelief.

"Yes. We are family after all. It's high time I finally got to know her a little better, don't you think?" He shot her a sideways glance, his chin framing a mischievous grin.

"That's a grand idea," she said, her words dripping with sarcasm. " I bet she would love a few months alone with you. You'd be great writing fodder."

"I suppose I would be, wouldn't I?" He laughed.

She turned to face him, smirking. "You do know her earlier work was about a murderous baker who cooked his victims into pies, don't you?"

"Sounds a bit like *The String of Pearls* to me," he said, tapping his chin. "But more importantly, my uncle agreed that a man of my position ought to have a bodyguard with him."

"You?" She tilted her head. "The capable Master Bertram Steepe hardly needs someone to watch his back."

"Be that as it may, I did have someone in mind for the job." He kept his eyes on the fire.

Once more Laoise's heart started to race. "You think Charlotte would make for a decent bodyguard?"

"Oh no, I was thinking someone a bit more... accustomed to my dealings."

"Someone accustomed to cooking and cleaning for you, you mean?"

"God forbid you ever set foot in a kitchen again." He snorted. "But I could use someone who's not afraid to smash a stick over someone's head. And someone with the ability to clean the mess up afterwards."

"Must be quite the capable young lady you have in mind."

"She really is something," he said in agreement. "And I'm willing to offer her all the coffee she can drink. Warm sunny beaches with magnificent views of the ocean." Laoise's heart skipped a beat. He remembered. She looked over to find him preening. "...among other gorgeous views."

"It sounds like a dream. No one in her right mind could refuse such an offer."

"I expected as much." He set his cup down to steeple his hands together. His expression turned somber. "I thought the trip would be a good way to start over. To show you I can be a better man when I'm not at my lowest point."

Her breath caught in her throat. "And why would we be getting to know each other better?"

"...she was found engaged in a most unsavory act with his favorite horse. The discovery did not please him..."

Laoise's head snapped in Louie's direction. "Did you hear that? That can't possibly mean what I think, right?"

"I'm sure it's nothing." He crossed the room to shove Louie into a cupboard beside his uncle's desk.

"...angry at her plan of running away being discovered, the two quarreled..." Louie continued as Bertram slammed the cupboard shut. The teapot continued droning on, though his voice was muffled now.

"Martin is happily married now. One sister is expecting a proposal any day now, and the other two entertained a stream of suitors while I was gone," said Bertram as he returned to his chair. "I finally have time to focus on myself and what I want in life. The Steepe Foundation, Remojo Coffee, and courtship."

"Courtship?" The rush of emotions made her dizzy, and she nearly dropped her cup of coffee. "You mean with me?"

"Yes," he said, looking down sheepishly. "I think I'd like to get to know you better, Miss Hughes. Preferably under less stressful circumstances."

She held her hand to her chest, steadying her emotions. They threatened to burst out of her at any moment, and it took every bit of her willpower to not wrap her arms around his broad shoulders right then and there. "Didn't you once say I was as stubborn as an ox?"

"You are. And so am I." He reached up to adjust his cravat, looking pleased with himself. "We have that in common, which has got to be a better starting point than a magic teapot, don't you think?" His gaze flickered toward her. Nervous energy radiated off him.

Relief soothed her stomach. He was interested too, but she didn't have to make a decision about the two of them right away. Starting over was exactly what she needed to be sure of how she felt.

"Then I accept the job offer, Mr. Steepe." She held out her hand. "I look forward to working closely with you."

"Oh you'll be working very closely with me, Miss Hughes. "Bertram shook her hand, giving her a sly smile. "As my bodyguard, I will be depending on you to stay close and keep me safe. We'll have plenty of time alone to get to know each other better."

"Alone, you say?" She fluttered her eyelashes at him. "There is one part of me you'll need to become intimately familiar with."

He licked his lips. "And what might that be?"

"My appetite," she said, her voice sultry. "...for coffee. You said I'd have all the coffee I could drink, didn't you? Don't underestimate how much I can handle."

"I'll see to it you're satisfied." The smile he gave her made her cheeks warm. She couldn't recall a man ever looking at her with such obvious affection. "If you can keep up with me, that is."

A sprig of mistletoe floated into the room, followed by two girlish giggles. Bertram's youngest sisters peeked into the room, darting back out of sight when they noticed Laoise looking. "Looks like your sisters have taken notice of us."

He watched the sprig dancing overhead out of the corner of his eyes. "They went through the trouble of learning the spell to levitate the mistletoe. I'd hate to disappoint them." He leaned forward.

She met him in the middle, caressing the back of his neck as he dipped her. "Are you certain you want them to know about us already?"

"I think they'll have it figured out when I whisk you away to have you all to myself." He leaned toward her. The giggling in the hallway gave way to excited gasps right before something buzzed loudly around their heads.

She opened her eyes to see a pair of hummingbirds chasing one another. They both zipped away in a pair of emerald blurs. "Was that Pepper?"

He waved the birds away. "And her new beau. We still haven't managed to catch her since the gala, so Martin decided to get her some company." Once more he leaned in, and once more he was interrupted. This time by the jingle of the bell on Oolong's collar. They both looked down to see the two dachshunds weaving between their legs as they scrambled after the birds.

Bertram sighed. "It seems fate is conspiring to make this as difficult as possible."

"No use cryin' about the interruption. Or letting it stop us." She pulled his face close and pressed her lips against his, smiling at the chorus of cheers they received.

Irish Soda Bread Recipe

Dear Charlotte,

Ma finally shared the recipe for her Irish Soda Bread with me. Since I'm to be traipsing about all over South America for the next few months, she figures I ought to have some way to have a taste of home until I return to London. Really I think she just wants me to make it for Bertie. I still can't believe how much he loves the stuff. He has a big slice slathered with butter every time he visits my family. With a big cup of Irish Breakfast tea, of course. And far too much milk.

The trouble is that I cannot for the life of me figure out how to bake it right. I know there's no yeast or proofing or any such fancy bakery nonsense, but it never seems to turn out, even as I'm looking at the recipe!

I know you've been hounding me for the recipe since we were children, so I'm willing to do you the favor of sharing it. But you must promise to show me what I'm doing wrong. Do that and I'll consider us even.

Ingredients:
- 3 1/2 cups flour
- 1/3 cup sugar
- 1 teaspoon salt
- 2 teaspoons baking powder
- 1 teaspoon baking soda

- 1/2 cup butter

- 2 cups raisins

- 1 3/4 cup buttermilk

- 2 eggs slightly beaten

- (Optional) 2 or 3 teaspoons of caraway seeds

Instructions:

1. Heat oven to 350°F

2. Grease a large casserole dish

3. Sift dry ingredients together

4. Mix in butter until mixture resembles coarse crumbs

5. Stir in raisins (and caraway seeds if adding)

6. Combine Buttermilk and eggs and add to flour mixture

7. Bake 50 to 55 minutes

P.S. It figures that Ma would wait til after I wrote it down to tell me she made a change to Granny Hughes' recipe. Apparently the dish I've been using to bake this isn't a casserole dish at all! I thought it was strange seeing as I've never had a ring-shaped casserole before. It's actually a tube pan for making angel food. To think Mrs. Hammond threw away a perfectly good pan all those years ago just because it had a little dent in it. I swiped it, Callum fixed it, and now Ma's been using it to make soda bread.

Granny would have a conniption if she knew Ma was straying so far from the traditional recipe, but she told me it's to make sure the bread cooks all the way through. I'm not sure I believe it since mine is still raw in the middle!

That's two Hughes family secrets for you, Lottie. Now you really owe me!

Very Truly Yours,

Laoise Hughes

Thank you for reading. If you enjoyed this book please consider leaving a review. If you would like sneak peeks at future titles, access to ARCs, and a free short story join my newsletter at https://katevalent author.com/steeping-notes/